Consider Lily

Also by Anne Dayton
and May Vanderbilt

Emily Ever After

Consider Lily

a novel

By Anne Dayton
and May Vanderbilt

Broadway Books

New York

This book is a work of fiction. Names, characters, businesses, organizations,
places, events, and incidents either are the product of the authors' imagination
or are used fictitiously. Any resemblance to actual persons, living or dead,
events, or locales is entirely coincidental.

PRINTED IN THE UNITED STATES OF AMERICA

BROADWAY BOOKS and its logo, a letter B bisected on the diagonal,
are trademarks of Random House, Inc.

Visit our Web site at www.broadwaybooks.com

Book design by Donna Sinisgalli
Illustrated by Bonnie Dain for Lilla Rogers Studio

Library of Congress Cataloging-in-Publication Data
Dayton, Anne.
    Consider Lily / by Anne Dayton and May Vanderbilt.
        p.   cm.
    1. Fashion—Fiction.   2. San Francisco (Calif.)—Fiction.
I. Vanderbilt, May.   II. Title.

PS3604.A989C66 2006
813'.6—dc22

2005058112

ISBN-13: 978-0-385-51830-7
ISBN-10: 0-385-51830-7

1 3 5 7 9 10 8 6 4 2

FIRST EDITION

For

Beth Meister

and

Pastor Kyle

Consider how the lilies grow. They do not labor or spin. Yet I tell you, not even Solomon in all his splendor was dressed like one of these.

—Luke 12:27

Acknowledgments

Thanks to Claudia, Trace, Darya, Kate, Laura, Julia, Trish, Charlie, Meister, Haymaker, Joan, Jen, Christine, Maria, Kristen, Rakesh, Tracy, Sarah, Brie, Laura, Dan, Ursula, Talia, Nate, Karyn, Nora, Dudley, Shannon, Ginia, Joel, and all the good folks at Waterbrook and Broadway who are crazy enough to publish a second book with us.

And a big thanks to Kateigh Axness and Staci Nakayama for the "inspiration."

Special thanks to Mom and Dad for the support and lame science jokes, the Slater/Burns clan for the laughs and inspiration, and Nick and Peter, the prettiest bridesmaids in the world. And thanks to Wayne. You poor sucker.

—*Anne Dayton*

Thanks to Dad for the fishing lessons and waffles, Mom for "raising me right" and for taking my emergency phone calls, Matt for the talks about Walker Percy, Diem for putting up with Matt, Isaac for the crazy hair photos that keep me laughing, and Sandy for good old-fashioned sister support. Thanks to all the Bransfords for being my booster club out in Colusa and for being my other family. And most especially thanks to Nathan. Without you to bail me out and give me a hug, I'm confident I'd be stranded somewhere.

—*May Vanderbilt*

• Chapter 1 •

The spotlights swirl and then land on the back of the catwalk in one solid beam. I hold my breath. This is it.

The first model stands at the end of the runway. She's wearing a Diesel swimsuit and strappy high heels. She gives me a big smile and begins to strut down the catwalk, just like we practiced. Someone asks me a question through my headset, and I answer quietly. I look around at the seated crowd of glittering A-listers. They're nodding their heads in approval, and the fashion journalists are taking frantic notes. Flashes are popping. I glance at my mother at the back of the crowd. She looks like she's watching *Schindler's List*. I take a deep breath. It's going to be just fine. It's going to be the best fashion show San Francisco has ever seen. And it will all be because of me and my hard work.

I try to read the crowd's reaction to the first model. I begged and pleaded with Mom to let me use the fashion show as a benefit for the San Francisco YWCA. She agreed, reluctantly, saying she hoped that this would help us get extra press. All of the clothes worn today by the models will be auctioned off to benefit the girls club. I'm going to give something back to the city *and* prove myself to my parents.

I am the only child of Roland and Joan Traywick—the über–fashion couple who made Prada a household name in the Bay Area. They are the clothiers behind the most high-end department store in the city, Traywick's of San Francisco. The haute couture temple of my mockery.

Tomboy. Awkward. Wallflower. Late bloomer. Ugly duckling. Old maid. That's me. Lily Opal Frances Traywick. Hear me roar! (Actually, hear my grandmothers roar, since each insisted I be named after her, hence my crazy middle names.)

I still can't believe my parents trusted me with organizing the annual Traywick's spring fashion show. If all goes well, this could be my chance to get out of my pastel prison, the Silver Spoon, the Traywick's children's wear department. Management position here I come.

I didn't always want to work in the children's department. In fact, the plan was to avoid fashion at all costs. Having grown up at my parent's store, I was desperate to strike out on my own. However, I was forced to abandon my immediate postcollege plan, which was writing a bestselling novel, when I realized that the only plots I could think of were old episodes of *Saved by the Bell.* For a while I had actually convinced myself that I had invented the Sprain. Next I applied at the Family Crisis Intervention Center so I could make my mark in this world, help my fellow man, ask not what this country can do for me but . . . is that my salary?! Sadly, things didn't work out at the Intervention Center.

That's when my parents offered me a job at the store. At first I scoffed at their generosity, but as my bills started to pile up, I came around to the idea. It was no secret I was expected to take over the store someday. I guess that's why they felt justified in inflicting on me their ridiculous philosophy, "hard work is good for you," which directly translates means *no handouts,* not even for their only child. Plus, Traywick's was home, in a sense. I grew up hiding in the coatracks and wreaking havoc on the gracefully ascending escalators. It felt safe, and I knew I'd get something else soon enough. Now it just feels like my tombstone will read *It was supposed to be temporary.* I guess the road to hell, or Traywick's, is paved with good intentions. In the four years I've been rotting in kiddieland I've been brainstorming ways to get out. So when Dad asked if I would like to have a go at organizing Traywick's annual publicity stunt, I mean fashion show, I jumped at the chance. He hinted that if it went well I could leave the Silver Spoon behind. It has to go well.

I watch the runway breathlessly as the next model comes out. Shelly is missing one of her front teeth due to a field hockey incident. I've tried to remind her not to smile, but as I look up, there she is at the end of the runway in a Kate Spade sundress, beaming her gappy grin. I feel a pinching, icy death-grip on my arm.

"What is the meaning of this?" Mom hisses at me. As the fashion editor from the *San Francisco Chronicle* passes by, Mom looks up quickly and throws her a big, calm, patent Joan Traywick smile.

I gulp. "What?"

"Where did you get these models?"

"The YWCA."

"The what?"

I steel myself against her venom. "It cut our costs in half and—"

"This is unacceptable. Unacceptable. I said it could *benefit* the YWCA. Not that you could use their ragamuffins as runway models."

"Mom, shhhhh. Calm down."

I look up at the runway and thank God as I see Chloe coming down. She could be a model, even though she's not. The point of using the girls from the YWCA was not only to get them involved, but also to show the fashion world women of all shapes and sizes instead of those preening giraffes Mom usually hires who make young girls hate their butts and freckles.

My mother stands with me in the back of the crowd with her lips rolled in like a perfect seam. She won't look at me.

"It's fine, Mom. At the end of the show, I will thank the models and announce that they are from the girls club, and everyone will be moved and impressed."

She turns to face me. I can sense that she still needs more coaxing.

"You just need to believe in people. If you just elevate culture to be more aware of those less fortunate, then—"

I hear the crowd gasping. A woman near the runway springs to her feet and runs quickly to the back. Several others are trying to hide behind their programs or duck under their folding chairs.

Oh no. Ginger. I should have known.

Ginger is the YWCA spitfire, who they warned me was a bit immature. Ginger is standing on the end of the catwalk in a cute little camo-print skirt and white silk top. There is just one problem. She is launching cream pies from the stage and yelling something about saving the earthworms.

As chaos erupts, with powdered and primped ladies mowing down photographers, my mother finally speaks.

"Maria Shriver has whipped cream in her hair, and the style editor at *Vogue* is crying over her vintage Chanel. Tell me, Lily, is this what elevating culture looks like? Because I already feel less fortunate."

I roll over and look at the clock. Eleven thirteen. I roll over again. I just can't go down there. I'm too embarrassed. I'll just play dead. They'll come up here to my bedroom and find me dead and feel terrible about not appreciating me all along. That's what I'll do. I'll just die on them. And since I don't have a boyfriend, maybe the man of my dreams will show up at my funeral—never had a thing for punctuality, did he?—and wail over my beautiful porcelain skin and ruby red lips. He'll beat his chest and ask, Why God, why?

I hear a gentle knock at the door and ready myself to play dead.

"Lil?" It's my grandmother Opal, who lives with us. The only sane person in this house.

I don't answer her.

She comes in and clomps over the *San Francisco Chronicle* spilled all over my floor. She's seen the article. I've seen it. My parents have seen it. And now I must die.

Gran sits down on the edge of my bed. "Hey, sweetie, why don't you come on down to breakfast now, hmmm?"

I guess she's not buying that I'm asleep or dead. I groan. "I can't go down there. I can't ever go outside again. I have to stay here in my pajamas for the rest of my life."

"So you saw the article then?" Gran asks.

After Ginger unloaded her pies on the audience, I felt we made quite a graceful comeback. I coaxed the crowd back into their seats, assuring no more special effects, and the rest of the girls were perfect. At the end of the show, I gave a speech about how the benefit worked and whom it benefited. And then I called out the models and introduced them to the crowd. Everyone clapped politely and went home. Sure it wasn't perfect, but really, it was fine. Not a fiasco at all. But unfortunately, the *Chronicle* fashion editor did not agree. Today in the Weekend Style section the lead article was "Fashion Victim." It recounted the Traywick's fashion show as "an evening of garish fashion, fat models, and activism." I was crushed. Deflated. I mean, sure, I didn't mean for the style editor of *Vogue* to get smacked with what I later found out was a vegan lemon meringue, and it really didn't make any sense that Ginger threw the pies at women wearing fur to promote her Save the Earthworm club. But the article also claimed that the benefit angle was just "another pathetic attempt by the fashion world to seem humanitarian when in fact all the Traywick's Corporation clearly wanted was some good press and a little free publicity." Why were they being so cynical? The girls from the Y loved being in the fashion show, and we raised thousands of dollars. So much for my big promotion out of the kids' department. This was the biggest scandal at Traywick's since the sixties when a group of women did a sit-in in the lingerie department and set off the fire alarm by burning their bras.

But the absolute worst thing that the fashion editor said had nothing to do with the stupid fashion show. It was a personal shot. Below the belt.

The biggest problem, however, was not with the show itself but with its coordinator, Lily Traywick, who has been working for her parents since she graduated from college. It seems the fashion gene skipped the young Miss Traywick altogether. Not only did she organize the ill-fated fashion show, but she herself came dressed like a WNBA star. One can only wonder whether the notoriously persnickety Joan Traywick is asleep at the wheel where her own daughter is concerned. Or perhaps young Lily is so hopeless that Joan has tossed up her hands in disbelief and cried, I give up!

Above this is a photograph of me, mouth open, looking stunned and helpless.

I guess I'm staring blankly across the room again because I come to to the sound of Gran talking.

"I just don't care what that nasty viper woman said about you, it's simply not true. Now buck up, Lil. You're tougher than this," she says.

I smile weakly at her.

"And you're my Lil' Opal."

I laugh. She just loves that I'm named after her. "Love you, Gran."

She smiles, and then the doorbell rings. "I'll get it," she says and goes downstairs.

I lie back on my bed and try to fall back asleep when I hear Gran yelling from downstairs. "Lil?"

"What?" I yell back. I'm not going down there. In fact, I'm never leaving this room. I'll just tell people my pajamas are sewn to the sheets.

Gran doesn't answer. I guess she doesn't need me anymore. Good.

I hear a knock at my door and sigh. "Yeah?" I call to the closed door.

It opens. "Hey, you." It's Steph. I have two best friends in this world, Reagan Axness and Stephanie Harold. They're as different as can be and are definite proof of my multiple personality disorder. I met Steph on the leadership team of Campus Crusade at Stanford. She divides her time between medical school, the San Francisco Symphony, and volunteer work, and looks like she stepped off the pages of a

J. Crew catalog. Men look at her and dream of raising lots of flaxen-haired babies and tending fields of wheat. Meanwhile, Reagan is half Norwegian and half Chinese and is coolness defined. She has more fashion sense in her little toe than I do in my entire body, and her prowess in the dating game would be envied by Elizabeth Taylor. For a girl named by conservative parents after their beloved Republican governor (later to be the "Don't Worry Be Happy" Republican president) she turned out pretty wild. All that she and the late president share is a deep and rarely paralleled love of the eighties.

"Mm," I say.

"How are you doing? I haven't seen you in a couple of days," says Steph.

"Fine. I'm fine. Busy, I guess."

She comes over and sits on my bed. I try to pull up the sheets to cover my pajamas and then try to mat my hair down with my hand. "Busy? Busy growing bed sores? You're not worried about that silly article, are you?"

I shrug. "What article?"

She points with her finger at my floor where the article has been since I ran downstairs to see the press we must have generated at the fashion show. Now the article is all crumpled and tear-stained. "I'm *so* sorry, Lily. It was a stupid article. It really was. My mom agrees with me completely, and she always reads the fashion pages. Everyone says so. It was a personal shot. And it wasn't fair, nor is it true. Any of it."

I smile, weakly. "Right. So I'm not a fashion victim. And my mother isn't persnickety. Hmph."

I hear Steph laugh. "Okay, the persnickety part is true. But the other parts weren't. You're not a fashion victim. I've always liked you just the way you are."

I look at myself in the mirror. "That doesn't change that I've still never had a date."

"You've had a date. I'm tired of talking about this with you. We've already been through it. Tell me your dates."

"No."

"Yes. For my personal sanity, I need to hear you list them so that *I* know that *you* know that you have in fact had a date. Now go."

I sigh. "Okay fine. But you and I both know they don't count."

"Go."

"Once for a middle school dance my mom 'surprised' me and arranged for me to take my cousin Christopher as my date. Everyone laughed. We spent the whole night avoiding each other."

"I've seen a picture. He's hot. Continue."

"Another time in high school, Reagan and I went to the movies with two guys. My date chose to sit next to Reagan's boyfriend instead of next to me."

"You probably were so shy that you didn't talk to him so he gave up."

I roll my eyes. "Finally, the worst of them all, in college *you* arranged for me to be auctioned off for a date at a Crusade fundraiser."

She's laughing. She loves that story. "And . . ." she prompts.

"We had a really great time until his mom called and said he had to come home."

"Yeah. Tyler needed to cut the old apron strings, but I think he really liked you."

"Sure he did, only he was crazy. He said he liked me, but that his mother felt that he was too young to be in a relationship. Which is why I don't count it or any of the dates. They're bogus. Rubbish."

"You know, the only person who believes you are undatable is you."

"And the editor of the Style section."

"Lily. I know it's hard, especially after an article like that, but try to stay focused on what really matters. God calls us to be beautiful on the inside. The outsides don't matter. Plus, your outsides *are* beautiful. You just don't adorn them with the latest fashions or care about brand names. That's all."

"Yeah."

We're both silent for a while.

"I don't think wallowing is a good idea," she says.

"I'm not wallowing."

"Gran answered the door. She told me you're wallowing."

"Okay, I'm wallowing. A bit. And my goodness. Is my grandmother opening the door down there and saying, 'Hello, how are you, my granddaughter is upstairs but she's going to the state hospital later'?"

Steph laughs. "You seriously need to do something to take your mind off this. You got knocked down. Think of something that will help you come back up swinging. Maybe write a response article back to her. That might feel good."

"They'd never print it."

"Really?"

I nod.

"You vengeful English-major types." She shakes her head in astonishment. "Maybe you're right. But, Lily, I can't help but feel you need to start venting your feelings a little more. I'm worried about you."

"I'll be fine. It was just some dumb article."

"I'm not worried about the article. I'm worried about you. The zip has gone out of you lately," she says.

"Mm," I say. "Maybe a little."

Chapter 2

"Posture, posture," my mother sings at me in a nauseatingly fake-sweet voice as she sits down across from me at the overlong, dark wood table.

I sit up and push my shoulders back until it hurts. Even at a family dinner on a Thursday night, my mother feels the need to wear an impeccably tailored white Prada suit. Her dark brown hair is expertly bobbed and recently colored. For being so fashion-forward, my parents are commonly described in the press as *"très* Old World." I have to agree. We still eat dinner as a family every day of the week, unless the two of them are at a show in Milan or a trade fair in Paris. Even then, my grandmother Opal is eternally at home. Gran generally cooks the family meals and is round, jolly, and an eternal reminder to me that my mother was not always the sleek, polished woman she is today, much to my mother's chagrin. While Dad grew up wearing the finest fashions, attending the best schools, and vacationing all over the world, Mom, try as hard as she may to forget it, is from a small town just outside Des Moines. *Day MWAHnuh*, she says breathily, as if pronouncing it with a French accent makes it any closer to Paris. Fortunately for her, she was—and still is—an extremely beautiful woman, and she easily won the heart of my young father *that summer on the Cape*. In telling the story, she usually forgets to mention that she was paying her rent there by working as a waitress at a seafood restaurant and slipped my father her phone number along with his bill one night, but after marrying him she adapted to the Traywick lifestyle nicely.

"You don't want to be a humped-over old woman, Lily," she says. "Oh, and I saw a dress that would look stunning on you at the store today. It's such a nice fuchsia color."

"Mom . . ." I whine. She always does this. She tries to make me wear clothes I hate, and I'm supposed to act grateful when she points out things I'd never wear.

"Fuchsia is in this season," she says, rolling her eyes like I'm the one who's crazy. She lets her eyes travel back to the newspaper by her plate. I watch her eat, chewing her food slowly, drawing out every bite. I still cringe whenever I see the paper, though my parents have not mentioned the article once since it appeared. Mercifully, someone else is getting the criticism today.

"He just looks too stripy in all those ties and button-downs," she says, shaking her head. I crane my neck to see what she's looking at.

"Kofi Annan?" I ask, quickly asking God to help me not kick my mother. She narrows her eyes to read the caption.

"Yes, I guess so. Kofi Annan," she repeats.

"Mom, he's the head of the United Nations. He has more important things to worry about than fashion."

"If he's so important, he should try all the harder," she says, screwing up her face. "He's obviously going to be photographed all the time." She pauses, holding the paper at arm's length. "If he just wore only the tie or only the shirt . . ." I roll my eyes.

"Oh and look at this, dear," she says, flipping a page. "Your friend Mary from school is getting married." She slides a section of the paper to me.

I look at the paper. It is indeed Mary from school. Mary who went from one boyfriend to the next in one codependent relationship after another. I slide the paper over to Gran, who is leaning way across the table to get a peek. She *loves* the wedding announcements section. "Great," I say and shake my head.

"Oh Lily. There's no reason to be annoyed. I mean, that off-the-rack dress is hardly anything to be jealous of."

"That's so rude, Mom. What if she doesn't have any money for a nicer dress? Or even still, maybe she has money, but like most people doesn't believe in wasting it on clothes!" I can't believe I'm defending this girl. She once told people that my jeans were so short I was probably building an ark.

"What do you mean 'wasting'?" she asks.

Maybe I shouldn't have said it. Granted, Jesus was hardly tap-dancing in heaven as I won my mom to the Lord with that little doozie, but I can't hide that I find the fashion world utterly worthless and frivolous.

"Those clothes are going to be yours to sell someday, so you'd better learn to like them," she says, looking away. "And you certainly don't seem to mind the life those clothes bought you," she says, gesturing at the room around us.

Dad looks at me. "Ladies, please. We're having dinner." His charcoal Marc Jacobs suit gleams, and his short auburn hair, just starting to gray around the temples, shines in the light of the chandelier. I wonder how long he has until Mom makes him dye it.

Mom glares at me and mumbles something under her breath.

"I think I'm going to spend the weekend at Reagan's," I announce to no one in particular. Reagan hasn't invited me . . . yet. But I need to get away from these fashion-bots called my family.

"I don't see why you girls don't make more use of our house. Didn't you say her futon makes your neck ache? We have three guest bedrooms going to waste." My mother looks at me as if I'm foolish. And, hey, maybe I am foolish for opting to stay in Reagan's cramped apartment in Russian Hill with the vintage furniture from her dead grandmother and the one tacky splatter-painted futon circa 1984, but sometimes our Art Deco Woodside mansion feels like a prison.

I have been saving up for a down payment on my own place, preferably somewhere far away from Traywick Dungeon, for a while. But right now I only have enough for a geodesic dome in Golden Gate

Park, and that's if I can sweet-talk Buckminster Fuller down on the price a little—from the grave no less. Sure, Woodside is an enviable place, and with five acres of land selling for more than a million dollars, it had better be. But I hate driving into the city every day for work, and living with my parents seriously impedes my dating life. I mean, it would, if, you know, I was dating.

I shrug at my mother, and she shakes her head in disbelief as an answer. Her diamond earrings glisten.

"And don't forget that this Sunday night is that thing I go to once a month with church. I'll just see you guys at work on Monday," I say.

"What's that *thing* called again?" my mother asks, cocking an eyebrow at me.

I groan internally. I love my church, I really do, but whoever named my favorite event should be shot, or kicked out, or . . . okay, well, maybe they should just have nursery duty for a year with lots of poopy diapers to change.

"Super Single Sunday," I say, and wince.

Adding the word "super" does not make the rest of it better. It's like saying Super Toe-Jam Problem. The crud is still under your nails. But I am too old for the college class now and there are some good-looking guys there.

"I really don't think you're going to ever meet a man that way," my mother says.

"That's *not* why I go," I lie. Her comments about my singledom are increasingly frequent the older I get. Granted, they started when I was nineteen. I try to change the subject.

"Gran, how's the owl coming?"

My Gran, a true original, makes "art" sculptures constructed entirely out of California almonds, using only a glue gun. She's even sold a few on eBay. She's working on an owl at the moment. But she doesn't answer me, deep in thought over her roast.

"I just think that it would be nice for you to get married someday. You're going to need help running Traywick's. You can't do it all alone."

"Mom, that's so unfair—"

"So I'm the villain, then. I'm the villain because I suggested you try to meet someone. I should think that my concern for you would make you realize I'm a nice person. Isn't that right, dear?" My mother puts her hand on top of my father's.

"Hmm?" he says.

"Isn't that right that I'm a nice person and that I love my daughter?"

"Oh yes. Certainly," he says.

"I want to meet someone too, Mom. You're not listening to me. It's just hard, that's all. I can't just marry someone I meet walking down the street."

"Oh, did you meet someone?" Gran asks, suddenly interested in the conversation.

"No, I was just telling Mom that I—"

"Oh. That's too bad, dearie," Gran says.

I get up and start scraping the food off my plate, while my mother recaps her point to Gran. I've got to get out of here, fast.

"Argh!" I can't sleep. Again, that is. I haven't gotten a good night's rest since I read that article about myself in the *Chronicle*. I lie down and my mind just whirs and whirs, and I can't make it stop.

I reach for the phone. It's one in the morning. I wager that Reagan will still be awake and dial her number quickly.

"Hey you!" she yells into the phone. "What are you still doing up?" Loud music thumps in the background.

"Trying to sleep, actually. Where are you? It's really loud."

"Hm? Oh, sorry," she says quickly. "Hold on." I hear vague muffled noises and a deep bass beat, then it gets quieter and Reagan reappears on the line. "Sorry about that. I'm at this club where Zack's band is playing. But I'm outside now. What's up?"

"Is Zack that guy you met last weekend?"

"Uh huh," she says, giggling. "He's really hot, Lily. What? Oh, here you go," she says away from the phone. "Sorry, someone asked to bor-row a lighter."

"Mm," I mumble. Somehow this isn't making me feel better. Why is dating always so easy for her?

"Are you okay, Lily?" she asks. "You aren't usually awake this late." Reagan gives off the impression of being flighty sometimes, but she is one of the most caring people I know. She can always tell when something is wrong. We met in sixth grade because some boys were picking on her in gym. I offered each and every one of them their very own knuckle sandwich if they didn't stop. What did I have to lose? I was already two heads taller than every boy in our class. And God bless her, she'll never forget it. She's loyal to a fault. This was great for me because she ended up being the class president all four years of high school and even Prom Queen our senior year. She wore a little white cropped sundress, white knee socks, and slippers. She somehow looked so cool next to all the other girls in sequins. Meanwhile, I was pretty shy. I wasn't the coolest kid in school, but Reagan never cared.

I take a deep breath. If I tell her what's really wrong, she'll leave the party and come straight over and listen to me whine all night.

I just can't do that to her.

"I just wanted to see how you're doing, is all," I lie.

"You're so funny. I'm totally fine!" she says, laughing.

"Well, okay then . . ." I say, trying to sound upbeat. Inwardly, I just want to cry.

"Lily, are you sure you're okay?" she asks quietly.

"I'm fine." I sigh. "Go back in and have fun."

"Ok. I'll give you a call tomorrow?" Reagan asks. The loud thumping resumes.

"Have a good night, Reagan."

After I hang up the phone, I don't feel any better. I consider calling Steph, but she's probably been asleep for hours by now. I listen carefully to see if I can hear Gran moving around, but the house is still. They must all be asleep. I lie back in bed and think.

Eventually, I can't stand being still anymore. I get up and fumble with my robe and slippers. One of the drawbacks to a high-gloss hardwood floor house is that it's always freezing to walk around. I shuffle into the upstairs office and turn on the computer. Maybe a little Internet surfing will ease my mind.

I go to salon.com. Lately I've been reading the blogs that people write. It's kind of lame, just a bunch of amateurish writers pouring out their hearts to no one, but much like with chick flicks, you get sucked in. Some of them are so personal and interesting, it's like reading a stranger's diary.

By two in the morning, I'm quite delirious after having read all the top-ranked blogs—who knew that cooking all the recipes from *The Mastery of French Cooking* would be so difficult or that knitting was so fulfilling—I can hardly see straight. But I'm still not tired. And then something catches my eye.

Say your piece on the Web—with Salon Blogs, you can be up and running in five minutes!

Fashion Victim
Transmissions from Fashion Land

single
Bible-reading
fashion-hating
boy crazy
only daughter
twenty-something still living at home
speaks out

Hmmm . . . let's see. What can I tell you, dear reader?

    1. This is my first blog, ever (as if you couldn't tell).

2. I am twenty-seven years old and have never been kissed, unless you count when I was five and a classmate pulled me behind a bush and the teacher caught us and he got a spanking.

3. I have famous parents. I am supposed to take over the family business someday. Whether I actually want to or not is irrelevant.

4. I currently live at home with said famous parents and mutiny is in the air.

5. I am most likely one of the last Christian women in my age group because the rest of them got married while I was watching *Wheel of Fortune* in college and studying for my important career, which now, after college, I'm still trying to locate.

6. I've wanted to be a writer since second grade when the first book I ever wrote won first place at the Young Author's Fair.

7. I don't like bananas. I never have.

8. I have two best friends—one Christian, one not—and apparently a multiple personality disorder.

9. I played four sports in high school and believe that the batting cage would be a great first date. I'm speculating, of course.

Go with God! Down with fashion!
Fashion Victim

• Chapter 3 •

I grip the steering wheel and close my eyes. Too good to be true.

It's a double-crush Sunday, with an all-too-rare appearance from Stephanie to boot. God is my best friend, and I tell him so, if not just to make up for all the times when I let him know how unfair he seems. Normally all it takes is one J. Lo video and I'm asking him where my butt went and why I'm a five-foot-ten ogre. But not tonight. Tonight is my night. As one of the few members of Super Sucky Singles to actually own a car—living in the 'burbs does have some advantages—I have been elected to drive a carload of the group to this month's event, which tonight is, wonder of wonders, miracle of miracles, a San Jose Sharks hockey game. I needed something good to happen to me. Something just like this.

"Do you know the way?" Miguel asks, pulling the seat belt tightly across his nicely defined chest.

"To San Jose?" I ask, rolling my eyes. Thank you, Dionne Warwick. For the rest of our lives, we Californians will have to endure your song.

"Yeah," he says, flashing a shy smile my way. I melt inside, and it's not just the sun-streaked hair and big brown eyes. He has a way about him. A junior lawyer and soccer fanatic, Miguel always seems so sweet and vulnerable, and his natural tan only accentuates his muscles. He could convince any girl there is a God. But he was so quiet when I first met him that I thought for sure he found me utterly and completely dull.

Turns out he's just shy. When he plays the bass in the worship band at church he often forgets to face the congregation. But he's been opening up, and his dumb joke is a good sign . . . Maybe he is finally working up the courage to ask me out. I grab the directions out of his hand.

"Not that you were *really* curious, Miguel, but San Jose is just south on 101 all the way," I say, skimming the page. "Let's go. We have to hurry. Only the first ten thousand fans get Sharky bobblehead dolls."

Steph is in the backseat with Daniel, who is the youth-group intern and all-around fun guy. Steph almost didn't come, since, being from Hawaii, she's never been a big hockey fan and hates long car rides (they call it the Big Island, but it's a lie), and she has a biochem final coming up. I tried to bribe her with a can of Betty Crocker frosting and a tube of raw cookie dough, which was our favorite snack in college. When that weirdly didn't work, I begged her, saying I needed her to help me win over one of my crushes. Any of my crushes. At this point it doesn't matter who.

Steph has this uncanny way with men. With such a petite frame, blond hair, and a sweet, easygoing nature, any guy in our singles group would love to take her out. But none of them even try now. She's told them all no over the years. She used to date some in college, but now she's too busy with volunteering and med school to be around much. She's been formally proposed to three times now! Three times! She actually dumped her last boyfriend, Dave, because when they were in Union Square, he *suggested* they pop into Tiffany to "take a quick look." She said she started hyperventilating on the sidewalk and refused to go in. She hasn't accepted a date since then.

"Miguel! Please take the map and pay attention," Steph says from the backseat. "You called shotgun so your punishment is to keep our girl on track. I doubt anyone forgets the last time we let Lily drive anywhere." Okay, so I'm not the best driver.

"Do you know the way to Honolulu?" Daniel sings in Steph's face.

"Hysterical," she says. "A joke about Hawaii. I get it. That's new.

Maybe someone has another joke about Hawaii they could try out? C'mon, mainlanders. Pick on the girl from Hawaii, why don't you?"

Steph is cracking me up.

"Did you guys eat Spam instead of turkey at Thanksgiving?" I ask, jokingly. I take off the parking brake. Hawaii, I once learned on *Jeopardy*, is the largest consumer of Spam in the world, and I haven't let Steph forget it. We all love to tease her about being so "Hawaiian." Steph's father was stationed at Hickam Air Force Base and though she is a *haole*—a white ghost—her family has been there since before she was born. I have a mix tape of her singing the "Twelve Days of Christmas," as she thought it was until she went to college on the "mainland." They learn their own version out there, which starts, "Numbah One day of Christmas, my tutu give to me, one mynah bird in one papaya tree," and involves five big fat pigs instead of five golden rings. And once Daniel sent her a bogus e-mail inviting her to join the Neo-Mainlanders Club of San Francisco. She actually tried to join.

"Do we really have to wait for the rest of the group?" I ask, looking over my shoulder at the group standing around the other three cars, parked in a circle, still coordinating. We are supposed to drive to the game in a four-car caravan, but I really love a good hockey game, and I don't want to be late.

"Lily! They're planning," Steph says, shaking her head. "They're trying to make sure we all get there. Be nice." Steph has this annoying habit of always thinking the best of others and trying to be kind and compassionate.

"I have my cell phone on. I think we can go ahead and go. They can catch up at the game," Daniel says. Hooray, let's go! I mean, Sharky bobblehead dolls are at stake!

I pull out of my parking space in the grocery store parking lot, the designated meeting place in this parking-nightmare of a town. Daniel rolls down his window to yell, as we go by the rest of the group in a huddle, "That first shall be last thing is a sham!" and then pulls his head back in and buckles his seat belt.

I'm feeling good. I can smell someone's cologne—Daniel?—I've got the cruise control set, and Miguel is chatting with Steph. He's making fun of Steph's compulsive habit of making lists and scheduling every second of her time. She tends to be a bit of a perfectionist. She laughs goodnaturedly and quickly changes the subject.

"Daniel, have you looked into which seminary programs you're interested in?" she asks sweetly.

Daniel swallows hard, and I stifle a giggle. He hasn't even started looking. He mumbles something about planning to start researching this week, then says, quickly, "You guys need to meet Miguel's new girlfriend."

What?! My mouth falls open in shock.

Miguel laughs. "Don't be so surprised, Lily! I'm not as bad as you think. Some girls don't mind a guy like me."

"Lily!" Steph says, alarmed. "Ahhh!"

I look up and realize we're swerving into the other lane! Thankfully, there's no car in it, and so I just put us back in our proper lane. My cheeks are hot, but Daniel is cracking up in the backseat and begins to say a prayer of protection to tease me.

"Sorry, guys. I think I need a soda at the next In-N-Out," I say. And then I go for the recovery. "That's great that you met someone. What's her name?" I ask, sweetly. Bathsheba, perhaps? What about Jezebel?

"Becky. She's great. I met her at a soccer game. She's sporty like Lily."

Like Lily? Is he serious? Why go with "like-Lily" when you can in fact have Lily, the genuine article. I *love* soccer. I love all sports. Was Miguel a complete dolt? I've been crushing on him for a year! And now, he dates Becky who probably only plays intramural soccer and is like-Lily. *Argh!*

"What, Lily? Did you say something?" Steph asks.

Uh oh. Did I *argh* out loud?

"Ha ha ha. Me? Oh no. I cleared my throat is all. I really need that drink. Keep an eye out for fast food, eh?" I say to Miguel and hit him playfully in the arm.

Steph painfully pulls every detail about Becky out of Miguel, and by the end of it, I have to admit, she does sound like the kind of girl I'd be friends with.

"You should bring her to S3 sometime," I say, impressed by my own maturity. Who is an adult? I am!

"Yeah, I don't know," he says.

"Why?" Steph asks.

Daniel cracks up. "He's missionary dating!"

I glance at Steph in the rearview mirror. She is wide-eyed and staring at Miguel, who is looking at the car floor.

"She's not a Christian?" I ask.

"No," he says.

No one knows what to say. I certainly don't since I have never even been on a date, much less in a relationship. Stephanie saves us.

"All the more reason to bring her to church. She might have fun. It could be a first step."

"Yeah," Miguel says and goes quiet again.

"Hey, can I trade seats with you?" I whisper to Bill as he climbs into the seat next to Daniel. It's an awful thing to say, but Bill is probably my least favorite person in Super Single Sunday. He always has this weird hot dog breath and has a strange fascination with spiritual warfare. He has even painted his face turquoise in support of the Sharks tonight. He turns and looks at me blankly. I hold my bobblehead doll nervously.

"Why?" he asks loudly, looking down at his ticket and then at the row of empty seats behind him. Daniel turns and watches us. "This is seat number 128 F 12. I have the ticket for number 128 F 12." He looks up at me, confused. "I don't see why you want to change seats. I'm supposed to sit right there next to Daniel."

Why do I even try? Last year when he got laid off, he passed up a job offer that would have taken him off of the church's charity fund because he felt that God didn't *want* him to take it. It was a respectable job, but apparently God wanted him to live off the charity of others when he had the chance to provide for himself. Plus he always prays for a good parking spot and then says *Thank you, Jesus* again and again when he finds one. As if God cares where he parks his teal LeBaron.

"Never mind," I say quickly, noticing that Daniel is staring at us, and walk away, sitting carefully down in 128 G 10. No matter about the seating arrangement. I'll at least be able to see Daniel from here, although sitting next to him would have been more ideal. At least Steph is on my right, now smirking at me, having watched my attempt at maneuvering near Daniel's side. But when I look to my left, I realize I am stuck sitting by the Super Sucky girls who clearly intend to talk instead of watch the game. On my left is Maggie, who with her round face, curly brown hair, and the scarf that she is currently knitting—*at a hockey game*—looks a little bit like a rendering of a young Betsy Ross. I notice there's something in her hair. It's a bug! I lift my hand up to try to swat it away from her head but stop my hand just inches from her curls.

"Ahhh," she yells, shying away from my hand.

I lean in closer to get a better look. "What *is* that in your hair?"

She touches it lovingly. "Oh. This is my butterfly clip."

I study it and see that it is in fact a butterfly made out of fake rhinestones—it has a startling lifelike quality. I look her over and then spot tiny butterfly decals on her fingernails too. "You really like butterflies, I guess."

She beams and elbows her best friend, Alex, who is sitting next to her. Alex, who prefers to be called by her full name, Alexandra, is gorgeous, self-centered, and the ring-leader of the church girls. No one is a better Christian than she is. "See, Alexandra, it's working!"

"What's working? Oh hey, Alex," I say.

"It's Alexandra," she says quickly, shaking her head. "She wears a butterfly every day as a symbol of her rebirth in the Lord. It's a part of our Creative Adornment Outreach initiative," says Alex. They both look happy that I noticed a bug crawling in Maggie's hair and tried to save her from it sucking her brains out. It would have starved anyway.

"Right. But I'm already a Christian so . . ."

They both look at me confused. I stifle the urge to make a joke about larvae and look down the long row of church girls instead. Yep. They're all here. A few of them smile and nod at me as only aging Christian women in the presence of marriageable men can.

"Who's Nabokov?" Alex asks me. While Maggie is meek and mild and so sweet she'll give you a toothache, Alexandra's long red hair and green eyes just about sum her up. She is beautiful, and she wants to make sure you know it. Oddly enough, in spite of her striking looks, her career in the male-dominated world of banking, and her desperate desire to be a good Christian wife, she is not dating anyone. I like to think it's because her blunt personality, her love of lace curtains, her habit of bossing sweet Maggie around, and her transparent attempts to snare a man scare the guys away. They sure scare me away. I lean back a little.

"Nabokov?" I ask, incredulously. I glance to my right and see a wry smile from Steph as she turns away, pretending not to hear, now examining her nails. Thanks for the help, Steph. Remind me not to put you down as one of my lifelines. "The writer, or the guy whose name is on the back of my jersey?" I ask Alex, taking pains to tone down the sarcasm in my voice. Steph gives me an elbow in the ribs to remind me to be nice.

"Uh. I guess the guy whose name is on your jersey? Is he one of the players?"

"Yes. He's their legendary goalie."

"I don't like hockey," Maggie says. The girls all nod in unison.

I bite my lip. Is it wrong to ask why they came then? "Oh," I say. There. I just didn't say anything at all instead of something not nice. A victory.

Maggie leans in and drops her voice. "I just like all the cutie-patooties," she says. They all begin to twitter in agreement about the cutie-patooties and the two on the end give each other a high-five but miss each other's hands twice before they finally connect.

I know, I know. I come to Super Single Sunday for "the view" myself, but I also *like* hockey, honest to God, and I have never, ever, used the word "patootie." I'm at a loss with Alex and the girls so I just smile, nod, and then focus all of my attention on the rink, thinking of my rotten, low-down, no good, sensational bad luck.

When the Sharks score early in the first period, I jump out of my seat and scream. And when one of the opposing players knocks a Sharks player into the wall, I boo him loudly. And when Nabakov makes a great save, I stand up and wave my arms around, knocking Maggie's head by accident and interrupting the gossip session. "Sorry!" I scream, and she smiles politely before turning back to her conversation. Daniel turns around and gives me an overly enthusiastic high-five that leaves my hand red and smarting for about twenty minutes, but I don't mind. I might not wash that hand again.

At the end of the period, the girls all go to the bathroom en masse, but I don't feel like waiting in an eternal lavatory line and pretending to care about makeup, so I stay behind. Steph grimaces at the girls but has to use the bathroom, so she goes along. "If I'm not back in ten minutes," she whispers, "send a search party. They'll have accosted me with frosted lipstick." While they are gone, I can focus on Daniel. Or at least stare at the back of his head. He must eventually feel my eyes boring a hole through his head because he turns around and smiles when he sees me sitting alone.

"You didn't go with the giggling gaggle?" he asks.

I shake my head. "Nah. I have a bladder of steel," I say, then cringe. That's right, Lil. Wow 'em with talk about your bodily functions.

"That's why I like you, Lily," he says, laughing. Did he just say he liked me? I think he did. My heart is pat-pat-patting. He likes me! "You're not like the other girls." I am not like other girls!

"That's right, I'm not," I say, hoping I sound confident, then putting my fingers to my mouth and letting out a shrill whistle as the Zamboni comes onto the ice. The whole row turns to look at me. I just shrug.

"And now . . ." a man's voice booming from overhead says, "it's time for our first intermission drawing." I sit up and pay attention. I have to win something—it's my lucky day! "We have lots of prizes to give away, so grab your ticket stubs and pay attention," the voice thunders. Lights flash across the ice from above the scoreboard. I pull out my ticket stub from my back pocket.

"If your seat number is called, please go to the box office to claim your prize," the voice says, resonating throughout the arena. I look again at my ticket stub, and pray for him to call seat 128 G 10, grimacing as the girls come back loudly to their seats.

"Our first prize, two tickets to Great America amusement park," the booming voice says dramatically, "goes to the fan in seat number 222 M 38." A woman in the balcony starts screaming. The JumboTron camera lands on her, and we all watch her hug her entire family like she just got picked to be on *The Price Is Right* and then run down the steps to collect her prize.

"A family pack of tickets to Marine World in Vallejo," he continues, "to seat 118 B 16." I cross my fingers.

"A meal for two at Chez Panisse," he says, slowly, drawing out the suspense while I pray for him to pick me. My parents often take important clients to Chez Panisse, but I have never been there, though I have always wanted to go. If I win, I could casually ask Daniel to go with me because he was there when I won it. He'd say yes, I just know it. I simply must have these tickets. I need the excuse to ask him. I will win. I will win. "Goes to seat number 128 F 12."

128 F 12?

Bill jumps up, arms above his head, pumping his hands, yelling, "Yes! Yes! I won!" I feel a righteous indignation coming over me. That should have been my seat! Why he's an ungrateful, unchivalrous . . .

How could he win with *my* seat? He doesn't even have anyone to take to a fancy restaurant! Bill stops to point up at the ceiling and mouths "The glory is His!" before he pushes past the other guys, who slap him on the back as he makes his way to the aisle. Rejoice with those who are rejoicing, I think. Rejoice. I am so busy trying to convince myself that I am rejoicing for him that I am not paying attention to the disembodied voice until Steph, who has returned unscathed from her adventure in the bathroom, starts pounding me on the back.

"That's you!" she says, smiling broadly at me. Everyone around us is cheering. I stare back at her confusedly. The spotlight searches section 128 and finally stops to focus on me.

"That's right, seat 128 G 10 is our grand-prize winner!" the voice says enthusiastically. I look up and see my bewildered face on the JumboTron. "Come on down to the ice," it yells, "and enjoy your ride on the Zamboni!" I stand still, in shock. I see my mouth hanging open on the giant screen and close it immediately.

"Go!" Steph says encouragingly. I take a tentative step toward the aisle. The girls lean back so I can pass. I won a ride on the Zamboni! I've always wanted to ride a Zamboni! As I step into the aisle, I raise my arms over my head. I run down the stairs—luckily we're on the first level—to the ice. A man in a giant plush shark suit and a turquoise jersey helps me to the door in the high plastic wall that keeps pucks out of fans' laps, and I step uncertainly onto the ice. The giant red ice-smoothing machine pulls up right in front of me. Sharky helps me climb up onto the seat next to the driver, and we take off, swirling around the ice.

I'm riding a Zamboni! Wow, I never realized quite how high these things are. And somehow it didn't occur to me that everyone in the arena would be watching me . . . I try to forget about it and just enjoy my ride.

The announcer plays "Ice, Ice Baby" loudly over the loudspeaker. The crowd cheers, and I catch a glimpse of the JumboTron. That's me on the Zamboni! Take that, *San Francisco Chronicle*. Take that, Maria Shriver. I raise my hands triumphantly.

"Now that's a true fan!" the announcer says, laughing. "She brought her Sharky bobblehead doll with her!" I did? I look up. Oh no. I forgot I still had it in my hand. Oh well. I shake it for the JumboTron camera, making the head bounce back and forth.

"And check out that jersey!" he yells. "Folks, I would have to say we have one dedicated fan here." I start dancing in my seat. The driver laughs at me, turning gracefully around the oval of ice.

"Who loves the Sharks?" the announcer asks, and I stand up on the moving machine, pointing to myself. The crowd roars. "I'd say we have a super fan here!" he says, laughing at me. "Super Fan, show us how much you love the Sharks!" I remain standing and dance, doing the Macarena, the twist, and the hula as the driver pulls the Zamboni back around to the clear plastic door. The clapping grows louder. I am bringing the house down.

"Aw, Super Fan," the announcer says dramatically, "it looks like your ride is just about over," he says as the machine slows to a stop. The giant Shark helps me climb off. "But to show our appreciation for being such a good sport," he says, "you get your very own limited-edition Sharkhead!" A man in a teal shirt comes over carrying a giant piece of gray foam in the shape of a shark's head. He places it ceremoniously on my head. It must be at least three feet high and three feet in diameter, and the jaws open straight out of my forehead, lower jaw straight out in front, upper jaw raising at an angle toward the ceiling.

It is . . . well, it's terrible. I may not know much about fashion, but I know this falls somewhere between pegged jeans and shoulder pads. A fashion no-no. Sharky pats my back, and I look at him uncertainly. He nods enthusiastically, and I doubtfully walk toward my seat. So now I'm taking advice from a giant plush shark. The crowd cheers as I push past the first row of fans.

"Ouch!" a woman in a teal sweatshirt yelps, rubbing her head where I hit her with the brim of my giant Sharkhead. I turn to apologize, but I whack a little boy on the face with my lower jaw.

"I'm so sorry!" I yell, then reach up to take my hat off. I keep walking toward my seat. Why is the camera still on me?

"What's this?" the announcer says loudly. "Super Fan, what have you done with your Sharkhead?" They must have put me back up in the giant screen, because suddenly the whole crowd is booing. "Put your Sharkhead back on, won't you, Super Fan?" the announcer asks sweetly. I walk up the stairs to my seat, see Steph, who is winking at me and pointing toward her head, and resignedly put the Sharkhead back on. The crowd erupts into cheers.

I groan. Okay, the stunt is over. Time to go back to regular hockey.

I push my way past the row of church girls, knocking Alex in the face with the brim. The girls after her have the foresight to lean way back as I pass. I paste a smile onto my face.

"That was so great!" Daniel says, standing up to give me another high-five.

"Yeah, that was really cool," Miguel says enthusiastically. I smile, willing him to turn back around and stop acting so excited so the camera will focus on something else.

"And the Sharkhead is awesome!" Bill yells. Bill thinks the hat is awesome? That's definitely a bad sign. You know what's really awesome, Balding Bill? A dinner for two at Chez Panisse! The Sharkhead has to go.

I start to take it off but am stopped by a round of boos. I look up at the screen, see myself blushing furiously, wanting to disappear into the floor. I put the Sharkhead back on slowly. The crowd cheers wildly. This could get old really quickly. I pray for the game to start again soon.

It does, but I only get to see a little bit before the man behind me yells, "Move! I can't see!" The Sharks charge up the ice and shoot the puck into the goal, and the man behind me starts cursing. "I missed it!

Take the Sharkhead off!" I quickly slip it off, turn to say I'm sorry, but immediately hear the cheering that greeted the goal turn to booing.

"Super Fan!" The announcer scolds. "We all see you!" I am once again on the screen. People begin to chant, "Sharkhead. Sharkhead. Sharkhead." I could leave now, I think to myself. I could just get up, leave, and drive home. I can't wear the Sharkhead anymore. I don't want to be the center of attention anymore. I see all of the hockey team standing still on the ice, players chanting along with the crowd. Reluctantly, I put it back on. The chanting turns to cheering again. I want to sink into the floor.

This is going to be a long game.

I can't sleep. In the dark I can tell my cheeks are still burning. That was the worst hockey game of my life. Sure, it was fun to ride the Zamboni, but having my face plastered on the JumboTron for half the game isn't my idea of fun. Once I got my Sharkhead, it seemed like no one cared about the game anymore. In addition to getting booed whenever I tried to take it off, I had to stand up during the second intermission (or look like a jerk with the cameras on me) and stretch my arms out in front of me, lifting them up and down to simulate a shark's jaw opening and closing. This might have been fun with just friends, but it was not fun to have the whole arena imitating me. There's a reason I did not go out for cheerleading.

But the worst was that nobody seemed to understand why I didn't want to stand up and cheer and wear a stupid Sharkhead. Bill thought it was the greatest thing in the world and kept laughing whenever I had to perform. Steph was the first to start the booing when I tried to unobtrusively slip the hat off during the third period. Daniel kept giving me high-fives.

I roll over in bed. And of course, now, he will never go out with me. Who dates a girl with a Sharkhead? I am cursed. Daniel was supposed to fall in love with me last night. How did loving sports somehow get used against me? The worst was at the end of the game: Daniel said I could hang out with him and Miguel anytime because after that game, I was officially cool enough to be *one of them*.

There we go again. One of the guys.

How does Reagan do it? She can just walk into a room and have every man mesmerized. She gets so many guys in such rapid succession that I can't even keep up with who she's dating. I always liked to think just hanging out with her made me a little bit cool. I mean, I always had boys trying to talk to me. Sure, they wanted to ask me about Reagan, but it was something. And Steph? Too driven to notice that she could have any guy she wanted. She has some indescribable charm that makes Christian men fall for her every time. She says it's because she teaches Sunday School so all the guys wrongly assume she wants be a mother to their children, but I know it is more than that.

I will never get a date.

You'd think that I would have had at least one boyfriend by now. It is no secret that my family has money—it's hard to deny you share a name with the most chichi store in town—so surely I should have at least run across a gold digger or two? But no. Why?

I get up and walk into the bathroom. I stare at myself in the mirror, tears welling up in my eyes. Am I so awful? I study my face. I do have a nice long neck, even Mom has admitted that, and I am very tall, but I look like I never really filled out. I'm long and coltish. My lips are rather standard; I guess they would benefit from being highlighted by a little lip gloss. And my eyes are a nice warm brown color. I pull in close to the mirror and blink back the tears. Yes, I seem to have longish eyelashes. Maybe if I learned to put that awful black goop on them . . . And my hair. I've always gotten compliments on it. It's sort of boring, dropping well below my shoulders in a straight, one-length blunt cut, but it's very shiny and thick and the same rare auburn color my father has.

I shrug. I just don't get it. What's so wrong with me?

And suddenly I know what I have to do.

I need to ask Reagan for help.

Fashion Victim
Transmissions from Fashion Land

STILL SINGLE
fashionably in pain
boy crazy
shopophobe
about to change her life
speaks out—okay, rants today

Whew! I thought I'd never get to write. Gran was *monopolizing* the computer, conducting a hot eBay auction for one of her Almond Art pieces. The Fashion Victim family would like to take this opportunity to wish Hoot the Owl well in his new life beyond our home. I can't believe someone bought it. It just goes to show there are a lot of crazy people in this world.

And operating further on that premise, how come a *sane* (okay, mostly) girl like myself can't get a date? Surely I could offer an insane guy, say, a nice shiny object, and he'd take me out on a date to the roller rink or something? Where are all the wackos? I mean, I know the normal guys are all gone, but I was hoping there were some nuts left.

And . . . you know, I'm just going to keep ranting here. I'm tired of being an "adult" about it. A few nights ago I hung out with a bunch of guys and wowed them all with my encyclopedic knowledge of the San Jose Sharks, and at the end of the night, I still had not been asked out. *No!* Instead I found out that same night that one of the most datable guys I know (he had the look, the manners, the Bible) is now dating a non-Christian who he described as "just like you, Fashion Victim!" Why am I like, This little light of mine, I'm gonna let it shine, all alone in the corner while the Christian guys are out picking up random girls who don't even know the Ten Commandments let alone the Twenty-third Psalm, who remind them of me. I'm here! We Christian girls are here! Date us! We're wasting away in the church nursery!

Breathe . . . breathe . . .

Okay, I'm back and armed with a mouthful of brownie. Whew. Sorry things got a little ugly above.

On the upside, I did get an e-mail out of the blue from a guy named Daniel. I was jumping up and down and freaking out until I read it. It didn't say anything except, "I thought you might think this is funny," and it had a link to a Chapstick of the Month club. But in the PS it said, "I need a suit for an interview. Maybe I'll stop by and see you at work sometime this week." Please write me, loyal readers, with an interpretation of the e-mail if you speak Boy. Chapstick? Is that some kind of code?

Another plus is that my parents are in Paris for the week at . . . well, let's just say a trade show. Cue Handel's Hallelujah Chorus. Oh man, it's so nice not feeling judged every time I walk into a room.

Oh rats! What a night. Okay, Gran is letting her art go to her head. She just came in and demanded to get back on the computer so that she could download a picture of Benny Hinn. Gran is *obsessed* with Benny Hinn, who is this preacher on TV she watches every Sunday morning.

I have already heard from legions of you, dear readers, and it has been great. I guess I'm striking a chord with some of you, and the rest of you just can't turn away from the train wreck that is my life. Keep writing me! Tell me who you are! (No, I won't return the favor.) Oh, and Earle? Yes, you, earle@sfw.com. Whoever you are, I am naming you my number-one fan. Seriously, readers, so far I have gotten four e-mails from him in the past week. Sure, one was supposed to be a picture of himself but turned out to be a jpg of a plate of peas and another one was an online quiz entitled "How Fashion-Savvy Are You?" but still! Halloo to you, Earle, and thanks for reading.

Go with God! Down with fashion!
Fashion Victim

• Chapter 4 •

"Is everything all right?" the waiter asks. My face is a mess of tears.

Reagan and I are at Traywick's café, The Good Life, where every day we have frozen yogurt on our afternoon break. The place disgusts me—it caters to the high-maintenance Traywick's customers by offering only healthy menu options and by serving everything with a sheet of nutritional information—but it is convenient. Reagan and I have a policy never to read the handouts, but every day we get a new sheet about every item we order. I think of shouting at the waiter's beautiful face, *No! I'm twenty-seven years old and have never been on a proper date. I will die alone with only my six cats to mourn my death!* Instead, I just sit there a sniveling mess.

Luckily, Reagan handles him. "She's fine. Bad day at work. Maybe some napkins please?" she smiles at him. He smiles back and then bumps into a chair as he walks away. Her lily-white, square-toothed smile has turned him into a fumbling mess. I sigh. I've seen this all before. Men find her funny ways irresistible.

"You want me to stop?" She slides her chair over to mine, placing a hand on my arm, plastic teal bangle bracelets jangling on her wrist.

The waiter reappears with some napkins, places them on our table, and smiles at me. I smile weakly back and then stare at the table. Reagan puts a napkin in my hand, and I press it to my face. I try to blot, not rub (my mother's voice eternally echoes through my head) my tears away.

Reagan knows what she is talking about. I'd be a fool not to listen. "No. Keep going. I need to know," I say.

I love Reagan for *finally*—after our fifteen-year friendship, during which time I have watched her date every available guy we've come across—leveling with me. I asked her just ten minutes before the question every ugly duckling wants to know: Why not me? And she had told me, truthfully. No one had ever done that before. And I guess while I knew all along on some level that I was a fashion catastrophe, that I probably scare guys away with my vast knowledge of sports and because I look like I would wear sneakers under my wedding dress instead of Blahnik's from Traywick's, it was still hard to hear. It always is.

"We just need to channel all of your finesse on the softball field into finesse in the dating game."

I nod, staring at my vanilla frozen yogurt. "And . . ."

"And, well, you need a new look. We can go shopping! We have a lot of raw material here that is going to waste. You have great, thick, shiny auburn hair. You could get a cute haircut. And you're so tall you could be a model."

I look down at my giant, flat feet and feel less like a model and more like the urban-Amazon woman I apparently am. I also look at my black Keds sneakers with the hole in the right toe. I only bought them four years ago. I hope these don't have to go.

"I'll help you, Lily, but you have to be ready to make this step. I'm not going to lie. There are some dramatic changes we're going to have to make to your wardrobe, your hair, okay . . . your look in general, but more importantly, *you* are going to have to change. Lily is going to have to come out. No more being shy. I don't want to do this unless you're wholeheartedly behind it. I love you the way you are, but sometimes I feel like I'm the only person who gets to see the real Miss Traywick. You're going to have to let the cool person inside of you out. It's going to be hard. But I know you can do it."

I spoon a glob of yogurt in my mouth. Did I really need to change my hair to make guys like me? What about being beautiful on the inside? I glance at Reagan's perfectly made-up face. She really knows what she's doing. I swallow back the lump in my throat. "I want to do this. I'm in." A clear stream of snot leaks out of my nose.

Reagan gives me another napkin, laughing. "We've got our work cut out for us. You promise? No backing out?"

"I promise."

"I need more than a promise. Let's bet on it. You *love* to bet," she says.

"I only like to bet on sports. And even then only for a free dinner or something."

"But you like a challenge. Bet me . . . bet me you won't back out, no matter how hard it gets."

"Why? I won't back out."

"Remember when I tried to perm your hair in middle school? You only let me do one side, then you panicked and made me stop, and you had to wear your hair in a ponytail every day until the perm fell out."

"It looked awful!"

"You didn't let me finish. Why, with a little teasing and some hairspray I think you could have looked a lot like Jennifer Beals in *Flashdance*."

Reagan had always been much more adventurous than I was when it came to things like haircuts. While I am content to let mine grow for six months or a year until the split ends get so bad I can't stand them, Reagan always has the latest styles, often before celebrities show up with them in the fashion magazines. And even though working at Traywick's isn't my dream come true, working in the European Fashions department is the perfect job for Reagan. She's already moved up to a buyer in her department, and Mom thinks she's the brightest fashion merchandising major they've ever seen from Berkeley. I look at my sports socks poking out of my black sneakers and sigh. "Fine. What do you want to bet?"

"If you let me transform you in the next six months and really, actually fall so deeply in love I don't recognize you, then I'll go to church with you five whole times."

"Fifteen times," I counter immediately.

"No. Ten times, but only the fun events. None of that big church stuff for me. I did that once as a child, and I vowed never to return, even if it meant never wearing my awesome little patent leather shoes again."

I consider the terms of the deal.

"Seven fun outings, and three Sunday mornings," I say slowly, narrowing my eyes.

"Fine. But! You can't refuse any step of the process of your transformation, as deemed by me, your Makeover Fairy, Reagan Axness."

"Wait a minute. You can do whatever you want to me?!" I ask.

I look under the table at Reagan's hot-pink, authentic, vintage 1980s Sam and Libby's slippers with the little obnoxious bow on the toe. The thought of a makeover from Reagan terrifies me. Sure my mother adores her fashion sense. Reagan's probably the only person I know who can pull off wearing Old Navy flip-flops with a pair of Dolce and Gabbana trousers and a vintage top, but not everyone can get away with a look like that. Not everyone, namely, me.

"Just think. All those years you wanted me to go to your dorky church outings. I'll go ten whole times. No complaining."

Reagan is right. I do love a bet, and there is nothing I want more than to see her start attending church. I've been after her for fifteen years straight. I just know that if I could get her around some Christians and away from the local party scene, God would do the rest. I *have* to agree to it. Even if it means she will have the ability to turn me into the next Madonna, complete with a diamond-studded belt buckle that says Juicy and long blond tresses. Hey, it's ministry.

"Let's shake on it," I say.

"Certainly," Reagan says, raising her eyebrow.

As she pumps my hand, I feel my life changing.

"You really expect me to give up my rent-free life?" I ask as we walk quickly through the cavernous first floor of Traywick's. The crystal chandeliers sparkle above us as we pass the sleek glass cases of perfume, the rich mahogany counters. We walk toward the breathtaking curving escalator bank in the middle of the store and step on. As we rise, I look down at Harry, our longtime piano player—my parents insist he adds *atmosphere*—and smile. He's like a grandfather to me. I turn away and look up at the arched mosaic tile ceiling. I will never stop feeling insignificant in this place.

We get to the second floor, and I head straight for the clearance racks, but Reagan pulls me over to the display in the front. She starts rifling maniacally through the expensive clothes.

"What about my free dinners? My cushy bedroom? We have maids! Reagan, we have a pool!" I say.

"Come on, the maid only comes once a week. And yes, I do expect you to. See how the other half lives," she says, pulling a pair of tan pants off the rack. She holds them up to my waist thoughtfully. "Here, try these on."

I take them doubtfully and decide it's time to change the subject. "So how's Zack?"

"Who?" she asks, distracted by a white sweater.

"Zack? The guy you're dating?"

"Oh, him. Yeah, I ended that last week. But remember that drummer in the band?" She moves her eyebrows up and down. "I'm going out with him tomorrow night."

"Oh, um, okay. We should figure out some kind of system so I can keep up."

"Oh, please, Lily. There aren't that many guys." She laughs. "But did you see that new guy in women's footwear? He's totally hot. And built. You could bounce a quarter off his abs."

"What? Who? A hot new guy I haven't seen yet?"

"I'm surprised myself. But whatever. It's not like you'd ever date him. He seems to be a bit of a partier. I already chatted him up this morning." She holds up a plain white tank top. "What do you think of this shirt?" I nod uncertainly. "Anyway," she says, tossing her hair flippantly, "he's a surfer, and his name is Sam, and he is delectable. But I am wary of any guy who works in shoes. He probably has some kind of foot fetish or something," she says. She stops and looks at me wide-eyed. "You've changed the subject."

She walks right past a whole rack of black shirts that seem perfectly fine to me toward a rack that looks like a box of Crayolas spit up all over it. "You have to explain something. You're always talking about wanting to get out of your parent's house. Why are you so resistant all of a sudden?" She sorts through the rack.

"Of course I want to get out. But actually making the move . . . well, that's a big step. So much work. So much money. I don't have enough for a down payment on my own place, and I don't want to just throw my money away on rent . . . And Gran is there, and who knows how much longer she's going to be around," I say, slowly. "I'm comfortable, if not exactly happy. I mean, as much as my parents bug me, they're better than starving."

She rolls her eyes. "You're not going to starve. I promise. And rent isn't ideal, but it's a part of life," she says, pulling out a bright lime-green skirt. I see her eyes light up.

"No," I say defiantly, and she slowly puts the skirt back.

"It's not like I'm asking this of you for my amusement. And I'm hardly telling you to move into the wilderness and survive on nuts and berries. It's for your own good," she says, shaking her head. "My point is that most single, independent men want a woman who knows how to take care of herself. Who can remember to pay her own rent. Who doesn't live in the boondocks. And," she says, narrowing her eyes, "whose parents he doesn't have to face every time he wants to sleep over."

"Come on, Reagan. You know that isn't an issue," I whine.

"We can address that later," she says with a mischievous smirk. She picks up a blue collared shirt, squints, holds it away, frowns, and puts it back. "Regardless, you're never going to get a guy if you live out in the suburbs with your parents."

"It's not the suburbs. Woodside is a part of San Francisco, it's just a little further out." I don't even know why I'm fighting this battle.

She glares at me with one eyebrow raised. "Get real. Are you going to listen to me, or not? You made a bet."

"I know I did. I know. I'm going to try. It's just—"

"Yes?" she asks, smiling mock-sweetly.

"The money. How am I going to afford it? I don't make a lot peddling Valentino to tots." She stares at me.

"What do you think I make? Squat is what," she says. "And I have student loans I'll be paying off until I'm forty. But I make it work. Trust me," she says, shoving a tiny, sleeveless pale blue top into my arms, "you'll be fine."

It's not much bigger than a piece of paper, but it is delicious to touch. I turn over the price tag. Surely this won't be too bad. Hardly any fabric at all. "Three hundred and fifty dollars!" I yell.

"*Shhhhh!* You are totally embarrassing me, Lily."

I'm in shock. She cannot be serious. I'm trying to hand it back to her as though it's a rattlesnake. "Take it! Take it!"

"Cut it out. You're trying it on. That is Balenciaga, and it will be stunning on you. You need some tops to go out on the town in. Buttondowns and sweaters are fine for work, but this is California, sunny California, Lily, and you're going to show off that slim, hot bod of yours, or I'll walk off the job, and you'll lose the bet."

I stop trying to force the shirt back into her hands. It *is* beautiful, but . . . "Fine. I'll try it on. But for the record, there is no way I can afford this. In fact, I couldn't even afford this if I dipped into my children's college funds, if, you know, they had one, or if, you know, I had children."

She glares at me. "I work and I slave and what thanks do I get? Nuthin! And cry me a river about how much the Balenciaga top costs when the rest of America has to buy it full price. You should appreciate what you have."

I know immediately that this statement has two meanings. I'm being stubborn and ungrateful for all her help, and I'm ignoring how blessed I am. Guilt sweeps over me. "I'm sorry. And you're right. I can admit I get a big corporate discount." I look at her pink sweater with the feathers around the neckline. "Is that how you do it? You just discount your way into always looking like a million bucks?" She pauses, stares at me a little uneasily.

And then she laughs. "How else would I be able to afford this stuff? Why do you think I work here?"

"I thought it might have something to do with your fascinating best friend," I say with just a little pleading in my voice.

She smiles at me and cocks her head to the side. "Of course it does, pookins. I love you. Now get your head in the game. I want you to be looking fabulous by the day's end," she says pulling out a filmy pink dress. "This will be so sexy on you. You have the perfect body for these clothes."

"Where am I ever going to wear that thing?" I exclaim. "I'll look like an anorexic Energizer bunny. Like the Pink Panther on drugs. Like Pepto-Bismol on its way . . ." I hear someone shhhhhing me and turn. Sheila the Hun! Sheila the Hun! Sheila the Hun, who plays a winged-devil-monkey to my mother's Wicked Witch of the West, is the ultra-stern Traywick's general sales floor manager. Also my mother's snoop.

"I hope you're both on break," she says. Her hair is in a tight bun, and she's wearing an immaculate bone-colored Chanel suit.

Reagan slips into what I like to call authority figure mode. "Oh hello, Sheila. Yes, we are on break. We know better than to abuse company time. I was just helping Lily here put together some new ensembles." Reagan beams at Sheila, and I try it too. Sheila meets my smile with suspicion.

"Just remember that no one, ahem," she says, throwing a knowing glance in my direction, "*no one* gets special treatment around here. Be sure the clerk in this department rings you up for everything and with only the Traywick's associate discount."

"Yes, ma'am," we say in unison, although I've stopped smiling altogether. I can't believe she is accusing us of cheating the store.

"And no double-discounts. If something is already on sale, you can only use your Traywick's discount to bring it up to 35 percent off and no more."

"Oh yes, ma'am," Reagan says. "I learned all of that during orientation. We would never—"

"Good then," Sheila says and marches away.

Reagan sighs loudly. "Back to business."

We've got two armfuls of clothing. She starts walking, and I follow her as she weaves her way to the dressing room, grabbing things with lightning-fast arms as we pass them, adding them to her pile. "Yes . . . Comme des Garçons for the evening and a little DKNY for the daytime and maybe some Tocca for the beach . . . Oh! Perfect. Some Campers to knock about in." I try to understand her, but she's now speaking Fashion fluently, and I don't know what she means.

"What about my car?" I ask, trying to bring her back from her Tourette's fashion fit.

She opens the door to a changing room and hangs up her pile and shrugs, her gigantic green hoop earrings swinging. "You can sell it. Or leave it at your parents' house. Then you can use it when you need it."

"How am I going to get around? Am I going to have to take FART?"

"Shh . . ." Regan hisses. "Do you want that crazy Sheila person to come back? It's BART. Bay Area Rapid Transit. You're going to have to start calling it that. And yes, that's one way. Buses, cable cars. The way the rest of us do."

"I hate FART. And no one rides cable cars except tourists."

"In certain parts of the city they do. Just think. You could commute on a cable car. Wouldn't that be fun?"

"I guess," I say. "But not as convenient as my car."

"Lily, are you going to do this or not?" Reagan asks, staring me in the eye.

I pause. I imagine Daniel holding my hand. I imagine us lounging in Golden Gate Park on a summer day. I picture Reagan sitting next to me in church. She's right.

"Yes," I say slowly. "Whatever you say, master. I'm in."

"Good. Now get into the dressing room and try these clothes on. Then we'll head over to accessories." I look at her accessory choices today and see that in addition to her hoops she is wearing an orange studded belt. I am doomed.

The guy next to me rolls down his window, looking at me, and instinctively I roll mine down too.

"Crazy female driver!" he yells at me.

"What?" I say, shocked.

"Hey, lady. You cut me off back there. I almost hit the cable car. I ought to write down your license and report you."

He just keeps going, and tears flood my eyes and drip down my cheeks as I stare at him in shock. That is, until I hear honking behind me. The light is green again. I pull forward much too fast, blinking hard to try to get the tears to stop. One tear drips right onto my new top, and after I brush it away, I force myself to stop crying immediately. These clothes are too expensive to ruin with salty tears, and I can't possibly wreck my face after the makeup took so long to put on this morning. I turn on the radio and leave the window down. I see the angry man turning left and relax a little. What a day. It's not even nine yet.

Driving in San Francisco is a nightmare, with all the hills and streets going off at crazy angles and cable cars cutting through intersections. On the basketball court, I may have nerves of steel, but the streets of this beautiful city can turn me into a tense, quivering mess. Lucky for me, Traywick's has an underground parking garage—where else would the Bay Area's richest leave their Bentleys while they shop?—and since I know the owners, I get to zip past the valet line and have a place to park when I drive in to work.

This morning, though, I'm running really late. It took me almost an hour to pick out an outfit that didn't clash too horribly and wasn't extremely uncomfortable. I tried on a flirty lavender sundress, a pair of red pants and a green turtleneck, and a short skirt and knee-high boots, trying to figure out if any of them were acceptable to wear to work, before I settled on what was undoubtedly the most boring of all the possible choices. I made a mental note to ask Reagan to tell me exactly what I am supposed to wear with what from my new collection of ridiculously expensive clothes. The gray pants alone had a $700 price tag, which is way too much for anyone to ever pay for a pair of pants. Granted, my employee discount took a hefty chunk out of the final price, but I still have to pay for them, no special privileges, and from the money that was supposed to buy my ticket out of my circus of a home. Surely there must be a happy medium between thrift-store cargo pants and Prada, I think as I race into my regular parking space. The black cashmere sweater I finally chose is soft, and I don't mind it so much, but the shoes are killing me. Some French guy made them, and they make me feel like I'm playing dress-up. I clump-clump my way to the store entrance, trying not to fall off my towering heels. And I'm really not so sure about my makeup, which also cost a small fortune. Who knew a guy with a humble name like Mac would charge so much for eye shadow? I bet I look like a clown. Or better yet, a clown who's been crying. Ms. Weepy Buttons, or something.

I swipe my access card at the employee entrance and pull open the door, racing to the elevator. So late. Mom's going to kill me if she hears. The elevator button light is already lit, but I hit it again, just in case. I look around. The cute security guard is also waiting patiently. I'm surprised I didn't notice him first. My radar must be on the fritz. I smile at him. He smiles back and then lets his eyes travel slowly down my body. His gaze is broken only when the elevator dings and the doors open. He flashes a big grin and holds the door for me.

Once we're both inside he says, "You look nice," looking me over once again. I feel his eyes on me as I hit the button for the third floor.

"Thanks," I mumble. I am both embarrassed and pleased. He is so cute. And if the look on his face is any indication, right now he thinks I'm pretty cute. Is it working? Really? At long last? I could have sworn he didn't know I drew air. It's about time he noticed.

I stare at the floor. My mind has been swept clean by his glance and is a complete blank. I don't know what to say. I doubt I even know my own name. I just keep staring at the floor, but then I notice that the elevator doesn't seem to be moving.

"Isn't this your floor, Lily?" he asks.

Oh. He knows my name. "Lily . . . huh. Right." What am I saying?

He looks at me quizzically and then at the door.

I look at the door too and realize it's closing. I instinctively put my arm out between the doors to stop it. The doors don't stop in time and close on my arm. "Oh!" I gasp.

He quickly moves forward and forces them apart and then presses the door hold button. "I'm so sorry. Are you okay?"

"Silly old elevators," I say and practically run out. But I stop as I hear the doors closing and turn back to read his face. He must think I'm such a dork.

He looks a little stunned. "See you," he calls. And the doors shut. Did he just wink?

"Um, have a nice day," I say. Right, Lily. Next time, say that *before* the doors close.

Well, I botched that, but he definitely looked twice. Or three times. And he does know my name. Yes, we did learn that today. If you look at it the right way, it was a small first victory, right?

A little more confidently, I walk through the employee break room. I emerge onto the sales floor to the marble path that leads through Men's Accessories and past Footwear before eventually ending up at Children's. I walk quickly, my shoes clicking like a grown-up's on the shiny floor. My new shoes are kind of tight, but they'll loosen up, and I kind of like the way they—*who is that?* The most gorgeous man I have ever seen is straightening the display of Jimmy Choos. His dark brown hair just touches his shoulder, his skin is tanned, his broad shoulders fill out his blue collared shirt nicely while his muscles stretch it tight, and his features are finely chiseled. I know instantly it must be the new guy Reagan mentioned. Was it Sam?

I watch him check the size of a pair of shoes and arrange them carefully on a table. He looks up, turning his head toward me, and smiles. A hot flush comes over my face as I realize I have stopped walking and am blatantly staring at him. I close my mouth, moving my feet purposefully and quickly over the polished floor. I stare at the ground. Maybe he didn't notice. Maybe he—

"Watch it," says a high-pitched nasal voice I immediately recognize as belonging to Stanford from Men's Accessories. I stop just short of running into him. I notice that he is craning his neck to get a better view of Women's Footwear too.

"Oh, sorry," I mumble, as he pulls back and scowls at me. He is one of Traywick's worst fashion bots. I frown back. It's not like he was looking where he was going either.

"New outfit?" he asks, looking me over clinically. Stanford and I have always been cool toward each other. He worked very hard to get to where he is, Traywick's head men's accessories buyer and manager in charge of all the necktie displays, and I always get the feeling he resents me for bringing my untouchable cluelessness into his house of worship.

"No," I say, deadpan. "Why do you ask?" Why do I get such great joy out of tormenting poor fashion slaves? Because they silently torture me every day with their inborn knowledge of fabric blends? Because they can pronounce the name of every foreign designer without stumbling over the accent? Because it boggles my mind how anyone can care so much about neckties?

He gives me another once-over, nods, and begins to walk away. Then he stops, turns back to me, and touches his fingertips together.

"It's a good effort," he says, squinting, "but you could use a little flair." I stare at him blankly. "You could have a bright shirt peeking out from under your sweater," he says, nodding, and flinging his hands up, "or a shiny belt. You know, something to brighten it up. A little sparkle," he says, smiling and turning away. I shake my head and begin to walk away. "But I like the Louboutins!" I hear from behind me. I turn to see him sashaying back to accessories.

Flair? Sparkle? I want to go on a date, not be a Vegas showgirl. I shake my head and hurry toward the Silver Spoon.

Ah, children's wear. Mindless drone reporting for duty.

"Sheila tells me you were running up quite a bill the other day at Traywick's, Lily," my mother says.

I nod. Thanks, Sheila. It makes me a little ill that my mother looks like she has hope for all of humankind because she heard a rumor that I bought some decent clothes for a change. "Mmm," I say. I reach for my cup of coffee. Too early. Must have more coffee. Must not engage in warfare with Momzilla.

"Your father and I have both noticed that you're making a concerted effort with your appearance lately, and we think that it's very professional of you." She flashes a canned Jackie Onassis smile. "So I brought home a great Jill Stuart dress for you as a surprise!" she says nodding. "It's fairly formal, but it'll look great on you. It's just the right emerald green for your hair."

An emerald green Jill Stuart dress. What happened to no handouts? I guess my popularity at home is up. I roll my eyes. She looks at me expectantly. "Thanks, Mom."

I shrug. I mean, I knew they'd notice, but I'm stubborn and don't want to give her the satisfaction of agreeing with her. After all these years, I'm not going to magically turn into the little fashion-plate daughter she always wanted. I'm still the same Lily, just different packaging. I reach for my coffee mug.

"I've noticed too! Lil, you've been looking so cute lately. Why, you'll get a boyfriend in no time now!" says Gran.

I grimace. Gran's harmless, but she doesn't realize how much of a disappointment I feel like because I'm such a dunce in the dating game.

"Which reminds me, honey, you got an e-mail from someone called Danielman last night. I heard it beep and checked it for you," says Gran.

I almost spit out a mouthful of coffee. "Gran!" It's too early in the morning for me to cope well with this. I had been doing a heroic job of enduring family breakfast in silence while I woke up, but now I'm outraged.

"Lil. I didn't *read* your e-mail. I just saw who wrote you and made a note to tell you!" says Gran, defensively.

I look at my mom for some intercession. Gran is getting out of control.

"What, Lily? I think that was nice of your grandmother to do. Don't you like it when she gets your mail from the mailbox too? Would you rather just have her leave it there and not tell you?" she says.

I sigh. Does no one at my house understand the basic rules of e-mail privacy?!

"Who's this Danielman?" my father asks.

I do my best to convince them all that we are organizing something for church, but I see my mother raise her eyebrow to Dad, and my face burns red. I clear my bowl of strawberries and cream and excuse myself, vowing to *always* remember to close out my e-mail program so Gran won't be able to be such a snoop. And then I vow to apologize to Reagan for resisting to move out and beg, beg, beg for her help on how to begin my apartment search posthaste.

I check my watch again and look up just in time to see Stephanie yank open the door of Café della Artista and scramble inside.

"Oh, Lily, sorry I'm late," Steph says, swooping down into the chair across from me.

"That's okay," I answer quickly. "What happened?" Steph is always on time. Always. She's a bit OCD, this one. I move my bag off the chair across from me quickly, hoping she doesn't notice it. I have been nervous about this meeting, since last time I saw her I was dressed like I had been hiking for a week and today I am dressed more like Gisele Bundchen. When I had told Steph about Reagan's makeover idea a few weeks ago, she had exactly the reaction I expected her to, which is to say negative. She hadn't said much, but the way she shook her head when she asked me not to change too much made it clear what she thought.

"My study group ran over, and I tried to get away, but as I was trying to leave, the Habitat for Humanity project leader called and said there was a big problem with the place we're going on Saturday. And then, I tried to rush over here, but the bus was going so slowly. I waited at the stop for almost . . ." she trails off. "I can't keep making excuses. I'm really sorry, Lily. I really hate to be late. Lateness is a failure to plan ahead, and I hate making you wait. I'm sorry," she says. I want to laugh. She can be so dramatic. I don't like waiting, but she doesn't have to do *everything* perfectly.

"This place is really cute," she says, looking around the café. I nod, taking in the dark paneled walls, the eclectic mix of funky furniture, the imposing fireplace with candle wax drips forming a massive wax sculpture on the mantel.

"Um, are those new?" she asks, narrowing her eyes. She is looking at my black Manolo Blahnik slingbacks that I have been wearing all day and have not fallen over in once.

"What?" I ask, though she is glaring at my shoes. "Oh, the shoes?" I laugh nervously. "Heh, yeah. They're kind of cool, huh?" She doesn't look convinced. I eye Stephanie's khaki pants and blue buttondown shirt. She doesn't exactly exude the aura of a fashion risk taker. "They were on sale!" I add, hoping that Steph will be won over by thriftiness. She's not.

"Was the shirt on sale too?" she asks skeptically. I look down at my light-green low-cut Stella McCartney top.

"It was, in fact," I say quickly. "Should I get the menus?" I signal for the waiter's attention, but he is idly staring at the ceiling, twirling his brown curls with his finger. He is on another planet. I get up quickly to get them from him and end this interrogation but knock my hip into the table in the process. My *ow*ing, though, is enough to startle the waiter. He makes eye contact with me and motions that he'll be right over.

"Wow, those are some stockings," Stephanie says, staring at the inch of black fishnet she can see peeking out of my shoes.

"Oh," I say quietly, looking down at them. "Yeah." I take the menus from the waiter, who walks away with a bored expression. "I'm not really sure what to think of them, but I'm trying them out. They kind of make my toes feel like little fish caught in a net, but I also think they're kind of fun . . . So you don't like them?"

"I didn't say that," she says, swallowing. "It's just, um . . . are these part of Reagan's makeover project?"

The waiter interrupts by coming over and taking our order. I ask for a large crème de menthe mocha with extra whipped cream; Stephanie orders green tea. I cringe. Why doesn't she just order a cup of warm dirt? Water with the taste of just-raked leaves? Blech.

"Yes, these are part of the makeover project, but if you think these are bad, just know that it could have been much, much worse. For instance, the other day Reagan was wearing hot pink leg warmers at work," I say. "She had them on under this jean skirt. Hot pink! Leg warmers!"

Stephanie looks at me quizzically. "Are leg warmers ever okay in California?"

"Precisely what I thought. But of course Reagan said I should get some too. I told her no way would I ever wear leg warmers. Certainly not hot pink ones. But, as you know," I say, "she has complete artistic control over the Lily makeover project." I see Steph wince. "So we had to compromise since I rejected the leg warmer idea. She said I could start with black fishnets instead. And I could wear them under pants as long as I let a little bit peek out from underneath the pants. Reagan just wants to make sure I'm branching out some. I think she has a good point." I smile hopefully. Steph doesn't look convinced.

"I'm glad you're starting to take risks, I guess." The waiter places our drinks in front of us silently. "But don't you think . . ." she pauses, curling her perfectly manicured fingers around her brown ceramic cup.

"What? Would white have gone better with this shirt? I have no idea what colors match," I say quickly. "But, I did get whistled at as I walked through Union Square today," I add triumphantly.

"I guess that's something then," she says.

"It never happened to me in jeans and a T-shirt." I can tell Stephanie doesn't find this something to brag about, but what does she know? Stephanie probably gets whistled at all the time with her long blond hair and her perky smile. She has always had guys following her around like lovesick puppy dogs.

"Lily, you look great," she says, taking a sip of her tea, "but you always have. I like you the way you are."

"It's too bad you're not a six-foot-two lawyer."

"I'm serious! And changing how you look on the outside might not attract the right kind of guy. You want a man who likes the real Lily."

"Right about now, I want any man who likes me," I say, taking a sip of my drink. She scowls. "I guess that's what I'm trying to unearth," I say, sighing. "The real me. I'm still deciding right now." I glance down at my fishnets.

"Just be careful."

I smile. Even though her tone is cautionary, it's also loving. I don't know what I'd do without Steph to keep me in check and love me all the way. "I will. Scout's honor," I say, holding up my middle three fingers in the Girl Scout salute. "So how are you coping with that insane schedule of yours?"

After taking two years off to work for peanuts at the Ronald McDonald house in Palo Alto, she is in her second year of med school at UC San Francisco. She also heads up the Habitat for Humanity ministry at our church and hopes to join Doctors Without Borders and live in developing countries when she graduates.

"Man! I have been *so* busy," she says. "The Habitat apartment we've been working on in the Tenderloin is just a wreck. The plumbing is ancient and has to be completely redone. And also there's this monster class I'm taking that I swear is taught by a vampire, advanced physiology, I mean, Lily, I'm . . . I'm . . . it's just so hard. I haven't sat still for days."

I nod silently.

"And I got an A on that big test? In biochem, the revenge. So that was good. And I have a concert coming up in a few weeks, so I've been really busy practicing for that," she says. In addition to curing diseases and saving souls, Steph also plays the cello in the San Francisco Symphony. Is it any wonder I feel inadequate? I make a mental note to befriend some boring people.

"That's good. And how are the patients doing? Anyone die on you today?" Doctors love this kind of humor.

"No, not today, thank goodness," she says. "But I did visit this one interesting woman in the psychiatric ward this morning. She thought she was a mouse. She made me address her as Cheeser and kept sneaking around the room sniffing the floor. She stroked her imaginary whiskers and put her hand up to her face when she talked and asked me for cheese. She was—"

"Oh my gosh! Look, Steph, that's him!" I whisper, rather louder than I intended.

"Who?" She turns around and looks behind her.

"Don't look! He'll see you!"

She turns and stares at me. "Who am I not supposed to be looking for, Lily?"

"It's him. Sam! The new hot guy in shoes," I whisper. "Okay, now turn around slowly. Don't be obvious." She nods, then slowly cranes her neck around in time to see Sam and a guy I don't recognize sit down at a table on the other side of the café. I don't want him to see me. I sit up straighter and cross my legs anyway.

"Which one is he?" she whispers.

"Stop looking, they're going to think you're staring!"

She turns back to face me, exasperated. "How I am supposed to know who he is if you won't let me look?"

"Okay. He's the one with the long hair," I lean in and whisper conspiratorially. "Turn and look quickly, then turn right back," I hiss.

"Okay. Turning slowly," she says. "Long hair. I see him. Turning right back," she says, looking back at me again. "He's very cute. That's about all I can tell from here. Tell me about this guy."

"He started working at Traywick's a little while ago. Women's shoes. He just joined the company softball team, but I haven't talked to him or anything. I know he surfs, but I don't know much else. Kind of flaky I think. Probably dumb as rocks. But so cute."

"Is he a Christian?"

"Steph, I have no idea. And nothing is ever going to happen, so I don't care." She just grunts. "Reagan said he's not. But whatever. Oh, no, Steph. He just looked over here. We have to get out of here. I don't want him to see me."

"Why not? Try to make eye contact with him!"

"No, I can't," I say, grabbing my bag off the floor. I throw some money on the table and walk quickly toward the door. Steph is slow in gathering up her stuff, pulling her light jacket on precisely before walking. I am already at the door, but as I push it open I glance one last time over at Sam, and he sees me. I stop dead. He smiles. I almost manage to smile back before I run out the door.

Fashion Victim
Transmissions from Fashion Land

single
fashion challenged
boy crazy
shopaphobe

with new expensive clothes
about to change her life
speaks out.

Yes, faithful readers, another exciting week has passed in the life of Fashion Victim, and I'm still alive. Barely.

It turns out I am getting a makeover.

My best friend Reagan made me go shopping and buy all these fancy clothes. And I have to admit I like them. I hope she doesn't read this or she'll never stop gloating. And if my appearance-obsessed (did someone say superficial?) mother ever reads this, I'll have to fight the urge to vomit while she falls all over herself to finally love me now that I *look* like the kind of daughter she'd always wanted. But it is amazing how these new clothes just seem more . . . quality, somehow. They kind of fit better. I guess for what I paid for them they better. After I blew a large chunk of my savings on "the essentials," I felt more than a little guilty. Talk about being a Fashion Victim. I mean, after I forked over the plastic all I could do was go sit down on the bench by Harry, my friend the septuagenarian professional pianist, and mope. I just plopped my bags down and stared at the floor for a good while, thinking of all the orphans that money could have fed, and tried to talk myself out of flinging the bags off the Golden Gate Bridge. He didn't say a word to me, but played "My Funny Valentine," my favorite song, over and over. I wonder if there's such a thing as grandpa adoption. I never got to meet either of mine and could use Harry as my "Poppa."

In other disastrous makeover news, I got a haircut today. Reagan took me to this tiny little salon in the Mission. It was about the size of my closet and had exactly three chairs. The walls were plain white except for a tiny red sign by the glass front doors that said Tino. I guess Tino was this hairstylist guy's name, but all I know is that he was extremely flamboyant. I insisted that he could not give me any haircut that would require blow-drying or any other time-consuming, labor-intensive style, as I would not do said labor and would give him a bad name. To which he responded, "You are tying Tino's hands up!" But he figured something out, clearly, because I almost cried when I saw how much hair was on the floor when I got up. I admit my head is a lot lighter now. It has some layering kind of thing, and I don't know what all else. He wanted to put in highlights, but I threatened to walk out, and since I was still wearing his cape, he relented. Reagan assures me it looks fantastic. I'm afraid it makes me look like a drowned border collie, but since I am stuck with it, I am going to do my best to be positive.

But some good things did happen. Daniel did appear unannounced at my place of work and wondered if I could help him choose a suit for a job interview. He is *very cute* so I just neglected to mention how fashion ignorant I am and took a break. The best part about it was that I got Reagan to help me, and he seemed not to notice that she is way hotter than me. Of course, now I'm walking through the Valley of the Shadow of Doubts, wondering if it was just a fluke or if I can expect a phone call from him or an e-mail. We did have a lot of fun together, laughing at funny tie patterns and suspenders.

Go with God! Down with fashion!
Fashion Victim

• Chapter 5 •

As soon as I get home, I sprint to the computer to check my e-mail. Daniel said he might drop me a line, and ever since he came to the store I have been checking it obsessively. The computer is off. It takes forever to gear up. "C'mon, c'mon, c'mon. You can do it. Let's go." I try to remain calm. Sure Daniel has been showing more interest in me now, but an e-mail from him could just as easily be a mass e-mail to our group of friends with an online quiz attached or a group movie night suggestion. Finally, I get my e-mail open and see an e-mail from Danielman@ yahoo.com. Stay calm, Lily. Stay calm. I click on it greedily.

It's pretty typical at first, not that my hand isn't shaking as I read it. He thanks me for helping him pick out the suit, but then it says, "I'd love to take you out to dinner sometime this week if you're available. Let me know."

This is it! This is the moment I have been waiting for for twenty-seven years. An actual date. A date! A date! I spontaneously begin to sail around the room in the rolling computer chair, pushing off the walls with my feet, and sing, "My boyfriend's back and you're gonna be in trouble . . ." And then I stop and run to the mirror in the hall and look at myself. I look like a mess. What will I wear? I'm going to have to ask Reagan.

Oh and he's so perfect. He's a Christian who's adorable and funny and his eyes crinkle in the corners when he laughs and he's great on the basketball court and so am I . . . maybe we'll play basketball together. I think that would be so cute. And didn't I hear him say he cooked? I mean, he's perfect! Perfect! God, if I had to wait twenty-seven years to get a real date, you have rewarded my patience with the perfect man. Thank you, Jesus! Thank you! This is going to be the perfect first date. I run back to the study, grab the chair from the corner, and then pull up at the desk again, now calm, to write him back.

I compose a brief reply, which I have to draft six times, saying yes, I'd love to get dinner, and telling him I can't tomorrow because I have a softball game but any other night is great with me. And then, I make a wise move. I say, "Call me, and we'll organize it." Reagan will definitely approve.

I accidentally sigh out loud. When I hear myself, I stand up straight and stop daydreaming. Every time I think of Daniel's e-mail and our date, my stomach flips. I'm so nervous, excited, happy, terrified . . . I can't think. Good thing nothing is happening today in the Silver Spoon. I've only helped one customer so far, and she was just returning something.

"Ahem." I hear someone clear his throat in front of me.

I look up. New guy. Sam. Oh no. I drop the pen I was using to doodle Daniel's name and bend down quickly to pick it back up.

"Hey, Lily. I'm Sam."

He knows my name? Yes! Yes! I begin to raise my arm to pump my fist in the air, but I catch myself. I mean, of course he knows my name.

"I was chatting with your friend Reagan and she told me your name and that your parents are, that they, uh—"

"Own the place?" I ask.

He blushes. "Yeah. But anyway, since women's shoes is so nearby I thought I'd pop over and say hi to you. But you look pretty out of it today." He laughs.

"Oh, right. I guess I'm just not awake yet." Oh I see. He's going to chat me up about Reagan. I frown. And what does he mean I look out of it today? I frown some more.

"I mean, you look great. I can just see that I startled you. You look, uh, really good."

I feel warm inside all of the sudden. Who is this man, right before my eyes, making me forget all about Daniel's e-mail when I thought nothing, not even aliens from another planet with a brain zapper, could do such a thing. And somehow Sam looks all the more masculine by being surrounded by the tiny little penny loafers and the pomp of our "Usher in Easter!" display. Yes, the exclamation is really there on the sign. Sheila appears to have a very poor grasp not only of what Easter is really about, judging by the bunnies, the mounds of colored candy, and the traditional seder plate that sit under the daffodil-covered paper cross that make up the display, but also of when it is appropriate to use the exclamation point, my least favorite punctuation mark. The whole display makes me want to vomit all over the marshmallow Peeps she has set up by the register.

"So what's up?" I ask. I smile and tell myself to be cool. My chest is thumping so hard I am momentarily afraid my telltale heart will give me away, but Sam doesn't seem to notice. This is particularly refreshing, since the chest is the first place guys seem to look when they notice a girl.

His eyes are dark brown, rich and deep. "Now that you ask, I am on a mission of sorts. Do you happen to know where the softball game is tonight? I lost my schedule," he says, laughing. "I've asked a lot of people, and they've all looked at me like I'm nuts. I can't remember who is on the team and who isn't from the reminder e-mails."

"Oh, softball." Softball? I knew he was on the team, but ours isn't the kind of league where you really practice, and our first game wasn't until tonight. "Of course. It's um . . . it's at Golden Gate Park. We're playing the Nordstrom Knickerbockers. Are you ready? I hear they lost their best hitter in a freak accident involving platform shoes. We're going to kill."

"Oh, yeah. I'm ready," he says, flexing his muscles. Oh my, what does this guy bench? "I can't wait. Golden Gate Park, huh? What happened to the Presidio?"

"It was all booked. I guess the bocce world championships are being held here this weekend? I don't know. But, um . . . ." Be brave, Lily. "I'm driving over there from work. I can give you a ride if you want." I can't believe I just said that.

"Really?" His beautiful tan face breaks into a wide grin. "That would be awesome. I have to work late tonight so I wasn't sure if I would make it on time."

"Why do you have to work late?" I say, picking up a pair of tiny overalls to put back.

"Oh, I had to rearrange a bit this week to make sure I could get Saturday off. There's a surfing contest that I've been practicing for for months down in Santa Cruz." Now, I have always had a thing for surfers, but I am a little afraid of how seriously they all seem to take it. Oh, and also how the sun and salt water seems to have cooked the brains of every surfer I've ever met. Still, all those hours in the water almost always lead to very nicely built chests and deep tans. "You know, because, dude, surf's up," he says, laughing as he pulls his three middle fingers down to make a "hang loose" sign and wiggles his hand around. At least he is able to make fun of himself.

"*Totally,*" I say, laughing. "I'll be here, earnestly working to clothe the next generation," I say, rolling my eyes at a $200 boiled lambswool sweater with a snowflake on the front that looks like it would be much more useful in a chalet in the Alps than here in balmy Northern California. "They are our future, and I refuse to allow them to go forth into the world poorly dressed."

He laughs. "I'll come by when I get off." He turns his head, then looks back at me. "By the way, nice haircut. It looks really good," he says shyly. Does that means he noticed it before? Is he blushing? Strong, confident Sam, embarrassed?

Embarrassed by my hair?

Oh no.

"Oh, thanks. I'm not sure quite how I feel about it."

"No, it looks really great. Now you can't hide behind you hair any-more," he says, winking.

"I never hid . . . hey now. What about you?" I look at his shiny shoulder-length dark hair. Most girls would kill for hair that thick. "What's with your hair?"

He laughs. "Oh, I decided to let it grow out a bit a few years ago, and here it is now. I'm not going to cut it for a long time," he says, pushing a piece behind his ear. "You'll see me someday sitting with the old hippies in Berkeley, gray hair all the way to the ground." He laughs. "I'll try to sell you a dirty bumper sticker." I smile, thinking of the tables lining Telegraph selling everything from incense to handmade jewelry and the alarmingly large number of hippies who don't seem to realize that the sixties are over. "Besides, I like it because it helps me fit in with all the high schoolers at the beach. Makes me feel like a real surfer," he says, laughing.

"Aim high," I say, smiling at him.

"Oh, I always do," he says, narrowing his eyes and looking into mine. My stomach turns. I hold his gaze for a few seconds, then turn away quickly.

"So I'll see you after work?"

"Yeah," he says. "But now, the shoes are beckoning to me. I must return." He starts to walk away and then turns back. "By the way, why did you run away when I saw you at Café Della Artista the other day?"

"I thought I saw the Bat signal," I say. Great, Lily. Just deflect the question. Act cool.

"A crime fighter, huh? I like that." He chuckles and walks away.

I look at my watch. Man. An hour until my break.

"So tonight, you'll come to my apartment, and we'll go on Craigslist and find you a suitable roommate," Reagan says at our after-noon break in the Traywick's café.

"One problem—"

"Have you thought about what area of town you want to live in? Is a three bedroom okay because I think I have this friend who might have a room coming open soon, but you know, I don't know, three girls in one apartment might just be too much."

"I can't tonight because—"

"You're definitely going to need to live off the Powell-Hyde cable car so that you can get to work easily."

"Hey, *Reagan*."

"Oh, huh?"

"Can't tonight. I have a softball game. Tomorrow night?"

"Oh, sure. Whenever. Sorry, I'm so excited. You have to live in Russian Hill I think. We'll be in the same neighborhood, and the shopping is really the best. Oh! Skip softball! What has softball ever done for you? This is important!"

"I am *not* skipping softball tonight. Something happened."

"What? Aside from getting an e-mail from your church crush *and* deciding once and for all to move out on your own? I can't take too much more of your new and exciting life. It's bad for my blood pressure."

"This isn't quite like the others because they are real and this one is make-believe. Sam—"

"Samuel March of Women's Footwear?"

"The one and only. God's masterpiece. He came over to Silver Spoon this morning and asked for a ride to the game." Okay, so this is a bit of an exaggeration, but he did *accept* the ride when I offered it. In fact, I would say he accepted it *heartily*, I reassure myself.

"Lily. I knew it. Ever since I started to make you over, you've gone from a famine to a feast. Those clothes really did the trick."

I wince.

"Miss Popular. What did you say to Sam? Are you giving him a ride?" she asks.

"Uh . . . I think I did all right. I don't mean to brag but . . ." Reagan raises her eyebrow at me.

"*Did all right* like the incident with the security guard in the elevator, Lily?"

"No. I promise. I made him laugh and made a joke about Batman. I think I was really—"

"You mentioned Batman?"

"What?" I ask, baffled.

She just shakes her head. "This is serious. We have got to go over how to flirt immediately."

"What's wrong with Batman? Boys like the Caped Crusader."

"Yes. Maybe they do. But girls don't. And girls are certainly not supposed to know Batman's nickname. Or profess to have read Batman comics as a child or anything like that."

Steph's warning about changing myself is swirling around in my head. "But that's who I am. I don't want to be different than I am."

"But you also don't want another guy who sees you as his 'buddy,' right? I think there's a happy medium somewhere in there. I don't want you to be an airhead, just make sure you're also being flirty and not just chummy."

"So what should I have said?" I ask.

"Hmmm . . . dare I ask how Batman even came up?" she says.

"He asked why I bolted when I saw him at the café." I realize, upon remembering that I literally ran away from him, that perhaps I really do need to learn how to interact with men I find attractive.

"Right. Great. Okay, that was what we'll call your 'window of opportunity.' You should have responded, 'Run? Who me? No, I just thought I saw Brad Pitt outside on a white horse.'" She smiles, pleased with herself.

"I don't know . . ."

"Okay, maybe not that exactly but something to say, I'm a girl and I like cute guys and I like to go on dates and I like you and you should ask me out."

"Oh, is that all?"

"Lily," she whines. "You can do this. You have to develop your own style. I mean, I say really weird things to guys all the time, but they love it. But I don't act like their friend, either. If I like a boy, I act confident and hint that I like him. I try to say, I'm not easy, but I'm possibly interested."

"I just can't think what I could have said differently."

"He was doing what I call researching with that comment, Lily. He was basically asking you, 'Do you like me? It sort of seemed like it when I saw you last.' Your Batman comment said back, 'No. I just want to be friends. What do you think of Robin?' You see what I'm saying or am I not making any sense?"

I take a bite of yogurt and play the scene back in my head. I definitely don't want Sam to think I just want to be friends. "What if I had said, 'Oh. When I saw you, I got nervous and bolted. Sorry about that.'"

Reagan hits her head. "You can't say that! That says you have no confidence. We have so much work to do."

"What's wrong with that? It tells him I like him, and it's the truth."

"But flirting isn't about being forthcoming. It's about encouraging while remaining aloof. You want him to suspect you like him and then he must decide if he wants to chase you. That's how you get flowers and dinner. Forthcoming is for once you're officially dating. That's when you tell him why you really bolted from the café."

This flirting lesson is taking a long time, and I really need to go back to work. But with our carpool to the game tonight, I'm desperate to learn the basics. I can't botch this. Sam's so cute. And then there's the real date with Daniel. Okay. Forget Sheila the Hun. This is men. This is important.

"Hello in there? Lily? Try again. I'll be Sam." Reagan drops her voice two octaves and pretends to shake her hair out of her eyes like I've seen Sam do. I crack up. "So, Lily. Why'd you bolt from the café the other day when I saw you?"

I'm laughing hysterically. This is just so silly. I raise my voice three octaves so I sound like Betty Boop. "Oh Sam. Was that you? I thought it might be you, but I wasn't sure. I had to run because I was late to meet a friend. I wouldn't run from you. I don't know that many surfers who know so much about women's shoes."

I'm still laughing, but Reagan isn't. She's staring at me wide-eyed. "What?" I ask.

"You do have it in you after all, Lily!"

"Oh. You can't be serious. I was just goofing around."

"Granted, no Minnie Mouse voice, but the right elements were all there. You're being flirty and aloof. You're saying you didn't notice him, but isn't it funny he noticed you? You're saying you wouldn't run from him because he's great. You're being funny, but you're not his softball teammate. You see?"

I shrug. I think I do understand her point. We're both quiet for a while, processing. Can I really do this? Will it make clear to Sam or Daniel or men in general that I'm a girl and I like them?

Then Reagan looks up at me, wide-eyed and smiling. I brace myself.

"Do you think we could throw a big pool party at your house when you move into your apartment in the city as a sendoff? It's a shame we never took more advantage of your house," she says.

"I have to warn you, I'm a terrible driver," I say, sitting at the exit of the Traywick's parking garage. I inch my car slowly toward the street as cars race by on the busy boulevard. There is no break in traffic in sight.

"Nah," Sam says, laughing. "You've only been trying for five minutes. You're doing fine."

"I just like to make sure there's enough room," I say defensively, edging a few inches further out of the driveway. I lean forward more. The steering wheel is almost melded to my bra.

"There's your chance, right there," he says, pointing to the gap between two cars down the block.

"I don't think that's enough space," I say, edging forward again to look. The car waiting behind me begins to honk its horn. Wwwwaaaaaahhhhhh, wwwwwaaaahhhhhh.

"You've got plenty of room there," he says.

"You think? I'm not—"

"*Go!*" he yells, and I press my foot down hard on the accelerator, shooting us across the street. Our bodies fly back into our seats. "Nice work," he says laughing.

I immediately sit forward again. I need to see the road. "Uh, yeah. Sorry about that. But I did warn you," I say, scanning the street signs for the right I'm supposed to make.

"That's okay," Sam says, turning his big brown eyes toward me. Then he puts a hand on my shoulder and pushes it gently backward. I sit back, uneasily. "Try to relax."

I realize that I looked like a grandma the way I was pulling the steering wheel up around my ears and laugh. "Is that one of your weird surfing voodoo techniques? Try to relax, feel the wave . . . uh, taste the spray?"

"Taste the spray? What?" He's cracking up.

"I don't know. I don't get out enough."

"Get out enough? How about you don't watch enough TV. Haven't you seen any of the classic surfing movies? The pope probably knows more about surfing than you do."

"Guilty, guilty. Let's go over what we've learned so far. I'm, one, not a good driver, two, not much of a TV watcher, and three, clueless about surfing. I will only plead to the court, though, that I can hit a home run in fast-pitch softball against a bunch of men and I have been known to make a mean brownie when called on to do so."

He's chuckling at me. I've used my humor to talk to boys for so long that I don't know any other way to relate to them. I need to refocus on flirting.

"Miss Lily. You are most humble. For your reward, I suggest that you come, as my guest, for a private surfing lesson, whenever you have an opening in your calendar on a Saturday morning. I would also chip in a private driving lesson, but since we're being honest here, I'll confess that I'm not what you might call the world's best driver myself."

Eek! My stomach is tying itself in knots. A private surfing lesson? I'm really clueless when it comes to men, but that has date written all over it, even to me. What should I do? This was not covered in my flirting lesson. Okay, make a joke. Deflect, don't answer. "A private surfing lesson with Samuel March? *The* Samuel March? I wonder what that's worth on eBay?"

"You're a big eBay person too?"

Too?

"Uh, no. My grandmother is, and she lives with us. I can never get on the computer because she's always selling her almond art—that is creatures and portraits done entirely out of California almonds—on eBay." We're both laughing, but I realize that I've revealed that I still live at home with my parents and grandmother. I will never get the hang of this flirting stuff. He must think I'm one of those weird girls who is best friends with her mom and wears matching Easter dresses with her. Not that it matters. I mean, I'm not really interested. I'm going to be Daniel's girlfriend any day now.

"Almond art. Hmm . . . yeah, it's not worth *that* much. But it would be fun," he says.

What should I say? I guess I can just accept it. We're friends, right? I mean, he didn't say date. I'm probably just jumping to conclusions. And before we go, I'll just tell him I'm a Christian and that will ensure that he will never hit on me. I've seen it do the trick many times when men hit on Steph in the bars. I'm a Christian. I'm not going to have sex until I'm married. See you later! "Then I accept your generous offer and warn you that if I die or am the victim of a shark attack, my grandmother will most likely commemorate my short and sad life in the medium of almonds."

He laughs. And then I begin to worry about how I will look in a swimsuit. I need to start doing some situps. I should have started yesterday, in fact.

"Don't miss our exit," he says.

"Oh, thanks," I say and actually turn smoothly. I take a deep breath and decide to try, for the sake of personal growth, to start a conversation. Here goes nothing. "So what brings you to San Francisco if you're a surfer?"

"I surf. I'm not sure that I'm a surfer, per se. I suspect there are more important things in life than surfing, which means I can't possibly be a surfer. But the reason I'm here is kind of funny. I had planned on moving to San Francisco this fall, but first I was supposed to spend this summer as a counselor at a summer camp. Unfortunately, I got unexpectedly kicked out for property destruction. So I decided to move to San Francisco a little ahead of schedule, and then I got a job at Traywick's."

Definitely not a Christian.

"I can't believe you got kicked out of summer camp."

"Me neither! But it was so innocent. We were all off-duty counselors, and no one was using that canoe anyways. Plus, the camp director definitely thought it was funny and said he just had to fire me because of a technicality."

"You destroyed a canoe?"

"Not exactly. A bunch of the guys were making this whole big deal about how much I can bench—"

"Don't tell me," I say, interrupting. I don't want to like him one bit more than I do. Plus his head is big enough already.

"Anyway, as I was saying, they dared me to drag the canoe with three people sitting in it. I told them I could do it, but they placed bets for or against."

"And?"

He chuckles almost shyly. "I dragged it with three people, four people, five people, but after that no more people would fit in the canoe, and well, the bottom was messed up from the pebbles on the shore and the middle bar got pretty bent from someone sitting on it."

"Did everyone get fired?"

"No. Just me. I took the blame. I knew I was leaving for San Francisco anyway so it wasn't important. Besides, I'm still pretty close with the camp director."

"Fair enough," I say. I hide that I'm still shocked. I can't imagine I'd ever be fired from any job. I guess he left that off his résumé for Traywick's. "Why Traywick's?"

He shrugs. "I needed a job. They hired me."

"You just waltzed in to Traywick's and got a job? Do you know how hard that is to do? Do you have any interest at all in shoes?"

"Not really. But at my interview I smiled a lot at that old bag Sheila—oh sorry. I forgot—"

"Oh, you don't have to worry about offending me. I never liked her anyway. She snitches on me to my parents. If I'm late, if I wear sneakers to work, if I say 'fart' really loud in front of customers."

"That's about what I would expect from her," he says, smirking. "Anyway, I sweet-talked my way into an interview and rattled off some designer names, gave her a little sales demonstration, and she offered to give me a try."

I am amazed at how he manages to sound humble and cocky at the same time. It disturbs me how comfortable I feel around him. I am going to fall in love with Daniel, who is perfect, and not Sam, who is the kind of person who gets fired and has long hair and surfs . . . I should probably tell him now that I'm a Christian. It'd be the right thing to do. No sense in waiting any longer. One more question.

"And why were you coming here anyway?" I say, looking over my shoulder to dutifully check my blind spot. "Why were you planning on moving to San Francisco in the fall?"

"Law school."

"Law what?" I ask, slamming on the brakes. "I'm sorry, what?"

"Law school? You know, lawyers? Courtrooms? John Grisham?" he raises an eyebrow at me.

"You were going to go to law school?"

"Go to law school," he corrects. "Yes, I am a law student at San Francisco State."

"You're a what? But you work at Traywick's. How do you go to law school?" My jaw is hanging open. Is it possible that he's really gorgeous, funny, and smart, too? Does he also have some kind of special power that can stop time?

"Mostly at night. Traywick's is ideal since the regular nine to five thing doesn't really work with school, but I still need to pay my rent. I can arrange my schedule around my classes. I'll start classes soon." I just stare at him.

"So you went to college then?" He laughs, shaking his head.

"Of course I went to college. Though I didn't study anything useful."

"What did you major in?" I ask, cocking my head.

"Comparative literature. My other languages were Greek and Italian."

"I had no idea. I thought you were . . ."

"You thought I was what?" he asks, looking at me knowingly.

"Oh, I just thought you were, you know . . . um, into shoes," I finish lamely. Thankfully, I have just pulled the car into the parking lot and am inching into what must be a smaller than regulation parking space.

"Ah, shoes," he says, leaning his head back against the headrest. "Sadly, no. Touching that you thought so much of me though."

There. I get the car between the white lines, or close enough that it doesn't matter. I slug him playfully in the shoulder. "Now, now, my own parents make their living at fashion. I just didn't assume you were in law school, which is a policy with me. I never assume people are in law school. Yup. That's what makes me such a fine person." I open my door slowly. "And what are you planning to do with your law degree?" I ask, climbing out of the car. He is in the process of unbuckling his seat belt but stops to look at me.

"Save the world, of course," he says, then climbs out and shuts the door softly behind him.

Fashion Victim

Transmissions from Fashion Land

single

fashion-able

twenty something

with housing woes

begs for help

Look outside your windows, readers. The sun is shining—if you're in California like me—the birds are chirping, everywhere there is summer and there is love.

Yes, indeed the makeover has worked, and I am now a better, more attractive person. The man of my dreams, Daniel, e-mailed me for a date and then called to set it up. *A real date.* And it's on a *Friday night.* That's not like a Tuesday night date (at least, according to my trusted advisors). And it's not like I'm going out with a leftover. This guy is a great catch. I'm more than a little worried about the date itself, but the fact that I'm finally going on a *real date* is a big step.

Speaking of big steps, guess who went looking for her very own apartment this week? It turns out it's not as easy as it sounds. Now, my faithful readers know that I am not really a big shopper, but I thought apartment shopping might be kind of fun. A kind of innocent voyeurism. A fun way to check out the different neighborhoods. Oh, naïveté!

I started out on Craigslist and searched for one bedrooms in a few select areas of the city, but, upon nearly choking on my Doritos at the prices posted, quickly widened my search. Then I widened it again. Finally, I found half a dozen possibilities that weren't too far out of my price range, in any kind of weird Satanic commune, or in the Tenderloin, and I set out, my friend Stephanie at my side. If Reagan is my, well, uh, totally eighties best friend, then Steph is my Girl Scout best friend. She is kind and good and moral and loves Jesus and always keeps her fingernails clean. Plus, with all that goody-goody work she does for Habitat for Humanity, she can spot a stinker of an apartment blocks away.

The first apartment we went to see was on the second floor of a Victorian row house. It was perfect—cute, clean, lots of light, a bay window, and the girl who was renting out the second bedroom, we'll call her Mindy, was really nice. Her roommate had just left to move in with her boyfriend, she said, and she needed someone quick. I told Steph we needed to look no further, and I pulled out my checkbook. Unfortunately, Steph pointed out about four other people ready to do the same. Mindy did not seem at all fazed by the hoard of people trying to throw money at her but calmly asked us all to leave her our names and phone numbers and promised to get back to us with a decision soon.

Who knew that getting a roommate was a beauty contest? I tried to get her to like me by smiling at her a lot and writing my name in really cool-looking stylized letters (you can tell a lot about someone by their handwriting!) on her sheet, and I even made a joke about how I couldn't wait to see my Barbie collection in its new home on the mantel above the fireplace. She didn't laugh at the Barbie crack, but I was still feeling pretty confident as I left the place. It was fate! It was meant to be! This apartment wanted me to live here. I wanted to just go home and wait for Mindy to call, but Steph insisted we keep looking. I went along grudgingly, her mumbling something about no more Barbie talk.

We went to a couple of dumps next—the handle for the hot water fell off as I washed my hands in the sink in one of them—and we trudged resolutely on. One was just a giant room in which a woman with a tool belt and a mullet who asked us to call her Jo had erected a plywood wall down the center of the room and called it a two bedroom. The kitchen was on one side of the wall, the bathroom in the other "room." We also found a room available in a house full of recent Berkeley graduates, all of whom had been on the men's crew team and were at least six-foot-five, except for the coxswain, named Wally, who came up to my shoulder. Tow headed, J. Crew–model-looking Steph was quite a hit with the boys, much to her dismay, so I dragged her out of there as quickly as possible while the bros were calling out their home number to her. No way was I going to live with five smelly jocks, no matter how good-looking they were (and, oh how they were).

Six hours later, I had traipsed all around our fair city and found nary an available room I could call home, except for the place with Mindy, which Steph says I have about as much chance of getting as Charro does of being a star anywhere but on *Hollywood Squares*. Okay, actually she said something about camels and a needle, but whatever. So if you know of any "affordable" apartments in San Francisco that don't have a shower in the living room or bunk beds, please let me know.

Please let me know quickly, in fact. I might have to kill my parents otherwise. If they don't stop making comments about how nice I look every time I enter a room, one of them will have to die. They're just trying to make me let down my guard. I am not falling for it.

Sorry for the long posting today. I guess there's a lot going on, and I know you find every detail fascinating. Or at least Earle does.

Incidentally, last week I made the top-ten blog list. I'm blushing, you guys. I really am. Thanks for reading! E-mail me your questions and responses.

Go with God! Down with fashion!
Fashion Victim, I mean, Vixen

I edit my blog one last time and then post it. The little picture of Jesus Gran has taped to the corner of the monitor catches my eye. It is a very detailed rendering of the God of the Universe with pale skin, long flowing brown hair, and clean white robes facing a blinding white light. He stares off into an undefined point in the distance. It looks like Jesus' senior portrait. Actually, with that long hair, it almost looks like . . . no. That is so wrong.

"Lil dear," Gran says, as she comes in the study. "What are you doing on the computer? You're on here all the time. Are you e-mailing your friends?"

I can't tell her about the blog. I've decided that no one can know about it. It's going to be my secret diary that keeps me from exploding from the pressure of my bizarre life. Plus, I'd hate for them to read all of my postings where I vent about them. At the end of the day, I love my friends and family very much, faults aside. "Yeah. I'm mostly e-mailing. And getting my Google on."

Gran looks at me funny, and I'm cracking up. Long ago I realized how much fun it is to teach older generations how to use slang, and now I make a point to keep Gran, Mom, and Dad up to speed. I'll never forget the time I taught them how to use "bad" to be mean "good" in the eighties. Unfortunately, Gran hasn't let that go, and still calls things "bad" instead of good. And Dad was really killing me after I taught them all that "cool" was good. He decided to invent a new term that meant really, really good, which was "totally frigid." Even now when he and Mom are plying through a catalog of potential fashion lines from smaller designers and he sees something awesome, he'll say, "Wow. That's totally frigid."

"Have you used Google yet, Gran, to look things up on the Internet?" Gran's better than most grandmothers with the Internet, but her knowledge is patchy sometimes. We just went over cutting and pasting last month. How she could have gotten along for so long without cut and paste, I'll never know.

"I think I usually just Ask Jeeves. He's so cute in his little tuxedo."

"Oh. You should switch to Google. It's the best."

"What?"

"Uh . . . Google. Here. I'll show you." I type it in and the search screen comes up. I type in "craft supplies" and a page full of sites comes up. Gran is very impressed and begins clicking around on them. After about ten minutes she says, "I got my Google on now, Lil!"

I'm cracking up. I'm going to miss having her around. "Oh. That's not exactly what that phrase means, though. It means when you Google-stalk someone you're interested in."

"What? That doesn't sound very nice."

Though in public I say I don't agree with Internet stalking, in practice it turns out I'm a regular pharisee. "Hmm . . . that's up for debate I'm afraid, but it is interesting. Let's Google-stalk Mom and Dad." I type in their names and article after article comes up on them, and it even shows a map of where our house is located.

Gran looks nervous. "Oh. I don't like this at all. Who were you looking for?"

I pause for a moment. I haven't told my family about my date coming up. I'm twenty-seven years old, and they don't need to know about my personal life, but maybe I could tell Gran. I might need some advice later. "Can you keep a secret?" I ask.

Gran breaks into a big smile. "Of course."

"I have a date Friday. So I was just about to get my Google on when you came in. I'm curious what he's all about. I think it'd be good to know in advance if the guy is a chess champion or hosts a Teletubbies fan site."

"Dial him up, Lil." Gran's morals, at the idea of her granddaughter traipsing around San Francisco with a wacko, have quickly gone by the wayside.

I type in Daniel's full name and some hits turn up. I click on the first one.

"What is that?" Gran asks with something like horror in her voice.

I stare at the screen in shock.

The first link for Daniel shows a picture of his head pasted on the body of a llama. By way of explanation, the page, which was an old profile from his college basketball team's Web page, says that this is the evidence that Daniel had been abducted by a UFO for alien experiments during his sophomore year.

Why can't I just find a normal guy?

"Let's do someone else," she says. I think I've created a monster.

"Okay, we'll do a friend of mine." I type in *Samuel March*. We find out that he is an amazing surfer (he's won something like six of the last ten competitions he has been in), he was a weight-lifting champion in college, he was once arrested for chaining himself to a tree, and he led a (successful) campaign to eliminate dissection and institute humane ways to learn anatomy in all biology courses at his college.

"Hmm . . . he must be one of those green people," Gran says.

"Yeah."

"He's cute though. No llama body. In fact," Gran says, clicking back to the picture of Sam with a surfboard, "I'd say that's a perfect body."

I crack up. Sam really does have enough might in his muscles to power the island of Fiji for a year. "He's not a Christian though. And he's a little, uh, impulsive as far as I can tell."

"Being a Christian is important. I'm sure this llama boy is very nice too."

"You guys will definitely like Daniel. I met him at church. If everything goes well on our date, I'll have him over for dinner or something."

I look at Gran, but she's wearing this funny, droopy frown on her face. "Gran, why so glum?"

"It's just that I'll miss our little talks like this. I was just downstairs watching a little TV, and it hit me, Why am I watching TV when my own Lil is upstairs and I could be visiting with her?"

"Oh. You're not sad about my moving out, are you?"

Oh, the pain of your grandmother's frown.

"Gran. Oh no. I'm so sorry. But don't worry. I'm just moving in town. I'll still be over here all the time. It will be like I never left."

She sighs. "No. It will be different. But I'm proud of you. This is a big step, and I think it will bring peace between you and your mother."

"Hmph. Maybe. I think that only comes when she accepts me for who I am and stops thinking of me as a little nursey old maid or something."

"And when you accept her for who she is and stop thinking of her as materialistic and shallow. She really loves you, you know."

I look at my lap and feel the internal burn of shameful recognition. I know Gran has a point, but I'm not ready to admit that yet, not after so many years of torture from Mom. She needs to start the acceptance chain of events, not me.

• Chapter 6 •

"*The guys* are all very excited for us," Daniel says and smiles at me. Somehow, since the last time I saw him, I've completely forgotten how hot Daniel is. What a crime. He is beautiful.

The date is going marvelously, which, considering my usual bad luck, means that God must have sent me some Grace Angels for the night to keep me from tripping and falling or slamming Daniel's fingers in the door or knocking over my glass.

Daniel and I talked on the phone on Wednesday night and agreed that I'd come pick him up at his apartment in the city since I had a car and he didn't. But from there, he had it all planned, and it was going to be a big surprise, he said. I was glad to hear he was so excited. It was going to be my perfect first date.

I arrived at his apartment about ten minutes late. I would have been about five minutes early, as is my custom, but Reagan and I had already been through every detail of the date that she could think of and one of her big requests was that since I was picking him up, I had to arrive fashionably late so that I didn't look too anxious. Whatever. So I arrived right on time—that is, ten minutes late—and rang his doorbell. He opened the door about two seconds after I rang the bell, making me think he must have been sitting on a chair just inside the apartment door.

When he swung the door open, I was a bit taken aback. Normally, when I see Daniel, he is dressed in beat-up khaki cargo shorts with so many useless pockets that he could store a dozen doughnuts in his pants. Almost always accompanying the cargo shorts is a T-shirt saying things like "Spring Crush" or "All-University Luau" that he clearly got for free in college. Apparently he was very popular at the University of Texas and got "a lot of cotton," which means that all the girls invited him to their dances, formals, and themed parties, each one for which he received a free cotton T-shirt. He usually tops off these stellar ensembles with a battered, sweat-stained ball cap for his favorite team, which is, rather inexplicably, the Mets. And I must say, I fell for Daniel in this outfit because it is a look that works for him. His wild brown curly hair tries to escape his ball cap and his piercing blue eyes burn right through you. He is the ideal image of the cute Youth Group intern. And there isn't a woman from the ages of twelve to forty-two at the church who doesn't have a crush on him.

But tonight he looked entirely different. He was wearing dark blue slacks that were not only pleated at the top but also still had that unwashed sheen to them and a crease right down the center of each leg. Plus, he was wearing the ultraconservative shiny brown loafers with the tassels on top he bought to match the suit I helped him pick out, and a buttondown, crisp-white shirt with a tie. A *paisley* tie.

I didn't know what to say. I was simultaneously flattered and embarrassed for him. It dawned on me he was as nervous as I was. But I couldn't help but wish he'd change clothes before we left.

I was wearing an outfit Reagan helped me pick out that was both flirty and nice. It was a funky, filmy lavender skirt that fell to my calves and a white, embroidered tank top with silky spaghetti straps. And to top it off, I was wearing strappy high heels that tied the whole outfit together. I'd even pulled my hair up in a loose knot and put on a little lip gloss and eye shadow. I looked like myself, but like myself on a really good day. Daniel looked like Mr. Rogers. And he looked uncomfortable.

But I soon forgot about his odd outfit (although he didn't apparently, since he kept sticking a finger in his collar and sliding it around as if trying to loosen the noose around his neck) because in his hands were two dozen beautiful red roses. He gave them to me, and like a sap in some kind of romantic movie, I burst into the biggest smile.

"Th-th-thanks," I stammered. Did roses have a power over women I had never before realized? I loved them. Loved them. Funny, I always thought they were overrated. But here they were in my arms, and I loved them so much.

"You're welcome," he said and kissed me on the cheek.

I melted. Forget the weird look he was trying out. He was all that I had ever dreamed of.

Now he's sitting next to me in my car, giving me directions for where we're going to eat, a place he described on the phone as "a really nice restaurant." The only thing that baffles me is that I thought all the really nice places to eat around here were in San Francisco, not outside of the city, which is where his directions are now taking us.

"Yeah. The youth group is having a lock-in tonight and the guys really wanted me to be one of the male chaperones, but I told them I had a date. The little monkeys just went nuts when I told them, and especially when they found out it was with you," he says.

Our youth group is really big, and the awkward guys in it have always had a special place in my heart. Sometimes I help out, and I know a couple of them by name. "That's so cute."

"Yeah. Working with the youth really brings meaning to my life. I hope to someday meet the right girl, finish up seminary, and then have a youth group of my own."

I burst out laughing.

"What?" he asks, a little wounded.

"That makes it sound like you want to have enough kids to *make* a youth group of your very own. Your poor wife!" The thought of Daniel being the father to twenty curly-haired kids is really cracking me up.

"Ha ha. Yeah. I meant run a youth group of my own. But I'd also really like to have a lot of kids."

"Uh, like three kids or something?" I ask. I can't even imagine having a sibling. Thanks, Mom and Dad.

"Oh. That's not enough. Lily, you must be kidding. Kids are the greatest. I want at least eight."

Goodness. Is talking about marriage and eight fat babies appropriate on the first date? This isn't something that Reagan prepared me for. I thought this was going to be just like all the other times I hung out with Daniel, only with a kiss on the cheek at the end of the night. But he's very serious. Who knew dating was so weird? I take a deep breath and try to relax and be natural. Okay, Lily. Just make a joke.

"If you do trick some woman into giving you eight children"—good, distance yourself, you're not the woman bearing all those offspring—"then I insist you call them the *Ochos Niños*."

"I like that," Daniel says, but I can't tell if he's kidding or not. "*Los Ochos Niños*." He squeezes my shoulder. "You're going to make such a great mom."

I gulp and then an uncomfortable silence spreads through the car.

By the time we pull up to the restaurant, things are going a bit better between Daniel and me. The awkward silence and the talk of children has been forgotten, and we're laughing like old friends about the girls at church who can't even throw a football much less name ten teams in the NBA and bonding over our shared love of vanilla but not chocolate ice cream. Only insane people like chocolate ice cream, and we make a formal decree outlawing all chocolate ice cream from the Bay Area. I'm being funny again, and Daniel almost seems relaxed in his uncomfortable outfit.

"So here we are, milady," he says with a grin.

I look up and realize that this faux-castle we have arrived at is not in fact a Hearst estate but Medieval Times. I frown.

"Oh no! You've already eaten here?" he asks.

I smile, bravely. I can't bear to tell him that the idea of paying fifty dollars a head to eat with my hands and watch a staged joust just isn't my idea of a "nice dinner." "Oh no, I haven't. This is a wonderful surprise," I say.

"I'm so glad you think so. I ran it by the guys, and they agreed with me that it was an awesome idea. Granted, they're only in high school but a lot of them have been on more dates than I have." He chuckles to himself. "Those guys," he says like a proud father.

I step out of the car and steady myself on my heels while I process the fact that my very first real date was planned by someone just as clueless as myself—no, more clueless than myself because he took advice from the youth group guys and I at least had the good sense to ask Reagan for help.

"You are the most beautiful princess in all the land," Daniel says, and kisses the top of my hand. He stares wistfully into my eyes. No smile. Why isn't he smiling?

"And you are the wartiest frog," I say, laughing. Only I'm laughing alone. Daniel is taking this whole medieval thing very seriously and desperately wants me to play along.

"Does milady find fault with her knight?" He pouts.

"Uh . . . your armor isn't shiny enough?" I try. What does one say to this? I'm wearing the little Burger King crown on my head, I'm eating the pheasant thing they served me with my hands, and I'm drinking water out of a goblet. I'm trying to play along but if he just wouldn't be so serious about it.

He doesn't laugh. "It dost hurt mine heart to hear so. I shall rise tomorrow morning and shine mine armor all over again for to win your esteem." He smiles a little. There, he's joking a little.

"Try using Windex. I'll bet that would do the trick."

He smiles at me. "Really, Lily. I've liked you for a long time. I'm so glad I finally got the courage up to ask you out. Now I can pamper you like the princess you really are."

I stare at him like he's nuts. "What took you so long?"

"I don't know. I never dated much, you know, because I only want to date someone I think I could marry and that kind of girl is hard to find—"

"Especially if you aren't looking for them." I laugh, mischievously, and then stop. He looks a little hurt. What? I think a good ribbing is deserved. If you can't laugh at your faults then you're lost.

"Point well taken, Lily. I haven't really been looking. Plus, uh, I guess you never really seemed interested before. I tried to flirt with you in the past, and you just seemed like you were too busy or too sensible to ever consider a guy like me."

"What? Me? I've always thought you were cool. I just didn't know how to show you. That's all. My best friend and I have been working on that."

"Hence the haircut and the new clothes?"

"Yeah. You like them? I'm sort of taking a poll at this point."

"I love what you're wearing tonight, and the haircut and makeup look great. Some of the other outfits aren't exactly my taste, but all the same, change is good and you seem more—"

"What?"

"I don't know. Mature? Self-possessed? It's not the clothes. You just seem ready to be an adult and have a relationship. I think that's always been a problem with me. I know sometimes girls are interested, but I've just been having too much fun in the past to sit down and plan a date or devote myself to a relationship. I tried to casually date this girl in college, but I realized later I really hurt her feelings by never calling much or investing in her in a real way so I swore off dating for a while."

"But now you're ready to date?" I ask.

"I think so. Miguel is dating Becky, and they're doing really well."

I blush a little at the mention of Becky's name. Maybe I was too hard on her in my blog. But since then she's come to S3 and is really nice. I caught her rolling her eyes when Alex starting bragging about how powerful she is at work and how it's weird that people at church didn't seem to recognize it, so she must be okay. "I'm glad to hear they're working out."

"I guess it's just time, you know, for old dogs like me and you to learn new tricks. We don't want to die alone."

I control my face from contorting into a look of horror. Old dogs? Die? I'm only twenty-seven.

"And you're so perfect for me. We're both Christians and love all the same things like sports and stuff. And if I get my own youth group some day, you'd be such a big help with ministering to them."

I feel myself taking in a lot of air. It's like, suddenly, in this dumb, dark arena, I can't get enough oxygen to fill my lungs. I smile at him and then reach for my stupid goblet of water. Thankfully, the joust begins, and Daniel is rooting with all his might for the Red Knight to save our kingdom, so he can't see me sitting next to him, having something of a panic attack.

I just wanted to go on a romantic, light, fun date. Was dating really only about going a courtin' to find a husband? I don't even know what I want to do with my life, much less if I'll be up for helping out with his youth group someday. I have very big dreams of my own. I'm going to be a writer. I'm going to do something great. I'm going to, to, to . . . I'm going to save the world.

I pull into my driveway, exhausted. I open the door, and the house is pristine and quiet. I say a little prayer of thanks. Soon, I'll be moving out to live with one of Alex's coworkers. I'm a little apprehensive, since Alex's voice is like nails on a chalkboard to me, but it was nice of her to hook me up with her friend. I don't really know the girl, Inie, but she seems nice enough, and her apartment is just a few blocks from Reagan's in Russian Hill and comes with a bay window. Every man, woman, and child who lives in San Francisco gets a bay window. It's written into the city codes. And sadly, Steph was right that Mindy wasn't going to call me back about that other apartment. One little crack about a (fictitious!) Barbie collection, and you're homeless in this city. Even still, I know my days of coming home to peace and quiet in a home once featured in *Architectural Digest* are numbered.

I had promised Stephanie that I'd call her when I got in so I dial her up. I get her voice mail. I try to sound desperate so that I can get her to call me back immediately. "Steph, it's me, Lily. I just got in from my date. I really think it's one for the books. So call me back first thing when you get this. I need to talk to you. Tonight." I momentarily contemplate calling Reagan, but I realize there's no way she'd even be able to comprehend a guy like Daniel. No sense.

I pace around the kitchen floor for fifteen minutes, waiting on Steph to call me back but she doesn't. Fine, be busy, Steph. I walk into the kitchen and put my two dozen roses into water in a nice crystal vase that only Mom and Gran have gotten to use before. I prick my thumb on a thorn. I stare at the blood. Perfect ending.

After a shower, I lie in bed, exhausted and agitated. My phone rings. I look at the display. Steph! I forgive her instantly for being busy earlier.

"Hey!" I say.

"Hey, sorry about that. I am trying to retile my floor tonight, and when you called I had, well, grouted myself into a corner so to speak," she says.

I look at the clock, and sure enough it's one a.m. Talk about overachieving. "Steph, you really frighten me. Were you watching Martha Stewart again? Because you know where all the obsession compulsion got her, right? Camp Cupcake ring any bells?"

"Yeah, yeah, yeah. Not why you called. So . . ." She prompts me to get talking. I love best friends.

She clearly thinks I had a wonderful time. I decide to have a little fun with her. "Well . . ." I say, slowly.

"Yes?" she says.

"So . . ." I say.

"Lily Opal Frances Traywick, if you don't spill the beans right now and tell me about your date with the youth group Justin Timberlake then I will never speak to you again."

I cave and tell her all about it. It's weird but, as I recount it, my spirits begin to lift. I mean, if I look at it right, it was really a very funny evening, aside from the minor panic attack. By mid-story, I am pouring out the hilarious details, sparing poor Daniel not one ounce of dignity. She occasionally interrupts me to say, "Oh no!" or "Oh, he didn't," but I just keep going. I finally finish and feel so much better.

"Oh man, Lily. That should really go down in the Clueless Guy Hall of Fame. Oh wow. I'm still in shock. Let me just clarify one point."

"Uh-huh?"

"He really said he wanted to treat you like a princess?"

"You betcha."

"No. It's too good to be true. I mean, too bad to be true. Either way."

"What about the I-want-you-to-bear-me-*ochos-niños* part?"

"This is historically bad. Although, if it makes you feel better, on my first date the guy tried to kiss me but instead did a maneuver I like to call the 'head-butt' kiss and broke my lip open on his braces and made it bleed. At least there was no actual physical harm done to you tonight."

I'm cracking up. "No, just some very serious emotional scarring. Incidentally, how's your womb? Daniel's in the market for a girl with some good childbearing hips."

We both explode into laughter once more. I love this feeling, the "in" feeling. I did it. I went on a date.

We slowly stop laughing, and I wipe the tears from my eyes. "I mean when I saw him in that outfit—"

"Okay, Miss Traywick. We've got to stop. This is getting a bit cruel."

I roll my eyes and smile. "Yes, ma'am." Spoilsport.

"We've had our fun at poor, super-sexy yet utterly clueless Daniel's expense, and now we must stop. That was sweet of him to drop well over a hundred bucks on you."

I sigh. "You're right," I say. "So another one bites the dust. Steph, what am I going to do? Daniel was the only adorable, non-booger-eating single Christian guy I know. I think I'm going to retire from dating."

"Already? What a wimp! I think you've got a good hundred dates in you before you'll find the right one."

I gasp. "I will never last one hundred dates. This one nearly killed me. The hours, the minutes, they were creeping by."

"C'mon. Take one for the team. I mean with stories like these, I'm practically looking forward to your next bad date."

"Very funny."

"Seriously. You can't worry about these things. God's timing is the perfect timing."

"I know," I say. Especially if you're a gorgeous, sweet-natured Martha Stewart–obsessed creature named Stephanie.

"I'm going to bed, Lady Lily. You've worn me out."

"Thanks, Conscience. It's good to know I can always give you a call."

"Ah yes. Moral clarity is my strong suit. It's grouting I struggle with."

I hang up, but I'm all wound up. I lie there giggling for a moment until I see my new outfit across the room and remember how much hope I had going into tonight. My skirt is lying in a silky puddle on the floor and one shoe is on the chair while the other is across the room. I'm already back in a beat-up old T-shirt and boxer shorts, in my childhood bedroom, still the same person. Not changed by love, not thinking back to a wonderful good-night kiss.

Suddenly, I realize something just awful and sit straight up in bed. I'm going to have to tell Daniel I don't want to go out with him ever again, that I don't see him as anything more than a friend. My stomach feels like a stone and that weird, small bird I ate at Medieval Times doesn't seem to be digesting right. How can I do that to Daniel? I mean, he wasn't the perfect date, but he was really, really sweet. And I know from experience that the last thing you want to hear from your crush is that she only sees you as a pal. I groan. Oh, this will be terrible.

I lie there thinking for a while about my new dilemma and cursing Steph for helping me remember how great Daniel was to me. I decide to get up and go and write an entry in my blog. Maybe it will take my mind off things. Lately, I blog so much that I think I'm becoming addicted. The weird thing is, so are my readers. I'm always in the top-five blogs on salon.com. Yup. If I can beat out the rabbi who finds secret Jewish references in *Star Trek*, then I'll be big number three. The number-one blogger is an ER doctor who tells in gory detail all the weird stuff he sees every day, and the number-two slot is a schizophrenic young fashion model. Yes, I'm very proud to be counted among this elite group. Whatever. It's something. I'm huge in Finland. I get quite a bit of e-mail, and I try to respond to the serious messages and laugh at the weird ones. And then there's Earle, of course. He always e-mails me to ask astute questions about my blog and then he usually says I'll be president someday or makes a joke of some kind. He's sort of a fun nuisance, and if I have time, I write him back something short. He's my number-one fan, after all. Still, I really don't understand why people like it. Is it the intrigue about who I am or my wisecracking comments about the fashion industry and my nutty mom?

I go into the upstairs office and turn the computer on in the darkness, the weird white glow from the screen welcoming me.

Fashion Victim
Transmissions from Fashion Land
Single by choice, finally
Fashionable
Twenty-something
Insomniac
With prince trouble

I can't sleep. Why? Oh possibly because there's a pea under my mattress.

What, you ask, dear readers? You didn't know I was a princess? Well, I am. According to my date this evening.

I know men must hear women say all the time that they "want to be treated like a princess." But listen up, women, the reason that whole princess thing went out of style is because it's dull, dull, dull. No sports. No humor. Just talk of marriage and other serious topics.

I went on my first date tonight and the guy was really nice and treated me like a princess all night. So what's my problem? I'm a rotten girl, it turns out. I hated being a princess. What's more, he kept talking about getting married and how he wants his bride to stand by his side and help him with his job. As in, no career of her own.

I freaked out.

I thought I was going to come home and write you all a blog saying I was no longer single. That I was in *love* at long last. But I've given up on myself. Daniel, my date, went from being a hilarious friend to a dull date. Let me let you in on something people never tell you: five hours is a long time to spend with just one person. How in the world will I ever get married?

And then there was the end of the night, after our dinner at a faux-medieval castle, we came outside only to discover that the guys from the youth group where he interns had stolen the tires off my car. I was exhausted and ready to bolt, but I had no tires on my car. Who knew high schoolers were so crafty? They left us a note with trivia on it. When we had the answers, it said, then we could call one of them on his cell phone, and they would deliver the tires.

We sat on the hood of my car for an hour and tried to re-member all of the Ten Commandments, the name of the lazy-eyed sister of Rachel, the names of all of the apostles, and all of the plagues of Egypt, among other things. Daniel loved this game. Apparently the youth group was having a lock-in across town, and we were now a part of it, against our will. Once we had all the answers right, we called in. Thirty minutes later, the white Dodge church van appeared and fifteen high school boys piled out. They coated us in Silly String, which I am still finding in my ears, and then begged us to kiss in front of them while they put my tires back on.

I'm a good sport, really I am, but this incident made me realize that having a crush on somebody is not the same as dating him. When he leaned over to give me a kiss on the cheek when he dropped me off, my stomach just turned. Surely that's not how love is supposed to feel? I guess I had all kinds of ideas about him, but they weren't really him, they were just what I had made him in my head. The reality was not nearly as attractive as the ideal. I don't want to be a youth group director's wife.

But now, readers, I'm in a really bad place. I'm so confused about this whole dating thing. I suppose, in the meantime, I have all of you out there in the blogosphere. So write me back. What's wrong with me? How could I not fall in love with the perfect man God put right in front of me? I am so ungrateful. And who knew falling in love was such hard work?

Go with God! Down with fashion!
A Blue Fashion Victim

When I open my free Yahoo account, I see a message from Earle, of course, and then a couple of others. I answer the others first. They mostly have the usual questions about my identity. Then I go to earle@sfw.com and see what he has for me today.

Dear Fashion Victim,

Even though you will never reveal yourself to me, I'd like to tell you who I am after all this time. I've been teasing you for a while, and I hope you weren't put off by it. In fact, I am a sincere fan of your writing.

I am the editor in chief here at San Francisco Weekly. But you knew that, right? From my e-mail address? I believe you must live here in the city, what with all of your talk of moving to Russian Hill. I hope so anyway. Every time I try to ask you about yourself, you won't say a peep.

I am writing you to ask for a meeting at our offices downtown. We're looking for some new freelance writers to work the Around Town beat. Would you be interested?

Here's hoping you're not some convict in Missouri.

Sincerely,

Edgar J. Arle

(not Earle as you keep calling me)

• Chapter 7 •

I pull my head and neck up in a crunch, lie back down, and start all over again from the top.

"One, two three, four . . ."

I don't know if Sam was serious about that private surfing lesson thing, but if he was, there is no way I am going to let him see me in a bathing suit with my flabby tummy. Eight-Minute Abs promises a sleek, toned belly in just four weeks, and I'm doing sixteen-minute abs.

"Fifteen, sixteen, seventeen . . ."

In any case, having a stronger stomach will certainly boost my overall athletic ability, which is a good thing since we've got a big game against the Gumps' Greyhounds that we must win after we took an awful beating from the Nordstrom Knicks last week.

"Twenty-two, twenty-three, twenty-four . . ."

And I would certainly like to hit a home run in front of Sam. We had the best time at the game last week and now we even talk some at work, which is so confusing because we get along so well—finish each other's sentences, interested in all the same things, make each other laugh—but I can't have him. Why would God make two people perfect for each other if he didn't want them to be together? I know I came down pretty hard on Miguel for missionary dating Becky, but now, in weak moments, I consider it myself. I know it's not a good idea, but something I learned from my date with Daniel is that being a Christian isn't enough. So now I spend my time picking through the petals of daisy in my head that go something like this: He loves me; I promise, Jesus, I don't love him; He loves me; I promise, Jesus, I don't love him. At least Sam accepted my offer of a lift to the game again. Either he has a very poor short-term memory, or he's willing to risk his life to be with me (which, knights and princesses aside, is kind of what every girl wants).

And again. "One, two, three . . ."

I guess I have to face it. I really, really like him. I try to imagine what tonight will be like. We'll drive over together after work, he'll confidently yet casually ask me out, everyone will notice how he sure seems to like me, and they will all be jealous, especially that sniveling little blond girl Lisa from Housewares who is always trying to talk to Sam in the dugout and offering him some of her Evian. She couldn't catch a softball to save her life. She probably just joined the team so she could talk to him. *God, please let him like me. Oh, and please let him become a Christian too. And not just so I can date him. For his own good.*

"Eighteen, nineteen, twenty . . ."

Oh man. Who am I kidding? I can't even convince myself that my motives are unselfish, why am I trying to convince God? I really want him to like me. *Please God.* I can't wait to see him tonight. I'll make it through the day by thinking about how I'll get to see him tonight.

"Thirty, thirty-one, thirty-two . . ."

"*H*ey, Ump! You need some glasses?" I shout from behind the plate. He holds up his pointer finger to tell me that I now have my first warning. Oops. But *please*, anyone could see that the runner's foot was clearly on first base before the ball got there.

I am hoarse from yelling. This has been a really exciting game, which is actually saying a lot, considering what I'm working with here. I mean, the Greyhounds are all wearing silver spandex tops, for goodness' sake, although they don't look nearly as ridiculous as the Neiman-

Marcus Nymphs, whose female players wear short hot-pink tennis skirts and whose men wear much, much too short hot-pink shorts.

Two summers ago there was a scathing humor piece in *San Francisco Weekly* about the long tradition of intramural softball leagues among all the premier clothiers of the Bay Area. The article paid special attention to the ostentatious outfits of the teams, and while it should have shamed the teams back to the standard T-shirts and shorts uniform all the other leagues use, it had the opposite affect of upping the ante and making every team try harder to outdo the others.

Hmm . . . too bad that story was already written. I would have been perfect for that story. I've got to think of some prospective story ideas for Earle—I mean Edgar. Edgar J. Arle. Edgar, Edgar, Edgar. I try to say it to myself over and over again. I need to reprogram my brain. Months of calling him Earle isn't going to serve me well at our meeting later this week. If I don't totally blow this, he could be my new boss. Should I tell Mumsy about the meeting? Enh. It's not like—

"Lily, you ready?" Mitchell, our shortstop, calls to me from the field.

Right. Mind on the game. It's the top of the ninth inning, and we're beating the Greyhounds 4 to 3. Their runner on second just tried to steal third, but Sam, who is our star pitcher, throws a quick pickoff to third and catches him in a pickle. Two guys from PR toss the ball back and forth for a while. I love playing catcher, I really do, but sometimes I want to get up and run to where the action is and really do something useful. Plus, it's so hot under this turtle shell of a catcher's mask. It has to be at least eighty-five degrees outside, and probably closer to a hundred and twenty in here. Finally, though, Sylvia tags him out, and I let out a long shrill whistle. Sam turns and winks at me. My heart skips a beat. I shake my head. I have to focus. We just have to keep them from scoring for one more out and the game is ours.

Señor Sketchy, the business office manager from Gump's, whom I saw hitting on two of our players at different points before the game, steps up to the plate. He swings the bat around by his feet, spits on the ground next to me, and knocks home plate with the bat. I half expect him to grab his crotch so he'll really look like a baseball player, but he digs his feet into the dirt and brings the bat up to his shoulders. Sam throws the ball. I hear the air around me whistle as he swings and misses. He cusses under his breath. I toss the ball back to Sam. He smiles.

This uniform is so uncomfortable. Our team captain took tight red T-shirts and sewed sequins onto them to make them "dazzle" our opponents. I am stuck running the bases with a shiny red shirt that says Traywick's Trojans across the front. I didn't have the heart to tell him that the Trojans lost the war. The worst part is that he silk-screened our last names on the backs of our shirts, so I look like a Traywick sandwich with my name on my front and back. He then got us all matching white pants with red pinstripes. Bootcut, of course. Though they are made of some kind of stretchy fabric, they are definitely designed more for style than function.

El Sketcho gets himself ready again and takes a deep breath. Sam throws a pitch, but it goes far to the left, and the batter doesn't swing. Ball one. I get up, grab the ball, and then toss it back to Sam. He's rolling his head around, stretching his neck.

I squat down again. Sam just holds on to the ball, looking at the batter. He looks tense. I try to catch his eye. We lock eyes, and then I direct my eyes down. I stretch my arm low, extend my middle and index finger, and pull the rest of the fingers back to make a peace sign. He looks at me, puzzled. Then I do the Spock greeting. He is squinting at me, probably trying to figure out what the heck I am doing. We don't usually use hand signals in our games. I make the sign language sign for I Love You, although I kind of hope he doesn't know what that means. I spell my name in sign language. A hang loose symbol. Little Bunny Foo Foo. I am about to do the only other hand gesture I know and raise my middle finger when I see him cracking up. The Sketchmeister turns his head to look at me and glares. This, of course, makes me laugh, which makes the batter all the more nervous. He turns back around, and Sam quickly throws the ball; he swings. The ball lands neatly in my glove. Strike two. Sylvia from Outerwear is doing the Cabbage Patch in right field to show her excitement. I throw the ball back to Sam, grinning. He shakes his head, smiling.

He stands resolutely on the mound, looking intently at the hitter. His eyes narrow. I know now I would never want to meet this man in a courtroom. His cold stare could make you confess to anything. Sketchman doesn't meet his eye, but brings his bat to his shoulder and waits. Sam winds up, then lets the ball go hard and fast. I see the bat swing, then hear the crack of the ball against the bat. It flies up in slow motion, and the batter starts running for first, but before he gets there Sam is holding the ball triumphantly in his glove above his head.

It's over!

Lisa from Housewares comes skipping in from the dugout, screaming, and Sylvia from Cosmetics rushes toward the pitching mound. Sam is silent, unmoving, looking at me, smiling. I get up, run to him, throw my arms around him (and I could swear he leans forward, but due to my pads, I really can't tell), and then quickly pull back as Sylvia and Lisa rush in. Oh my gosh. I just hugged Sam March. I am so bewildered and unintelligibly happy that I can block out the fact that Sam is now hugging everyone on the team, even Lisa, who is not sweaty like I am since she has been riding the pine for most of the game. But he hugged me back.

"On the count of three, we start. One, two," he says, but before he gets to three, he is digging into his triple scoop banana split.

"Hey! That's chea . . ." I say pathetically. Instead of arguing, I dig in to my own triple scoop banana split with a cherry on top. Sam March the cheater. The cute cheater.

Part of me can't believe I'm here. All of me can't believe I'm here eating a banana. I hate bananas. I mean, sure, for the past two hours from behind my catcher's mask I was willing him to ask if I wanted to hang out after the game, but I was still shocked when he actually did. Well, asked might not be the right word. He basically tricked me into eating ice cream with him by telling me he had to pick up something for his sister at a little store a short walk away and asking if I wouldn't mind helping him. I said I thought Jude Law wasn't going to be at my house for another hour or two (Reagan will be so proud!), so we went, and he led me down a series of streets that I didn't recognize. We kept walking and talking about softball and Traywick's and our mutual disdain for any movie starring Governor Arnold Schwarzenegger for what seemed like forever, and although I asked several times if we were anywhere near the store he was thinking of, he kept saying "almost." Of course I didn't mind. Eventually we stopped.

"Oh, look at where we are," he said mischievously as we strode into the open courtyard with a fountain in the middle.

"Um, it looks like Ghirardelli Square," I said, looking around. "Where did you want to go?" There were shops all around us, but he wasn't walking toward any of them.

"Hmmm . . . I don't know," he said, raising an eyebrow and looking into my eyes. Dusk was falling, and the light was silvery and soft. In this charming square, quiet except for the murmur of some tourists across the way and the gurgle of the fountain, Sam's eyes lit up and his smile seemed more vivid than ever before. Stop it, Lily. Just pretend he's not attractive at all. Pretend he's a . . . pretend he's . . . a box turtle. Yes, pretend he's a box turtle.

"You mean you don't know what store because you forgot its name or that you don't know because you're turned around and—"

"Maybe," he said, shaking his head at me and chuckling, "we should just get ice cream over there," he said, pointing to the entrance to the Ghirardelli Factory.

Oh man. The Ghirardelli Factory. Home of the best chocolate in the world. In addition to a store full of their famous candy bars in every flavor, they have a great little café where they serve these gigantic sundaes just dripping with whipped cream and chocolate. Once when I was ten Grandma Opal brought me here, and I ate so much ice cream I made myself sick. I love this place.

"I would *love* some ice cream right now," I said. "I'm starving."

"Let us go then, you and I . . ." he said, cocking his eyebrow at me, putting his arm on my hip to guide me toward the door.

"Oh, you might not want to do that," I said, gesturing toward his hand, "I'm pretty sweaty from the game and . . ."

He just smiled, laughing to himself.

"I mean, not that I mind, but . . ." What did my mouth just say? I didn't make it do that. "Oh, I mean, uh . . . never mind . . . So sometimes that catcher's mask gets kind of sweaty, and . . . wait a minute," I said, stopping short, recognition slowly dawning, "were you just quoting Eliot?"

He laughed again, steering me toward the entrance. "Who, T.S.?" He winks. "Naw. They don't teach that poetry hoo-hah in surf school. Bet I can eat my ice cream faster than you."

Reagan did not warn me about poetry-quoting men who are fond of non sequiturs. How do I answer that? I have no idea what she would say to do, so I just said what came naturally. "Please. You don't stand a chance."

I am shoveling ice cream into my mouth as fast as I can—banana and all—but he is somehow able to eat far more quickly. I spoon a gob of whipped cream into my mouth, then dip my spoon immediately back into my dish. Chocolate sauce is running down my chin. I am really full, but I continue resolutely. My head is lowered to reduce the amount of time it takes for ice cream transportation. I will not let him win. Just as I spoon a big mound into my mouth, trying desperately not to spit it back out, I hear Sam drop his spoon into his dish and look up. He raises his arms triumphantly. "I'm out," he says proudly. His dish is empty.

"Huw din yup," I start to ask, incredulous at his empty dish but realize there is so much ice cream in my mouth that opening it is not a good idea. I look down. My dish is still half full, mostly of banana.

He laughs as I work to swallow my mouthful. He has a smear of whipped cream on his nose. I finally manage to swallow.

"You're neglecting the only healthy part there," he says.

"Yeah, sorry, monkey. I don't actually eat bananas."

He's cracking up. "Why didn't you say anything when I ordered two triple threat banana splits from the waitress. That *was* you sitting here, right?"

I laugh. I can't possibly say that I was too tongue-tied to pipe up about my bizarre aversion to America's favorite fruit. I reach across the table and pat his hand. "I didn't want to hurt your feelings, little fella. Besides, I knew if I lost that the banana would be a good excuse to prove that the contest was totally unfair." I glance at his empty bowl. "How in the world did you do that?" I demand.

"It's just a gift," he says, laughing. "My big mouth usually just gets me in trouble, but sometimes it works to my advantage."

"Ugh. I'm never going to be able to finish this," I say, poking a banana spear.

"I guess we'll have to mail it to the starving children in Ethiopia then," he says. "We don't want it to go to waste."

"Good point," I say, steeling myself up to take another bite. I look at him and start laughing. "You, um, have something on your nose," I say, pointing to my own nose. I pick up a napkin and try to hand it to him, and he laughs. As he reaches to take the napkin from me, his hand brushes against mine. It is warm and soft. My head spins.

"Thanks," he says, wiping the white cream off. I nod, putting a bite of banana into my mouth. I try to force myself to swallow, but it's so gross that it's difficult. He just laughs at me.

"I don't think I can ever leave. I'm so full, I'm stuck to this chair," I say, leaning back in my seat.

"That's too bad," he says, signaling for the check. "Because I know what we should do next." He wants to do something next? This just gets better and better.

"Shave our heads and wear sackcloth to show our repentance for our gluttony?" Uh oh. Are Bible jokes funny to non-Christians? Actually, is that joke funny at all?

"That, too." he says, giving me a weird look. "But also something that doesn't involve sitting in ashes." The waitress places the bill on the table, and I reach for it, pulling my wallet out with the other hand. He narrows his eyes at me, grabs the bill from my hand, and lays money on the table.

"Like I'm really going to let you pay," he says, shaking his head in mock disgust.

"But I really don't . . ." I start, then think of what Reagan would think. She would definitely let him pay. But does that make it a date, then? Can it be a date if it happens by accident and you're wearing sweaty softball clothes? This is all too complicated.

"Let's go," he says, standing up and putting his wallet back in his pocket. I look down at the money he has left as I stand up and quickly count it in my head. Oh my gosh. Not only has he paid for both of us, but he has left a tip. A 20 percent tip. My heart sinks. There is no way this guy is a Christian.

We walk out into the warm night air, and I breathe deeply. It smells sweet, and I am so happy, and he is so beautiful . . . I need to get out of here. I have to tell him that I'm a Christian. Here I go, telling him. Look at me, opening my mouth. I really am just about to when he turns to me and asks "Are you ready for your surfing lesson now?"

"Am I what?" Just when I thought this guy couldn't get any crazier.

"Let's go," he says, and he starts to walk away from the square. Where is he going? I may not know much about surfing, but even I know there has to be a large body of water involved. Oh, and boards. Boards are involved. He looks like he's . . . oh wow. He is really heading toward the bay. Oh no. Nuh-uh. I am not getting in the nasty bay for anything. And certainly not in my softball gear. One of those terrifying sea lions might come and take me away to a floating pier to be his mate for life. I stand still.

"Lily. C'mon," he says.

"C'mon where? The bay? I hear there are sharks in the bay," I say.

"Yeah. The bay. It'll be fun. We're already gross from the game."

"Listen, Mr. Fired from Summer Camp. No. Never." I eye him to see if he could possibly be serious.

He rolls his eyes and walks back. He plops down on the edge of the fountain in the center of the square. "You should take some risks in your life, you know. Me and my friends in college would do some really crazy stuff, and it really keeps you . . ." he takes a deep gulp of air, "I don't know, alive."

I walk over to the side of the fountain and sit down with him. He looks so cute and pleading. Do I risk the sharks and sea lions for him? "Sam, some other time. We'll have a surfing lesson when we've planned it, and there are surfboards and bathing suits involved. Okay?"

"Okay," he says, not bothering to hide how lame he thinks I am.

It gets quiet, and we just sit there for a moment. I reach into the fountain and splash him just a little on his leg. "Brighten up. You'll get to watch me make a fool of myself on a surfboard soon enough."

He stares at the few droplets of water on his legs and sighs really loudly. "I'm afraid, Lily, I just can't do that. It's just not going to work."

Wait? What's he saying? Ah! Is this just because I wouldn't get in the stinking polluted bay? I'm not the most spontaneous person, true, but Sam, we can make this work. Why are you giving up?

All of a sudden, Sam throws his arm around my middle section and tackles me backwards into the fountain with him. I stand up gasping and sputtering, drenched from head to toe. "Wha, what?"

"I can't wait to see you make a fool of yourself. I need to see it now!" he laughs. We're both standing in the fountain now. He's cracking up.

"Sam! Do you see that sign right over there? No people in the fountain!" I hiss.

He laughs and splashes me playfully. "Who cares? What's going to happen, Miss Traywick? Are you scared?"

I look around. I don't see anyone I know. I don't see any police. Sam is just standing there, looking at me, smiling and looking like heaven itself, his T-shirt soaked and sticking to his chest. I don't want to get caught, but still, I do want to show him I'm no stick in the mud. Do I really want to walk back to the car wet? Can I stand to hurt his feelings and get out? Then I realize that the old Lily would never do this, and I reach out for his arm.

I pull him down, perhaps a bit too roughly. Dainty, dainty . . . I'm coaching myself as he totters. He doesn't want to date a gladiator named Flash or anything.

He looks at me when he comes up and then proceeds to start splashing me mercilessly, to which I can only retaliate not-so-daintily. This is war. Forget flirting.

We are laughing and chasing each other around the bronze statues in the middle. I'm yelling his name and kicking up water over the sides. This is so fun. He was right. It's good to let go.

"Mommy, can I go in the fountain too?" a little boy walking past asks loudly.

"No," she says quickly, grabbing his hand. "They're just dirty hippies. Stay away from them."

We stop splashing each other and burst into laughter. We wait till they pass by and then continue.

He leans over and dips his head into the water and comes up with his long hair in front of his face. "Hey look, I'm Cousin It."

I splash him.

"Lily, I need you to be serious for a moment."

I wipe my smile away and look at him. "Okay."

"Come here for a moment."

I walk over to him in the middle of the fountain, where there are bronze mermaids tanning themselves in the moonlight.

"Right now I have to show you the most important rule of surfing.

You must remember," he says, placing his hand on a scaly tail, "to be nice to the merpeople you meet out in the ocean." He begins to pet her as if she's a dog, or alive, or a live dog. "The ocean is their home, and though they don't mind letting us use it—"

"Hey! Get out of the fountain!"

I'm blinded by a flashlight. It's a security guard, and he's coming toward us.

"Let's go," Sam yells. He makes for the edge, and I'm right behind him. It's hard to run in the water, but we both get to the side quickly. We jump out and take off sprinting down the courtyard. I can think of nothing but the squishy sound my sneakers make as I tear through the square. Once we turn onto a side street, I finally look over my shoulder.

"He's gone," I say breathlessly, slowing.

"Oh good," Sam says, stopping beside me. "Well, that was an invigorating little jog. Are you ready for the biking portion of our triathlon?"

"No way," I say, gulping for air. "That was great. But what if we had gotten arrested? I'd be dead. Disowned. Cut off."

"Nah, I've been arrested before. It's not so bad."

"Oh yeah, the tr . . ." Oh no. I'm not supposed to know about him chaining himself to a tree. I can't admit I Google-stalk! "So, um, when did you get arrested?"

"Back in college. I was really involved in this environmental group, and we heard that a developer was going to cut down some redwoods on campus to make way for the new student center. So we went out there the night before the site was supposed to be razed and chained ourselves to the trees and got ourselves arrested. Course, it didn't really count. It was just the campus police so I don't have a record or anything, though it was widely reported in the school paper. Can you imagine? Chaining yourself to a tree? Is there any stupider way to get arrested?"

"Canoe trashing?"

"Hey, I wasn't arrested for that. Just fired," he says, nodding. "Though I'm sure I've done dumber things. I'll think about it."

I can't imagine being arrested. I fall quiet and try to ignore the voice in my head that wonders if this sort of boy would be good for me in the long run. He's been arrested, he's been fired, he just got me to jump in a public fountain and then flee a security guard on foot. Reagan's right. He's pretty impulsive. I gulp.

The Presidio is quiet now except for a few voices and the slow, mournful sound of a saxophone. Who's playing in the park this late? As soon as we hit the grass area, I take off my wet shoes and socks and walk barefoot. Sam laughs. He walked me back to my car, but the stars are just too much for us to not stop and enjoy them for a moment. We both stare up in amazement. This will probably be one of the few non-foggy nights of the year in San Francisco, so it'd be a sin not to stay for just a moment. The bay in front of us is black and still, and several boats move slowly along its surface. All along the edge of the water clusters of yellow lights blink and glitter. To our left, the Golden Gate Bridge spans the mouth of the bay, its towers like shining ladders to heaven.

"It's really a beautiful night," he says quietly, brushing his hair back behind his ear. He begins to lower himself to the ground. He lies back, looking up at the sky again. I stare at him.

"Join me," he says, patting the grass next to him.

"Uh, sure." I get down beside him. I'm nervous, but I want to be near him. I want him to hold my hand. And yes, I admit, I want him to kiss me. I lie down on the grass near him but not close exactly. Our feet are almost touching. I should have tried to get closer. Can I get up and do it again?

"Look, there's an elephant," I say, pointing to the sky. Nice one, Lily.

"I think that's the Little Dipper."

"No it's not, see there's the trunk" I say, moving my arm to the left, "and the legs are over there—"

"Is that vague cluster of stars up there what you're trying to pass off as a pachyderm?" he asks, lifting his arm to point at the sky.

"Yep," I answer simply.

"Huh," he says. His arm falls back down, closer to mine. I can feel the heat from his skin. "I always wanted a pet elephant."

"I wanted a monkey. Or a potbellied pig," I say. Weird. I haven't told anyone that. No sense. No pets allowed in the Traywick's prison in Woodside. Mumsy won't have the hardwood floors desecrated.

"You should get one now."

"A monkey? I don't think so."

"What about starting out with a dog and working your way up?"

"I can't even keep a plant alive. No way am I going to risk the life of an innocent animal."

"Don't say no one ever encouraged you to follow your dreams."

"It was hardly a lifetime dream. It's not like writing a novel or feeding starving children."

"You've got to start somewhere," he says, shrugging. We both fall silent.

"Oh my gosh!" I say, sitting up suddenly. "We never got the present for your sister."

"Hm?" he murmurs, still looking at the sky.

"Your sister? Didn't you want to pick her up something?"

He turns his head, looks directly at me, and says, a little guiltily, "I don't have a sister."

"What?" I shriek.

"Man, Lily. I'm so sorry. I thought you knew that hours ago, when I suggested we get banana splits. I thought it was obvious that . . ."

He doesn't have a sister? Then why did he drag me all the way out there? Why did he . . . Oh.

Yes! Yes!

Oh no. Again with the crazy behavior.

Oh God, I know I should tell him now that I am a Christian and can't ever go out with him. But I can't. Not right now. This is too perfect.

"I can't believe you'd pick on a poor, innocent girl like me. Why Samuel March, I am appalled," I say, in a voice I usually reserve for Momzilla impressions.

"Whoa. You were practically drowning me in a mermaid fountain earlier. I'd hardly call you poor or innocent. Plus, I've always had a weakness for beautiful women. How was I to resist your charms?"

I smile in spite of myself. He's so charming. But then with great determination, I regain my mock-indignation. "How was *I* to know you were so deceiving?" I say and punch his arm, making sure to do it softly. I lie back down slowly. And carefully. Our shoulders are now touching. Barely. But touching nonetheless. "So you don't have a sister."

And let the record show that I was tricked into coming.

"Nope. I'm actually an only child."

I look up at the heavens. Crazy boy. We lie in silence for a while, enjoying the soft warm breeze, the sweet scent of the California air, and the low music. I enjoy being here with him. Slowly, I see his hand move. I feel it brush against mine, and for an instant I am afraid he is going to take my hand, then I am afraid he won't. Slowly, he places his hand on top of mine and rubs it a little.

I can't breathe. I'm afraid he'll move his hand if I try. Maybe I don't have to do this. Maybe he doesn't want to date me. Maybe he just wants to hang out.

Then why is he moving his hand up my wrist, slowly stroking my arm?

We lie in silence for a few minutes, then I slowly sit up, moving my hand out from under his. This is the most difficult thing I have ever done. I want him to be my boyfriend so much, but it can't happen.

"Sam, I have to tell you something," I say uncertainly. My voice is shaking. I really don't want to do this. *God, why did you make him so great?*

He sits up slowly and looks at me expectantly.

"I really like you, but I can't really go out with you. Ever."

"Why not?" he asks, looking both shocked and wounded.

"Um, because . . . because I'm a Christian. And as much as I like you, I don't really want to date someone who doesn't share my beliefs. It wouldn't work. I guess I just feel like unless someone believes what I do they'll never really understand why I am who I am, and . . ." Don't start crying. Why is he grinning? It's not funny!

"Is that all?" he asks, laughing. "I was afraid you were going to tell me you had a secret boyfriend or had pledged yourself to a nunnery or something."

"No, but you see, it's kind of a big deal, because—"

"Lily? I knew you were a Christian."

"Oh," I say. "Wait, how?" I haven't worn my cross necklace in years.

"I talked to Reagan about you. She told me."

That's weird. She didn't tell me that. "All the same, that doesn't really change our problem here because—"

"So am I."

"You're what?"

"A Christian," he laughs. My mouth is hanging open. "I have been since, well, before I was born. My parents couldn't have children for ages, and then they prayed and prayed and finally my mom became pregnant with yours truly. They really believe that God answered their prayers so they sort of promised God to raise me in the church."

"Um . . ." I can't think rationally. How could I not know? This is way better than suddenly finding out someone is secretly a law student. My heart is beating wildly, my pulse racing. How did this happen? "Really?"

He nods. "I know it's hard to believe that anyone would think that I'm an answer to prayer."

"So was Reagan just like, 'Oh hey, what's up, Sam? Lily is a Christian. I love the eighties'?"

Sam cracks up. "No, no. I was asking her about you. To see if you had a boyfriend. And she mentioned it. And I was really excited to find out."

"But why . . . why didn't I know that about you?"

"I guess you never asked," he said shrugging. I take a deep breath. He continues. "I was raised in the church but got into all kinds of crazy stuff in college and kind of walked away from it. But my dad was always pretty strong in his faith, and when he died, I started thinking about it a lot. And I realized what a mess my life had become and that I needed help. And I have never looked back. I stopped the drugs. I swore off girls for a while. I applied to law school. I stopped paying so much attention to what people thought of me and how I looked. I let my hair grow long," he says, taking a chunk in his hand as if to demonstrate, "because stuff like that didn't really matter to me anymore."

I am still staring at him in shock.

"How about you?" he asks, putting his hand back on mine. "How did you become a Christian?"

"Televangelists," I say quietly.

"What?"

"Um, yeah," I say, taking a deep breath. "My parents aren't really into the whole God thing, but my grandma is, except that she's pretty old and doesn't get out much. So she watches church on TV. She has for as long as I can remember. And when I was young I would watch with her. And I was convinced. I believed."

"You're for real?" he says, incredulous. I nod. "You are a piece of work, Lily." He shakes his head. We stare at each other awkwardly.

"So, um, wow. I guess that changes things," I say awkwardly. He leans toward me.

"Yes, I guess it does," he whispers, as he bends and brushes his lips against my cheek.

"*Who* kissed you?" Reagan yells shrilly. A waiter looks over and raises his eyebrows. Ahh, another exciting break in the Good Life.

"Shhh . . . keep your voice down!" I hiss. "The last thing I need is for everyone in the café to hear. And it was just on the cheek."

"Okay," she says, a little quieter. "So Sam March. Long-haired Sam from shoes? Sam the hottest guy at Traywick's?"

"Yes, I guess," I say sheepishly.

"So when did all this start?"

"Not that long ago. After the makeover thing, mostly." I look down at my short orange skirt and realize how far I've come. I would never have had the guts to wear such a bright color until recently. Come to think of it, why did it start only after the makeover? I guess I should take a lesson from the peacock—it's all about your plumage.

"And how many times have you gone out?" she says, eyes wide.

"None, really. We just hung out for a long time after the softball game last night."

"So how did it happen?"

"We just got to talking, and I told him I couldn't go out with him because I was a Christian—"

"*You told him what?*" she shrieks. An old man at the next table whips his head around and frowns at Reagan's explosion. "Do we need another flirting lesson? When you're out with a gorgeous man, you do not tell him that. You do not tell anyone that. That was not part of the deal."

"No, we don't need another flirting lesson. And it worked out just fine anyway," I say smiling and sitting up straight in my chair. "You see, it turns out he's a Christian too, and—"

"He's a Christian?" She looks dumbfounded.

"Yeah, and he said that he already knew that I was from talking to you, which makes it better because if he didn't know and had been trying to get me alone, I wouldn't have been so . . ."

Reagan's face has gone white suddenly.

"What's wrong?"

"Oh, nothing. I just, I was just thinking about that time Sam talked to me. I thought . . ."

"Reagan, what's up? And, yeah, why didn't you tell me he was asking about me? What did he say?"

"He . . . he just came over to my area and was chatting with me. He asked about how long we had been friends and stuff. I think he said something like you seemed like a live wire, and I laughed and said that actually you were a good Christian girl. It just didn't occur to me that—"

"That he was one too? I know, it's crazy."

"No. I mean, yes, crazy," she says with a dazed look on her face. "I guess . . . I mean, I just . . . our whole conversation . . . I know we talked about you, but . . . he kept talking, and he's so cute, and . . . well, the whole time I thought he was flirting with me!"

"With you." Uh oh. Does she like him? Oh, please no. If she likes him I can't. That's the first rule of friendship. I know I'm supposed to choose friends over boys, but I *really* don't want to. "Do you, uh, like him? Um, because if you do I can tell him I can't see him anymore, if that's what you want."

Please don't say yes, please don't say yes.

"No. I mean, he's great, and totally hot," she says, breaking into a grin. "But I'm dating George now." I've never heard of George before. Interesting. "And I'm really happy for you, actually. It's just . . . it's just that this whole thing is going to take some getting used to. A whole new Lily . . ."

We are both silent for a moment. Everything has changed so fast for me.

Reagan clears her throat and looks pained to speak again. "Come to think of it, I guess this means you won the bet."

The bet? The *bet*. Oh yeah. I did. Awesome. "I had totally forgotten about it."

"Yeah, well, congratulations. Mission accomplished."

"I won!"

"So I guess I better start shopping for some patent leather Mary Janes to wear to church then," says Reagan, shaking her head.

As I am about to get in my car to drive to church this morning, I remember that I'll inevitably see Daniel, and I begin to panic. He's written me twice, but due to my excitement over Sam, I just haven't had the will to write him back yet. I have been hoping, no, praying, that Daniel would have sensed that we had a, well, we weren't a love connection. But no. His e-mails have been very flirty, and he point-blank asked when he'd see me again. I did feel a little bit better after he made a joke about the *Ochos Niños*. At first I wondered if I was just being too hard on Daniel, but after my date with Sam, I know what it feels like to fall for someone in a headlong rush, like they always show in the movies.

I spend the whole service trying to avoid poor Daniel. I slipped in late and sat next to Alex in the back. Granted, I don't like sitting next to Alex, Maggie, and Bill—the little Jesus club—but of course Daniel is sitting next to Becky and Miguel in the front. If I join my usual crew, it would instantly be a double date. Steph is working the church nursery this week so she is no help.

After the service, I run to the women's bathroom to hide out. I put down the lid to the toilet and just sit there, trying to remember all the names of Oakland A's starting lineup when I hear a voice.

"Lily?" It's Steph.

"Yo," I say.

"Sorry to, uh, interrupt you in there, but everyone was thinking of doing something cheesy for lunch, and I was hoping you were coming for backup," she says.

I smile and walk out of the stall. "How'd you know I was in here?"

She looks into the stall. "Becky, Miguel's girlfriend, tipped me off. She mentioned that you sat with Maggie and Alexandra during church so I knew something was amiss. Were you hiding in there?"

I shrug. "It's possible."

Steph studies me for a moment. "Oh no. I know what's up. You still haven't told Daniel?"

I frown at her. Oh this is so awful. "Yeah. I don't know what to do," I whine.

She laughs. "What have you been doing that you haven't talked to him yet? He must have at least called you."

I gulp. Why oh why didn't I just write Daniel back? Sam! Your infectious impulsiveness did this to me. Now I look so rude. "I should have just written him an e-mail."

"Yeah. You should have. But you'd be surprised, as uncomfortable as it is, it's always better to do it in person. C'mon. Alexandra's making us all ride a streetcar to Fisherman's Wharf for some clam chowder. You can pull him aside and tell him then."

I stand in the bathroom, feet planted and not moving.

"C'mon, you. I need you. I can't do something this touristy without support." Steph loops her arm in mine and walks me out of my hiding place.

We catch one of the vintage streetcars on Market so that we can have a nice long ride to Embarcadero. Yep, a streetcar. Don't ask me how it happened, but we have cable cars, streetcars, light rail, BART, ferries, and buses. I always pictured a big town meeting where someone said, "We need mass transit!" and everyone agreed. But then because this is San Francisco and everyone gets a vote and everyone's opinion is valid and has to be considered and no one should have their feelings hurt, they decided to go with *every* kind of mass transit suggested.

As the vintage green metallic car pulls up, I notice that it is the streetcar that the city bought from New Orleans. It's named Desire. Maggie and Alexandra start jumping up and down and clapping their hands.

"Yay, yay. We're so lucky," says Maggie.

"This is the most perfect one," says Alex.

The guys all look confused at their hysteria and allow the women to board first. I make sure Bill, not Daniel, is behind me. I feed my money to the little machine and step on to find a seat.

"A buck fifty?" Bill says. "That's pretty steep, isn't it?" he says to the conductor. The conductor just scowls at him, and I roll my eyes. Cheapskate. This is an authentic streetcar from the City of New Orleans built in 1923. This is a piece of history.

As I file through the middle aisle I quickly realize that the seats are all for two people. I also notice that—and this is weird—Alexandra and Maggie have sat down opposite each other, each leaving the seat closest to the aisle empty. As I move to pass them, Alex pipes up.

"This seat is taken."

"What?" I ask. "Oh, that seat, Alex?" I ask with a smirk, pointing at the seat next to her. As if I was going to sit with her.

"Alexandra," she says, pointing to herself. "I'm saving it for Bill. I heard him say he wanted to sit on the side of the car that has a better view of the waterfront."

I look at Maggie, and she just smiles extra bright. I am guessing she had tried to sit with Alex too, but Alex wouldn't let her. Poor thing. I keep moving back and find a seat to myself. I'm just waiting for the inevitable. I guess Daniel and I are going to have our little talk on the way to lunch. I'm going to try to keep it light and funny.

Bill files on behind me and plops down next to Maggie. My eyes widen.

"Bill, I thought you said that you wanted to sit on this side of the car," Alex says, pursing her lips. She lovingly pats the seat next to her.

He shrugs. "This is fine. Either way."

Maggie looks a little panicked, not wanting to incur the wrath of Alex. "You should sit over there. Alexandra saved it for you," she says.

"I'm fine. Thanks, girls," Bill says. And then he turns to Maggie and says, "Last night I dreamed a giant butterfly came in my window. I really think it's a symbol from the Lord."

Maggie claps her hands excitedly. "It must be a symbol of rebirth!"

"Stella! Stella!" We all turn our heads and see Daniel yelling as he boards the car. I have to smile, but notice everyone else is giving him a weird look. Typical. I would guess that Alex and Maggie know of *A*

Streetcar Named Desire, but they haven't seen the disturbing film, let alone read the classic play. They just think it sounds romantic, which cracks me up.

"You're impressed, aren't you?" Daniel says as he plops down next to me. I spy Steph sitting down next to Alex. Steph gives me a thumbs up, while Alex leans across her to try to talk to Bill.

"Yeah," I say, awkwardly. I'm such a mess. I swallow hard.

We're both quiet for a moment, and I'm willing him to realize what I'm about to say. I'm sorry, I tell him telepathically. So so sorry.

"Lily . . . uh, I think that we should uh . . ." he says.

"Daniel, I'm so sorry. It's just that . . ."

"No, no, no. Don't say it. I've got it. Let's just go back to being friends. Like it never happened."

I sigh. "Really?"

"Oh yeah. Really. I'm sure."

"I mean, you're really hot but . . ."

He laughs. "Yeah, I mean, I *know* that," he says.

I laugh. "I just think, we, uh, want different—"

"Right. I know. Better as friends."

We both laugh a little and then are quiet again.

"Can't blame a guy for trying," Daniel says, finally. And then he reaches over and messes up my hair. I beam back at him.

I open the window and let the fresh air hit my face. I need to calm down.

After wringing my hands for hours and pacing back and forth, back and forth, on the kitchen floor last night, I finally cracked when Gran asked me what was going on. I told all of them about my meeting with Edgar J. Arle today at the *San Francisco Chronicle*. I explained that he had by chance seen some of my writing on the Internet and that he had invited me in for a prospective interview at the paper. The weird thing was, they were very supportive. Dad said, "Good for you, champ."

And Gran suggested several pitches to me for Edgar: a profile of Benny Hinn, an exploratory piece about craft circles in the Bay Area, and a humor piece about the eternal problem of keeping panty hose from being bunched up. Mom, predictably, was the one person who was able to keep her excitement well-girdled.

"That's lovely, Lily. But do make sure it doesn't interfere with your previous commitments like your current job. We don't want anything to take you away from your future store."

I grimaced and begged them all to keep expectations very low because this was only going to be an occasional freelance kind of thing that wouldn't pay well and even that was only if Edgar actually liked my first piece. They agreed to try.

Now I'm on my way to the *SF Weekly* office, and I am trying to keep my expectations low too. I grab the handwritten directions from the empty passenger's seat and study them at the stoplight. What luck. I'm still on track, have only had one near-miss, and I'm not even running late. I try to inhale slowly. Steph and I had spent hours on the phone last night developing the pitches Edgar asked me to bring with me. It's going to be fine, it's going to be fine . . .

I need to breathe into a bag.

"Fashion Victim? Is that you?"

I walk toward Edgar. The whole experience is so surreal that I could be watching myself like a fly on a wall.

"Uh, yes sir. Lily Traywick. Nice to meet you." I give him the firm but not-too-firm handshake that I practiced with Stephanie ten times.

"Edgar Arle. Please call me Edgar," he says smiling broadly and shaking my hand vigorously. "Or Earle. Whichever you prefer."

Edgar looks exactly like an alternative, free weekly paper editor should. He is youngish, his brown hair just a little gray around the edges, and he is wearing a faded black blazer over a green T-shirt that says *Say Yes to Michigan!* His office is a little natty and strewn with papers, books, paper coffee cups, and even a wadded up T-shirt in the corner. He grabs a stack of folders from the chair on the other side of his desk and moves it to the desk, and then, reconsidering, the floor. "Please, have a seat."

I've seen his type before at Traywick's in the buyers' offices. Creative people are assumed to be laid back and easygoing, what with their eccentric outfits and messy office spaces, but often they are the most demanding people to work for since they are driven by a very personal vision of how their work should be accomplished. The trick is to not underestimate them and strive to inspire them while staying within the realm of their vision. I sit down and immediately make eye contact with him. I try to appear ready for this kind of responsibility. Worldly and sassy. Creative and smart.

"It's just so wonderful to finally meet you. And you're a Traywick, hmm?"

"Yes, my parents are Roland and Joan Traywick."

He's laughing. "What do they think of your little writing project?"

I gulp. I really want him to hire me, but I can't lie about this. "I'm afraid no one knows that I write a blog. And so far, no one has guessed who I am."

"Now *that's* a great story idea. *Fashion Victim Exposed!* I can see it now."

Oh no! This is not what I wanted. I can't agree to do that. "I'm sorry, Mr. Arle—"

"Edgar."

"I'm sorry, Edgar. I just can't do that. My family would be too hurt. It isn't worth it to me to get a byline at their expense."

He sits back, wrinkling up his nose. "Vicki?" he yells.

I jump. Is my name Vicki? No. Wait. Does he think my name is Vicki? Is he yelling at me?

A thin woman appears at his door. "A coffee, please." Vicki scratches this down on a pad and turns to leave without saying a word.

"Oh, wait, just one moment. Lily, would you like a cup of coffee?"

"Sh-sh-sure," I stammer.

"Two coffees, please, Vicki. Black?"

I'm picking up on his laconic conversational style now. "One cream, please."

Vicki nods and slips away noiselessly.

Edgar turns back to me, looking very serious. "This is my paper, Lily. I have my hand in all parts of it. Some people don't like that, but you know what I always say?"

I shake my head no.

"You don't like me? Take a number."

Uh . . . okay.

"But I'm fair. And I've got a sense of humor. And I'm always on the lookout for young talent. I respect your integrity, and I already like your writing. And my probing has revealed that you have a sense of humor, which I like. I had to make sure of that. So pitch me something you think would be right for us. I assume you've read *SF Weekly* quite a bit?"

"Oh yes. Of course," I say. The moment he e-mailed me, I got online immediately and read every back issue feature I could. And I loved it. The stories were quirky and honest. Their only theme was the Bay Area. It is exactly the sort of publication I want to be writing for. I want this job. I need this job for my sanity.

"Good then. What ideas have you brought me? A writer is nothing without her ideas."

Right. "Well, I was sort of thinking the other day about the traffic here in the city and uh it's really bad and I thought—"

"Okay. We'll work on this, but the first rule is that you have to pitch faster. I believe any decent story can be boiled down to a sentence or two."

I take a breath. "I could interview people from out of state about the traffic and ask what ritual they do to keep calm in their car."

He shrugs. "What else?"

I look in front of me and a steaming cup of coffee with a little cream in it has now appeared as if by magic. Goodness that Vicki is a ghost. "Uh . . . well . . ." Stop it! Stop it! Spit it out! "The farmer's market outside the Ferry Building." Whew, I spit it out. "I'd like to do a profile of some of the vendors there. I think many are family farmers or small start-ups."

He nods a little. I can see he likes that one a little better. Good thing I've been saving the best for last. Let's hope he nibbles on this one. "Or I could do a profile piece about Harry Lloyd, the Traywick's piano player."

He cocks his head to the side at me and then waves his hand in the air to urge me to keep talking.

"Harry comes from an old rich East Coast family. He became a professional piano player when he turned twelve. He first played Carnegie Hall when he was nine. He traveled the world, playing in concert halls in every major city, and eventually fell in love with his wife, a hotel manager in South Africa. His parents didn't approve, so they settled out here, where they lived happily for several years. Unfortunately, their only child, a girl, died from leukemia when she was ten, and Harry was lost. With all the money in the world, but nothing to live for, he quit playing and became a sort of recluse. A few years later, he had a severe stroke and lost the use of most of the left side of his body. He started playing again as a kind of physical therapy. It brought him back. He moves a little slowly, and sometimes has a hard time speaking, but he's almost totally recovered. He doesn't need the money, but these days, he gets paid to play the white Steinway grand piano in Traywick's. I was thinking I could do a feature about him and talk about the redemptive power of music."

Whew. That was kind of long, but I can tell Edgar is definitely listening. I lean back in my chair and take a sip of my coffee while he turns and stares out the window.

"Hmm . . ." he says. "You're sure you don't want to write about your blog? Or a scathing piece about the dark underbelly of San Fransisco's fashion world?"

I nod resolutely.

"Okay. Give the old man a try. But try to keep it from being dull or sentimental. It should be fast-paced and engrossing. Keep it on the short side. I'll put it in the Local Profiles section."

"Okay."

"Get it to me in two weeks. We've got a couple profiles lined up for the next two issues. And this piece is on spec. Okay?"

Thank goodness I know what that means, although it is bad news. On speculation. No moola. "Fine."

"If I pick it up, you'll get the standard payment for freelancers. And if I really like it, I'll call you again."

I nod and smile.

"Thank you for coming by." Now that business is over, he starts smiling again. "And good luck with that surfing lesson. That guy totally likes you."

I blush, lean down, and grab my purse. I turn around to see Vicki ready to usher me out the door. How did she know? Does he have a little eject button behind his desk? At least it is over, and it wasn't a complete catastrophe, but I do sense he's still deciding about me. I'm going to have to really knock myself out on this piece.

Fashion Victim
Transmissions from Fashion Land

Newly dating
Lovesick
And livid
Twenty-something
Surfer chick
Rides the wave

Fashion Victim is steaming mad. Remember the fun little romp in the fountain I regaled you all with a couple weeks ago?

Well, it turns out Mumsy's old friend who she "lunches" with, aka her secret spy, happened to be in the area of said fountain and spotted poor Fashion Victim frolicking. Of course she told mother dear, and did I get an earful. "Disgracing our family name . . . acting like a child . . . your position in society . . . blah, blah, blah." Disgracing our name? It's not like I pulled a Paris Hilton; I played in a fountain. I could have done so much worse! She doesn't know how lucky she is to have a well-behaved daughter like me. Only five more days until I get out of here . . .

At least my Free-at-Last Luau is this weekend. I'd say I can't wait, but really what I can't wait for is for the end of the toothpick wars between me and Gran. Reagan, who really should be a party planner instead of a fashionista, sent out the invitations and arranged for the decorations. Stephanie—a walking copy of Gourmet magazine—planned the menu. All I have to do is assemble the really easy stuff like ham on sticks. Okay, it's really called Hula Half-Bites, but basically it's prosciutto and grilled pineapple on toothpicks. But the toothpicks have these cute little umbrellas on them, and Gran keeps running off with the umbrellas. She insists they make perfect parasols for her figurines. When I tried to argue, she said I was keeping her from her "art." Five more days.

Also, here's a fun surfing fact for all the Midwestern readers: You surf in a wetsuit in Northern California. Not a bathing suit, a wetsuit.

I finally had a real surfing lesson. You know, at a real beach. I was able to get up on my board—my new beau's spare board—pretty easily, thank goodness. Of course what I was most nervous about was him seeing me in a bathing suit, but ten thousand situps later, I was feeling pretty good. And then as soon as we got to the beach, before I even took off my shorts, he tossed me a wetsuit. I pulled it on, zipped it up, and could have been an Oompah Loompah for all anyone could tell. Who knew?

Got to go pack. Did I mention I only have five more days?

Go with God! Down with fashion (and crunches)!
Fashion Victim

• Chapter 8 •

"Lily," *Reagan* says, holding up my navy blue Speedo racing suit, "you cannot wear this."

"Why not? There are no holes or snags or anything!" I insist, grabbing it out of her hand.

"Hey, that suit looks good on her," Steph says. This is a showdown between Reagan and Steph. What will Lily wear to the pool party? Does anyone actually ask Lily what she wants to wear? Oh no. Of course not. We've got agendas clashing here.

"Isn't it time to take the baked brie out of the oven, Steph?" Reagan asks, smiling sweetly. Steph laughs and gives a definitive no. She takes the blue suit from my hands and feels the fabric. "I don't see what's wrong with it," she says defiantly.

"This is the old Lily," Reagan says, reaching to grab it back. "It's vintage Lily. Come on," she says, looking at me pleadingly. "You've changed. This is your coming-out party!"

"It's not a coming-out party!" I say defensively. "It's a going away party! A goodbye to this house party!"

"A goodbye to this *life* party! Lily, admit it, you've changed. For the better. And *this*," she says, finally grabbing the suit back, "is a relic of your old life." She tosses it on the bed.

"Whatever, Reagan. You didn't change her genetic code. Lily, you should wear whatever makes you comfortable," Steph says and hands me back the blue suit as if to say, *this* makes you comfortable. I look at her intently. I look back at Reagan. No one speaks. I'm not sure what I want. I had just assumed I'd wear my blue suit, Old Faithful, as I call it, but maybe I should try something new.

"I don't actually own anything else so I guess this time I'll just wear—"

"I know, Lily. I remember how you resisted my pleadings to buy that cute white one at Traywick's, even though it looked amazing on you and also happened to be 60 percent off. But never fear. I brought you some options," Reagan says nearly singing with glee. She pulls a handful of fabric scraps out of her Kate Spade beach tote. "Now, you're taller than I am, so these might not fit perfectly, but they'll be close," she says, rummaging on the bed for two pieces that match.

"I am *not* wearing this," I say, pulling up a string with two tiny silver lamé triangles on it, which I guess was supposed to pass for a bikini top.

"Of course not," she says, shaking her head. "That's Gucci. And that's what I'm wearing." She grabs it out of my hands, laughing. Reagan's generous, sure, but not with Gucci. There wasn't enough fabric there to keep my wrist covered. "Now, this one isn't really the right color for your skin," she says, holding up a lime green bikini top, "but it's fun. The trim here is really cool," she says, pointing to the sparkly yellow and red piping on the top.

I shake my head. "I'll look like I was attacked by a bag of Skittles."

"Reagan. You can't be serious. Why wear anything at all with that little fabric?" Steph says.

"Fine," Reagan says, throwing it back onto the bed. "How about this?" she asks, holding up a bandeau top. It's just a purple band of fabric—no straps or anything.

"Too much . . . of not enough," Steph says quickly.

"One of my legendary jack knifes off the diving board and that thing is on the bottom of the pool," I say. "I don't mind trying something new, but let's be practical here."

Reagan shakes her head and tosses the bandeau back onto the bed. She grabs a reptile skin print bikini. How does she have so many bathing suits? It's not like these are cheap-o Wal-Mart brands. These are all Traywick's classics.

"How about this?"

"I don't know. I don't want to look like a snake. What are you wearing, Steph?" I ask.

"A tankini. It's cute," she says a little defensively.

"I wash my hands of this. I'm done, kid," Reagan says. "All of your options are here on the bed. Take one if you want. Or don't. Wear that blue thing. I don't care," she says.

Steph looks at me, and I shrug. I realize that Reagan could never understand. Steph genuinely tries to dress modestly for the sake of guys, visual creatures that they are. I've never been a bikini fan myself, but that's mostly because I spent so many years at swim practice in baggy, holey suits that anything smaller makes me feel like I'm naked. But, sadly, we both know how judgmental Christians can be. Someone once brought a friend to a Super Single Sunday beach night, and the poor girl didn't know any better and wore a little pink bikini. The girls shunned her all night. And of course the guys were too scared to talk to her. She never came back. It's like an unwritten rule that bikinis are a part of secular culture, and anyone who wears one might as well be Bathsheba, trying to lead the poor innocent church boys astray.

On the other hand, is it my fault if men sin? I should think not. We are accountable for our own actions. Plus, I've been the awkward girl in the tank suit my whole life. And I did all those sit-ups to go surfing, now I could finally show them off. And Sam will be there. Hmm . . . I believe the Bible says that in Christ we are truly free. I should just choose a suit that I feel good about myself in and not worry about what the Christians will think. If they judge me, that's their problem.

"This is all right," I say quickly, picking up a light blue bottom from the pile and holding it up. The legs are almost boy cut, and though it is still very much a bikini bottom, it is definitely more modest than the others.

"I'm not sure how the church guys would feel about that," Steph says.

"If they have one ounce of testosterone in their bodies, they'll love it," Reagan says.

"That's exactly what I'm afraid of," Steph says.

"You're afraid that guys will like the way you look? Is this some kind of weird Christian thing? You can't wear anything that boys might find attractive?" she asked, rolling her eyes. "Why not just shave your head? They won't be tempted then." She stands up straight and looks at me. "How in the world do Christians ever get married?"

I laugh. Oh Reagan.

Steph stares at me coolly. "Christians just don't objectify women," she says calmly. "And I guess they just care about more important things than appearance." Reagan meets her gaze. They stare at each other, and we're all up to our ears in tension.

"Ahem. We all have our own dating theories, of course." They both stare at me now. I have to make peace. I grab the bikini off the bed. "I'll wear this bikini, but I'll also wear a sarong to, uh, keep warm when I'm not in the water." I smile.

I slip into the bathroom to try the suit on, and I almost don't recognize myself. I'm a knockout in this thing. I turn from side to side to see myself, so, so much of myself. Reagan's right. I am different. She's transformed me from a girl who'd never been on a date to the girlfriend of Sam March. Hooray for the power of fashion.

"*Dive!*" Daniel yells. Miguel leans forward, throwing his hands down toward the water, but he hits the surface more chest-first than headfirst. As a wave of chlorinated water washes over the side of the pool and splashes Reagan's ankles, the guys from church cheer. Reagan gives them a dirty look and keeps walking with the drink tray.

"Almost, bro," Bill yells, then climbs up on the diving board. Seeing him, I am starting to doubt that this pool party thing was a good idea. In my obsessed craze to make sure I looked decent in a bathing suit, it never occurred to me that there were certain people I'd rather not see without their clothes. Did all the hair from Bill's head pack up and move to his back? Now Sam on the other hand . . . I glance over at him, talking to Steph on the steps of the pool, and try not to let my eyes dwell on his broad, tan shoulders.

Steph catches my eye, and I try to pretend I was looking at her in the first place. I see her studying me. Her face says she is not pleased. Maybe the bikini was a mistake. She, on the other hand, looks like a model. A model of Christian virtue. I wish my hair shined in the sun like hers does. In fact, I wish I looked as good as Steph does all around right now. Her pink tankini with little embroidered flowers is so simple it's charming, her skin is inexplicably and perfectly tan, and she's so thin. When does she have time to exercise? I start to walk toward them, carefully balancing my tray of hors d'oeuvres, willing it not to tip and spill ham chunks into the turquoise water.

I look back at the diving board and see Bill's hands folded in prayer. Oh goodness. He even prays for his dives. I hear three loud steps, the groan of bending fiberglass, and the squeak of the diving board curving back up, and turn to watch, waiting expectantly. Bill has brought his hands in front of him and is starting to curve down in a dive when Daniel yells "Jump!" Bill throws his arms back and gets his feet under him just before he hits the water. A cheer rises from the guys waiting in line behind the board.

I am so thankful Mom had to be at a dinner party (with *Donatella*, she reminded me obnoxiously three times) and can't see her award-winning landscape getting soaked with chlorinated water. And Gran wouldn't care, but thankfully she has promised to stay in her room and out of the way, though she said she was at least going to come downstairs at some point and check out my cute new boyfriend so that she can tell Mom and Dad she chaperoned the party. But she promised not to stay long.

"Good one Bill!" yells Maggie, who is wearing a long flowered dress and white sandals. She is surrounded by the church girls, fully or mostly clothed and gathered around a round glass table, who are clapping appreciatively. Becky, Miguel's girlfriend, sits uncomfortably among them in shorts and a black bikini top. She looks around and meets my gaze. I smile. She hangs herself with an imaginary noose as Alex leans in to examine Maggie's nails. I laugh back at her. How can they seriously just be sitting around watching this? Sure "Jump or Dive" is fun, but this game—whose only rule is that you have to be in midair before someone yells whether you are supposed to enter the water feetfirst or headfirst—is so simple even a two-year-old would get bored after a few minutes. I guess the cutie patooties are fascinating.

I walk toward Steph and Sam. Sam turns and watches me coming, smiling and raising his eyebrows.

"You look hot!" he says as I put my feet on the first step and sit down on the edge of the pool next to him.

He noticed! But then I see Steph's glare. "Thanks," I say quickly. "Hula Half-Bite?" I ask, holding the tray out.

"No thanks," Sam says quickly, wrapping his arm around my leg. Steph shakes her head no.

"Oh, come on you guys, they're not that bad," I say, resting the tray on my knees and putting one in my mouth, sliding the toothpick out.

"I don't eat pork," he says, laughing.

"Why not? Peter saw the animals up in the clouds, and now we can eat creatures without cloven hooves," I say laughing. "It's in the New Testament."

"Yes, I've read the New Testament. Lily, I'm a vegetarian," says Sam, laughing.

"Fine. What about you?" I say and turn to Steph. "I know *you're* not a vegetarian."

"They look great," Steph says quickly, shaking her blond head. "But I don't know . . . pork? I just don't eat pork anymore."

I stare at her in shock. "This from the girl who forced me to eat a fried Spam sandwich in college?"

She's laughing, and Sam wrinkles his nose at us.

"No really, Sam. Steph also once accepted a ten-dollar bribe to eat a whole package of hot dogs on a Crusade camping retreat," I say.

"Yeah, but things are different now. I mean the chemicals in hot dogs are enough to . . ." she trails off.

"Medical school is really having a negative effect on you," I say.

"Pork is so fatty. It just disgusts me."

"One Hula Half-Bite? One?" I wave the tray under her nose. I'm cracking myself up and Sam too. Steph is looking at me like I'm crazy.

"You know you want one," I sing. I wave them under her nose again.

"Gross, Lily. Just stop it!" she says much too loudly and shoves the tray at me. I stop dead still for a moment. Wait, is she mad, or did I just carry it over the line again? I notice Sam is looking a little surprised too.

We both look at her, trying to read her face. Then she snorts like a pig and puts her finger on the end of her nose. I start cracking up. She grabs a Hula Half-Bite and slides it in her mouth. "You happy?" she asks through a mouthful of pork and pineapple.

"Yes, little piggy," I say.

"*Dive!*" Daniel yells, as one of the guys lands on his stomach, hitting the water with a loud thump. Several gasps come from the corner and then high-pitched cheering.

Reagan, shaking her head at the shrill sounds from the church girls, walks over to us, carrying a tray of Blue Hawaiians effortlessly, her silver bikini sparkling. It's no wonder all of the guys here are watching her every move—even the guys from church who are valiantly pretending not to be. She looks stunning with her long brown hair hanging straight down her back, her giant hot pink hoop earrings dancing as she walks, and every inch of her skin perfectly tan (which is saying something, since she is exposing is lot of it).

She nods coolly at Steph and sits down next to me on the side of the pool, her legs dangling into the water.

"Drink?" she asks sweetly, holding the tray out in front of us. Sam takes one quickly. Steph smiles hopefully at Reagan as she takes one. Good old Steph, always the first to try to reestablish peace. Reagan nods and waits for her to take her drink.

"Doesn't Lily look great?" Reagan asks Sam, smiling and nodding.

"I'll say," Sam responds, winking at me. Regan looks triumphantly at Steph. "But then she always does," he says, planting a kiss on my cheek. Steph looks at Reagan, raising her eyebrows as if to show she was right too. Reagan won't meet her gaze.

"Shouldn't you be passing out the snacks, mingling with your guests?" she asks me.

"I'm taking a break," I say, lunging for and successfully grabbing a glass. "I don't know how many more times I can describe what the new apartment looks like and how much I'm going to miss living here and all that." I take a sip of the blue liquid through a little pink straw. From our little corner of the pool, we can see the whole patio and observe all of the little groups talking, laughing, and drinking, and can see just a hint of the hills beyond the low fence.

"Good," Reagan says, leaning back. "I'm taking a break too. I'm tired of trying to convince the cast of *Little House on the Prairie* over there," she says, nodding at the church friends, "that it won't kill them to have a drink."

Sam snorts. "Who are they anyway?"

"They're from church," Steph says, taking a sip of her drink. "They're harmless enough."

"From church?" Reagan asks, wrinkling up her nose. "Should I point out to them what Jesus' first miracle was?"

"You know what Jesus first miracle was?" I ask, openmouthed.

"Oh, come on," she says at my shocked expression. "I'm not a complete moron. I had to take confirmation class. I know a little bit about religion," she says indignantly.

I smile. "Good. Then you're going to fit in nicely at church."

"Not if everyone dresses like that," she says under her breath. "It's no wonder the guys are keeping a safe distance."

"Reagan . . ." Steph starts. I can see she's torn. On the one hand, she knows she should defend the church girls, but I know how little she wants to.

"Seriously," Reagan continues. "Look at the girl in the straw hat," she says, pointing to Maggie, who is braiding another girl's hair and smiling sweetly. "Do you want to know why she's not dating anyone?"

"She kissed dating goodbye," I say uncomfortably.

Steph clears her throat. I stare at the water. It's one thing to help me with guy problems, but I am not really comfortable with Reagan making fun of girls she doesn't even know, even if I don't find them fascinating either.

"More like never said hello," Reagan laughs.

Steph looks very uncomfortable, stirring the surface of the water with her fingers. She opens her mouth to speak, then closes it. She tries again. "Reagan, did you say you're coming to church?" Steph asks brightly, turning to look at Reagan and smiling.

"I suppose so," she answers.

"*Jump!*" We are sprayed by the enormous splash of Miguel unsuccessfully trying to get his feet under him before he hits the water. He comes up laughing and winks at Becky. She smiles and shakes her head.

"That's great!" Sam says, then seeing Reagan's dejected face, continues, "I'm going to go too. I haven't found a church I like in San Francisco, so I haven't really been going to church, but Lily swears hers doesn't involve snake handling or virgin sacrifices or anything," he says, playfully punching Reagan on the shoulder. "We can tough it out together. So what prompted you to start going? A burning bush?"

"Um . . ." I interject quickly before Reagan can answer. She can't mention our bet in front of Sam. "Speaking of burning, does anyone have sunblock handy?" I stretch out my arms and try to look concerned. "I'm going to get roasted." Sam gives me a weird look.

"I just helped you put some on half an hour ago," he says. "And the sun is going down."

"Oh, ha ha! You're right," I laugh, and then turn quickly to Reagan. "In any case, there are plenty of cool people at church, right Steph?" Steph nods.

"Yeah," Steph says, scanning the patio. "Like the girl Becky over there in the black suit? She's cool. She just started coming. She dresses really well too . . ." she says, offering Reagan a tenuous olive branch. Reagan smiles a little. "And like those guys over there," she says, pointing toward Miguel and Daniel. "They're from church."

"Really?" Reagan says, looking over the top of her sunglasses and narrowing her eyes. "Who's the one in the blue shorts? He's really cute."

"That's, um, Daniel," I say, giving her a please-shut-up-in-front-of-Sam look.

"Daniel? *The* Daniel? Look at those pecs!" she says as he raises his arms to cheer for the next guy climbing onto the board.

"Yeah. And I hear he's looking for a princess," Steph says, laughing. Steph and Reagan both laugh, and I look nervously at Sam.

"Who's this guy?" he asks, eyebrows raised.

"Uh," I say.

"Tell me. It's okay. I won't be jealous. Reagan, will you tell me?" he asks.

"He had a thing for Lily right before you guys started hanging out. She didn't like him though," she says to Sam. And then she turns to me, "You didn't tell me he was hot!" She checks out Daniel again.

"Down girl," Sam says to Reagan, laughing. And then he looks at Daniel too. "He seems pretty cool, but I'm glad I stole you away," Sam says to me.

I smile from ear to ear. "Me too. Reagan, aren't you still dating . . . what's the new one's name? George? Aren't you dating George anyway?"

"Yeah," she says, nodding and pushing her sunglasses up her nose again. "But he's gone so much for work. He's in sales," she explains to Sam and Steph. "He's not coming back for like two weeks. I just like to keep my eyes open." I smile, knowing full well how Reagan likes to keep her eyes open.

As another wave of chlorinated water hits us, Reagan stands up, saying, "This stupid game has got to stop." She picks up her tray, walks over to the picnic table near the barbecue, stands on a chair, and loudly asks for everyone's attention. It takes a few minutes to get the guys to stop with the diving board and join the rest of the party.

First she thanks Sylvia from Cosmetics for handling the food all night. When she and my other non-church friends arrived they naturally gravitated to the bar area by the food. Sylvia then took charge of the barbecue, insisting that she is a gourmet cook and can handle the goat cheese and asparagus-stuffed hamburgers Steph has prepared. Tricia and Charlie, fellow slaves in Children's Wear, are here too, as is the entire softball team. Well, almost the entire softball team. I may have accidentally on purpose forgotten to invite Lisa.

"Also, I would like to propose a toast," she says, raising her glass, "to everyone's favorite Lily. May her move go well, her new life be full of surprises, and her radio always be playing Wham!" I blush beet red and am even more embarrassed when, with all eyes on me, Sam wraps his right arm around my waist. Embarrassed and yet somehow very pleased. There is polite clapping in the Super Sad Singles corner and cheering from the Traywick's contingency. The cheering dies down slowly, and then the patio is silent.

"And the food is ready!" Charlie yells suddenly. An even louder cheer goes up, and the church girls get up to make their way to the barbecue. Becky follows them, reluctantly, glaring at Miguel, who is still across the pool with the guys.

"We've got to help Becky," Steph says, walking up the steps of the pool. She grabs her towel, immediately wraps it around her thin waist, and walks over to Becky, who smiles gratefully when she sees Steph approaching.

Sam and I are left alone in the still, blue pool, and he wraps his other arm around my waist, resting his chin on my shoulder. The sun is slowly sinking down behind the hills, and the sky is glowing as if from within. Beyond the low wall that surrounds our spacious hilltop patio, we can see the valley spread out below us, and beyond that row upon row of breathtakingly beautiful golden hills turning purple in the twilight. Reagan has turned on the rows of paper lanterns she painstakingly strung around the patio last night and is now chatting up Daniel, who looks both delighted and horribly uncomfortable. I see Steph showing Becky how to light the tiki torches stuck around the patio.

It's beautiful. Everything about this moment is perfect. I'll almost be sad to leave, but I remind myself that my new life has only begun.

Fashion Victim
Transmissions from Fashion Land

Coupled
Fashionable
Young writer
With her life in order
And her future before her

Well, I did it. I just threw the first successful soiree of my adult life. It was amazing! Aside from one little ham incident that made me wonder if my best friend had suddenly lost her mind along with all desire to eat pork, the evening was perfect. I feel like an A-list celebrity.

And in two days I'm moving out. My roommate seems great, and though she couldn't come to the party tonight because of some work thing, I'm sure we're going to be great friends.

But there was one little snag in the evening. Everything was going so well at my party that I got to feeling magnanimous and decided to try to reach out to my nemesis from church, Alexandra. Yes, Alexandra. I just call her Alex even though she hates that. What is she, a Victorian?

I invited Alex and her sweet but prairielike friend Maggie to come and hang out in the pool with me and some of my friends. I thought, hey, maybe, they wanted to stop cheering on the boys' diving contest and meet some new girlfriends. Perhaps they haven't been mingling with us because they're too shy? So they came over and sat on the side of the pool. "Get in," I said. And then they just looked at each other. Actually, Maggie just looked at Alex because Maggie defers all of her decisions to Alex, who is the pious ringleader at church.

What do I have against Alex, you might ask? Well, she's mean to Maggie first of all. But also, she believes that she is the most godly creature on this earth, and I am an ingrate and a deviant in comparison. I'll finish the story for evidence to the above.

Alex then says to her adoring friend, "Maggie, you get in and swim with the other girls. I can't because Bill has a terrible crush on me, and I don't want to cause him to lust after me."

I just stared in shock at Alex. What an awful thing to say. Would Maggie not make the men lust? Was she implying that Maggie was too homely? Grrr. So I said, "I don't think the men are lusting after anything but the hamburgers at the moment."

"No offense, but I'm not taking modesty lessons from you," Alex said.

I just smiled back at her, wishing that all of her teeth fall out in old age.

Maggie did get in, and she was a lot of fun and got to know my friends from work. Alex maintained her position of being much too sexy to swim and just sat on the side of the pool, ogling clueless (and balding) Bill.

I'm sure Reagan looked like a common whore to the two of them in her string bikini. Granted, I think Reagan would have been pleased to hear so.

I hope God will have mercy because I probably shouldn't have written that but I can't make myself erase it.

So with that, dear readers, I sign off. I need to pack away my computer. The next transmission you will receive from me will be from the big city.

Watch out world—Fashion Victim on the loose!

Go with God—Down with fashion!
Fashion Victim

• Chapter 9 •

I take a deep breath and look at Sam. He smiles and nods. I press the doorbell.

"Hold on a minute," Inie yells from the other side. A minute passes with us leaning into the wooden door, trying to catch sounds from inside. Then we hear some loud thumping and rustling. We wait. We hear some swishing. I am about to push the button again when the door swings open. Sam and I lean back, a little startled.

My new roommate is wearing a pair of red and green plaid pajama pants and a rumpled striped shirt, and she is smoothing her wild brown hair down. She looks like she's just rolled out of bed, but her blue eyes are wide and excited, showing no signs of sleepiness. "Come on in," she says, ushering us in. We walk inside the door, and she wraps her thick arms around me in a hug that takes me off guard, though I try to return it at the last moment. "Welcome!" she says, drawing back and sticking out her hand toward Sam. He rests the box he is carrying on the table by the door and grabs her hand, shaking it. "I'm Inie," she says, her round cheeks rising as she grins broadly. "Inez. It's an old family name. Inez Perkins."

"I'm Sam. It's nice to meet you," he says, smiling. "Did we wake you up?"

"Oh, no," she says, her blue eyes registering surprise. "Why?"

"It just took a . . ." he says looking at me. I shrug. "Um, never mind," he finishes. "So this is the place, huh?" He looks around the small living room, which looks more like the common area of a mental hospital and is devoid of all signs of life. The hardwood floor is covered by a beige area rug, and the walls are white and a little scuffed here and there. There are two small windows hidden by some dirty mini-blinds, and in the middle of the largest wall there is a small, faux-wood-paneled television on a yard sale metal stand. The room looked bare and uninviting like this when I came to see the apartment two weeks ago, but I figured her roommate had just moved out or something.

"It's . . . nice," he says, smiling. "Did you just move in, Inie?"

"No," she says.

"Oh, did your old roommate take a lot of stuff with her when she left?" he asks, wiping his brow with the edge of his blue T-shirt. There are those abs that I love. Out of the corner of my eye I see Inie's eyes widen as she sees them too.

"Uh uh," she says, sucking on the ends of her hair. "Why?"

"Um . . . I just . . . there isn't a whole lot of clutter, you know? It's nice. Nothing to trip over," he says, turning away from her and grimacing. "Is it hot in here?" he asks, and I nod in response. "Do you mind if I open the window?"

"I guess not," she says, biting her lip nervously as Sam tugs the bay window open. "I like to keep it toasty." Sam raises his eyebrows.

"So," I say quickly, "Sam, do you want to see the rest of the apartment?"

"Sure." He follows me into the kitchen. The apartment is on the second floor of an old blue Victorian. From the outside, it looks like a gingerbread house dripping with white frosting, and from the inside the bay windows and hardwood floors make the place feel old-fashioned and interesting. Inie even has a turret in her bedroom. The apartment was renovated and updated only a few years ago, so despite the architectural Old World charm, the fixtures are all new and shiny.

"Nice counters," Sam says, running his hand over the granite. "And the cabinets are deep." He opens a light oak door. Four bags of coffee sit on top the shelf. A small can of curry powder and a bag of rice rest on the bottom. Nothing else. "Big coffee fan?" he asks, looking at Inie. She nods, silently, her eyes following his every move. He walks to the plain white refrigerator. The only thing on the front is a takeout menu for an Indian restaurant, held up by a magnet that lists the phone number for Fog City Cleaner on Columbus Avenue. He pulls the door open. Five bottles of water sit alone on the top shelf. He flips open the butter holder, searching in vain for something more in her fridge. He pulls open the crisper drawer and spots a furry white half of a tomato. "I think it died of loneliness," he jokes, laughing. We both look at Inie. She is staring at Sam, smiling uncomprehendingly.

"I really like efficiency," she says. "I'm not home much since I work a lot of hours, so I try not to keep too much stuff around or it will just go bad." She watches closely as Sam nods and closes the door silently. He looks around, trying to avoid Inie's eyes.

"Shall I start bringing up some boxes?" he asks.

"That's a good idea," I say. "I'll be down in a second. I'm just going to test out the bathroom."

"Oh, it works. No need to test," Inie says, biting her lip. Sam meets my eyes, eyebrows raised, and walks toward the front door. As soon as he is outside, Inie turns to me and says in a whisper loud enough for the downstairs neighbors to hear, "He's cute!"

I nod, laughing uncomfortably. "Yeah, that's my boyfriend Sam," I say. "He's all right." I walk toward the bathroom.

"All right? He's adorable! You think he's just all right?" She looks incredulous.

"Um, I don't know," I mumble. "I mean, he's my boyfriend. I think he's more than all right, I guess."

"Oh," she says, disappointedly. "I'll take him if you ever decide you don't want him anymore."

"Um . . . okay," I say. Because *that* would be comfortable for everyone. Sheesh. "I'll be right out," I say, pulling the door shut quickly.

When I come out of the bathroom, Inie has gone into her bedroom and closed the door, and Sam is just coming back into the apartment, carrying a box marked "Sweaters, Dead Russian Authors, Softball Mitt, etc." He puts it down on the floor by the door. "I don't know where this should go," he says, straightening up.

"Um, right. There's fine, I guess. I'll come get another load with you."

He looks around, craning his neck and seeing her closed bedroom door. "Where did you find her?" he whispers as we walk down the stairs.

I shrug. "She's a friends of Alex's. You remember Alex from church? They work together," I say quietly. "She's a little strange, I guess, but she seems nice enough."

"Alex from church? The one who is trying to organize a letter-writing campaign to ban all books about Halloween from the Library of Congress?"

I nod.

"Oh man, Lily," he says, laughing. He leans over and kisses my cheek. "You walked right into that one."

I push Reagan's buzzer and hear her scream "Just a minute" over the intercom. It's been nice living just walking distance from her, and today we're going to meet up with Sam and take the cable car to church together. I whisper a quick prayer that all will go well today and that Reagan will really hear the message the pastor preaches. Two minutes later she comes flouncing down the staircase in—gasp!—a pink polka-dotted shirt with a plunging neckline, a black micro-miniskirt, and little black patent leather shoes.

"Don't look at me like that, Lily Traywick! If I am going to church then I at least am going to feel comfortable."

"That's comfortable?" I ask.

"Look, if your Jesus friend can't accept me for who I am then he will be no friend of mine."

I pause for a moment, thinking. I guess she's right. "Fine. And, hey, you'll at least ensure that the pastor will notice that you're a guest and personally come harass you after the service. No blending in for you."

"Hmph. I can handle some old crusty pastor."

After the service, I am really nervous and trying to read Reagan's face. The pastor, who is only thirty-five and not crusty at all, preached about how in the postmodern world, we as Christians need to learn to express our love for God in new ways. He even listed surfing and music as good examples of expression, so I was happy that I had finally gotten Sam and Reagan both organized enough to attend this morning. I was really excited to see Reagan taking notes until I looked over to take a peek at what she was writing and noticed she has scrawled "If God is love, and love is blind, is Stevie Wonder God?"

Oh well. Maybe I was expecting too much too fast. I'm sure to her singing old hymns in a converted warehouse on the waterfront isn't the coolest thing to do on a Sunday morning, but at least she came. I guess I have to trust God to do the rest.

"How was it?" I ask. "Not too painful?"

Reagan shrugs noncommittally. "Weird." Weird? Ouch. Remain calm, Lily. This is Reagan. She's always suspicious of new things.

"Yeah, huh, it's not a traditional church at all. Probably not like the one you attended as a child."

"Hardly." She folds her bulletin in half and places in it her purse. I look away and bite my lip.

I see that Daniel and Miguel have come up to talk to Sam behind me, and I'm really thankful for them trying to make him feel welcome. Especially Daniel.

"But the pastor didn't say anything you didn't agree with, right? I mean, it was pretty peace-love-kindness?"

"Yeah. He was fine, I guess. Hey Daniel!" Reagan says.

I sigh. I'm really going to have to let God do all the work here.

I can get her bedecked in polka dots but the rest is going to have to be him.

We morph into one big group, and everyone chats loudly about anything but church for about ten minutes while the sanctuary empties out. I do spot Pastor Kyle considering coming over to meet my totally eighties half Norwegian half Chinese guest and my long-haired surfer guest, but I see him resist and just wave to me. I smile back, thankful he's not going to try to welcome them, because I think Reagan's had just about all the church she can take for one day. Now, has she had enough Daniel? I see her squeezing his bicep. I should have told her years ago that cute guys attend church.

I punch Steph's number into my phone as I walk down the two flights of stairs from my apartment and out the front door of my building.

"Hello?" she says cheerily, picking up the phone on the first ring.

"Hey Steph," I say into the phone, pulling the front door closed behind me. "I didn't wake you up, did I?"

"Of course not! I've already run six miles and have been studying for like an hour." Of course. I should have known. No rest for the perfectionist.

"I was just trying to figure out a time when we could get together for dinner or something."

"Sure! Can you do it Tuesday? Ooh! Look at the time! I'm sorry, Lily, I have to run to pick up snacks for the Habitat meeting tonight before class. Can I call you back?"

"Sure," I say quietly, shaking my head. Even hearing about her life makes me tired.

I put my phone in my bag and walk toward the cable car stop. I still can't get over the fact that I take a cable car to work. I love flying down the hill over the old tracks, the wind blowing through my hair. I have even made friends with some of the conductors, and enemies with a particularly gruff one. All I did was sing the Rice-a-Roni (The San Francisco treat! *Ding Ding!*) song when he rang the bell a couple of times and suddenly I was persona non grata.

This morning as I walk to the stop, though, I am distracted. The new edition of the *San Francisco Weekly* is supposed to be in the news-stands today, and I haven't heard whether or not my article has been printed. I slaved over it all weekend, and I was actually pretty pleased with it when I e-mailed it to Edgar on Monday. I sort of expected some kind of reply, like, "Hey, good attempt, why don't you fix this?" or "You're the best writer we've ever seen!" or "Sorry, try again" e-mailed back, but many obsessive e-mail checks have revealed nothing. No response. As I walk to the red box on the corner where the free paper is distributed, my heart is pounding. I realize I am sweating. At least I haven't told anyone about this piece, so when they don't print it I'm not going to have to pre-tend it doesn't matter anyway.

I stop in front of the box and pull open the door. I shut it again. Maybe I shouldn't even check. They probably didn't print it anyway. I start to walk away but stop. I have to know. I open the box, lift out a copy of the paper, and place it on top of the box. The cover is a cartoon-like drawing of a beating human heart against a collage of Lombard Street, Coit Tower, Fisherman's Wharf, and the Golden Gate Bridge. The headline is "I Left My Heart in San Francisco?: The City's Black Market Cadaver Trade" by Edgar J. Arle. Weird.

I open the cover and page slowly through the paper. An article about the history of Alcatraz. A review of a dim sum place in China-town. I don't see anything. An editorial arguing that only electing actors for public office is California's best plan for fixing the state budget cri-sis. I keep turning the pages. Nothing. Wait, there's a picture of Harry. I scan the headline: "Solving the World's Problems, One Joplin Song at a Time." There it is! And underneath: "By Lily Traywick."

I'm a writer!

I close the paper, shove it into my bag, and take off running. I can't wait to show Sam.

"Harry! Did you see it?" I yell, bounding down the escalator with a copy of the paper.

"I saw it," he says, smiling, his deep voice alight with excitement. "You did great. You made me sound like a good man after all." He lifts his hands from the keys and stands up slowly. I walk around to his bench, and he leans in jerkily to give me a hug.

"All I did was report the facts," I say wrapping my arms around him tightly. "Has your wife seen it?"

"My wife has probably gone out and taken every copy in the city and mailed them to everyone she knows by now," he says, laughing and pulling back.

"I guess she'll have to fight for them with my grandmother," I laugh.

"Lily?" Harry says, smiling at me. "Thank you."

"Jewish. That's nineteen points, times three for the triple word score makes fifty-seven, plus fifteen for making *queen* into *queens*, is seventy-two," Sam says, writing down the number on the little pad. "Your turn."

"How badly am I losing now?" I ask, grimacing.

"One hundred and forty-two points," he answers triumphantly. "You wanna quit now?"

"No," I say defiantly. "And quit acting so proud of yourself. You don't have this game locked up."

"All right," he says, laughing, looking into my eyes. "Do you want some more wine?"

"Please," I answer, handing him my glass, never taking my eyes from the Scrabble board. He pours some Montepulciano into my glass, then turns to cut some more Saint André and baguette. I'm still thinking about how to use two *A*s, a *V*, a *P*, an *E*, an *L*, and a *Z* when he hands me a piece of bread with the triple cream cheese on top.

I look up. The sun, setting slowly in a fiery blaze, casts a golden glow on the deep rust stone of the classical colonnade behind Sam. The swans in the lake are flecks of white against a deep blue, and the lush green grass is soft and cool against the warm night air. The Palace of Fine Arts. This place was made for romantic late summer evenings.

"What did your parents say about the article?" Sam asks, refilling his own wineglass.

"Oh, they're off in Italy looking at shoes. They haven't seen it. I don't know, I might not even show it to them," I say, looking up from my letters.

"Lily, you have to. It's really amazing. You should be proud. And I bet they would be proud of you."

"I don't know. We'll see. But Reagan and Steph were really excited for me."

"I'm very proud of you. And to think no one even knew you were writing it. It's really great." As soon as I showed Sam the article, he had suggested we go out tonight to celebrate, then arranged all this. It's all so perfect that I can't help thinking there has to be some cosmic catch. "How did it all happen, anyway? Did you just write the article and send it to them for consideration or had you contacted them before?"

"Oh, um," I say quickly. I can't tell anyone—not even Sam—that Edgar saw my blog. If anyone found out about it and looked at it and saw what I'd written about them, well . . . Even Sam, who looks like a knight in shining armor in my online writing, can't see it. That would just be too embarrassing, if he saw what I've been saying about him and how long I've liked him. "One of the editors had seen some old writing I had done. You know. And he just sort of mentioned that I should submit something. So I did." There. That was technically the truth. I smile, praying he doesn't ask any more.

"Are you going to write another article?" he asks, taking a sip of his wine.

"I hope so. They said I should submit another one soon. And they told me their rates. Man, if I get a few more articles published, I won't worry so much about paying rent anymore."

"That's great," he says, then lets his voice trail off. I look at the board. I could spell *veal* with the *E* that's on the board as part of Sam's sixty-six point doozie *leering*. It's such a nothing word, but he played it as the first word of the game, for which he got a double word score and then a fifty point bonus for using all of his letters. I do the math quickly. *Veal* would only get me seven points. I have to do better than that. I'm too competitive to let him beat me at this game.

"I'd like to propose a toast," he says suddenly, raising his glass. "To Lily Opal Frances Traywick, the best Christian to ever rip off people just trying to clothe their children. And to her bright future. Our bright future." Our? Did he just say our? As in his and mine?

"Hear, hear!" I say enthusiastically, taking a sip of wine. "And to Samuel Sherman March. May he break many records of women's shoes sales and may he catch a wave and be sitting on top of the world."

"Add in that I'll someday sit on the Supreme Court and save the world, and I'll drink to that," he says, laughing. He stops. I look at him and wait. "You know, Lily, I was serious. You're the first Christian I've ever really dated, and I had no idea it was going to be so great." I take a deep breath. "I mean, when I had turned my back on God, my relationships were generally pretty physical."

I grimace. I guess I'd figured as much, but it was still hard to hear.

"I'm sorry to have to admit that, but it's the truth, and you need to know that. And that's all behind me, but since I've never really had a relationship that wasn't built on that, I was a little nervous about how this Christian dating thing would work." He reaches out and takes my hand. "But, Lily, it's amazing. I had no idea that there was a way to connect to somebody on a level that was deeper than physical. We're joined in a whole different way."

I nod, unsure what to say, but he continues.

"You understand me because you understand what I am, my deepest and most basic beliefs." He strokes my hand, looking into my eyes. "And I am so thankful for that. I'm so glad you're who you are, and I'm so glad you're a Christian." I am going to melt. "It's more than I ever dreamed it could be."

I can't do anything but stare at him. I wasn't expecting this. I gulp. But I love this. I stare back at him, certain I look like a dope. He leans over and kisses me.

The warm breeze blows a strand of his hair against my cheek, but I don't rub it away. I listen to the gulls, feel the warmth of his body. Slowly he pulls back.

"You're beautiful," he says, letting go of my hand.

"Mm hmm . . . you're all right too," I laugh nervously. I just look at him. What could he possibly see in me?

"Lily?" He asks after a few minutes.

"Yes?"

"It's your turn." What? The game. I pull my eyes away from his beautiful face. Oh, looking at the board is much less fun than looking at Sam. What can I possibly do with this *K*? I fall back into competitive Scrabble mode. Several silent minutes go by as I try to find a place to play *keep*.

"Oh, guess who e-mailed me today?" he says suddenly, taking a big bite of bread. I laugh at him, raising my eyebrows quizzically as I wait for him to swallow his gluttonous bite.

"Who? Miss Manners, calling about that private tutoring session?"

He holds up one finger, telling me to wait. "No," he says, finally swallowing. "But then I don't know that I really have much to teach her anyway." I roll my eyes. "But my friend Delia from college wrote. She's moving up to San Francisco next month. Isn't that great?"

Delia? I've never heard him mention her before. Who is this Delia person?

"She's very cool," Sam continues, "You guys have so much in common. You'll love her," he says, nodding. "I mean, I think you will. It's weird, she doesn't have a lot of girlfriends."

"That's weird. I wonder why?" If it weren't for this silly *P* . . .

"I don't know why. I think some women are intimidated by her."

"What's she like?" I look up from the board.

"Oh, you know," he says, taking a sip. "Pretty. I don't know." Pretty?

I am silent, drinking this in. Everything about this night says that I have no reason to be worried about this Delia, that Sam is really as crazy about me as I am about him, so why does this make me so uncomfortable? He has other female friends. There's Beth who he surfs with and Haley in his department, and that's never made me uncomfortable. But then, they're really cool. Who is this Delia that no one wants to be friends with? That can only be a bad sign. Stop it, Lily! Stop it. It's fine. It's fine.

"Did you guys date in college? I mean, because she's so great and all."

"No, we didn't. It's funny," he says, laughing as he watches two swans fight for a piece of bread. "I'm not sure why we never dated. We hung out all the time, and I was certainly attracted to her," he chuckles, "but I guess it just never seemed to work out somehow. The timing was off or something, you know?" He looks at me, shrugging.

The timing was off? Does he still like her? Has she heard that Sam is dating someone and has come back to take him away? What happens when she gets here and suddenly the timing is right? Are they going to hang out all the time again? I don't think I can handle that. Lily, stay calm. Stay calm. Sam adores you.

"But that was while I was 'in my rebellious phase,' as they say," he says, laughing, "so it's probably a good thing it never happened anyway."

"Yeah, probably," I say, uncertainly. I will not be jealous. I will concentrate on winning this game. "How did you meet her?"

"We had some classes together and stuff, but it's funny, I didn't really get to know her well until my dad died. Her father had died when she was twelve, and so she really understood. We grew really close. She meant a lot to me during that time."

I have to focus. I'm not jealous. I just have to block out Delia and her closeness to Sam. I have to get a lot of points on this word. Okay, I am jealous. But I will not show it. "It will be good to meet her." Score one for me.

I reach down and slowly move my letters onto the board. I put the K above the E in *leering*. I put my E below it. *V. A. L. A. P.*

"*Keevalap?*" Sam asks, raising his eyebrows.

"Not KEE-vel-lap," I say, "KEH-vel-lap. Don't tell me you don't know what keevalap means."

"I'm sorry to say I don't," he says, eyebrows raised. "Is it Latin?"

"Ha ha. No," I say quickly. I take a deep breath and try to think quickly. "It's, um . . . Middle English. A keevalap is a shallow-bodied bowl used in medieval liturgical services," I say quickly. Where did that come from?

"Is that right?" he asks, laughing. "I had no idea. And I thought I knew a lot about the church. I didn't know I was playing with a liturgical history scholar. Tell me, where did you learn such specialized knowledge?"

"Um, I learned it . . . well, you know, I've been to a lot of churches, and . . ." I trail off and pause. He waits. "Look, are you going to challenge it or not? That's my word."

He laughs. "Oh, no. You seem pretty certain that keevalap is a real word. I'm not going to challenge it. I know you wouldn't try to cheat," he says, laughing, "since God is watching." He winks. I laugh nervously. "So that's sixteen points for the word, plus a triple letter score on the K makes it twenty-six, plus your bonus for using all your letters is seventy-six points?" He looks at me.

"Don't forget the double word score under the L," I point out, moving the tile so he can see the little pink square.

"Oh right. The double word score. Which brings us to one hundred and two points for *keevalap.*"

"Right," I say triumphantly. Sam makes some marks on the score sheet, then looks up at me laughing.

"Lily?" he says.

"Yes?" I answer, trying to avoid his eyes as I very deliberately draw seven new letters from the bag.

"You're amazing."

Fashion Victim
Transmissions from Fashion Land

Happy
In Love
Scrabble-winner
Babbles about
Wonderful new life

Warning: this posting involves a discussion of nudity

It's been another crazy week, dear reader, in the life of Fashion Victim. My new roommate? Absolutely crazy. Also, she's naked 95 percent of the time. Do tell, you say? Pshaw. How could I resist?

She's not around much, so when she was home the other day I tried to make conversation and get to know her. The apartment is completely devoid of all art and decoration, leaving me little guidance for small talk, but I had noticed that in her bedroom she had a few framed pictures of people, so I asked her about them. She ushered me into her room, where I noticed for the first time that she had a Cinderella pillow on her bed. Cinderella. This woman is thirty-two. The first picture she showed me had her standing next to another woman who she identified as "my sister, the cow." "We're not very close," she confided conspiratorially. "She's always been jealous of me." I nodded and innocently asked why. Inie proceeded to tell me it was because she is so much prettier than her sister. "Oh," was all I could muster. Now, Inie is cute and all, but she's not

Angelina Jolie. More like Natalie from The Facts of Life on a good day. Then she showed me a picture of her closest friend, Maria. Maria was a few pounds overweight, but she wasn't actually any larger than Inie, which was why I was so surprised when Inie called her a cow too. All I can conclude is that Inie has a really robust self-esteem, which I guess is good.

But she's always naked. Naked! If she's home, she's naked. It's gross. I've taken to secretly calling her Hiney. Earlier this week I walked in the door with my boyfriend and had to immediately usher him back out until she put on some clothes. She was just sitting on the couch watching TV completely naked! She yelled for us to come back in when she was clothed. All she said by way of an apology was, Sorry, Roomie, sometimes it's hard to keep clothes on this hot bod of mine! And then she giggled and tromped out of the room. We might need to come up with some kind of necktie on the doorknob system so that I know if she has her clothes on or not. My boyfriend says I should say something to her, but I just moved in and it is her apartment.

Don't even get me started on how she only calls me "Roomie."

In other news, something perplexing happened. Well, two things.

One. My boyfriend announced that a friend from college e-mailed him to say she was moving to the city. Apparently she is hot, he used to have quite a crush on her, and oh, other women don't seem to like her very much. What. does. this. mean! I'm freaking out over here, dear readers, and I need your help. Blogosphere, unite! In your opinion can men and women be just friends, particularly if there is an attraction between them? I've always had a lot of male friends, but I've also always been attracted to them and would have made out with any of them if I had the chance, which makes me nervous about Sam.

Two. My mother called. Hiney left me a message on a sheet of paper I found in the kitchen. It said, "Roomie. Mom called. Said she loves you very much. Please call." I was shocked. I'll call her back soon. I must have forgotten to do something at the house before I left. Or maybe she's heard some gossip about me from work and since she can't nag me at the breakfast table about it had to call.

All for now. I need to go to bed if I'm going to face another day of a stark-naked roommate.

Go with God! Down with fashion!
Fashion Victim

Chapter 10

"*Hi, this* is Stephanie Anne Harold. I'm not available right now but leave me a brief message, and I'll call you right back. If it is urgent, please contact me on my pager." *Beeeeeep*. I roll my eyes. I can now recite Steph's voice-mail message from memory; I even get the beep pitch-perfect. I leave her another message. We've been trying to schedule dinner all week.

I can hear Inie in the living room watching reruns on TV. I passed her when I came home from work and she at least had a bra and shorts on so I was happy. I even stopped for a moment and chatted with her. It's funny. Living on my own is a little lonelier than I imagined. Granted, I'm supposed to be working on my piece for Edgar on the Bushman—that iconic San Francisco street performer who camouflages himself with live greenery, thus looking like a bush, and then jumps out at the unsuspecting tourists strolling along the wharf, scaring them and then winning their admiration and spare change—but I'm doing my favorite trick from college. Procrastinating. I snap my laptop shut and decide to call Sam. He'll cheer me up.

He picks up the phone, laughing.

"What are you laughing about?" I ask. I hope it's a good one. I need some cheering up. This place just doesn't feel like home yet.

"Huh. Oh nothing. I'm just IMing with some friends."

"Oh." That was a dud. "Who?"

"Tim and Matt and Delia."

My heartbeat escalates.

"Oh."

"What's up?"

We chat for a little while and then Sam needs to go. I hang up unsatisfied still. I have to get out of this house, or I'll go crazy.

"*H*e's *so* cute. You must be crazy, girl," says Reagan. The waiter doesn't even bother to take our order anymore and just brings us our two small frozen yogurts, and, annoyingly, the same slips of nutritional information. He places them on the table, and I hand him our ID badges to swipe.

"I just still can't believe you went out with Daniel," I say.

"Why not?" Reagan asks.

I can tell she's a little hurt. Where do I begin?

"For starters, *I* went out with Daniel."

"But you never really kissed him, and you don't like him and never really did."

"Is that the rule? I mean, I don't really care I guess, but I'm intrigued with the rules on these things." To think I would have considered giving up Sam for her if she even had a crush on him.

"I think you have to take each situation as it comes. I say, your loss. You're clearly in love with Sam, and I can't just let some girl with bad fashion snatch Daniel up."

I laugh. "Good point." I am going to have to be the bigger person here. "Then, I guess we should all go out together some time."

"Yes. Let's. So how's it going with Sam?"

I smile. I love Reagan. She's really good about making sure that we don't spend the whole time talking about her and her problems.

"Uh . . . I guess we're in a new place now."

"What do you mean?" she asks.

"I'm new to this whole dating thing, but I don't know, things are all weird now."

"Why? Are you still spending time together?"

"Yeah. Several times a week."

"You're still going on your romantic Tuesday night dinner dates?"

"Those are sacred."

"He calls?"

"Virtually every day."

"Then what's up?"

"I don't know," I mumble.

"What? You can tell me."

"It's just that, well, everything matters now. Or something. I scare myself with how much I care about him."

She looks at me, shocked, wide-eyed.

"What?" I ask. She can help me. She knows what I'm saying.

"You're in love!" she says.

I look around to make sure no one heard that. "Shh . . . no. No I'm not. I'm positive that I'm not."

"Oh yes you are!"

"Not. Am not."

"Can you sleep at night?"

"No."

"Are you eating normally?"

"No. I ate a whole tube of raw cookie dough last night."

"Do you get jealous if other girls talk to him?"

"Wait. Yeah. I do. And it's not like me. Is that what I have?"

"Totally. You're in love! I can't believe it. I mean, I have *never* been in love, but I know from experience what it looks like."

"Why?"

"Sometimes the guys I date fall in love with me, and then I have to leave."

I laugh. This girl. "Oh, no." I stop. "Do you think he loves me back?"

She wrinkles her mouth up and looks to the ceiling, considering this. I stare expectantly at her. "You know. Yes, I think he does," she says finally.

I feel so relieved. He loves me too. "This explains everything."

"What?" she asks.

"I've been a little nervous about this female friend of his. That's all."

"Sam? Pshaw. You have nothing to worry about."

She's right. So, it's nothing to do with Delia. She just entered the picture right after I really fell for Sam. "I'll tell you something, Reagan Axness. No one ever mentions how heart-wrenching it is to have a boyfriend. Sam's got me so crazy, I hardly recognize myself."

I'm sitting in front of a little French café called Le Petit Robert. My bag is reserving the chair across from me. Sam and I have been meeting here on Tuesdays and having coffee or cocktails and just chatting. I love these nights, just the two of us, connecting and learning more about each other, since on the weekends we spend a lot of time with our friends or my family, who, incidentally have decided that he has fallen from heaven for their amusement.

I pull my cardigan across my shoulders. The cool night air announces that fall has definitively arrived.

Sam is running late. At least, I hope that's all it is. He hasn't called. I crane my neck to look up Polk Street, squinting. All I see are two figures walking in my direction. Not him. And then I see the taller figure wave. Who is that? Daniel and Reagan? We bumped into them the other day since she also lives in Russian Hill. I squint harder and wave back. No, wait. That's Sam. I wave him over. But who's the other person with him?

"Lily! Hey! Guess who arrived just today?" Sam is looking at the beautiful blond woman next to him. She is smiling at me uncertainly, her green eyes cold.

"I'm Delia," she says. She puts out her hand for me to shake.

I'm breathless for a moment. Delia? "Wha, oh, uh. Hi. Lily." I shake her hand. She gives me a quick smile and then turns and looks up at Sam. "Sammy Boy has been good enough to show me around today."

I can barely see. I'm so confused. I just sink back into my seat. Sammy Boy? This is all wrong. So wrong. What is she doing here?

"Were you surprised?" Sam asks. He's grinning ear to ear, as if he just surprised me with a new car or a floppy-eared puppy.

"Huh?" I say.

The waiter comes up behind us with an extra chair, and then they both sit down across from me.

"Were you surprised?" he asks again.

"Oh, yes. I didn't know you were in town," I say. I appraise Delia. She has long, shiny hair and perfectly carved features. Good skin, nice teeth. She's definitely cute. I mean, some people would think she's cute . . . like Sam, in college.

"I thought I'd surprise Sam," she says. "He loves a surprise."

Is this woman telling me what my boyfriend loves? I'll kill her. "Boy, he sure does. I remember this one time—" But then I stop talking because Delia is practically jawing Sam's ear off about some dumb old story from college about a professor who surprised both of them by bringing a keyboard to class one day and singing Happy Birthday to Delia in front of the whole class. Sam's laughing his head off.

"You should have been there, Lily. I mean, Deals was his favorite student ever, and then he just started singing Happy Birthday to her."

I smile. Of course. She was the teacher's pet. I hate today. Today is the day that I will always hate. Delia, pardon me, Deals, is clearly everything I wasn't in college. Me? Blend in at all costs. Her? Stand out. Loved or hated. Nothing in between.

Delia turns to me, and I feel a tiny spring of hope bubble up inside me. Maybe now she will include me. "That was the class that I met Sam in," she says. She turns and looks at him adoringly.

Oh.

"Delia would always draw these little cartoons about our professor, and I thought they were so hilarious," Sam says. Why do I feel like I'm listening to a couple tell me how they met?

For the next thirty minutes, Sam and Delia catch up with each other as if I weren't there. A story about their shared co-ed dorm morphs straight into a dance they both attended and ditched because it was boring. And on and on and on. At one point, I storm out and stomp off to the bathroom, half-hoping Sam will get it through his thick skull that I'm cross with him.

I try to calm down in the bathroom and throw some cool water on my face. This is no big deal. I'm sure Sam didn't even realize that our Tuesday evening dates were so important to me. And besides, he didn't even know she was coming today since she wanted to surprise him. No point in telling him how uncomfortable I am with this. I'll just get over it privately.

I take a deep breath. Sam is worth it. I will go back out there and be the bigger person.

"I'm so sorry I'm late."

I look up from my book and giggle at Steph.

She notices my book and says, "I see you came prepared."

"I'm an ex–Girl Scout. We're always prepared." After three voice messages and two conversations, we finally set a time for dinner. We're eating at Ristorante Milano on Pacific Avenue. As a slave to the Dining Out section of the paper, I've been wanting to check it out lately, and it's walking distance for me, plus it is close to the hospital where Steph is doing her rotations.

We both scan the menu, and I know immediately that I'm going to have gnocchi. I'm not a huge pasta fan, but gnocchi, those delectable little dumplings, is food from heaven. I look at the dessert menu while I'm at it and see that they do offer tiramisu.

"Do you want to split an appetizer?" I ask, salivating over the description of the prosciutto-wrapped figs.

"Um . . . I don't think so. I'm not that hungry," Steph says, taking a sip of the water the waiter has placed in front of her.

"Oh. Okay," I say, dejected. I can't get a whole appetizer just for myself, can I? Steph squirms in her chair. The waiter places a basket of bread and a bottle of olive oil in front of us, and I dig in. Steph twists her napkin.

"What are you going to have for your main course?" she asks quickly.

"The gnocchi. Definitely. You?" I pour some of the olive oil onto my plate and replace the lid carefully.

"Oh, uh . . ." Steph looks a little nervous. "I'm full, so I'm not going to get anything but a Diet Coke."

"What? What do you mean you're full?"

"I, uh, caved about an hour ago and had this huge plate of vegetables. I know I shouldn't have, but I was so hungry."

"You can't just not order," I say, exasperated.

"Why not? I'm not hungry. You shouldn't eat if—"

"Are you kidding me? Stephanie Anne Harold. What has gotten in to you lately?" I stab my bread into the olive oil. "First of all, it's rude to go to a restaurant and order nothing but a Diet Coke. Second of all, we've been planning to get dinner for several weeks, and now you're just not participating." I take a bite and chew angrily. She watches me, silent, until I finish. "Plus, this whole health kick you're on lately is just ridiculous. If you ate some crudités at work, there should still be room in there for some good old-fashioned pasta and meatballs. You love Italian. That's one of the reasons I chose this place."

"I'm just not hungry, Lily."

"What have you eaten today other than vegetables? How could that make you full?" I take another bite of bread and watch her expectantly.

"I've eaten plenty. You can't make me eat tonight."

Something in Steph's tone isn't right. She's like a mean old dog tied to a stake barking at anyone who goes by.

"I don't buy it. What's the real reason? Don't do carbs now either? Get some antipasto then."

"Yes, carbs are totally disgusting, but I don't think you're listening to me. I'm just not hungry. A Diet Coke will be fine."

"Steph, you need to eat. You're way too skinny. It's not healthy."

"Leave me alone. I can take care of myself," she says, putting her napkin on the table.

"I'm just worried that you're changing too much," I say slowly. "Look at you lately. You're über-healthy, which hey, I've tried to understand because I know in med school they're teaching how bad stuff is for you." I take a deep breath. "But you're also up at all hours doing weird home improvement projects. Or you're always with the Habitat crew and don't have time for your old friends anymore. Steph, the world isn't ever going to be perfect, no matter how hard you try to make it so. And you don't have to be perfect either."

"Hah!" she says, her voice becoming almost a yell. "Funny thing for *you* to lecture *me* about change. Look in the mirror, Lily. You dress differently, you act differently. I don't even know who you are anymore. And you're the one who never calls me now that you have a boyfriend. You're, you're, you're like Reagan's little clone!" she spits.

I narrow my eyes at her. I'm so mad. I knew it. I knew she was judging me for improving myself. This is why she was so against my changing. The moment she's not the "more attractive" friend in this scenario, she turns on me. "You're just jealous," I spit back.

She stares at me wide-eyed. "Jealous? Of you? I think not. I have my priorities straight, Lily. And that's at least more than I can say about you."

I just stare back at her. I'm shell-shocked. I need a moment to calm down. I count to ten in my head and then say a little prayer. Then I look up and see Steph staring in her lap, the condensation from her Diet Coke now making a pool on the table.

"If that is all you're ordering, I'd rather go," I say quickly.

"Fine, I don't have time to hang out anyway," she says.

I wince. "Fine," I say.

Steph picks up her purse and walks out, and I head to the bathroom to avoid leaving the restaurant at the same time she does.

I open my door and am staring down Delia. Sam's head peeks out from behind her. Anger washes over me. I can't believe it.

"I hope it's okay that I brought Deals," he says stepping out from behind her. "She needs to get some stuff for her new apartment too, so I thought she could just come with us." Delia just stands there smiling at Sam, her hair glinting in the sun.

No! I want to yell. *She cannot come ruin our day together. This was going to be our time!* But what can I say? My mother has always taught me to be saccharine in situations like this. "Sure. That sounds great!"

"Oh goody!" Delia says in a voice as fake as her highlights. "I just love shopping."

So off we go to the boutiques. Yes, the boutiques. Never mind that Sam and I had agreed to go to Bed, Bath & Beyond because I just needed a bunch of stuff cheaply. Oh no. Deals needs throw pillows and scented candles and can only get them from the small shops on Union Street in the Marina. Apparently she deems chain stores too déclassé.

She's Sam's friend, I keep reminding myself as we browse through shops full of silk paisley lap rugs. But I can't help thinking that if I wanted to spend too much money on my baubles, I'd go to Traywick's. All I wanted was an automatic shut-off iron and some under-bed storage bins.

"Oh! We used to keep one of these on our boat!" she exclaims, holding up a plaid wool blanket. "We'd use it for picnics at the yacht club!" she laughs, smiling at me, as if pitying me for not having a boat too. I smile placidly, for once grateful that my mother has drilled into my head that it's not okay to flaunt money. Talk about déclassé. She's a philistine. I will not tell her. I will let her revel in her presumptuous assumptions and then feel like an idiot when she finds out that my parents are on the board of the San Francisco Swim and Racquet Club. I look at Sam pleadingly. He's busy looking at a vintage movie poster of a sixties beach movie starring Annette Funicello.

"Oh, Sam! You know what that reminds me of?" she asks, practically shrieking. "That time in college where you taught me to surf!"

What? He taught her to surf too? Is that his standard pickup?

I bet she couldn't even get up on the board.

"Remember how I couldn't get up on the board and whenever waves came you kept having to save me? That was so fun. We should do that again!"

"Yeah, that was pretty great. Who knew you were so uncoordinated?" he asks, laughing. She purses her lips in a little pout. "But when I taught Lily, she was awesome. She picked it up right away and was surfing like a pro." He smiles at me, almost proudly. That's better, I think. Out of the corners of my eyes, I see that Delia is biting her lip. Perfect.

"Hah," she laughs, sounding ridiculously hollow. "Yeah, well. Sports have never been my thing. I don't like to be all sweaty and gross," she says, fingering a sleek modern-looking silver candleholder.

"You don't get sweaty surfing," I say raising my eyebrows. "You're in the ocean." Sam narrows his eyes a little at me. Maybe that was too harsh. Be good, Lily. Sam is worth it.

Delia glances at Sam, who smiles at her. "I guess not," she says quickly, laughing. She picks up the candlestick. "Though don't get me wrong. There are times I like to get all hot and sweaty," she says, winking at Sam. My stomach drops. "If you know what I mean." Did she really just say that? Sam is blushing. How should I react to that? I decide to play dumb and make a joke.

"No," I say. "What *do* you mean?"

Sam laughs.

Delia stares at me for a second, trying to read my face. "Oh, I think you know, if I know Sam," she says, laughing. My stomach clenches. "Unless you're one of those born-again virgins," she finishes with a sneer.

I am shocked into silence. I stare at Sam. Why isn't he saying anything? I look at Delia, whose eyes are shining, cradling the thick silver candleholder. No one speaks.

She looks from me to Sam, smiling. "I think I'll get this," she says, tossing her hair back. "Then we can go to Les Maisons for those pillows I wanted?"

As her cab drives off, loaded up with shopping bags, I look at Sam. I made it. After she had insulted everything I stand for and dragged us through stores where no one but she even remotely considered buying anything, we ended up at a sushi place—"I just love sushi!" she had exclaimed when we tried to think of a place to eat dinner— where Delia and Sam talked for hours about people I didn't know and things that made me uncomfortable. I knew Sam had something of a wild past, but wow. Sam finally started to tell Delia about me, my writing, my job, my life. Delia wasn't the best listener—stories about me kept reminding her of stories about herself. We never made it to Bed, Bath & Beyond. I never got my iron.

I am just going to let it go, trying to remember that Sam really loves me. I know that. Everyone says so. But then Sam shakes his head as we walk away. "Heh heh heh. Oh Deals . . ." We are walking up Polk Street, going back to my place. "Can you see why we were friends?"

"Oh, uh. Yeah. She's, uh, great."

"I always thought so. It's weird. She had such trouble making girl friends. I always assumed the other girls were just jealous of her. She got a lot of attention from guys. All ages even. I'm not kidding about that professor of ours who was just crazy for her."

"Mmm," I say. I clench my teeth and swallow hard.

"Plus she's hilarious."

"I didn't really think so, actually."

Sam looks at me at bit surprised. I try to relax my mouth. My lips are pinched tight. "Hm . . . I guess she's funnier if, you know, you get the jokes. Because at school—"

"No. I'd say she's just basically not that amusing. Done. Period. Over. I didn't laugh once. And I don't appreciate your insinuating that I don't get the jokes, because I did get them. I just didn't think they were funny. Especially when I was the butt of them. That's all. Just not funny." By the end of my sentence, I'm almost yelling at him.

Sam waits a little while before he answers, and I realize that I've really snapped at him. "I meant that a lot of her humor was based on college, and you weren't there. That's all. What's wrong?"

"Is that what you want?" I blurt out.

"Whoa! What?"

"Is that the kind of girl you want?"

"I want whatever kind of girl you are, Lily."

"No. I'm serious. She's an awful, miserable person. She flirted with you the whole time and hardly talked to me at all, and I guess you can't see it, but she still totally likes you, and at this point, I'm beginning to think you like her too!"

Sam stops dead still on the sidewalk. I keep walking and then stop too and walk back to him. "What are you saying, Lily?" He turns to look at me, narrowing his eyes. "I can't believe you would accuse me of having feelings for another girl! Don't you know how much I care for you?"

I stare at him. While he is not yelling, he is very, very mad. I'm instantly very sorry. I started this whole thing. With my paranoia. And my accusations. "Sam," I say, tenderly as possible, "I'm so sorry."

He looks into my eyes, and I want to swoon. He is so beautiful and clearly quite wounded by this whole affair. He comes over and takes my hand. "Lily. You're such a special girl. I care about you more than I've ever cared about anyone. But you can't start with this jealousy stuff. I don't think I can deal with it." He looks into my eyes. "I need space to have my own friends and be my own person."

We start walking again, and I lean my head into his shoulder. I even start crying a little. "I want you to be your own person too. And I'm not jealous about any other girl you hang out with. I don't know. Something about her is just really hard. She's just—"

"Lily," he says. His voice is an odd mixture of forced patience and irritation.

"Right. I'm over it. And I really care about you too. And I trust you. It's going to be fine."

I type in Delia's screen name, courtesy of Sam, who gave it to me when I told him I wanted to extend the olive branch to Delia. I am going to be the bigger person. I am going to show Sam how cool I am with his being friends with Delia. I am going to IM her and tell her what a good time I had hanging out with her at Le Petit Robert and shopping and welcome her to the city. I only wish my screen name wasn't eggplantlegs.

I log onto AOL instant messenger and type in Delia78. Oh good. She's online.

Eggplantlegs: Hey Delia—this is Lily. Sam's girlfriend.
Delia78: Oh hey. That's a weird screen name.
Eggplantlegs: Yeah, it's an old joke from college. It was funny then! But I won't bore you with it. Just wanted to say how great it was to meet you and hang out the other day shopping in the Marina. We'll all have to hang out again.
Delia78: Lisa, you're so great. I completely agree! I was just IM-ing Sam and even said how great you are.

I stare at the screen in disbelief. Wait. Why does it say Lisa? She's making a joke? She's joking. Right. Did I mention that people often think I'm named Lisa and right now she's pulling my leg? No. Wait. I didn't say that. In fact, I hardly said anything because she was just yammering on the whole time. Didn't I put my whole name in there? I look at the screen again. I did. Is she nuts? Okay, I'm sorry, but I'm just going to have to confront her. And why is she IMing Sam?

Eggplantlegs: Lisa??? Thanks for the kind words.—Lily

There is a five-minute pause while I pace the floor, listening for that little obnoxious ding noise. C'mon Delia. Write me back. Write me back. Tell me you were kidding. Finally, she does.

Delia78: Ha ha ha . . . sorry! I was thinking of an ex-girlfriend of Sam's who I never really clicked with. So funny! Freudian slip! Forgive me.

I snap the top of my laptop shut and stare at it in horror.

Fashion Victim

Transmissions from Fashion Land

Dating
neurotic
fashion vixen
Staring down the
Green-eyed monster

Hello all. Moments ago, the worst thing happened to me and having already exhausted my boyfriend tonight on the phone and being too embarrassed to call him again, I turn to you. I'm going insane. A friend of Sam's from college moved to the city just a few days ago. Delia. Now while he is friends with many girls, she makes me uncomfortable. But we were making a lot of progress. I explained how I felt like Delia ignores me, and he conceded that she's probably a little self-centered. But he stressed that she's not a bad person because he's not friends with bad people and that I had nothing to worry about because in his opinion I hung the moon and she is just a friend. He even pointed out that now that he's serious about his faith again he wouldn't date her even if he were attracted to her, which he isn't, he stressed, and I sort of believe him because, well, she has big ears. I promised to try to be more relaxed about him hanging out with her, and I was feeling so magnanimous that I IMed her to say how glad I was to meet her. You know what she did? She called me the wrong name! I just saw her two days ago, how could she not remember? I'm so insulted. Please write as to your reactions. I know I'm supposed to trust my boyfriend, but this woman is not to be trusted, I fear.

In other news, I'm really worried about my friend Steph. It has occurred to me that she's possibly anorexic. She's getting so thin, and she stormed out of a restaurant the other night when I insisted she order at least a salad with her Diet Coke. She's always been a perfectionist, but I wonder if she's taking the struggle for perfection with her own body too far. It's weird because while Reagan was trying to make me gorgeous, Steph was the one who kept telling me it didn't matter what I looked like and it is what's inside that counts. I don't know what to do. She's in med school and is applying for a rotation this summer in Honduras with Doctors Without Borders, but I don't see how she can go to a third world country to heal others if her own health is seriously compromised. Plus everything I read about this disease says that if I confront her, she'll only deny it and become cleverer about hiding it. Should I talk to her parents? The counselor at her medical school? I really don't want to get her in trouble but I can't stand by and watch her starve to death. I don't know. Maybe I'm overreacting. I'm going to just wait and see for now.

Oh, and do you remember Daniel? The guy that wanted to treat me like a princess? Reagan is going out with him! She didn't understand why I thought this was weird. Let's make a list of reasons why this is weird. One, I went out with Daniel. Two, she was supposed to meet God, not boys, at church. Three, Daniel is a Christian. It's his decision but . . . Four, doesn't Reagan have a boyfriend? Five, I always thought Reagan was too cool for Christians. Six, isn't he looking for a girl to marry and help him with his very own youth group? I guess the silver bikini thing is more powerful than I realized.

The rest of my life is going pretty well, and my roommate, since fall is finally coming, has taken to wearing more clothes around the house—that is, a pair of shorts—so we've been hanging out a bit more.

Go with God! Down with fashion!
Fashion Victim

I can't even face all the Fashion Victim e-mails I have. I really need to read my fan mail soon, but I promised myself that I would finish the Bushman story tonight and e-mail it to Edgar. My deadline is eight a.m. tomorrow morning. What a way to spend a Sunday night.

I just need to think of a closing. Instead all I see is Delia's face on my computer screen. What she did was so hurtful. How could she not remember my name? Did she do it on purpose? And who is this Lisa that Sam dated in college? I've never heard of her before. Why did Delia feel competitive with her? Does she feel competitive with me?

Argh! I wish Edgar had asked for a story on Delia. I could whip that out in about an hour. I don't know what to do. Usually blogging puts my mind to rest.

I pick up the phone. I need to talk to somebody. I can't call Steph.

I'll call Reagan. But as I start to dial, my fingers type in another number.

"Mom?" I say when she answers. I don't know what I'm doing.

"Hi darling."

"Oh, hi." I feel better immediately.

"What's wrong?"

How do moms always know when something's wrong? I blurt it out. "Sam's got a friend named Delia, and she makes me uncomfortable, and she just called me the wrong name."

"What'd she call you?"

"Lisa."

"Oof. I do hate that name."

"See!"

"Now, Lily. Samuel March is a very fine young man, and I'm sure there's nothing wrong with this Delia. Mistakes can happen."

"No. You don't understand. She—"

"Go get yourself a nice haircut. Maybe a set of highlights. That's always the way to make sure he won't even see her for you." Great. Highlights are the secret to getting Sam's attention.

"But Mom—"

"Lily, darling. I'm sorry. Unfortunately, you've caught me at a bad time. I'm just off to meet your father for dinner. It's for one of our accounts. We'll talk later."

"Oh. Okay," I say.

"Hugs, darling."

"Bye," I say. The tears begin to pour as I put the phone back on the hook.

• Chapter 11 •

"*Delia St.* Marks," I type. I think wistfully of Gran as I hit enter. When Mom called to say hi yesterday she told me that Gran has now Google-stalked every member of our extended family and has been writing them cryptic e-mails about that time they won the Tristate Chili Cook-off or wrote a scathing letter to the editor of the *Sacramento Bee*. I miss Gran and her crazy ways. I can't wait to see her at family dinner on Sunday.

Aha. The first link leads to some kind of March family Ofoto page with different photo albums. Oh yeah. I remember this. But wait, why did Google direct me here for Delia? I start hunting around in the albums. There's only three—"Stuart's Funeral," "Sam's Graduation," and "Mom W/ Friends in Cabo"—and I already looked through the graduation one. It's just a bunch of pictures shot from what must be the top floor of the auditorium at a collection of black-clad ants waiting to graduate. Also there's a few of just Sam in his cap and gown. He's hot even in a dress with a square hat on his head.

I hit the back button to the Google page and check the "cached" button so that it will highlight Delia's name and then hit forward again. This time I'm quickly led to a picture of Delia with an almost solemn look on her face holding a giant, and I must admit gorgeous, casserole. Underneath it someone has written, "Sam's friend Delia St. Marks and the casserole she made for us during our tough time. What a precious lamb!" I gulp and look around on the page. Oh no. I'm in the album with the pictures from Sam's dad's funeral. Delia is in several pictures—sometimes just in the background doing dishes with his mom. I feel very small. Not only is Delia obviously an awesome cook, but she also appears to be a good person. I swallow back some tears. Maybe I should give her a second chance. I suppose all of my complaints against her up until now could have been innocent blunders on her part? I mean, being called Lisa isn't so bad, is it? But at the same time, it hurts a little to see the picture of Sam giving her a hug. She was there for him during the worst time in his life, and I just wasn't. That's something they'll always have.

I push the back button on my browser and click on the next link Google gives me. This one is from the college paper. It is an article about an annual party called the Big Score. After the first football game every year, the senior guys and the freshman girls all gather in the quad and—can this be right?—make out with as many people as they can. I scan the page. There's a picture of Delia, several years ago. "They say you're not officially a student until you've scored! So I did my best. I kissed thirty-two boys tonight! No one can say I'm not a real student now!"

Thirty-two boys? In one night? I think quickly. If it was senior guys and freshman girls, Sam wouldn't have been one of them. But three years later . . . he wouldn't have, would he? I close the window in disgust.

"Great article, Lily," Sylvia from Cosmetics says as we walk toward the field. We are here at Golden Gate Park for the first game of the fashion league playoffs. The Knickerbockers have been on fire the past few weeks and are going to be hard to beat, but we've got new long-sleeved play-off shirts, so maybe that will help. "I've been reading the *San Francisco Weekly* ever since you stared writing for them, and I really liked what you did this week. I've always thought that the Bushman was creepy too."

Creepy? I haven't had a chance to get a copy of this week's paper yet, but I'm pretty sure I didn't call the Bushman creepy.

"I haven't seen it yet, actually. Do you have a copy with you?" I ask.

"Sure," Sylvia says, pulling it out of her bag. "Take a look."

I stop walking and flip to the Profiles Page. "Bushman Backlash: San Francisco Icon's Scary Past." I skim the article. My mouth is hanging open in shock. I turned in a happy little profile about how he got the idea of scaring tourists for money and how much he likes his job. Sure I was surprised to learn that he earned as much as $30,000 a year just by panhandling, but the story, as I wrote it, was light and happy. Now it has a decidedly mean tone. It does indeed call him creepy, a word I never used, and also dwells on the time he spent in prison, and ends calling for an uprising to get this dangerous man off the public streets. It also goes on to point out that all of his "earnings" are tax-free, so he is currently cheating the government in addition to being a former criminal. The part about raising his two daughters alone since his wife died has been cut, as have his pontifications on love and world peace. As has my assessment that he is a gentle, if off-beat, person.

This is not my story. Maybe there was some mistake? Maybe Edgar assigned two people to the story and printed the other? And yet there's my name in the byline. How did this happen? Edgar had made some changes in the other stories I turned in, and the first time I questioned it, but he insisted it was his paper, and he was going to have to do things his way. But still, those were minor changes. The stories were essentially the same. But this! This is different. This is just . . . well, this is just wrong. The poor man has been made out to be a criminal. Is this what sells papers? Do I want to take part in the lies if it is? Am I willing to give this up if that's what it takes?

Stupid Earle.

I walk silently to the field. I don't think I can say anything to him. This means too much to me.

"Hey Lily!" I barely have my phone up to my ear before Reagan is yelling excitedly at me. "You're going to this Bigger or Better Hunt on Sunday night, right? Daniel was telling me all about it—say hi, baby."

"Hi!" Daniel yells from her end of the phone.

"So he was telling me about it, and it sounds so fun!"

What? Reagan is calling to make sure I'm going to Super Single Sunday?

"I guess so . . ." I say hesitantly.

"Oh good. I'll see you there, then. We have to run to make it to the bar before the Maples start playing. But I can't wait!" Click.

Reagan can't wait for a church event? Daniel is going with her to see a band playing at a bar? And did she call him "baby"?

This world has gone mad.

"I know what you should do, Sam," Dad says, wiping his mouth with his napkin. "You could make laws about footwear. I mean, have you looked around? People need some firm guidelines about what they can and cannot wear in public."

Ah, dinner with my family. Actually, it hasn't been that bad so far. My mother and I haven't fought even once, and we're at two hours and counting. That's probably close to a record. And when I walked into my old room I found a perfect pair of black heels Mom had picked out for me. I can't wait to wear them. Plus, having Sam here takes a lot of the pressure off, since my family adores him. He's been over for the Traywick family dinner several times, and of course Mom and Dad know him as the shoe-selling wonder boy from work, so that's enough for them. Gran doted on him from the first moment she met him, telling him, to my embarrassment, that he was the first boy I had ever brought home and that if he was good enough for her Lil, he was good enough for her. She then tried to sell him a macaroni sculpture (she's branching out) that she insisted was the Samaritan woman at the well. Sam gamely bought it for five dollars but insisted I take it home with me to beautify my new apartment. And while Dad tries to pretend that he only likes Sam because he brings in good money for the store, I've seen them talk about weird science things for hours—who knew Sam was a physics minor in college?—so I know Dad also approves. Even Mom, except for one uncomfortable conversation where she urged him to cut his hair to look less feminine, has been perfectly pleasant to him, suggesting several times a week that I invite him over for dinner. I didn't move out just to come home for dinner every night, so Sam's been spared for the most part, but they do insist I bring him along when I come home for Sunday dinner every few weeks.

"No, really," Dad is saying emphatically between bites of pot roast. Gran has cooked Sam a special fettuccine dish with roasted olives and vodka sauce, which on one hand makes me glad they are accommodating his veggie food habits, but on the other enrages me when I think about all the times growing up I begged for something to eat other than mussels and shallots. "You should go into fashion law," Dad continues. "You could make a killing on all the intellectual property disputes. Why, just the other day, Ralph was complaining to me about how every knockoff of his clothes costs him thousands. You could prosecute stuff like that!"

"Ralph?" Sam asks.

"Lauren," Mom says kindly. "They're longtime golfing chums."

"And he's got a terrible slice, if you want to know the truth," Dad says, taking of sip of wine. "You'd think with all that All-American bravado he's got going for him, golf skills would be part of the package, but I guess he must have spent too much time playing polo recently." He shakes his head. Sam nods as if my dad is actually making helpful suggestions.

"Or you could do something more corporate," Dad continues. "Maybe you could help us with the thefts we've been having. We're losing a ton of money on it, and Sheila thinks it is people within the company, but we just can't pin down how they do it. As if our employee discount weren't generous enough. You could deal with that kind of thing."

"He's not going to be a security guard, Dad," I say, laughing.

"Yeah, well, it's too bad. If ours doesn't start spending less time flirting with the Housewares girls and more time keeping the merchandise on the shelves, he's going to have to start . . . looking for a law school to attend . . . or something like that," he finishes lamely. Sam is laughing, and Dad starts laughing too.

"I guess I never really thought about fashion law," Sam says, looking as if he is actually giving the idea serious consideration. "I was kind of leaning more toward human services—solving poor peoples' housing disputes, something at the DA's office, public policy, that kind of thing. I want to help people."

"Fashion helps people, Sam," Dad says, cutting his meat.

"Fashion," Mom says, smiling, "makes us better people. The right clothes can make you feel great. They can transform you," she says, sitting up straight and raising her chin. "Fashion makes the world a more beautiful place." Wow. I am almost touched. I have never heard her talk about why she likes what she does. She almost makes it sound a little bit noble.

"And having good fashion sense," she continues, "means you'll never wear a vintage sea-foam green one-shouldered caftan to the Oscars. Really, what was Jennifer Lopez thinking?" I groan inwardly. "When she came into Traywick's looking for a dress, I showed her a nice demure black Galliano number that looked stunning on her, but she insisted on that dreadful green thing. She looked like she spilled a health shake on herself." I roll my eyes and grimace at Sam. He winks back.

"Lily, I saw that," she continues. "And you of all people should back me up on this." I stare at her, waiting for her to continue. This should be good. I see Sam sit up straight to listen. "I mean, Lily, until Reagan took you under her wing and showed you how to dress, you were a mess." What? I feel my face flush pink. "You didn't know *what* you were doing, even after years of my trying to imprint the value of always choosing reliable brands, and it showed." I look at Dad, silently begging him to make her stop, but he avoids my eyes. She continues, "Remember the tomboy look you had going?" I wince. "How many guys asked you out then? None. In all those years, you didn't have one boyfriend." Please stop. Please stop. I want to look at Sam, but I'm too embarrassed.

"And now look at you," she adds, meeting Sam's eyes, nodding conspiratorially, "one little makeover and you bring this home," she laughs, widening her eyes in mock surprise at Sam's appearance. "Just imagine if you had been paying attention to your appearance all that time!"

I am going to kill her. I am going to kill her.

I take a deep breath.

I am not going to blow up at my mother at the dinner table in front of Sam.

I look up and see Mom smiling at me expectantly. She doesn't get it. I shake my head, seething silently.

"What?" Mom asks, taken aback.

"Gran, could you pass the gravy?" I ask politely. Gran nods worriedly, biting her lip. Sam is looking down at his noodles.

"Lily, look at me," Mom says firmly. I do, reluctantly, feeling the three other pairs of eyes at the table boring into me. "I'm proud of you. I'm not sure if it came out right, but that's what I meant," she says firmly, then looks around and asks quickly, "May I have the gravy when you're done with it?"

I nod, keeping my eyes on my plate. Proud of me?

Why is she only proud of me now?

"You have two hours. Each member of the winning team will win a free dinner anywhere in San Francisco," Pastor Kyle says through the bullhorn. "Go."

"*Woohoo!*" Reagan yells, holding our penny up in the air enthusiastically. "Let's go!"

I try to feel excited, if only for her. I remind myself that Sam and I could win dinner anywhere in San Francisco. Perhaps a romantic date at Gary Danko?

A Bigger and Better Hunt is one of those things that probably would seem fun if you'd never done them before, like sliding down a banister. It's only when you get to the newel post at the end that you realize it's not all it's cracked up to be. Free dinner, I remind myself.

Bigger or Better Hunts are, like the song about Zaccheus climbing a tree, one of those weird things that you only know about if you've grown up in the church. We must have played this game dozens of times in youth group. You start out with something small, like a pencil or a penny, and go out in a team and start knocking on random people's doors or going into stores and asking them if they have anything bigger or better they'd be willing to trade you for it (reminding them that they won't get it back). At the first house you might get a hairbrush, then you'd trade that up at the next house for a basketball. Whoever comes back with the biggest and best item wins. I've seen people come back with broken TV's, Christmas trees, and children. While it's fun to see what everyone brings back, it's always struck me as wrong to disturb people at their homes at night to trade them for junk. And I sort of lost my taste for it when my team got disqualified in college when it came out that in trying to trade a broken stereo for a ladder, I sweetened the deal by offering the man five dollars. So I wasn't very excited to find out that this month's Super Single Sunday event was a Bigger or Better Hunt—in Berkeley, no less, as if walking into stores selling tie-dyed shirts and liberal bumper stickers and asking them to trade you something for a penny might be less awkward—but I had to go. Reagan was so excited.

I look around. Not a bad group. Stephanie has not shown her face, but we have Reagan and Daniel, Becky and Miguel, Alex, Maggie, and Bill, plus me and Sam. A few liabilities, but overall fairly strong.

"So where do you guys want to start?" I ask, looking around. Our official starting point is the parking lot of a church run by Pastor Kyle's friend on Dana Street, just a block from Telegraph Avenue, about two blocks from the UC Berkeley campus. One group has already taken off toward Shattuck Avenue and its wealth of chain stores; another has decided to try the standard door-to-door approach in the surrounding residential neighborhood.

"I saw an old couch on the street a few blocks away," Becky says quickly, pulling her brown hair into a ponytail. "Let's just go get that and get some ice cream and wait for everyone else to come back."

I knew I liked Becky. Miguel flashes her a grin too.

"That's totally cheating!" Alex shrieks. "That would not be a good witness."

"Yeah, where's the fun in that?" Reagan asks. Did she really just agree with Alex?

"You might as well just put the penny away and replace it with a twenty dollar bill if you're going to do that," Maggie says, shaking her butterfly-barrette-covered hair. She is so earnest and soft-spoken, I almost feel appalled at Becky's suggestion myself.

Luckily, I get over it.

"I've got a ten," I say, reaching into my bag.

Reagan rolls her eyes at me. "Come on," she says, walking toward Telegraph. The group starts to follow her tentatively. A man with a long gray beard walks past us, mumbling about fascist pigs. Ah, Berkeley. Home of incessant protests, power to the people, and aging hippies. Indelibly marked by its position as the seat of the radical movement in the sixties, it still maintains a free-love, free-spirit air in addition to one of the biggest and best universities in the country, and I have always loved its vibrant feel as well as its excellent burritos.

"We should just find a student and bring him back," Bill says. "We'll trade him the penny. Students will do anything for money." I turn to look at him. Maggie looks tentatively at Alex, who begins to laugh like this is the funniest thing she's ever heard, so Maggie starts to laugh too.

"Oh Bill," Alex says, cracking up and putting her head on his shoulder.

Everyone else is looking at him like he has two heads.

"What?" he asks, "I was serious." He moves away from Alex.

"I know the perfect place to start," Reagan says quickly, leading us to a dark store with pictures of mushrooms that glow under a black light, pounding techno music, and a suspiciously sweet smell. "I used to come here all the time when I was a student." We walk, en masse, into the store. The man behind the counter, in a black shirt and dreadlocks, stares at us.

"What's this?" Maggie asks, picking up a glass pipe with a tall glass tube. She turns it around and over. Bill and Alex shake their heads, shrugging.

"That's a . . ." Sam starts, then pauses. "Um, never mind," he says, shaking his head.

Reagan walks up to the counter and asks, "Do you have anything bigger or better than this penny that you'd be willing to trade me?"

The student behind the counter stares at her. "Huh?"

Reagan starts again. "We're on a Bigger or Better Hunt. We've got this penny, and we're trying to trade it for something bigger or better. Do you have anything?" Daniel walks up to the counter to stand next to her. "You'd get to keep the penny." Reagan flashes him a big grin.

"You can't buy any of this stuff for a penny," the man behind the counter says confusedly.

"No, I'm not trying to buy anything. I'm just wondering if you would trade us something." She looks around the counter. "Like that pen you're using." He looks down at the blue ballpoint pen he is holding. "Will you trade?"

He looks at her silently, raising his eyebrows in confusion. "You want my pen?" She smiles and nods, leaning over the counter. "Okay," he says, holding it out slowly. "Here you go." She takes it, and he retracts his arm as if he's afraid she might bite it.

"Thanks!" Reagan says cheerfully, putting the penny down on the counter. She turns and walks to the door, smiling. We all follow her out. "That was easy," she says, laughing. "This is going to be a piece of cake.

Who wants to go next?" We all stare at her. She looks at me, raising her eyebrows. I shake my head vehemently.

"I will," Bill says, coughing. "I mean, if no one else wants to."

"It's all you," Reagan says, handing him the pen. "Where do you want to go?"

"Maybe that store over there?" he says, shrugging at a store with plain windows called Agent Boudoir. Reagan nods.

"Maybe we shouldn't all go into a store at once," Miguel suggests, his black hair shining in the late evening light. "That poor guy looked kind of overwhelmed."

Reagan nods, thinking. "Okay, we'll go in twos," she says, putting her arm around Daniel. Miguel reaches out to Becky, while Sam touches my arm. Alex and Maggie both move closer to Bill, who just looks confused. The two girls give each other uneasy looks.

"How about groups of two or three?" Becky suggests.

"Okay," Bill says, turning toward the store. "I have a good feeling about this. God will go before us." He starts walking away and is almost to the store entrance when he realizes Maggie and Alex aren't with him. "Are you coming?" he asks, his face blank. Slowly they follow him, looking at each other warily. They're fighting over Bill? Has it come to this?

As soon as they are inside, Miguel starts laughing.

"What?" Sam asks, snickering a little himself.

"Who knew Bill was such a hot prospect?" Miguel blurts out, laughing. I snort. And Daniel gives Miguel a high-five.

"Miguel Dominguez Santiago. What has gotten into you?" Becky asks.

"Sorry, *Rebecca*," Miguel says. She playfully punches him in the shoulder.

"Becky's right," Reagan says. "Bill's got two available girls interested in him. So maybe he isn't the smoothest player on the block. We should help him."

"Does he want help?" Daniel, says, laughing too now. "I mean, have you seen the choices? Alex and Maggie?"

Reagan's eyes widen. "That's so mean!" she says, elbowing Daniel. I look at Reagan, wide-eyed. The black skirt she's wearing today goes all the way to her knees. Who is this person? Is this the same girl who was wearing a string bikini and making fun of Alex and Maggie at my party just a few weeks ago?

"Oh, don't look at me like that," Reagan says, seeing my shock. "Aren't you the one who's always pulling out the 'Jesus loves everybody' on me?" I nod. "They're actually nice girls. Maggie even said she'd show me how to make a cake. They just don't know how to highlight their best features," she says, looking at me knowingly. I gulp. "I'm going to help them," she says.

I don't know what to say. Sam is the first to speak.

"Good for you," he says. "And good for them, too." He grins at me. I'm still looking at Reagan in shock so I am almost glad when I see the infamous three emerge from the store. Bill is still clutching the pen in his hand.

"They, um, didn't want to trade," he says, quietly. Maggie and Alex are silent, eyes wide. Sam tries to find out what happened, but none of them will talk about it. All Bill will say is "Satan has his hand on that store." We quickly decide to move on.

Sam and I go into a café next, and come out with a chipped mug. Becky and Miguel trade that for a used dustpan at a pizza shop. Reagan and Daniel take it and disappear into a record store. Alex and Maggie stare after them.

"How long have you known her?" Alex asks me, nodding toward them.

"Reagan?" I ask, slightly taken aback. "A long time. Elementary school." Alex nods. There is silence. Sam is scraping the ground with his shoe.

"She's not a Christian, is she?" Alex asks. Miguel puts his arm around Becky and tries to move her away, but she is watching carefully.

"Um, no," I say slowly. "She's so great, though. I really love her."

"Why is he dating her?" Alex continues. "He should know better."

"What?" I stare at her in shock. Who is she to judge? At least Reagan is excited about church now, which is something I've never seen from her. And to say something like that in front of Becky?

"If she's not a Christian, he shouldn't really be dating her, you know?" She looks up. Seeing Miguel's icy stare, she looks quickly at me. "I just thought maybe you could say something to her or something," she says. "Or at least tell her what's not appropriate to wear to church."

"Say something to her?" I ask angrily. "What do you want me to say? 'You shouldn't be going out with Daniel because you might be a bad influence on him?' That would go over really well. Or 'Reagan, you can only wear skirts that go down to your ankles, and while you're at it, could you please cover your head too?' Surely that would win her to Christ," I practically spit.

"All I'm saying is that Daniel would be better off with a good Christian woman," she says, looking around. "Particularly if he wants to be a youth pastor. He can't be unequally yoked." She shrugs. She looks at Bill, who is examining his nails.

"A good Christian like you?" I ask archly.

"Lily," Sam says, but the tension is relieved when Reagan runs out of the store.

"Look what we got!" she yells. She holds out a record, and we all lean in. Neil Diamond is posed in a tight white sweater in front of a roaring fire. It is a copy of the Neil Diamond Christmas album.

"Isn't Neil Diamond Jewish?" Becky asks, screwing up her face.

"That's why it's so great!" Reagan yells. "Come on!"

We try trading the record in at a Jamba Juice, a grocery store, and with a man selling bumper stickers on the corner (where Sam briefly contemplates buying a sticker that says *Hunt Meat Eaters for Sport*), but no one will take it. Finally, with only ten minutes to go, Reagan has an idea.

"I'll go into Moe's," she says, pointing to the four-story bookstore across the street.

"All right, let's go," Daniel says, following her. Reagan stops.

"Actually, I'll go on my own this time. It'll be easier that way," she adds. "I went out with a guy who worked there for a while. I don't know if he's still there, but if he is, it'll be a lot easier to use my charm on him without you," she says, winking. Daniel concedes reluctantly. A few minutes later, she comes out of the store. There is nothing in her hands.

"I got it!" she says, shooing us away from the front of the building. Reaching into her bag, she pulls out a copy of the Bible. "We're totally going to win! Someone may bring something bigger, but Pastor Kyle can't say anything is better than the Bible!"

I have to admit, that was a smart move.

"Does he still work there?" Daniel asks.

"Who?" Reagan asks, taking off into a sprint.

"The guy who . . . never mind," Daniel says.

We all take off running to make it back to the parking lot before time runs out, but inwardly I am in turmoil. When she reached into her bag, I could have sworn I saw the corner of the Christmas record still inside. I shake my head, deciding I must have been seeing things. If Reagan didn't trade in the record, how else could she have had the Bible?

Fashion Victim
Transmissions from Fashion Land

Single girl
Had by the church
All for a Swanson dinner

Microwave dinners. That's right.

This past weekend, some friends and I suffered through a terrible scavenger hunt event at singles night at church. I wasn't motivated about it. I mean, I'm an adult! I should be beyond these sorts of high-stakes mixers by now. But Reagan insisted on going and, I told myself, eyes on the prize, Fashion Victim. At least, the prize was very mature: dinner anywhere in San Francisco. Thus when Pastor Kyle declared that indeed we had won—we brought back a Bible, which was deemed the best booty of any of the groups—we were jumping up and down, high-fiving and congratulating ourselves. So when Kyle produced TV dinners for each of us and said, Eat it anywhere in San Francisco!, I nearly collapsed in bitter disappointment. They even offered us the use of the church microwave to warm them up. How good of them. In fact, I just fired off a joke e-mail to Pastor Kyle holding him "accountable" for misleading his flock and for treachery in general since we all know that those meals are inedible!

And for Salisbury steak and a frozen brownie, my fledging church-attending friend Reagan stole a Bible. Don't get me wrong, it was brilliant. Of course we were going to win by bringing back a Bible, but it wasn't worth stealing for. She just went into a bookstore, and then came out with it in her bag. The rest of the group seemed too naive to think of it, but I mean, it was in her bag! And you should have seen her face. It spelled *guilty*. I've thought a lot about what I should do, and I've decided nothing. She probably didn't do it, right? And even if she did steal, it was the Bible after all. Maybe she'll read it?

One funny thing did happen, though. A few of the more clueless members of our team went into a store that none of us recognized and came out shell-shocked. It turns out they tried to trade a pen for something bigger or better in a kinky lingerie store. They apparently went in, looked around, tried to get up the courage to ask the salesperson for a trade, but were so embarrassed by the feathers and lace that they turned around and ran out. Why does it give me such joy to imagine them running away, tail between their legs? Ha ha. Life . . . it's out there just waiting to pounce on them.

After our victory, we had a prayer time, and one of these esteemed individuals, Bill, got up and asked us to pray for him. He was recently fired from his brand-new job, he said, and he knows Satan is behind it. He asked us to pray that God would show his power and defeat the evildoer. I dutifully bowed my head, but I couldn't help smirking. I mean, really. Satan cost him his job? Newsflash, Bill: Playing video games at work cost you your job. It's not Satan's fault you're a dork!

On the plus side, things are better with Sam. Earlier today, we met up to shop for a birthday present for his mom. He got really excited, telling me story after story about how cool she is and then he said, "I really hope you can meet her soon. She'd like that." That made my stomach flip. It's not like we're about to jump the broom, but it's nice to hear that I'm important to him. Plus I love hearing how important his mom is to him. He really opened up to me about his father's death and his wild rebellion in college after his father died. Hearing it from him, his "wild" past didn't seem threatening and foreboding but sad and painful. I sort of understand his turning away from God, and it was cool to hear him talk about how happy he is now, on the other side of the pain, and finally able to be in what he called "a real relationship." Even now when I think of what he said I smile.

We still don't exactly agree on his friendship with Delia, but I have decided to just let it go and trust him to take my feelings, which I have made perhaps a little too transparent at this point, into consideration in his friendship with her. It's not like they're best friends, and I don't want to lose him over her. I am trying very hard to be cool. Delia is just a little fly buzzing around my head but please, shoo fly, you don't bother me.

Now if only Steph would call me back. I swallowed my pride, became the bigger person, and wrote her an e-mail the other day, and have yet to hear back. At least I tried. It was hard.

Go with God! Down with fashion!
Fashion Victim

Chapter 12

I'm licking my ice cream cone in pleased-as-punch silence. The fall is coming on, and we're sitting on a bench in the middle of Union Square, a town square so beautiful it could rival those of Europe, and eating ice cream and letting the sun set upon us. We have nowhere to go, and all is right with the world.

"Have you heard from Steph yet?" Sam asks, taking a lick of his pumpkin ice cream.

I shake my head, not daring to take my eyes off my cone lest a rogue drip stain my skirt. "Nope. I called her again, but her phone is always turned off. Or else she's screening my calls. I don't know," I say, taking a big bite.

"That stinks," Sam says, shaking his head. "Friends are so important. Especially friends you've known for a long time. I'm remembering how much they mean." Hmm. Old friends? I wonder to whom he could be referring? I bite my tongue. I am going to be cool.

Sam reaches over and pinches my cheek and smiles at me. "I'm so glad everything's calmed down about the Delia thing."

I laugh uncomfortably.

"I mean, it was really no big deal," he says, licking a drip off his hand. I furrow my brow at him.

"I don't know if it was no big deal exactly . . ." I say slowly.

"Oh. Yeah. I mean, I know it was a big deal to you, but, like, it's not to me."

I take a lick. What is he trying to say? Is it no big deal that she feels like she has to compete with me? That she flirts mercilessly with my boyfriend? And calls me by the wrong name? Lily . . . Lily . . . stay calm. Shoo fly! Shoo fly! It doesn't matter. "Yeah," I say. It's so nice and noncommittal.

Then we sit in silence, and I can't help but wonder when was the last time they talked. I haven't asked him to report back to me on his every move, but now that I think of her, I wonder. Should I just ask? I mean, no harm in asking, right? I'll just ask, but no matter what he says, I'll make sure I say, "Oh, cool. Whatever."

"You talk to her lately?" After I ask it I feel a moment's relief for getting it out there and then begin to dread the response.

"Sure. Just the other day," he says.

I take another bite of my cone. Things have been so much better. I won't press this any further.

Okay, one more.

"What did you talk about? Uh, school and stuff? How's she doing?" I'm particularly proud of the final question. I'm so mature! Yes, how is she doing? I care. I am confident, secure, trusting, charit—

"Eggplant parmesan, mostly," he says, absently taking a lick of his ice cream. "I didn't realize how good eggplant is. And, yeah, I think she's settling in some." He smiles at me.

"Eggplant?"

"Yeah. Deals and I were going to get drinks together the other night, but then when I called her after I talked to you on Monday she said she was trying to save money so could we just cook dinner together."

"What?" I feel the air going out of my lungs.

"What?" He shrugs at me.

"She cooked you dinner?" I ask, incredulously.

"Sure."

"Where?" I ask. At this point, my tone plummets from neutral to angry.

Sam pauses for a moment and then looks exasperated. "At her place," he says, quietly. And then he looks at the buildings across from us in a blank stare.

"Alone?" I ask.

"Yeah. Her cousin wasn't home. She was still at work or something."

"So let me get this straight," I say, sitting up straight. "On Wednesday night, you went to Delia's apartment because she wanted to save money by not getting drinks in a public place and there she cooked eggplant for you for dinner?"

"I made the salad," he says.

I shoot him a look. "You know what I mean."

"Yes, she cooked me dinner," Sam says. His lips are tight, and he's looking at the sidewalk. "What?"

"First of all, how in the world is that saving money? For the price of an eggplant parmesan you could have bought drinks. What else did she make you?"

"Asparagus, and uh, wine, and a salad. I made the salad."

I roll my eyes and fight back the tears. I feel so betrayed. So betrayed. Haven't we spent untold hours going over how uncomfortable she makes me? Is this his best attempt to make things easier for me? I'm so mad. Spitting tacks mad. How dare she? How dare she arrange a date with my boyfriend. How dare she cook a formal dinner for him? How dare she?

"Listen, I don't deserve this, Lily. It was harmless. Nothing happened. I didn't realize it would make you uncomfortable. I see now it does. I'm sorry."

I am fighting back big tears of frustration. "Can't you see how she is? Why can't you see this? Cooking for someone, alone, in your apartment, with wine, is a deep level of intimacy."

"What? I was hungry." He is looking at me, but I am hunched over, silent, fighting back tears. "Lily, say something." He waits. "I don't understand. It was just dinner."

"It's not about the dinner!" I burst out.

He looks at me, his face showing surprise and shock. "What? What is it about then? You're being so ridiculous about this." There is a twinge of anger in his voice.

"What? Did you just say I'm being *ridiculous*? I can't believe you'd say I'm being ridiculous." I take a deep breath. A trickle of melted ice cream drips down my hand, but I don't move. "I have ignored and ig- nored her behavior and tried and tried to get over this issue for you. And now when I'm trying so hard you tell me that I'm ridiculous?"

He sits in silence and stares back at me. His face is unmoved.

I sit in silence for a moment. I'm at the end of my rope. Sam is not helping me feel better about Delia, and I know I can't do this on my own. How could he treat me with so little respect? He had dinner with her at her apartment alone and did not tell me or invite me along? I can't do this. I'll just tell him I can't do this, and then we'll go from there.

"Sam. I'm sorry. I know Delia is an old friend, and you just moved here, and you could probably use more friends, but I can't handle it."

He waits for a moment. "What do you mean, Lily?"

"I mean," I say, taking a deep breath, "that I can't handle Delia."

"Are you asking me to not hang out with her anymore?"

Is that what I'm asking? "Yes," I say finally.

"Lily, she's an old friend. She was so good to me during that awful time," he says, looking away. "I can't forget that. We go back too far."

"Please, Sam."

"Is this some kind of ultimatum?" He leans back, eyes boring into me.

"It's not. I just wish you wouldn't hang out with her."

"So you're asking me to choose between you two?"

"No," I start, then falter. Am I? "I hadn't really thought about it like that. I mean, maybe in a way I kind of am," I say. "But it's not like you can't ever hang out with her," I say quickly, steeling my face. "I mean more like, don't hang out with her unless I am invited to come along. Don't hang out with her alone." I pause. "I'm just going crazy, and something has got to change. I can't handle you being friends with this girl. The other female friends of yours are not a problem, but Delia, I can't handle it. I'll just go mad."

"Lily, don't do this. Please," he says, taking my hand between his.

I take a deep breath.

"We can't go on like this. It's ruining our relationship."

"Don't make me choose. I care about you so much, but I need to be able to have my own friends. I need freedom to have my own life. You can trust me. You mean too much to me."

"Sam," I say, slowly. Her big evil grin flashes into my brain. "Please. Anyone but her."

He nods, slowly and sadly.

"If you're forcing me to choose," he says, taking a deep breath, "I guess we have to call it quits."

"*What?*" I yell. I see a few people in Union Square turn around and look at me. I am *shocked*. Shocked. "You're breaking up with me?"

"I can't be in a relationship where I don't have freedom," he says sadly. "It's just the way I am."

I can't breathe. This wasn't supposed to happen.

"That's not what I meant, I just—"

"Lily? Unless you can let it go, I have to."

It feels like I have no heart, like it's been stolen from my chest and all that is left is a hollow, gaping wound. I don't cry. I don't do anything but stare at my lap. I can't say anything.

"I should go," Sam says. I see him walk away and think of calling out to him, but I can't. I'm too mad, too hurt, too paralyzed.

I stay on the bench alone until nightfall, but it feels like five minutes. Finally, my body shudders in the cool that settles on San Francisco in the evening. I only have on a tank top and shorts so my whole body is chilled, but it feels good, like I'm dead. I stumble toward the cable car stop. I've got to get home somehow.

Fashion Victim
News Bulletin

It's over.

Sam broke up with me unexpectedly. It's now been . . . fifty-two hours since we broke up. Not that I'm counting. We had a fight, and I asked him to choose between me and his darling friend Delia . . . he chose his freedom, or her.

I want to dig a hole and climb in and never come out. I don't want to get out of bed. I can't remember the last time I ate.

I found out today he changed his work schedule. My spy said it was to accommodate his law school classes, but I know the truth. The less time we share in the same building, the less chance he has of seeing repugnant me.

I didn't know it would hurt this much. And I thought he really cared about me. How could he just walk away? Write me. Tell me anything, dear readers. Take my mind off this. I have a lot of time on my hands, now that I'm becoming the shut-in of Russian Hill. But please, if you write, don't forget to mention how crazy this boy must be to walk away from something so good.

Warning to all women: Never date a man who has the same haircut you do. It's just a bad idea.

Gowithgoddownwithfashion

Blah

I am straightening a rack of little Emporio Armani corduroy trousers. I look at my watch and see that it says five till eleven. I've been here for a half hour already. Whatever.

I enjoy mindless tasks right now. It's been five days since Sam and

I broke up. I miss him. I miss him with all my might. I miss him. It's all I think about.

Two X, two X, four T, four T, four T, six, eight . . . who thought up kids's sizes? I shrug and keep organizing. It's nice to put things in order. Yesterday, I cleaned my kitchen within an inch of its life. Inie looked at me as if I'd gone mad as I was pulling the crisper drawers out and bathing them in bleach and Ajax. She's one of the few people who know about my breakup with Sam, and that's only because she lives with me and was the person who greeted me as I burst through the door that night in tears. It was an awkward moment for the two of us, not really being all that close, but she made me a cup of tea and sat in the room with me while we watched bad TV sitcoms the rest of the night. Reagan has been great too. She called me this morning and sang "Breaking Up Is Hard to Do" over the phone. But she and Daniel are so happy together and coupley I just can't face her. And I can't call Steph. I've tried to get her a few times since our big fight at Ristorante Milano, but thanks to cell phone caller ID, she doesn't answer when I call.

"Miss Traywick?"

I look and see Sheila the Hun in a weird zebra-striped suit and clunky black heels. "Hi Sheila."

"Aren't you here early today?"

I look at my watch and see it's now eleven. "My shift starts at eleven."

"I guess I'm just unaccustomed to seeing you here right on time. Good work. And I also noticed you're going through the racks and organizing everything. I appreciate that."

No one, and I mean no one, likes to do Sheila's favorite task, that is, straighten and organize the sales floor. It's mind-numbing. You just go through each rack and put everything back in rising numerical order and take note of missing sizes. But right now, talking to people is too hard. I can't pretend I'm happy. I can't even allow myself to think. "No problem. It, uh, needs to be done so I thought I'd get on it."

203

"I'm going to talk to Tricia and make sure you're allowed to do this all day. I was just coming over here to reprimand Silver Spoon for the disarray."

I nod. Please, please make me do this all day. No parents, no kids. I can't face the world.

"Also, Lily, I wanted to tell you I've noticed a change in you lately."

Really? She's noticed that I'm happy? That for the first time in my adult life I'm happy? Was happy? Was. Was. Was. And now, I'm so depressed that—

"You are more professional in your dress and taking Traywick's more seriously. Good work."

Oh. I'm a better fashion drone. Never mind. "Thank you, Sheila."

"Although I must say today's outfit is not one of your best."

I look down at myself for the first time in days, and I'm a bit shocked. I have on some black slacks that I've been wearing for I don't know how long now, which are stained on the right thigh with what looks like toothpaste. And I've paired them with a crumpled, white buttondown shirt and black Old Navy flip-flops. "Yeah. I was a little uninspired today."

Sheila stares at my outfit one more time and then shrugs. "Very well." And then she turns to walk away.

Whew. But just after I go back to my wonderfully mindless task I hear the click-clack of her heels stop for a moment.

"Lily?"

I look up at her.

"Make sure you take your breaks today. That job can absolutely numb one's mind."

I smile and nod. She walks away.

I go back to my work and thank God that I'm having such an easy time at work. If anyone so much as looks at me wrong, I'll just burst into tears. Two X, two X, four T, four T, four T, six, six, six, six—I lose myself in the numbers.

I knock off for my break with Reagan a little early. While I am enjoying doing mindless work—especially as I hear the other Silver Spoon sales associates laughing and talking about their wonderful weekends—I am beginning to lose it. I weave my way over to European Fashions looking for Reagan. I spot her a ways off with her department's new hire, Cherie. Cherie glows with life and enthusiasm, could be Halle Berry's younger sister, and has just moved here from New York with a newly minted degree from FIT.

As I get closer, I can see that Reagan is buying something. Again. Oh Reagan. I hide quickly behind the wall just around the corner from the register. It will be funny if I hide behind the wall and then when she passes me to go to the café, I say, "I caught you! What'd you buy this time?" I lean my back against the wall and listen for Reagan to finish her purchase.

"This is gorg!" says Cherie.

"It's not like I need another dress exactly, but please, this will be perfect for church. Plus, it's Versace."

"I know! But how can you afford this? Eight hundred dollars!"

I lean in to hear her answer. Good question, Cherie.

"Oh, no one told you this yet? Here's what we do. Just ring it up as a clearance item, which takes off 70 percent, and then add on your Traywick's Associate's discount on top for an extra 15 percent off, and voilà! Eighty-five percent off. Even I can save up and afford seventy dollars for a Versace dress."

My eyes are wide, and my hand flies up to cover my mouth. Reagan! I listen for Cherie to tell her this just isn't right. To stop her from her fashion greed.

"Really? That's great! I didn't know we could do that!" she says excitedly.

I can't believe this. I can hear them finishing up the sale, but I don't know what I'll say to Reagan. She's stealing! She's stealing from Traywick's! I take off, weaving my way around the floor fixtures and duck down through the sportswear department. I have to get away from her. I need time to think. What can I do? Confront her? Tell my parents?

Chapter 13

I log into my Fashion Victim account and look at the hits I've been getting. Since my breakup news bulletin, I've become the second-most-popular blog. Not that I'm surprised. My life is like a sordid soap opera lately. I check to see if it's the same people checking every day or new people coming to the site. The only real pattern I notice though is that Edgar must check it about twice a day . . . every day. Goodness gracious, he is a fan. It's a little awkward to have your boss knowing all the gory details of your personal life, but then, I never actually see him anymore. He just e-mails me asking for a new pitch or giving me an assignment. And then I e-mail the story in by the deadline, he completely rips it apart and puts in some half-truths to make it juicier, and then off to press it goes. Hmph. It's certainly not the perfect writing job I once thought it was.

I hear a knock at my bedroom door.

"Yeah?" I yell, trying to keep the annoyance out of my voice. What does Inie want now?

"Lily?" she asks, poking her head in the door cautiously. Her eyes quickly scan the room, taking in my pajamas, greasy hair, and puffy, tear-stained face. I wait for her to make a comment about my appearance. "I was just wondering . . . Um, I'm ordering some Chinese food. Do you want some?" she asks, smiling sympathetically.

What? Where's my weird creepy roommate?

"I knew you were in here," she says, "and I hope you don't mind me saying this, but you look awful." I bite my tongue. "So I thought this might help cheer you up," she finishes.

"No thanks," I mumble, turning back to my computer. "I'm not hungry."

"Okay," she says. "That's probably better for you anyway." She walks toward the door. "You've lost all of that extra weight you were carrying around when you moved in," she says, smiling brightly as she closes the door.

I shake my head, too exhausted to do anything else. I open a new e-mail window. I'm going to try Steph one more time.

Just as I start typing, my phone rings.

"Hello?"

"Lily?"

"Oh, hi Mom," I say. I'm always a little confused when she calls.

"Listen, darling, your grandmother, father, and I wanted you and Sam to come over for dinner sometime this week. Do you have a free night?"

Tears of humiliation immediately begin to pour out of my eyes. How can I tell her this? It's so embarrassing. They loved Sam. They'll think I'm such a loser. They'll blame me. I begin to make the sniffling sound that always indicates crying.

"Lily? Honey? Are you okay?"

"MomSambrokeupwithmeeeeeee," I say. I'm not really talking or crying. I'm doing both. My cheeks are burning hot. This is so embarrassing.

"Oh there, there now. Oh darling. It's going to be fine."

"No! It's not!" I'm already tired of when people say this. They don't understand. I really loved him. I did. I'll admit it. I did.

"Oh Lily. I'm so sorry. Why don't we get together this week just the two of us? Hmmm? A little girl time?"

I slow my crying. Is this woman serious? We never hang out. I know from movies that some mothers and daughters always have "girl time" together, but we are not those people. "Uh . . ."

"Lovely. Are you free this week for tea at the St. Francis? You'll adore it. We'll get you a nice cup of tea and some sandwiches, and we'll just work this all out."

Before I can stop myself, I agree. We'll get together as soon as she gets back from Tokyo later this week. For some reason, as lame as tea at the St. Francis and "girl time" sounds, I need to see her. I need someone I know and love and trust to talk to me. I'm falling apart.

As my grandmother holds me in her big, squishy hug, I feel a moment's respite from the current sadness of my life. I know it's not just my imagination that she holds me a little longer than usual, probably saying a prayer for me silently. She pulls back, finally, and gently puts her hands on my face.

"Let your old gran look at you now, Lil." She looks into my eyes and seems to search around in them. She nods. "The first time is always the hardest." She gives a lopsided smile.

"What?"

"Getting your heart broken. The first time—it's always coming from outer space. You never see it coming, but it will be easier next time."

I put my head on her shoulder again. "Gran, please don't say next time. I can't think of going through this again. In fact, I can't even imagine ever loving again. It hurts too much."

She pulls me back to look at me again and says, "Oh Lil. Don't say that. Fourscore and for shame. It's just like Jesus says, 'Better to have loved and lost, than never to have loved at all.'"

I look at her. "Hey! That's not in the Bible."

"Oh yes it is." She looks at me with a poker face. Is she serious?

"No it's not." I'm cracking up. "Where, then?"

"Oh . . . uh, I guess it was Second Thessalonians."

I look at her askance. I think she's just taking advantage of the fact that *no one* can remember what's in Second Thessalonians, but I don't have the heart to tell her it was St. Augustine. Plus I feel like I should cut her some slack because I did miss that trivia question at Super Single Sunday Jeopardy Night about who first said a house divided against itself cannot stand. Turns out that was Jesus, not Abraham Lincoln.

I follow Gran as she ushers me into the kitchen, mumbling under her breath about respecting the wisdom of elders, while I giggle behind her. She produces a tube of raw cookie dough. "Do you still like to eat the dough raw?" she asks.

"Are almonds an art medium?"

She laughs, produces two spoons, and we get started on the chocolate chip goo. After a half hour, Gran has me all caught up on the house's gossip, and I'm feeling a little better. Thank goodness Mom and Dad are out of town right now. I tell her all the details about the breakup (Mom had made that Traywick family knowledge immediately, apparently), and she comforts me. The weird thing is, Gran doesn't blame Sam. I do, and I figured she'd be on my side, but all she says is "Everyone's got some coming up to do yet." I don't really want to talk about it anymore, so I decide to change the subject.

"Have you been reading my articles in *SF Weekly*?"

"Of course I have. I have them all right here. Although I do think you have become quite biting lately."

I frown. She produces a stack of my clippings, and I skim back through them.

"Why were you so hard on that bush gentleman? I've always admired his work."

I smile at her reverence for his "work." I guess eccentrics can appreciate one another. "That's the thing, Gran. I wasn't. My editor is changing my work around."

"Like, editing it? Or is he really changing it?"

"At first it seemed like editing but now, he's just putting lies in the stories to make them have a higher entertainment value."

Gran gives me her signature look—stern face and eyebrows reaching for the ceiling—that means *And what do you intend to do about that?*

Vicki escorts me back to Edgar's office. Just before I reach for the doorknob, she whispers to me, "He's, uh, busy today, and in a bad mood because last night he was attacked by a swarm of killer bees on his way home."

Has Robot Vicki lost her mind? Killer bees? I just decide to nod at her, and then she disappears.

I enter, and Edgar waves me to come in and sit down, but he's still talking on the phone. I immediately notice that his face is in fact swollen with bites. I look at the ground to avoid staring.

"Jack! Jack! Listen to me, just pay the ones that are threatening us with legal action, put the rest off until next month. In the meantime, I'll get the sales team to really hustle and bring in some lucrative ads. Fall's here. Big stories on the way."

He puts a finger up in the air to me as if to say *hold your horses*. I do my best to look really patient and unconcerned. I go over what I want to say to him in my head one more time.

"Uh-huh . . . Mm . . . yeah. I understand. Uh-huh. Yeah, well that's why we pay you Ha-hah! You dog! Yup! For your creative economics. Ha ha ha . . . uh-huh . . . uh-huh. Yeah, later." He puts the phone receiver down and then looks up at me.

"Yes, Lily? Go," he says.

"Yessir. I, uh, wanted to talk to you about—" I look up to make eye contact with him but am distracted by the giant swollen welts all over his face. I look back into my lap again.

"Oh, right. Killer bees. Last night. I'm fine. Front page tomorrow. Yes? Sorry, busy day today, Lily. What's on my crackerjack investigative reporter's mind?"

How does such a busy man find time to check the Fashion Victim blog as often as he does? "Sir, your editing of my stories can't continue. I'm uncomfortable with how you change what I'm trying to say."

"What? I just clean them up, spice them up. The old one-two. That's what I pay me for." He laughs hysterically at his own joke, so I force myself to smile.

"I know you see it that way, sir, and I really don't mean to be difficult, but I just can't stand for it. You often end up sending the opposite message I intended."

"So?" He straightens a disarrayed pile of paper on his desk.

"Well . . ."

"Spit it out, Lily."

"It has to stop, sir. It's wrong. It's lying. I want to make a difference in the world. I want my writing to count for something, not just be some flamboyant piece of half-truths and unfounded, sensationalist accusations."

He stops for a moment and stares at me with what can only be described as tenderness in his eyes. "That's really very sweet, Lily. I admire you."

I beam at him. Whew. He gets it. He knows what I'm saying.

"You're fired."

"What?" I screech.

"You're fired. Goodbye. Busy day. You understand."

I turn around, and sure enough Vicki is standing in the door. I walk toward her, confused, stunned. Fired?

Fashion Victim
Transmissions from Fashion Land

Job ain't got nothin on me.

You Bible scholars out there will remember the tale of Job. Job has everything his heart desires and then *boom*, God takes it all from him. I used to read the story and feel so bad for Job.

Bah.

Welcome to your friend Fashion Victim's life. She is Job-incarnate. No, change that. She makes Job look as if he is on holiday in St. Tropez.

Let's recap, shall we, what's going on in my life of late. (Those pregnant or with heart conditions should probably stop reading now.)

1. My best friend Steph is losing weight like there's a colonial tariff on each pound of flesh. And when I suggested to her that she eat a salad with her Diet Coke, she stormed out of a restaurant and has not spoken to me since. I fear she is anorexic and, now, unreachable.

2. My boyfriend, my very first boyfriend ever, the most wonderful and caring and special and talented and amazing boyfriend ever, ditched me unceremoniously in the middle of Union Square. Stick a fork in us, we're done.

3. I lost my writing gig. I was doing a little freelance work and I really loved it. My boss and I had a disagreement, and then poof! No more job, Job. In fact, irony of ironies, he's probably reading this right now. He's a fan!

I know you're all thinking, what more could go wrong? I'll tell you.

I caught my other best friend, Reagan, stealing. What makes it so much worse is that she's stealing from *my parents!* Apparently the way she is able to afford dressing like she does—i.e., like Nicole Kidman—is that she always has her friends at work ring up the clothes as clearance and then she smacks her company discount right on top. She gets everything for 85 percent off. Brilliant Reagan! Why not just put the clothes in your bag and walk out. *Eighty-five* percent off!

Plus, she's been doing it behind my back. She hasn't exactly lied to me but . . . it's definitely a sin of omission. I'm so mad at her. Really furious. And this just doesn't come at a good time because I've got her going to church some now, and I really think she's making progress in that department so if I confront her about stealing from my parents and the store, I think she will only get defensive, lash out, and then stop going to church to avoid seeing me.

All I can say for this life is: ajfka;lfjdka fl;dasfjk;dsafjkdj;ajk;

So help me God,
Victim

• Chapter 14 •

I can't believe it's already over. That couldn't have been nine innings, could it? How could we have already lost? To the Neiman Marcus Nymphs? They wear pink miniskirts, for goodness' sake. And how can Sam have managed to avoid meeting my eye for three straight hours?

I have been looking forward to this game all week. Sam and I haven't crossed paths too much at Traywick's recently, and he hasn't come to church at all, but I knew he couldn't avoid me at a softball game. I mean, we're on the same team, right? It's not like I expected him to ask if I want to go get ice cream after the game, but at least I would get to see him and hopefully talk to him.

I watch him as I slowly pull my gear off. He's already packing his glove away in his bag. Should I try to go talk to him? I shake my hair out of its tight ponytail, hesitating. I'll just go up and say hi casually and ask how he's been. There's nothing weird about that, is there? I miss talking to him so much. I take a step toward him, but stop as I see Lisa from Housewares approach him. He smiles slightly, picks up his bag, and starts to walk. She skips beside him, laughing. Why is she with him? Shouldn't he be shooing her away? Why isn't he telling her he has to go? And why is he getting into her car?

I can't breathe. Not Lisa.

He puts his bag down in the trunk of her car and walks around to the passenger door. I watch, transfixed. As he opens the door, he looks up. He sees me watching him and immediately looks away. He gets in and closes the door, and I trudge resolutely to the light-rail station. Sylvia is walking to the same station just ahead of me, and I slow down so I won't have to talk to her. As soon as I reach the train platform, I burst into tears.

"How's the Queen Anne?" Mom asks, looking at my pot of tea. She picks up her spoon to stir her tea and it slips through her fingers, landing on her plate with a clatter. She reddens slightly. I feel a rush of pity for her. I appreciate her impulse to hang out with me, but this whole tea thing is really awkward.

"It's fine," I answer, recrossing my legs uncomfortably. "Um, how's the Darjeeling?" I take a bite of my scone. This is mother-daughter bonding?

"Hm," she says noncommittally. She looks down at her plate. I scan the petit fours. I slowly reach out and choose one, placing it carefully on my plate. All around my elbows swarm spoons, forks, and knives in miniature, a tiny collection of real silver silverware for tea service. I don't raise my eyes. I can't think of anything to say to this woman.

"So . . ." Mom says, slowly. "Um . . ." She stirs her tea uncomfortably. "How is the newspaper going?" she asks brightly, pleased to have struck upon a topic of conversation.

"Oh, uh, well, I was let go." I gulp. Here we go.

"Mercy. Why?" she says, taking a bite of a cucumber sandwich. She looks down at her plate, takes a sip of tea. She is unflappable. Wow.

"Creative differences. He was changing my work around to make it sensational and, quite frankly, fallacious." *Quite frankly, fallacious?* I'm frightening myself with such properness. Who's a well-turned-out young lady? *C'est moi!* Mom is looking at me, really listening so I decide to keep going. "I talked with Gran about it and decided that even though I loved writing for the paper, I needed to take a stand with my editor. When I told him my concerns, he fired me."

I wait for her to give me a lecture on the permanent black mark of being fired or perhaps her favorite reoccurring lecture about how I'm always taking life too seriously and should adapt a moral code more in tune with practical day-to-day living.

"I'm proud of you, Lily. You did the right thing," she says.

I stare at her.

"I'm serious. I know, darling, we may not have always agreed in the past. Sometimes I don't understand why you choose to live the way you do, but I want you to know that I've always been proud of you. And since you've moved out . . ." She looks out one of the tall windows of the formal hotel drawing room at the rainy sky outside. I wait, but she doesn't finish her sentence. We sit in silence for a moment.

It occurs to me she actually misses me. We're so different that I thought my moving out wouldn't faze her. I can't believe it. She misses me. I feel warm all over.

"And you've always got the store in your future anyway," she says, smiling optimistically.

I gulp and stir my tea silently.

"So what happened with Sam?" she asks after a moment.

I tell her all about Delia and the escalating fights and then that day in Union Square. I find myself really opening up and telling her everything. She doesn't offer advice like Gran, but she listens. After talking for what must be the longest sustained period in my life to my mom, I fall silent. What is going on here?

"That's so difficult, Lily. I'm sorry. Why, I remember when my very first boyfriend broke my heart. I, oh, I suppose your grandmother already told you about that."

"No, no. She didn't. Someone before Dad? Who?"

"Joseph. Joseph Wright. Mr. Wright. He was my high school sweetheart."

"Mr. Wright?"

"Yes," she says, nodding, a far-off look in her eyes. "A little too perfect, no?"

This is so weird. I can't imagine Mom without Dad. I want to hear more. "Keep going."

"He was the drum major, and I was first flute."

"You can play the flute?"

"Of course not! I mean, not anymore. I just did it to be near Joe. He was two years older than me and just . . . the most . . ." She looks out the window again and loses herself in thought.

I smile. The most? Who is this warmhearted and lovable person before me? Where'd my mom go?

She looks back at me. "He *was* the most, I should say. He ended up being the least. Mr. Wrong. I was so wrong about him. He graduated high school, kissed me on the cheek after the commencement, and then said, I'll call you tomorrow. He never called again."

"Whoa. You were boyfriend and girlfriend?"

"Oh sure. I had his letterman sweater."

"He never called again?"

"Yes. Never heard from him again."

"What did you do?"

"Small town, of course. He started dating a girl in my class that summer and then went away to college."

I'm in shock. Who behaves that way? No one.

Mom giggles. "I'm so glad it happened though."

I look at her like she's nuts.

"No, really. I am. I learned so much from the experience, and afterward I was much better at dating. You have to learn to respect the other person and yourself. Plus, I'm glad I was single that summer on the Cape when I met your father."

I let this sink in. I hadn't really been focusing on what I was supposed to learn from the breakup with Sam. Frankly, I guess I thought we'd just . . . never break up?

Mom and I chat easily for another hour. I learn so much about her and Dad, and what it was like around the house when I was young and they were struggling to make a name for themselves in the fashion world. And then I remember Reagan. I feel so awful for betraying my parents. I know who's been stealing from the company, my own parents' company, and I haven't told them.

I let out a sigh. This is going to be hard, but I know it's the right thing to do. "Mom, I have to tell you something about Reagan."

"She's here!" Reagan hisses at me, her eyes wide. I instantly feel a pang of guilt at the sight of her. I haven't seen her since I squealed on her. My parents haven't told anyone or taken any action yet as they are still discussing what to do and still assessing how much money has been stolen from the company. I swallow the lump in my throat.

"Who?" I ask, wrinkling my brow, careful to keep my voice down so Sheila the Hun doesn't hear me. I'm carefully folding little yellow T-shirts and placing them on the racks. I've become the regular Silver Spoon custodian, which is just fine with me.

"Delia!" she whispers, practically yelling. She grabs my arm and tries to drag me away from the racks.

"Delia?" I lay my shirt down carefully. "How would you know? You don't know what Delia looks like. You've never met her."

"Lily," she says, stopping to look at me. "You don't honestly think you're the only one who Google-stalks, do you?" I think of the perky little picture in her college paper. "She's here. On this floor. I saw her, and I just knew it was her, and I came running. Let's go!" Oh, Reagan. You're too good to me.

"Go where?"

"To see what she's up to!" she says, rolling her eyes, pulling me toward the door. I scan the section quickly. I don't see Sheila. I follow Reagan.

We take off. "There she is." I whisper, pointing at a blond head approaching shoes. We run, hunched over, through Men's Accessories, keeping toward the back wall. Stanford gives us a dirty look as we scamper by dangerously close to a carefully arranged necktie display. We rush into Footwear from the back and crouch down behind the empty register counter just in time to see Sam emerge from the storeroom and smile broadly at Delia, who is nonchalantly examining a pair of pink kitten heels on a display table.

"Sam," she gushes, as if surprised to happen upon him here. "How are you?" She rushes up and gives him a kiss on each cheek. Reagan grabs my arms and squeezes gently.

"Deals," he says, smiling. "What are you doing here?" He puts the shoeboxes he's carrying down carefully on a low bench.

"I was just in the area and thought I'd stop by to say hi," she says, giggling.

"Oh. Okay . . . Well, that's great," he says, smiling. She pouts a little at his hesitation. "And you look great," he adds, looking at her pink miniskirt, tight black tank top, and high black heels. She beams.

"She looks like a woman of the night," Reagan mumbles.

"Shh . . ." I hiss, but Sam and Delia don't seem to have heard anything.

"So what are you doing?" Delia asks, leaning in to see his boxes.

"I was just about to bring these shoes over to that nice lady waiting patiently over there," he says, nodding toward a gray-haired woman in a Chanel suit who is watching the scene with interest. "But I have my break in a little while if you want to grab coffee or something at the café," he says, looking at his watch.

"Oooh, I don't know," she says, pursing her lips. "I'm in kind of a rush. I've got so much to do today," she says, grinning.

"What does she have to do? Does she even have a job?" Reagan whispers, and I elbow her. I want to hear this.

Delia reaches out and takes Sam's wrists in her hands. "Maybe I should just go," she says, leaning in toward him familiarly. He looks down at her distractedly. "But I'll see you tonight?" She kisses his cheek again. My stomach churns. He's seeing her tonight? Sam pulls away, smiles, and gives her a playful punch on the shoulder.

I brighten. He's not under her spell. Of course he doesn't want to kiss her back! He's still in love with me! Poor silly Delia. Even Reagan relaxes her death grip on my forearm.

"Sure thing," he says, reaching for his boxes again. He pauses, looking at her. She looks up at him, her eyes narrow, her teeth bared in her best attempt at a seductive smile. "I better take care of this customer," he says, stepping back. Then he stops, puts the boxes down, and steps toward her. Slowly, he leans in and places a kiss on her forehead.

Reagan digs her nails into my arm, and I stifle a squeal as I yank it away, but I lose my balance and fall against the counter with a slam. A bag of metal hangers crashes to the marble floor, clattering as the hangers settle.

"What in the world?" shrieks Sheila, coming quickly out of the storage room. I can't see Sam and Delia, but everyone else in the store seems to be staring at me. I try to sit up, navigating between the hangers, but I am still on the floor when she comes around the counter and finds us. Caught red-handed.

"Lily! Reagan!" she yells, her eyes wide. "What are you doing hiding behind the counter? Why aren't you at your stations?"

"We were looking for a contact?" I say sheepishly, grimacing.

"Looking for a . . . I never . . . Get up, both of you!" she yells.

Slowly, we pull ourselves up. My face is burning, though Reagan is doing a good job of looking like she doesn't care at all. Over the counter, Sam and Delia are staring at me. Sam is wide-eyed, his fists clenched by his side. Delia is laughing like she finds this hysterical. "That's so tragic," she says, smirking.

"Both of you, back to your posts," Sheila says coldly. "Your supervisors will hear about this." I look from Sheila to Sam and back to Sheila quickly when I catch his eye. I wish I could explain, but Sheila is already escorting us away. I take a last look as we're walking away. Delia is still laughing, but Sam is looking intently at me, his jaw clenched, his face stoic. His eyes follow me as I walk away.

"What do you think you're doing, spying on me?" he asks, coming into the Children's Department a few hours later. His eyes are narrowed, his voice brusque.

"I wasn't . . . Reagan . . ." I mumble. Why is he here? I can't meet his eye. "Sam . . . " I say, biting my lip.

"What?" he asks, exasperated.

"Why was Delia here?" I look up to read his reaction.

"Why was Delia here?" he asks, leaning in. "Because she's my friend. And she stopped by to say hi. Because that's what friends do."

"But you're seeing her tonight."

"I guess you were listening pretty closely," he says, cocking his head. "Yes, I am." I wait for him to go on, but he just looks at me. I look back, waiting.

"So was it all just lies then?" I finally ask. The tears I have fought so hard to keep back start pouring down my cheeks. "All that stuff you said about how great it is to date a Christian, about how you'd never date a non-Christian again, about me being special, was that just lies? Because it sure doesn't seem like you meant it." I swallow hard. He doesn't flinch.

"Lily?" he asks, raising his eyebrows. His eyes soften, and I nod. This is where he confesses he loves only me, and Delia doesn't mean anything to him. He's about to tell me he made a grave mistake that day in Union Park and wants me back, and I'll tell him I'll consider it, but he hurt me so badly that it is going to take a lot to trust him again. He opens his mouth, and I smile. "You're out of line." He turns on his heel, his long hair flying, and walks away.

I stagger up the stairs, grateful to be home. I'm going to put my pajamas on, make myself a bowl of oatmeal, and climb into bed with a book. I pray Inie isn't there naked when I walk in. She's been really nice since the breakup, going out of her way to be helpful, but I just can't face her sympathetic smile today. I already feel bad enough for myself. I don't need anyone else compounding the problem. I slide my key into the lock, lean my weight against the door, and swing it open.

I stop still. Why is Alex sitting in my living room? I step back outside and shut the door again quickly. Did I walk into the wrong house? A nightmare maybe?

I push the door open a crack and peek inside. I see Alex looking at me, confused. I open the door slowly and step fully into the living room, my living room. Maggie is here too, sitting on the couch. And there's Becky by the window. And Inie, grinning at me on a kitchen chair. What is going on?

"Surprise!" Inie yells, clapping her hands like a delighted child.

"Is something wrong with your door?" Maggie asks Inie.

"What?" I say, putting my bag down by the door. "What surprise?"

"We just wanted to . . ." Alex starts.

"We thought it might be nice if . . ." Maggie says.

"You've been looking . . ." Inie says quickly.

"Getting dumped stinks," Becky says clearly from the corner. Everyone turns to look at her quickly, and she reddens, then shrugs. "I mean, we've all been there," she says, smiling at me embarrassedly. All of them? I look at Maggie's darling curls. Is it possible she has been here too? Is this some cruel joke? They must have gathered here to laugh at me. To get me back for laughing at them? But then why is Maggie looking at me so sweetly?

"I made a cake," she says, gesturing to the giant shiny chocolate mound on the table, its glossy peaks fit for the cover of *Better Homes and Gardens*.

"And we thought we could pray for you," Alex says, looking into my eyes. "Ending a relationship is hard, and we noticed you seemed like you've been having a tough time recently," she says quietly. "And Inie said that you've been hiding out and sleeping a lot and not acting like yourself. So she asked us to come over. We hoped you wouldn't mind if we prayed for you."

They're serious. Inie gathered them here to cheer me up? That's the dorkiest thing I've ever heard. Inie isn't even a Christian. She's just Alex's friend from work. I don't want Alex with her perfect red hair to pray for me. I want Maggie and her sympathy cake to get out of my living room.

"I don't know . . ." I say slowly. "I was kind of thinking I just might go to my room. I have some cleaning I need to finish up, uh, you know old magazines up to my ears and uh—"

"Lily?" Becky says from the corner. I look at her. With her tight white tank top, flared jeans, and glittery nails, she looks out of place among these girls. She leans forward. "We don't have to pray if you don't want. I'm not so sure about that part. We just wanted you to know that we know what it's like to have your heart broken, and we're here for you. Please don't go in your room and sulk."

I look around at their smiling faces. Alex is looking at me, eyes wide. Maggie is smiling compassionately, fingering the butterfly charm on her silver necklace nervously. Becky is silently begging me to stay. Inie is grinning like she doesn't know what's going on but is glad to be here anyway. She meets my eye and smiles guiltily.

And then I lose it. The first tear runs down my cheek slowly, and before I know it I am bawling. I am beaten down and broken. I need to rest. I am crying so hard I don't even mind when Inie guides me to the couch. I don't mind when Maggie sits down beside me and starts to rub my back. I am grateful when Becky hands me a tissue. And I almost don't notice when Alex begins to pray, asking God to keep his hand on me to comfort me and to help me to look to him in my time of need.

They take turns praying for me, and I keep my head bowed as the tears keep coming. I only partly listen. The rest of me is thinking.

I can't believe they did this. I can't believe I've been making fun of them. I am humbled by their compassion.

I think about Sam. I thought he was the One. It never occurred to me that it would end. And I never dreamed it would hurt so much if it did. And yet, I can't help feeling, I'm okay. Despite the fact that I wake up every morning wanting to die, I wouldn't trade this. I am getting stronger, I realize, because of this. This hurts, but it's something. Gran's right. Feeling this awful is better than never having felt love at all. I smile. With this, I can go on. Maybe Sam isn't the One, maybe I am going to have to stop waking up in the night missing him. I have to let go. I take a deep breath as Alex mumbles something about grace. It's over.

I can't believe they would do this for me.

When Maggie says amen, I look up, embarrassed. Becky hands me another tissue, and I wipe my eyes quickly. My face must be bright red, and my eyes already feel puffy. I blow my nose slowly, afraid to look up. No one says anything.

"Do you want some cake?" Maggie asks finally. I nod slowly, not caring what Inie may say about my thighs. Inie gets up to find a knife, and Maggie and Alex follow her into the kitchen. Becky looks at me shyly from the other end of the couch.

"You know, when Alex called about getting together tonight, I wasn't sure I wanted to come," she says. I laugh, and she smiles, shrugging. "I know. They're nice girls, but . . . um, they're not like the rest of my friends, you know what I mean?" I laugh again. "And it's nice that they've tried to include me even though they don't like that Miguel is dating me," she says, shushing my weak protests. "No, it's okay. I know they don't mean it personally. On some level, I understand why. It's fine. And I think I'm coming closer to seeing things their way," she says slowly. I hear cabinet doors closing in the kitchen.

"I didn't come to hang out with those girls," she says quickly. "I came because I like you. And because when the last guy I dated called it off just two months before our wedding, I thought I'd never recover."

She takes a deep breath. "But I had to, and I slowly did. I know how much it hurts. I came tonight because I wanted you to know that, if nothing else, I understand this." She smiles.

"What? You were engaged?" I swallow hard. "I didn't know that."

"It's okay. I was. But it's over. And it's better that way anyway. It was not a healthy relationship. Slowly I'm learning what a good relationship is." She smiles, shrugging, as Inie walks back into the room. "I'm here if you want to talk."

My mind is reeling. Becky was practically left at the altar. And here she is, comforting me?

I gratefully accept the piece of cake that is shoved into my hands, though I can't take my gaze from the wall. How can I have been so self-centered?

Fashion Victim
Transmissions from Fashion Land

Ah yes, single again
Previously sad and blue
And . . . okay, and pathetic
Young fashionista
starts a new life
(and uh, did I mention that I am single again? Cute
brothers anyone?)

Readers, I want to announce something. I'm a new girl.

I wish you could see me—you can't, don't e-mail me for a picture—but I am. Something snapped inside of me the other day, and now I'm a whole new girl. I realized that I have been wandering around this town of mine like a zombie, never looking up to see the sunset, never smiling at a little girl turning somersaults in the park, never splashing in the mud puddles in the rain. Navel-gazing. Poor-me whining. I have been a little gloomy cloud of heartbreak.

But now that's over. *Finito. El Fin.* Done.

In fact, I'm almost glad the breakup with Sam happened. I've learned so much from it. What? Uh . . . I'm still putting it into words. Oh wait, here's one. Guess what? You probably aren't going to marry the person you're dating right now. Yup! You heard it here first. And if you and your significant other should break up, it doesn't mean that you are somehow unfit for human interaction, it just means there are other people out there. So many fish in the sea!

Really. I feel so great. I've turned the corner on all this moping, which is why, darling blogosphere, I can't talk. I'm off to the store to buy a new outfit. It's been too long since I spoiled myself. Plus, I'm going to need something to start off my new life tomorrow. Tomorrow is the day when I will be more mature, self-confident, sane, and beautiful than I have ever been before. Tomorrow! Tomorrow things will be different. Particularly my outfit. My outfit will be different.

Go with God! Down with heartbreak!
Fashion Victim

I post this entry triumphantly, then close out of my browser and slowly shut down my computer. As the last bit of light fades from the screen, a tear runs down my cheek.

• Chapter 15 •

New woman that I am, I have gotten up thirty minutes early today and am *walking* to Traywick's. My new red skirt with the slit up the back is edged with lavender ribbon, and I have my awesome black Prada heels in my purse and my walking shoes on. I figured that as long as I'm going to be a new person on the inside, I might as well be a new person on the outside too. Out with the Sam and in with the new. It's all a part of my total body, spirit, and mind wellness plan. And while I don't really need to lose any weight, it would be nice to stay toned in softball's off-season. Plus, I thought it would be good for me to have a little quiet time to myself every morning, a time of reflection, instead of riding the noisy cable car, where invariably we have near misses with cars and choke on the exhaust fumes, while I spend my time listening to tourists bicker with their spouses.

The sun is shining after a few days of rain, and there's a fall snap in the air as I weave my way up and down the streets of this jewel box city. Yes. I do like this. I will do this every morning. The new me! I pass a red news-stand holding the *San Francisco Weekly*. I pause briefly but decide to press on. No need to get the paper. I've put Earle and his silly little rag behind me now. In fact, I should really contact the *Chronicle* about doing some real journalistic work for them instead of the yellow journalism I used to do.

After a few more blocks I spot a Royal Ground coffee shop and decide to pop in. I volunteered for the early shift this month in order to minimize my contact with people so it's only seven-thirty in the morning, and I could really use a little dose of caffeine.

I wait in the line for a moment dreaming of my beloved mocha when I remember, hey, I'm a new woman. What would a new woman get? Something healthy, something sophisticated, but also something different. A shot of espresso? No, too Wall Street stressball. A low-fat, sugar-free latté? No, I don't have a stroller yet. Hmm . . . tea. I've always steered clear of the green stuff (how being green is a selling point for a beverage, I'll never understand) but the herbal teas look quite good. I chose a green apple mango blend. I take a deep breath of the steam when they hand the cup to me, and it smells so . . .

"I just want you to know, Lily Traywick, that I still love you because I have Jesus Christ in my heart."

I am staring at Alex. Oh right. I remember now. She lives in this part of town. I knew that. Alex has her pink-lacquered nails over her heart, indicating exactly where Jesus lives in her body. "Hey, Alex."

She slits her eyes at me. "Jesus says that if a man . . . a woman slaps your face, you turn and give her the other cheek." She turns a cheek to me and puts it in my face. I lean back to get her cheek out of my personal zone. Whoa. What is her problem?

"What are you talking about?" I ask, chuckling. Man, she is getting weirder by the day.

"You know what the worst part of it is? I really pity you. I do. *I am filled with the love of Christ and I am happy.*" At that, she turns and storms toward the door. What is she talking about? When she reaches the door she turns back to me and yells, "*Happy!*" And then she is gone.

I turn around to look at the rest of the people in the coffee shop, but they all seem as confused as I am. I shrug my shoulders and act like I don't know her either.

As I approach the usual group hovered around the register at Silver Spoon they all go silent. I decide to walk over and say hi. I've been too antisocial lately.

"Hey guys. What's up?" I probably came up in between stories, and now it will be just a moment before someone starts a new one. I can't wait to tell them all about the new me. Sam? Sam who? I don't even know any Sams. And maybe Tricia will have a guy friend to set me up with.

"I should go, uh, unpack some stock in the back. Sheila asked me to do it yesterday, but I never got around to it," says Tricia.

"Me too. I mean, I'll help you," Charlie adds, quickly.

I turn and look at him. "So will I," I say. I like working in the back. No annoying customers, lots of gossip time.

"No. Sorry, Lily. We need you out here. Someone needs to cover the floor," says Tricia. Tricia's our department manager so her word is law, but this is not like her. I just worked the floor last shift. Usually she is better about spreading the tasks around. Charlie is already halfway across the floor by the time she can complete her sentence, and so I'm all alone.

After a half hour, I still haven't seen a single customer. In the meantime, I've shot myself in the head with the scan gun four times, I've written "Beam Me Up Scottie" all over an old receipt, and have now taken to playing the drums with two pens on the countertop. I drop one of the pens right in the middle of my big drum solo and bend over to pick it up when I see, wonder of wonders, a contraband paper, hidden behind the counter. Awesome! Sheila never lets us have reading material on the job. I know I shouldn't read it, but I'm so bored that if I don't do something I'll just fall asleep right here at the register, and then I'll get a thumbtack in my eye so it's probably better that I do take a quick peek at the paper.

I immediately recognize that this is the *Weekly*. Oh well. It will be interesting to see how Earle flounders without me. I look at the front-page lead headline.

FASHION VICTIM EXPOSED

The Sordid, Totally Top-Secret Cyber-Life of Lily TRAYWICK

What?! This, this, this . . . it can't be. What? I read quickly through the column, written by Edgar J. Arle himself. "Beneath the shimmering world of San Francisco's most upscale department store lies an ugly secret," it begins. "Her name is Lily Traywick." My stomach drops. "The only child of the owners of the most chichi store in the city, she spends most of her time pouring out her heart and her friends' dirty secrets on her top-ranked Web log."

I swallow. I'm speechless. After pointing out my blog's Web address for all interested readers to check out for themselves, he makes a big deal of the "exclusive" angle, saying that he is the first and only writer to have cracked the ongoing "Web mystery." The article quotes my blogs out of context—"My best friend is a total klepto, Lily says"—and assures all of San Francisco that I have been dumb enough to use real names. Edgar tells everyone how I take cheap shots at my own grandmother, make fun of my nudist roommate, and fawn over my ex-boyfriend the surfer. He points out how I get angry about non-Christians dating Christians, citing as examples Becky and Miguel and Reagan and Daniel, and insists that I think "my friend Steph would get over her eating disorder if she'd just eat something." He relishes the Delia story, drawing out every detail I have ever posted on her and declares me a jealous green-eyed monster. He even ran that embarrassing photo of me from the fashion show last spring, snickering at my makeover as "her obvious and pathetic attempt to get a boyfriend." He writes, "Her angry rants are ironic, considering her ardent and frequently professed Christian virtues, particularly since Christians are one of her favorite targets," listing, as an example, the Alex pool party incident. "Sadly, her lofty virtues fall by the wayside when there is a stone to be thrown."

"Aah!" I scream aloud.

My scream calls Tricia and Charlie from the back.

"We were taking bets on whether or not you'd come in today," says Tricia.

"I lost," says Charlie.

I look at him.

"Did you see that part where he calls your blog 'at times a steamy love poem to her current man du jour, at times an angry rant against all of her parents' fashion inner circle'?"

"I need to sit down," I say.

"Oh Lily. I really thought you must have known. I'm sorry you found out this way," says Tricia, smiling sweetly.

"My stomach hurts," I say.

"Lily?" Tricia says, looking at me sympathetically. "Why don't you go home? I'll cover for you," she whispers. I silently thank God I've never written anything bad about Tricia.

"Would you really? I don't think I can face anyone right now," I moan.

Tricia nods slowly. I grab my bag and walk resolutely out of the Silver Spoon, keeping my head down to avoid making eye contact with anyone.

"Leaving already, Lily?" Sheila barks loudly from out of nowhere. I think quickly. Have I said anything bad about Sheila in my blog? My heart sinks as I realize that I have referred to her as Sheila the Hun on at least one occasion.

"I'm not feeling well," I mutter, not even looking up.

"I should think not," she answers, shaking her head and muttering as I walk away. I pray I won't run into anyone else. Unfortunately, God must be busy playing chess, since Stanford, seeing me walking down the marble path, jaunts from his tie tack table quickly toward me to hiss, "You don't even deserve to be here if you can't appreciate what this place is." I stop, raise my eyebrows.

"And what, Stan, is it, exactly?" I ask archly.

"It's the center of the West Coast fashion universe," he replies angrily. "This is a wonderful place." I roll my eyes and keep walking. "This is a special place," he says, but I ignore him, "And *the rest of us* have worked very hard to get here." I pretend I can't hear him, and I walk away. "And just so you know, Lily," he yells after me loudly, "those shoes do *not* go with that skirt!" I don't turn but hear him stomp loudly back to his cuff links.

Where can I go? I walk slowly, trying to think. I can't go home. Inie will be there, and she will probably greet me wearing nothing but a deadly grin and holding a revolver; I can't go to my parents' house, since they'll probably never want to talk to me again; I can't go hang out with Reagan or Steph; I'm afraid if I even sit in a park the Bushman will sneak up behind me with an especially sharp branch. I slowly walk toward the soft tinkle of the piano keys, not knowing what else to do. I haven't ever said anything bad about Harry. Maybe he will let me sit by him and think. I sit down next to him on the velvet-covered bench and bury my face in my hands.

"What's wrong, Lily girl?" Harry says softly as his fingers move gracefully over the smooth keys. I lift my head slowly.

"Haven't you seen the article?" I ask, shaking my head. "I don't have a friend left in the world."

"Of course I saw it," he says softly, switching smoothly to "Stormy Weather," shaking his head as he plays. "That doesn't mean I believe it."

We sit for a while as I listen to the sad, moody song. I put my head on his shoulder and sob quietly. The piano music helps me think. What have I done? What have I done to all of my friends and family? All the people I love so much. I mean, of course I have complaints about all of them that I wouldn't want them to know, but they should have never found out. I berate myself for believing they wouldn't. What a stupid, stupid girl I am for thinking my blog was safe on the Internet. Yes, it was nice to have readers, but once I became a top blog, I should have realized one snoop or another would expose me. I feel lower than low. Like dirt. Maybe if I go to confession I'll feel a little better. If only I was Catholic. Those Catholics really know how to get things off their chests. They also have nunneries, which also sounds pretty appealing right about now.

"Harry?"

"Yes, love?"

"Oh, Harry, that's the thing. Most of it was true," I wail. "I really wrote most of that stuff," I say, sniffing. "I just didn't mean for anyone to find out."

"Honey, I'm sure you didn't mean it. You're a good person," he says, smiling at me. His sincere belief in me makes me feel even worse. "You'll get through this," he says, launching into a lively rendition of "The Sun Will Come Out Tomorrow." I smile despite it all. "And just remember, Harry still loves you, no matter what," he says, winking at me.

"I'm afraid you may be the only one," I say, sinking my face down into my lap.

• Chapter 16 •

"*I am not a klepto!*" Reagan screams through the phone. I sit up on my bed, grateful Inie isn't here, since she would probably be able to hear Reagan's shrill yell through the wall. "I can't believe you would say that! After all these years! Do you realize I'm on probation at Traywick's?"

"Reagan, please lower your voice. You're hurting my ears. And just calm down, please," I say without enthusiasm. If I know Reagan, she's not about ready to stop. "I dress slutty, do I?" she yells, though slightly more quietly. "What else do you think about my clothes, oh fount of fashion wisdom?" I take a deep breath and decide to just let her finish. "And why didn't you ever say anything about not approving of me dating Daniel! I can't believe this is how I find out I'm not spiritual enough for you. Well, I'm spiritual enough for him, and we have a great relationship, thankyouverymuch, and you're just jealous because he likes me and not you and I have a boyfriend and you don't!" She pauses, and I start to open my mouth, but she starts up again. "Daniel's feelings were really hurt, by the way, especially by the part about Medieval Times. He really likes that place." I wait. Nothing but deep breathing. She must be catching her breath. I'll risk it.

"Reagan, I'm so sorry," I start. "The blog was never meant to be read by anyone I know. I'm really sorry I hurt you."

"Oh, it hurt me all right, Lily Opal Frances Traywick. It hurt me so much I'm not sure we can be friends anymore."

"But Reagan, listen, please—"

"No, you listen to me, Lily," she says. "After all I've done for you, after all we've been through together . . ." Her voice rises again. "I'm really going to have to think about this," she says, her voice cracking.

"Can't we just talk?"

"No, we really can't!" she yells. "I have to go." She takes a deep breath. "And just for the record, I did not steal that Bible!" She slams the phone down, and the line goes dead. I lie back on my bed and close my eyes, too exhausted to cry any more.

I can't ignore it any more. I have tried to convince myself I don't care what they think, that I can put if off for a while, and that they probably haven't even read the silly little article anyway, but I know I have to do it. I don't like that I've hurt all my friends, but it makes my stomach ache to think that I may have hurt my parents and Gran. Slowly, I dial their home number.

"Hello?" Gran answers. "Are you there? Hello? Is this the Salvation Army?"

"What? No, Gran, it's me. Lily."

"Oh," she says, then goes quiet.

"Gran, are you okay? Why would the Salvation Army be calling? Is everything all right?"

"Oh yes, Lily. We're all fine here. I had just called the Salvation Army to see when they could pick some stuff up. I thought it might be them calling back."

Oh no. Do they all hate me so much they're getting rid of all the stuff I left there? My old report cards? My trophies?

"Um, what," I say, taking a deep breath, "what are you giving away?"

"Oh, nothing much," Gran says sadly. "Just some old junk no one wants. Mostly my nut figures." She laughs quietly. "I guess I should have realized who the real nut was."

"Ooooh, Gran . . . I'm so sorry. I'm really, really sorry. I didn't mean all that about your almond art. I love your almond art."

"Oh, it's fine, Lily. You don't have to pretend."

"No—Gran, wait. Okay, maybe I think your art is a little strange, but I do love it. I love it because it's a part of you, and, contrary to popular belief right now, I love you more than I understand. I love your quirks. I love that you watch church on TV. I love that you are learning how to love the computer. I love that you live with us . . . lived with us . . . live there."

She is silent for a minute. "You're sweet, honey, and I know you mean it. And I know that bad man made most of that stuff up." She takes a deep breath. "But really, isn't there some truth in everything? It's so rare that you get to see yourself how others see you."

"That's not really how I see you—"

"Really, mostly I'm just embarrassed. I didn't know how strange I seemed. But even though it wasn't all nice, I appreciate that I got to see inside your world, Lily."

"Gran, if there is any way I can make it up to you—"

"Now don't you worry about that, honey. I'll love you no matter what you do. It's your mother I'm worried about. She loves you no matter what too, but I think right now she's having a hard time remembering that."

"Can I talk to her?"

"She's just in the next room. I'll go get her," she says quietly putting the phone down. I hear some indistinct murmurs and wait. Finally Gran comes back on.

"Your mother says she's not home," she says sadly. "Oops, I mean she's not home. I mean . . . she was, but she just went . . ." Gran breaks off. "Well, I expect she needs some time. But please don't let this be the end, Lily. Try her again tomorrow," she says sadly.

"Thanks, Gran," I say quietly, "I'll try again." As I hang up, I lean back on my bed and close my eyes. If I fall asleep this whole world will go away.

I wake up a few hours later, dazed. I look at the clock. It's ten o'clock at night. My contacts sting my eyes. Slowly, I drag myself out of bed to walk to the bathroom. I pull the door open slowly, sticking my head out first. The coast is clear. I go into the bathroom, take my contacts out, and wash my face. I have just put my toothbrush in my mouth when I see a shadow out of the corner of my eye.

"I just want you to know," Inie says from the doorway, "that I love my body." My toothbrush is in my mouth, so I don't even bother to try to respond. "And if you have a problem with my body, you can find another place to live." She turns on her heel and walks toward the living room, but pops her head back in quickly. "And, you're just jealous of me because I don't have cottage cheese thighs." She disappears quickly down the hall. Apparently I am the most jealous creature on God's green earth.

I spit quickly and put my toothbrush on the counter. As I rinse, I rack my brain for a new way to apologize, since nothing I've tried today has worked and my living space is at stake here. Even if she is crazy, I can't deal with moving right now.

"Inie," I say, following her into the living room.

"Don't you mean Hiney?" she asks, sulking on the couch.

"No, I mean Inie," I say, taking a deep breath. "Inie, I'm sorry that I hurt you. I love living here with you. Especially after you were so sweet to me last week. That was friendship above and beyond the call of duty. I hope I haven't ruined our friendship. Will you forgive me?"

She looks at me, assessing. She is quiet.

"Oh, of course I forgive you, you big lug," she says standing up and walking toward me, her arms wide. I lean in tentatively, grimacing as she wraps her arms around me. She wiggles right and left, squeezing me hard, then pulls back. "Just don't move out on me, okay?" She grins like a child.

"Um, okay," I say, flashing her a thumbs-up and smiling much too broadly. "Just don't make me . . ."

"Don't be silly," she says, staring at her cuticles. "Do you want to order some pizza? I'm starved."

"No thanks," I say. "Cottage cheese thighs, you know."

She bursts out in insane laughter, and I laugh with her. "Yeah, we shouldn't. You're right. I have my girlish figure to maintain," she says, checking her hair for split ends. "Just let me know if you change your mind." I nod as I walk toward my bedroom. Crisis averted. At least I have one friend. Plus Harry and Gran. At least I have three friends. Even though one of them is a nudist, and two of them are members of the AARP.

"Oh, and Lily?" Inie calls. I turn and look at her. "Since you're not dating that cute Sam anymore, can I have his number?" Her head is cocked, her eyes questioning. She is serious.

Make that two friends. At least I have two friends, even if one of them is related to me, and they're both up for the senior's discount at IHOP.

I wake up to sunlight streaming through my window. I open my eyes, stretch my arms, and then remember. I roll back over and pull my sheet over my head.

It's Day Two of the new Lily. I pull the sheet down slowly.

I have to do this. Please God, give me the strength to do this. I can face this day. I am a new woman. I will hold my head up high. I will make apologies where they are due. I will show that I am not cowed by the schemes of the evil one, Earle. I will not lie here in bed all day. I will go about my life. I will overcome.

I look at my clock. It's only six in the morning.

I pull the sheet back over my head and close my eyes.

Ten minutes later, I know I will not go back to sleep. I sit up and look around. I see my computer. The offending device. I start to move toward it and stop. Do I dare?

Slowly, I switch it on.

As it boots up, I look around my room. I should clean those blinds. Maybe hang something on that wall. I wonder if I should paint it blue? Eventually, I have to turn back to the screen and open my e-mail: 124 new e-mails. I take a deep breath. I scan the list quickly. I don't recognize most of the senders. Probably hate mail.

There's one from Becky Nesterenko. Thank God for Becky. Even if she says she never wants to see me again, at least I know her. I click on it.

> Lily,
>
> Ouch. If you need to talk, I'm here.
>
> Becky

I can't help smiling. Maybe this is a good sign. I scroll down the list, searching for another name I recognize.

There's one from Delia. Well, maybe it will be an unexpected dose of good cheer, à la Becky. I click on it.

> LILY:
>
> Did I get it right this time? Is that good enough for you?
> 1. I do not have big ears
> 2. You're pathetic
> 3. I'm dating Sam
>
> Delia

I close it quickly. She's dating Sam?
I was right.
I hate her.
I climb back into bed and slowly pull the sheet over my head.

I walk to my room, thinking about Mom and Reagan. How do I get them both to forgive me? And then how do I get Reagan back into my mother's good graces? I sit down at my computer and am tinkering with my e-mail, lost in thought, when my cell phone rings. I haven't heard the thing ring in a long, long time. Unpopularity gives you a lot of alone time so I jump when I hear it. The screen says Stephanie. It rings again as I stare at it. I hadn't thought about Steph in all of this. It's not like she was speaking to me before so I hardly think that now that I told the whole world that she's anorexic—it rings a third time.

I punch the talk button. "Huh, huh, hello?" I say. I have to clear my throat because suddenly my voice doesn't seem to be working. My heart is racing.

"Um . . . Hi," she says, very quietly.

"Oh Steph. I'm so sorry. I feel so awful about everything. I'm sorry I said you were anorexic. I mean, I have no proof. And I'm sure you're not. And I'm sorry we've been fighting. And I'm sorry about that night at Ristorante Milano. I'm sorry that I was trying to force you to eat. I mean, maybe I'm just a jealous cow who wishes she had a career that she believed in, that I could devote myself to. How have you been? I've missed you. I'm so glad you called!" I'm getting really good at boot-licking and groveling.

"I just wanted you to know that I'm the talk of the hospital," her voice sounds so small and tired.

"Oh that's awful. I'm so sorry. If it makes you feel better, I'm going to write a new blog, a retraction to set the record straight."

"It's too late. Thanks to your blog, I was just denied my dream: a post in Honduras with Doctors Without Borders this summer. They cited my 'anorexia' as too much of a risk to make me a viable candidate for the position."

I swallow. I am the most wretched and miserable creature. I am ruining people's lives! Crushing their hopes and dreams! "Steph, let me try to make it up to you. I love you so much. I care about you. I'm so sorry." I'm pleading with her.

I don't hear a response.

"Steph? Steph?"

I look at the phone and see it says "Call ended."

• Chapter 17 •

I fall back on my bed, exhausted. This will not be a Friday night for the record books. No hot date here. In fact, no people here. Just me, alone, exhausted. I decided to use yet another empty Friday night making my apologies official. I must have just posted the longest blog in the history of all of blogkind. It took me four excruciating hours to write because I had to go back and read all of the awful things I said about people, and then apologize to each of them and try, where I could, to set the record straight. I had to apologize for being so judgmental of Becky and Miguel when they first started dating and tell all of my readers that Jesus would not approve of my judgements. I had to apologize to all of the people I made fun of—Inie for her nakedness, Maggie for her meekness, Alex for her nauseating ways—but try as I might, I couldn't apologize to Delia personally. I tell myself she's included when I wrote, *I'm really sorry to anyone I'm forgetting and hope you'll forgive me.* But most of all, I had to beg everyone's forgiveness, even though I hardly deserved it. I made an open appeal to all who were slighted in the blog to e-mail me with their idea for how I could make it up to them. I was half-kidding when I did it, suggesting my maid services, but maybe some people will actually take me up on it. I'd love a chance to make things right.

The phone rings as I'm lying there, and I look at the clock. It's nine at night. My stomach rolls over. This can't be good. It's probably another person calling to chew me out. My phone displays a number I don't recognize.

"Hello?" I say.

"Hey there," a cheerful voice says. "It's Becky."

I sigh in relief. "Good to hear from a friendly voice."

She laughs. "Listen, I told my friends I was too tired to go out tonight because they were going dancing and Miguel is out of town with his parents. I rented *Pretty in Pink*, and I got four colors of nail polish and a face mask and my thought was, Hey, Beck, spend the night alone. Relax and pamper yourself. But now, I don't know. I kind of think it'd be more fun as a sleepover. So I called you. You're already in bed, aren't you? I woke you up?"

I look around at my sparse bedroom. "You mean you want to spring me out of friendless prison?"

"You're out on good behavior."

"I'll be right over. And I'll come bearing gifts of pizza."

My sides hurt. I don't think I've laughed this hard in ages. Becky and I really click. We've been quoting lines from the movie back and forth and comparing the characters to mutual friends for at least an hour now. We're lying on the living room rug of her chic, modern apartment, and we're being really loud because her roommate is out of town.

"Hey, Becky?"

"Yeah?" she says. She's staring at her toes in admiration. They are covered in Plum Crush.

"Thanks for this. It's so nice of you."

"Whatever. I've been wanting to be your friend since the pool party. Reagan's too. I was so relieved to see some girls at church that were normal. It's so important to Miguel that I go with him. Plus, I could really use some new friends. The people I hang out with are left-over from college, and we're, uh, moving in different directions now. So think nothing of it. My pleasure."

"And," I pause. Here I go again, "I'm really sorry about what I said about you and Miguel in the blog. I had a crush on Miguel at the time, as you know."

"Don't beat yourself up, huh? What you said wasn't so bad, and he's totally hot. I completely understand having a crush on him." She laughs.

I still feel a little uncomfortable so I can't help but add, "You know, that I'd never, ever, because—"

"Oh yeah. I know. I'm not jealous. It's cool. I see us as friends. And friends don't steal friend's boyfriends."

I sigh. "I couldn't agree more."

"I have to confess, though, I did read all of your blogs. They were fascinating. Like a cheap novel that you read in one day flat. How's Sam? Are you guys even talking now?"

I frown. I had been trying not to think of him tonight because it's Friday night, and I'm sure he's out gallivanting around and in love.

"Sorry. I shouldn't have asked," she says.

"Oh no. It's fine. I'm moving on." I take a deep breath and focus on sounding cool about the whole thing. "We're not talking yet. He left me for her. End of story. I guess we'll talk when he apologizes."

"Hm . . . I couldn't decide, reading your blogs, who was right or wrong about Sam hanging out with Delia. I mean, I can remember you guys together, and he was really into you, and I doubt that he would ever, ever do anything like that, but at the same time, he was really rash and immature in how he handled it and didn't really try to make you feel better. Sort of the stereotypical male ignoramus behavior. But still, I'm surprised he's dating her."

"Yeah. The consensus now seems to be that we both messed up. Royally. But I can't look back. I just have to wish them well, and with my next boyfriend, I'm just going to have to be more trusting." I think for a moment and then mumble, "They're probably good together, even. I don't know."

Becky looks me straight in the eye. "Really? You think so? You know she's friends of friends of mine, right?"

"No," I say, a little startled.

"I don't want to be a gossip, but from what I understand she's just not, uh, the kind of girl for a guy as great as Sam. He's getting a little out of control."

"What?" I say.

"Your blog painted him as being very, well, churchy. Is he?"

"I, uh, thought . . . uh, yeah. He is. Was. What do you mean?"

"I guess there was a crazy party last weekend at Delia and her notorious cousin's place, and all my old college friends were there. All my girlfriends could talk about was Delia's new hot boyfriend, who was really drunk and sort of stumbling around the whole time until he passed out talking to a plant in the corner with his face in the dirt."

"Shhh . . . shh . . . Please don't tell me any more," I say. I'm so sad. Sad for Sam. Sad for myself.

"Right. I understand. And like I said, it's just a rumor. Women, especially some of my friends, feel so competitive with one another. Let's just hope it's not true."

I sit there alternating between righteous indignation that I *knew* it, knew it all along that she was bad news, and overwhelming sadness that Sam is dating someone who will possibly lead him further and further away from God.

"But you know, since we're on the subject, I have a proposition for you. My cousin, Boris, lives in town and right when I met you, I thought you'd be perfect together, but then I found out you were dating Sam so I didn't say anything. Are you ready yet to get back out there, slugger?"

The laugh track on Inie's favorite Sunday night sitcom is driving me from the room. I'm glad I went to Becky's Friday night because the walls of this apartment feel like they're closing in on me, and TV has become a torture device. Am I the only one who's noticed that virtually all sitcoms are nearly indistinguishable from one another except for the city they're set in? It's just the same stereotypical people dealing with the same canned problems.

I go to the kitchen, open a bottle of wine, and pour myself a glass. I think I'll watch the sunset from our roof. One of the good things about living in the heart of San Francisco is virtually everyone has a set of rickety stairs that look like they're out of an old Western and lead up to the roof. Inie, in accordance with her interior design tastes, has furnished our roof with just two folding chairs, one of which is a little wonky and both of which depress me. I take a seat in the good one.

Thank God Becky and I have gotten closer lately because I feel as though I have leprosy. Church today was really difficult. I walked up to Reagan, Daniel, and Bill talking in a circle, and Reagan immediately walked away. Daniel told me not to feel too bad but that Reagan was still really hurt. Plus, I haven't seen any sign of Sam. It bothers me that he only went to church to please me. I thought he wanted to start attending again, and now I can see it was just an attempt to impress me. I suppose he spends his Sundays teaching Delia how to surf now. Or maybe they go Rollerblading or windsurfing or skydiving. Plus, I don't have Sunday evening supper at my parents' house to look forward to. Mom hasn't invited me over since the blog was exposed, and she won't talk to me when I call.

The sun is a great big orange molten mass, and it's staining the clouds bright salmon. It's breathtaking. A real fall sunset. I look out at San Francisco, and even though we don't have much in the way of fall colors, the cool air is crystalline and still and smells faintly of chimney smoke. It's clearly coming on Thanksgiving. A chill suddenly runs through me when I realize that, at the rate I'm going, I probably won't have anywhere to go for Thanksgiving. A soup kitchen? My phone rings. Though I don't recognize the number, I pick it up. At this point, what could it hurt?

"Hey Pumpkin," my dad whispers.

"Hey Dad," I whisper back as a reflex. "Why are we whispering?"

"I'm in my study. I'm calling you from the fax machine. I don't want your mother to hear."

I stay silent. I miss my dad so much. I miss them all so much.

"I was, uh, just going through some pictures here of you when you were little so I thought I'd call and see how you are."

I want to cry. Dad almost never calls me without Mom initiating it. He's just not much of a talker. "I'm fine, Dad. I just miss you guys, and I'm worried about Mom."

He sighs into the phone. "Lily. I tell you, we have to figure something out. I could help you from this end with coordinating, but it has to come from you. A grand gesture of sorts. She's . . . she's . . . I've never seen her this upset, darling."

A lump forms in my throat. "You're right, Dad." I'm such an ingrate. "I'm going to come up with something. I'll call you back in a few days."

"We love you, Honey. She still loves you, no matter what. And we all miss you."

"You too, Dad," I say, as a tear slides down my cheek.

I slide off my Prada pump and slump into my chair. Whew. What a day. I boot up my computer while I give myself a foot massage. I worked a double for Sheila because no one else would volunteer and Charlie had to go home sick. I'll do anything to make her see that I respect her and Traywick's. But I hadn't exactly planned my footwear around a double. I've just been doing my best to look like the height of fashion at work, hoping to earn back some respect.

I haven't checked my e-mail in days, and I'm curious what's happening with the Fashion Victim blog now that I've apologized. I open up salon.com and see, to my shock, that I'm now, after my longest blog ever, not even ranked in the top ten. In fact, I've slid to number thirty-three.

"Ha." I can't help but laugh out loud. I love it. Now that I've stopped dishing out my innermost unholy thoughts, my blog is not so interesting. Then I look to see who's been checking it. I notice there is just one hit from Earle on the day I posted my apology and nothing since then. Hmph. I hope thanks to my story he attracted some big advertisers who think that now his paper is an ideal place to advertise their tampons and skin cleansers.

And then I tackle the e-mail. I send most people my standard e-mail that says, *Hi, thanks for your interest. Unfortunately the Fashion Victim just can't respond to all mail personally.*" Then I look for addresses I recognize or interesting subject lines. I have one from Gran, telling me how proud of me she is for posting an apology and inviting me to stop by whenever and check out the mosaics she's now doing out of *exotic dried pasta*, as my *punishment—because you're just too cute to punish.* I have an e-mail from Maggie, Alex, and Bill that says they talked about it, and they've decided that as my punishment I have to sign up for the church work day they're organizing, and then all will be forgiven. Their e-mail is very good-natured, and I write back with an emphatic, *Sign me up.* I chuckle to myself, glad that some people are taking me up on my offer to make it up to them. It feels good to be able to do something other than recite hollow-sounding apologies again and again. And then I see another address I recognize.

Eggplantlegs,

    I have decided, as your punishment, that you will be my maid for the day. ;o) Let me know when you're available!

    Looking forward to seeing you again as always,

                                    Delia St. Marks

• Chapter 18 •

It's seven a.m. What do I have to be thankful for?

At least I'm not shivering on the streets of New York just to see a giant Bart Simpson balloon sail by. I flip the TV off. The Thanksgiving parade's so overrated. The scarves, the floats, the stars, the lip synching, the . . . joy. Okay. So I'm jealous. So what? I'm staring down a tough day here.

I look around to make sure I have everything. Dad will be picking me up any minute. The hardest part will be getting the defrosted, and therefore slimy, twenty-pound turkey down the stairs. I look out the window. In the rain, no less. New York gets snowflakes and ice-skating in the winter, and we get rain, torrential rain, spitting rain, and all-day rain. This is shaping up to be my worst Thanksgiving yet. And that's counting the time I choked on a turkey bone and was rushed to the hospital.

I rustle through the grocery bags to make sure I packed the cinnamon. The hardest part will be stuffing the turkey. I have never cooked a bird of any kind before, and I'm not looking forward to reaching inside its chest cavity to pull out giblets. Let me repeat. Chest. Cavity. Pull out. Giblets. *Giblets.*

I need to relax. I plop down on the couch. No, no. Certainly the hardest part will be walking in the front door.

I can't believe I'm going to do this. I don't know how to cook

Thanksgiving dinner. I don't even know how to cook spaghetti. Gran has always cooked the big meal, but this year she is in Florida spending the holiday with her sister Ruth, whose husband died in March. When Dad e-mailed me that Mom was planning to order takeout instead of cooking the traditional meal, I knew what I had to do. Mom may not want to see me, but there's no way she'll be able to turn down a dish of Gran's famous corn pudding, even if it was made by her least favorite daughter. Even her unborn daughters are more precious to her than me. Her godchildren. Probably even her childhood hamster Elvira Fuzzbucket, God rest her rodent soul. But I have a plan. There's no way Mom will be up when I get there to start cooking at the crack of dawn, and she can't throw me out once I've started messing up the kitchen. The cleaning lady won't come until Monday to tidy it up. I just need to prepare myself for her venom. I shudder.

I hear a horn honk and look out my window. I wave to Dad, pick up my bags, heft the turkey into my arms, and kick open the door. Here goes.

"Lily, did you add more butter than the recipe calls for?" Mom asks, blowing on a minuscule forkful of mashed potatoes.

I look at my mother, sitting smugly across the dark dining table in her black sweater with the giant Audrey Hepburn turtleneck. While it is good to see her indulging in carbs a little, I don't know what she's really asking. *Did I try to do it my own way? Was I rebelling against the recipe I had grown up with because I didn't think Gran's mashed potatoes were good enough for me?*

She had been surprised to see me, to say the very least, this morning when she came out of her bedroom. She had that must-find-coffee look in her eyes that immediately contorted to a face I can only describe as shock and horror. I was in the middle of making the stuffing. We stared at each other, and I waited for her to say something. I even did one of those loud gulps like you hear in the movies, but she simply went back into her room without a word. Forty-five minutes passed in agony, as I wrestled with various ingredients and hand-scrawled recipes, and then she came out and said hello and asked what I was making, as if we hadn't run into one another earlier that very morning. *Pumpkin pie*, I replied, and asked whether she would like an apple pie as well. *No*, she quietly replied. *No, thank you.* Dad stood by uncomfortably during this whole exchange, ready to break us apart if any hair pulling or high-pitched screaming started, but Mom just nodded and said, *The allspice is in the back of the pantry.* I nodded. And with that she walked out of the kitchen.

She had been cool but civil all day. Even if she hadn't said more than twenty words to me, at least they were all polite. I had begun to think that maybe I wouldn't be kicked out of the family after all. But what was this barbed mashed potato comment all about?

"Maybe a little more butter," I say.

She nods, taking a bite.

Dad looks around, bewildered. "Wow, these are mighty good potatoes, Lily," he says, raising his eyebrows and laughing uncomfortably.

Mom ignores him. "I thought so." She pauses, picking up another forkful. "I always thought they needed more butter." I look up at her. She meets my eye and smiles. I look down slowly. "I never knew you could cook, Lily. You never did it while you lived here."

"Yeah, well, Gran was always cooking, and . . ." I mumble, looking down at my plate. "I guess I never really had any real reason to."

"We should have let you cook Thanksgiving years ago. Your Gran could have relaxed and enjoyed the day off," she says.

"You know Gran would never have let me in her kitchen if she were here," I say, smiling.

"That's right! No one else allowed in the kitchen!" Dad says, smiling nervously. "Heh heh."

"Well, you did all right," she says, smiling at me.

"So, you don't mind that I made Thanksgiving dinner?" And, um, attended Thanksgiving without being invited, I add in my head. I look at Mom hopefully.

Dad looks at Mom hopefully.

"I was looking forward to mu shu pork," she says. "But other than that, no. I don't mind." She takes a sip of wine. "Thank you, Lily."

"To Lily!" Dad says very relieved, lifting his glass. I look at him as if he has lost his mind. Out of the corner of my eye I see Mom doing the same. Dad looks around, noticing he is the only one with a raised glass. Heroically, he keeps his arm in the air. "And to the Traywicks, together again," he adds.

"To the Traywicks," I say. I look at Mom.

"To the Traywicks." Mom says, winking at me. "All of us."

"I'll take care of the dishes, Mom. Why don't you go sit down with Dad," I say, gathering up handfuls of silverware.

"I'd like to help," she says, placing her plate and Dad's plate on top of mine and lifting up the stack.

"You've never washed dishes in your life," I say, narrowing my eyes at her.

"That's not true. I've washed far too many dishes in my life, so I try to avoid it whenever I can now," she says. "Never washed dishes in my life . . ." she mumbles, shaking her head.

We settle in at the sink, me washing, her drying. We have a dishwasher, but of course we have to use the silver and china for holidays, and they're not dishwasher-safe. We stand in silence, each lost in our own thoughts.

"So am I out of the doghouse?" I ask.

"You were never in the doghouse, Lily." Mom's quick answer makes me think this topic does not come out of left field for her. She wipes a plate dry and places it on the stack. "It's never fun to hear bad things about yourself. Particularly when you hear them because they have been published in the local paper." She lays down her towel. "But you know what? You didn't write anything that wasn't true. You were writing what you felt. And though I was hurt at first, seeing you here this morning . . . I saw you in a new light." She looks at me. "I finally knew what you were thinking, maybe for the first time. Sometimes, as you were growing up, I wondered if there had been a mix-up at the hospital. I just couldn't understand you at all. And you haven't exactly been open about things. I finally got to see inside your head. And, well, that made it . . . if not worth it, then much better. To have the chance to get to know my daughter better. I guess that's worth more than just about anything."

I look at her, speechless. She looks like she is about to cry. I feel tears well up, but I push them down. I can't let her see.

"Mom?" She looks up, and we're both a little weepy. "Thank you."

Delia,

My fingers hover over the keyboard. I take a deep breath. I try to think of my anger as a little red triangle or something like that. I try not to picture her with a little devil tail poking out from beneath her skirt. I try not to dream of her falling down the stairs in a very public place. I'm just going to do what Becky and I talked about.

Sure! Love to make it up to you! How about this weekend?

I have to pause a moment. The love part is a total lie. I sense my dead grandmother Frances rolling over in her grave. I hope Delia interprets all those passive-aggressive exclamation points as I intend them: miniature daggers.

Love,
Eggplantlegs

Ha ha! I'm so clever. I'll just reclaim that word so that she can't use it on me and have power over me. Oh no wait. Better idea. I delete it.

EGGPLANTLEGS

Mmmm . . . perfect. No missing the subtlety there. I reread my perfect little e-mail bomb to Delia and am very pleased. When I told Becky about Delia's suggestion that I be her maid for the day, I spent at least fifteen minutes on the phone dissecting how ugly Delia is and how Sam is an utter fool for leaving me for her. Finally Becky made me snap out of it by singing that song "They Will Know We Are Christians by Our Love" in a very sappy voice. When I demanded to know where she'd learned it, she confessed her grandmother used to sing it to her as a lullaby. I had to go through with it.

I hit send on the e-mail. I hope you're happy, God. I really do.

The broad smooth surface of the hibachi grill wraps around in a U shape, and Boris and I sit at the head of the U at a wooden table, watching the expert Japanese chef cook our meal right in front of us. He squirts oil on Boris's lamb, igniting the meat, and I gasp as he deftly flips and chops the meat, showing off his skill. Despite my lifelong fear of fire, especially fire near my face, I can't help but laugh. Boris has ordered some kind of blue drink, and mine is some pink fruity concoction, which I suck slowly as I watch my food in flames.

Boris is great. I should have assumed, considering that he's Becky's cousin, but it's still a nice surprise to be out with a man who is articulate and respectful and doesn't bring up the subject of our future children during the appetizer course. Okay, there's more. He's witty and charming and elegant-looking, like Baryshnikov. He brought me half a dozen orchids when he picked me up, he opened my car door for me, he called ahead and made reservations at the restaurant so we didn't have to wait to get seated. He has told me all about emigrating from Russia when he was twelve and the problems of being a teenager in New York City when you don't speak English. I insist that I would never have known. He doesn't have the slightest bit of an accent. He laughs, citing his pure determination not to sound like a foreigner and his hours of watching American television. He has made references to Foucault and Tolstoy without sounding the least bit pretentious. He even made a joke about his name, saying that he couldn't stay out too late because Natasha and Bullwinkle were waiting up for him at home. He's been a dream date.

So why do I keep thinking about how much Sam would have loved this place?

We talk about work—Boris is a fact-checker at a magazine, and though he laughs about the tediousness of it, he manages to make it sound fascinating to verify every detail of a story someone else has written. He seems surprised to hear that I work at Traywick's and even more surprised that my parents own the place. I tell him about my brief gig as a writer, and he laughs uproariously when I tell him how it ended. I'm almost able to laugh about it. Almost.

"So why aren't you looking into more jobs writing?" he asks, taking a sip of his fluorescent drink. "That's obviously what you want to be doing."

"Since I was outed, things have been pretty crazy for me, and I've mostly been trying to hide out and get my life back until the whole thing blows over," I say.

"But now's the time to do it, while people are thinking about you and before you get too comfortable with your life again," he says.

"Maybe," I say, picking up my glass. "I guess I'm also just not sure where to get started, and the idea of trying to find out just seems too overwhelming." I take a sip of my drink. "I can't just call up the *Chronicle* and ask them to give me a column."

"I bet I could help," he says, looking across the table to where the chef is lighting two bananas on fire for our dessert. I didn't have the heart to tell him about my banana phobia. "I have to call over there sometimes for information for my stories. I'll write down the contact information for the people I know." He smiles, shyly showing his slightly crooked teeth. My eyes widen.

"Would you? That would be great." My heart beats faster. He could help me get a real job. He is encouraging me to pursue my dreams. He is perfect.

So why does a small part of me wish it weren't him?

Maybe I'll get over it, I tell myself as Boris pays the check and walks me to his car. What was that thing Sally Jesse Raphael said? To really be over a man, half the amount of time you dated has to have passed. So Sam and I dated several months, and it's been, gulp, several weeks. Great. Who trusts that bimbo anyway because I *am* over Sam. Sam was practically cheating on me with a little blond girl! I'm sure the next time I go out with Boris, I won't think about Sam the whole time. Boris is so much fun and very sexy. Of course our next date will go even better.

We talk about our childhoods as he drives me home. My pink-canopied luxury seems a world away from Boris's crowded apartment in St. Petersburg. He makes his world come alive and makes me laugh.

When we get to my apartment building, Boris parks his car and writes down the names and phone numbers of his friends at the *Chronicle* before walking me up the stairs. Surely he can't be trying to come inside, I think, but he stops at my door and plants a gentlemanly kiss on my cheek. I grin big and goofily. God Bless little Becky Nesterenko.

"I had a great time tonight," he says, smiling.

"Me too," I say. I cue myself to smile. I look into his dark brown eyes and wait.

"So is this going to work out?" he asks. He gives me a very confident grin.

I open my mouth to say, Yes, yes, a thousand times yes, but then my head spins. This guy is so great. Of course I want this to work out. And yet . . . Couldn't he have shot me an e-mail? I can't date him. I'm not even supposed to be here. I'm supposed to be strolling down Polk

Street arm in arm with Sam. This charade has gone on long enough. I open my mouth again to say, No, I'm sorry.

But then I stop myself. What am I doing? Boris is wonderful. Perfect. And since I'm totally over Sam, I should have no problem saying yes.

But . . . why did he have to ask that question? Why couldn't he have asked if I wanted to go out again? Or if I liked him as much as he liked me? Why did he have to ask anything at all? Why's he asking about our ultimate destiny?

Sam's face pops into my head, and I can't do it. I start crying. Boris watches uncomfortably. I look at him, and manage to squeak out "I'm sorry" before I fling open the door and run inside, closing it sharply behind me. I lean against the inside of the door, panting, and wait several uncomfortable minutes before I hear him walking back down the stairs.

I haven't been taking my afternoon breaks since I've been trying to prove to Sheila how hard I work (and because I figure the less I leave this department the less likely I am to run into anyone who wants to kill me), but today my thoughts are so jumbled that not even doing mind-numbing tasks has helped me clear my head. Today I know only one thing will help—vanilla soft serve. With chocolate sprinkles. And maybe peanuts.

I walk to the cafeteria, trying to avoid making eye contact with anyone.

Boris was right. I need to get out of this job and into doing what I care about. I'll call his contacts when I get home. I'll tell them I'm a friend of Boris's and he suggested I get in touch with them, but I'll leave out the part about me losing my mind and slamming the door in his face. Oh Boris. I'm sorry. I remind myself to call Becky and grovel.

"Just one?" the waiter asks as I slide into the booth Reagan and I always used. I nod and order my yogurt. He places a napkin and a spoon in front of me and walks to the kitchen.

Why did Boris have to ask anything at all? I would have gone out on at least one more date with him . . .

The waiter places my cup of yogurt down next to the irritating little slip of nutritional information. I pick up my spoon and start to dig in.

"Mind if I sit here?" I look up and see a ripped hot pink sweatshirt with Madonna's face imprinted in black and white. Reagan. My mouth hangs open. Why is she here?

"Have a seat," I say gesturing to the empty bench across from me. "Be careful, though. I have rabies."

She shrugs off my comment and then slides in and places her white patent leather purse down next to her. She signals to the waiter, who brings her a cup of vanilla and her slip.

"How are you doing?" she asks.

"Recovering," I say.

She nods. "I'm sorry I yelled at you."

I look down at my frozen yogurt. "I'm sorry I said those awful things about you. I can't believe you're even talking to me."

"Part of me can't believe it either," she says, taking a bite. "But I miss you. And one of us has to take the first step, so here I am."

"I'm glad. Does this mean you forgive me?"

"I'm not totally sure about that," she says, picking up my nutrition information sheet. "But I'm working on the whole forgiveness thing." She takes a bite. "Do you know the first ingredient in those peanuts is 'partially defatted peanuts'?"

"It doesn't really say that, does it?" I grab for the sheet, and Reagan points out where it does, in fact, list partially defatted peanuts as an ingredient. "What does that mean?"

"I have no idea. You're the one who always eats them."

I smile, looking down at my cup. I swallow a big bite and then get up my courage to keep talking to her about the hard stuff. "Are you really on probation?"

"Yeah," she says, looking away. "But I'm on my best behavior now. Not just for the job, though of course that's part of it. We actually just had a departmental meeting. Despite what your father referred to as 'a series of unexplained merchandise losses,' European Fashions had a banner year, so they're all excited about that. And your mom called me into her office last week and told me that they thought I had great potential and wanted to keep me around, but if there were any more thefts I would be the number-one suspect. Which, when I think about it, is more than fair." She sighs.

"How are things with Daniel?"

"They're really good," she says, smiling guiltily. "He's been so supportive through this whole thing. He obviously wasn't very happy about the whole discount thing, but he's really encouraging me."

"That's great, Reagan. Really."

"And how are things in the guy department for you?" she asks. "Any more dates?" I launch into my tale about last night's ill-fated date with Boris, which makes her laugh. "I can't believe you slammed the door in his face. I mean, I believe you did it, this is you we're talking about, but still." She takes a deep breath. "His name was really Boris?" she asks, grimacing.

I nod. "He grew up in St. Petersburg."

"Een Russia," she says in her best Eastern European accent, "zere eez no door slamming. And zee veemen, zey no act crazy," she says, nodding seriously, putting her napkin over her head like a babushka. "Also, een Russia, vee no have zeez partially defatted peanuts," she says, shaking her head. "Een Russia, zee peanuts partially defat you!"

I stare at her for a second, then lose it. I laugh until I turn red in the face.

Lisa,

I would love to let you come be my personal servant this weekend but sadly, Sam rented us a charming bungalow in Napa! With an in-room Jacuzzi! Can't wait! Très romantique!

But never fear. I've always got time for you! I'll just pencil you in for the following Saturday. See you then.

Big Kisses,
Delia St. Marks

"Lily? Is that you?"

"Mnmhjgh . . ." I sit up in bed. I should know better than to answer my phone in the middle of the night. No one calls at this hour for anything good. "Hello?"

"Lily? This is Janice Harold . . . Stephanie's mom?"

"Oh, hi Mrs. Harold," I say. Why is she calling? Has Steph enlisted her to chew me out too?

"I'm sorry to call so late. I was just hoping . . . Steph didn't show up for a class this afternoon and her roommate called to let me know she hasn't seen her all day. It's not like her to not tell anybody where she is going, so I just . . . I wondered if you had any idea where she might be." My stomach drops. "We're trying not to get too concerned at this point, but we also don't want to lose any time in case . . . Well, we just hope someone knows where she is. Do you have any idea?"

"No," I say, shaking my head. "No, I don't. How long has she been gone? Who saw her last?"

"We're still trying to figure all of that out. You haven't heard from her?"

"I haven't heard from her in days," I say. I wonder how much Steph has told her mom. "I can't think where she might be."

"We'll find her. I'm so sorry to wake you. You'll call if you hear anything?"

"Of course," I say, staring numbly at my comforter. "Of course I will."

I stay sitting up in bed for a while, thinking about Steph. Where could she be? What have I done?

• Chapter 19 •

I look at the clock. Three a.m. Why can't I be one of those people who believe no news is good news? I'm worried sick about Steph. I mean, she probably just forgot to tell her roommate she had to work the late shift at the hospital. Or maybe she bumped into a handsome stranger and they decided to get a late dinner and, oh who am I kidding? This is Stephanie Anne Harold. The college student who never, not even once, missed a single class. She's hardly a risk taker.

I get up and go to my computer. Might as well do something productive with myself as long as I'm not going to sleep. I check my regular e-mail account. There's a message from Becky. I click on her message. I had written her a groveling "sorry I slammed the door on your cousin" e-mail yesterday, and Becky writes back to say it's no big deal and that she understands. She even apologizes for encouraging me to date again when I clearly wasn't ready. She's the best.

There's also one from Boris, who I had sent an I'm Sorry I Freaked Out on You e-mail a few days ago. Boris wishes me luck and encourages me to contact the *Chronicle*.

I decide to write an e-mail to Steph.

Steph,

    I know you're not speaking to me, and I really don't blame you, but your mom called tonight and said they can't find you anywhere. I just wanted to say, I'm up at three in the morning, worrying about you. You've always been the best friend anyone could ever hope for. If you get this, and you're fine, could you drop me an e-mail? You don't ever have to talk to me again, but I really need to know you're all right. I don't like thinking of a world without Stephanie Harold. It gives me the chills.

And I miss you, for what it's worth.

Love,
Lily

Out of habit, I check my Fashion Victim e-mail account. There's nothing. I mean, sure, since the apology blog I haven't written any new postings—where in the world would I go from that conflagration—but wow, my "fans" disappeared so quickly. Poof.

For the next hour, I reread old Fashion Victim blogs and marvel at how much I've changed. I cringe at my treatment of Sam. Looking back, I can see that this guy was quite clearly taken with me, and I blew it. A lot of my rants make me sound like some unstable woman named Velma on a bad TV talk show. Oh man. I sigh. Lesson learned, I guess.

How did I get so wrapped up in pouring my heart out in my blog, pouring it out to complete strangers, that I let my guard fall? I can't believe some of the things I wrote about people I loved. How could I have been so naïve? And so *mean*? Plus, it's not like "sharing" my innermost thoughts with my computer was healthy. I'm not going to beat myself up here, that's what the last few weeks have been all about, but hanging out with Becky and telling her how I feel is much better than getting to know the blogosphere.

And then it hits me, I may not be fully over Sam yet, but I'm over the Fashion Victim blog. I click around on Salon and relinquish my domain name. Someone else can be the victim now.

———————

I hate the way hospitals smell. I sit in the reception area with a handmade Get Well Soon card and a plant, trying not to freak out for Stephanie's sake. She needs me right now, after all, but if I'm honest, I'm on the verge of tears. I swallow the lump in my throat.

I finally fell asleep last night at four in the morning. At six this morning, Stephanie's mother called from the hospital. Steph had collapsed yesterday afternoon on her shift. The hospital had been trying to reach her mother, but they had an old phone number. They finally got the right number this morning and called. Steph had been admitted for exhaustion and, at this Steph's mother took a deep breath, anorexia. The blood work they ran on Steph showed she was greatly malnourished, but when they started asking questions about what she had eaten that day, that week, Steph lied and lied. Still suspicious, they had a specialist examine her for other signs of anorexia. Sure enough, the enamel on her teeth was deteriorating, her bone density was in a dangerous place, and her hair appeared to be falling out. Finally they had her favorite professor come and have a heart to heart with her. Mrs. Harold was in tears at this point on the phone. Steph finally cracked and admitted that she knew she had a problem because even now, she felt too fat.

"Would you come to the hospital, Lily?" she asked.

I briefly wondered if Steph had ever mentioned to her mother that she wasn't talking to me. "Of course, I will. I'll be there in about an hour," I said. I called my mom and explained the situation, and she said she'd tell Sheila I wouldn't be in today. I made a quick card on my computer, stopped by the florist, and headed over.

I knock on the door. How is anyone supposed to get better in a place that smells like disinfectant and mushy peas?

"Come in." It's Steph's voice, if a little weak.

I hope this is a good idea. Will she want to see me? Will she think I came here to rub it in? I swallow hard. "Hey there," I say.

She looks surprised to see me, and then she looks down at her lap. "Hi Lily."

There is an awkward moment. I set her plant down and bring the card I made over to her.

She smiles at me weakly.

"How are you holding up?" I ask.

"From a medical standpoint? Or actually?"

"Both."

"Medically, I'm not so bad off." She grimaces, then says robotically, "If the patient is put on a rigorous routine of counseling and nutrition and is supported by loved ones, the chance of complete recovery is quite high."

I nod. "I see that fancy education is paying off, Dr. Stephanie Harold."

She laughs. "Yep. And lucky for me, I was already in the hospital when I fainted, so I didn't have to go anywhere. And the people here know me, and, I think, had suspected for a while that something was wrong. People have made comments about me being too thin. So I'm in good hands."

"And how are you actually doing?"

"Actually?" She looks up at me and crumbles into tears. "I'm . . . so . . . embarrassed."

I hold her gently in my arms. "Why? Why? Shh, shh. There's no need to be embarrassed."

Through her sobs she says, "It's still hard to admit that I have a problem. My first impulse is to deny it. And I feel like I've let everyone down, and I'm going to have to take at least a semester off med school, probably a year, and I can't go to Honduras now, and I've been just awful to you and everyone else."

"Steph? Hey. I don't think you were awful. That wasn't you, that was that nasty old anorexia talking. Not you! You're the best friend I've got. And no one is at all disappointed in you. In fact, of all my friends, you're the most successful one I've got."

"Not anymore."

"Bah. You must be kidding me. I don't know anyone that could be as mature as you are going through something as hard as this. You're doing great. The doctor said you ate some eggs this morning and even had your mother bring you a doughnut."

She smiles. "I'm not going to lie. It was really hard to eat that doughnut. My mind keeps saying, Stop, stop. But thank goodness I've studied this disease enough in class that at least some small part in my brain knows that that's just nonsense."

I smile. I'm so impressed with her. "Yeah. *Stephanie* and *fat* just aren't allowed in the same sentence right now, nor were they ever. You're so beautiful. I've always been jealous of you. How many marriage proposals have you gotten in your lifetime?"

She laughs. "Only three."

I roll my eyes at her. "I'm still looking at zero. Plus, I'm stone cold single again, so it's not like I'm getting one anytime soon. But you. You're like the pied piper of men."

I hang out in her room for an hour, and we catch up on everything that's happened in each other's lives since that night at Ristorante Milano. It's so good to have her back. Eventually a nurse comes in and kicks me out, saying it's important for Stephanie to get some rest now. I tuck her in and give her a kiss on the forehead.

"Rest up, kiddo. I've missed you enough already. When you get out of here, we're going to start hanging out again. You won't be able to get me out of your hair."

She smiles. "Thanks, Lily. I'm not sure if I ever said it, but thanks, for everything. All along."

Dignity. People throw that word around saying it's important to maintain, blah, blah, blah. I see what they mean now as I am literally in

Delia's bathroom about to swoon from bleach fumes, scrubbing her bathtub with the nauseating red lip decals she has stuck to the bottom of it.

I discussed my plan of attack with Steph, and we decided that I should just focus on one of two pictures when I'm about to lose it and lob a sponge at Delia: either the image of Christ washing the feet of his disciples (even Judas) or that of myself, on a beach in the Caribbean, sun-bathing, drinking a piña colada that a hot cabana boy brought me. I came up with the second one when Steph kept suggesting that I would have to go to my "happy place" in my mind. I pause and try to feel the sun on my face.

"What are you doing?"

I look up and see Delia's perfect little head cocked to the side and realize I'm on my hands and knees in her tub with my eyes shut. "Uh, the fumes are hurting my eyes a little."

"You'll be fine. So when you have a moment, I'd like you to go to the kitchen and make me a cup of mulled cider. It's a bit cold outside today, but I'm just in the Christmas spirit, so I'll be reading on my roof, wrapped in a blanket. Just bring up the cider when it's nice and hot."

Christmas spirit! Is this her "Christmas spirit"? Remind me to duck for cover on Halloween. My anger at her is building. I try to calm down. Jesus washing feet. Jesus washing feet. Cabana boy, cabana boy. "Yes ma'am. You've got it ma'am." I try to keep my tone light. It's two-thirty. This ridiculous gesture will be over soon.

"Good then." She turns to leave and then spins back around and sits on the toilet lid for a moment. "Napa was so great, by the way. Sam's such a charmer, but then, I guess you know that." She laughs.

I take a deep breath and try to remember how many years one goes to jail for scrubbing the expression off someone's face with a Brillo pad. "Hmm, yeah."

She laughs again, and finally leaves, and I am left in the tub, trying to go to my happy place with tears stinging my eyes. I'm the private joke of their relationship. What was I thinking when I fell for that creep?

I shut off the vacuum because I think I hear the kettle whistling. Instead, it's the doorbell. I'm the butler too, woo hoo. I walk toward the door and reach for the knob to let Delia's guest in, when I do hear the kettle whistling in the kitchen. I'm briefly concerned about my appearance—hair in a sloppy bun, bleach-stained, beat-up old boxer shorts, long yellow rubber gloves on so that I can't contract any of Delia's evilness from her personal effects—but then I realize, what do I care? I swing it open and say "Come in" to a face I barely even glance at as I run to the kitchen for the boiling kettle, but halfway there I stop cold in my tracks. No. Not today.

"Lily? Wha, what are you doing here?" Sam asks.

"I, uh—"

"Where's Delia?" he says, looking around. He looks at me as if I'm some sort of crazy stalker. I open my mouth to explain when I hear Delia clomping down the stairs from the roof.

She flings open the door and runs to give Sam a kiss. "I missed you!" she says, wrapping him in her arms.

I look at Sam and then Delia. Sam is smiling at her, a slightly confused look on his face. I walk into the kitchen, pull the kettle off the stove, turn the stove off, and take my purse from the kitchen counter. This is too much. She orchestrated all of this so that I could witness her and Sam together.

"Sam, Delia, lovely to see you both, as always. I'll just get out of your hair." At that I walk out her front door, elbow-length rubber gloves and all, proud of myself.

I rub my palms together and then crack every knuckle in my fingers. Okay, now, I'm ready to begin. For the next hour I compose and recompose an e-mail to the contacts at the *Chronicle* Boris gave me. I decide to send the same e-mail to all three people separately. Each time, I make sure to double-check that I have remembered to include my writing sample and my résumé. Then I turn on some Bon Jovi Reagan gave me and dance around.

I hear a knock at my door and then Inie opens it. "I *love* these guys." She grabs the hairbrush off my desk and proceeds to sing into it, "Whoa-oh! Living on a prayer!" I grab a pencil and join in with her. Then we jump up and down on my bed.

"What are we so happy about?" she asks.

I stop bouncing. "I don't know. Life, I guess." I start bouncing again.

"Want to know what I'm so happy about?"

"Sure!" I headbang a little.

"I have a date this weekend."

"That's so great!"

I turn down the music and talk to Inie until she runs off to get the phone, worried it might be Cliff, her hot date. I lie back on my bed, beaming. Life is really turning around for me. I e-mailed the *Chronicle*, Steph's doing better, there's a Tacky Christmas Extravaganza at Super Single Sunday next week, no one's really mad at me anymore—except possibly Alex, who says she has forgiven me but still gives me weird looks at church and keeps her distance—and Gran and I are going Christmas tree shopping soon. Plus the annual Traywick's Christmas Gala is coming up, and even Mom and I are doing well.

I think of all the years we've fought and misunderstood each other and how much closer we've grown recently. Can I really risk all that by leaving the store for a writing job? I think I know how my parents would take that. And if I had to choose, I'd much rather be a part of my family and Traywick's than not. I got a little taste of having no family during the Fashion Victim fiasco, and I'm not going back there again. Maybe I could do both? Maybe I could just write little quirky features now and then for the *Chronicle* and still run Traywick's? Or maybe I could write about fashion and run Traywick's? I mean, it's never really appealed to me before, but I've also never given it a try. It might be fun.

I think about this for a while and sigh. I don't want to write about fashion. In fact, all I want to do is write. But at the same time, I want to be a Traywick. I want to be a part of my family. I want my parents to be able to count on me.

Chapter 20

"Lily?" I look up quickly. It's early and still really quiet, and I have been drawing a Nativity scene where all the characters are wearing spacesuits on a receipt. Oh good. It's not Sheila. It's . . . it's some weird guy who is looking at me like I am supposed to know who he is. His short hair is dark, but his skin is eerily pale and his eyes are bloodshot.

"Can I help you?" I squint. He is sort of attractive, despite the worn-out look in his gaze.

"Lily?" he says, staring at me. "It's me. Sam."

I open my mouth in shock. It is him. How could he . . . what is he . . . why does he . . . "What happened to you?" I say, then instinctually cover my mouth with my hand. He looks like a broken man. A broken man with short hair.

"The hair?" he says, his lips curling up slightly. "Delia cut it. About a week ago."

"Why?" Is she a barber now too? The barber of Eville?

"It was getting too long, and . . . I don't know. She wanted it like it was in college . . . I don't know. It was a symbol of . . . Whatever. It doesn't matter." He tries to smile, but his eyes still look lifeless.

"Sam?" I ask, staring into his eyes, looking for a hint of the man I knew. "Are you okay?" He sighs and takes a deep breath. He looks down at the counter.

"I'm fine," he says. He licks his lips. "Totally fine unless you count the fact that I was arrested on Saturday night."

"What? What happened?"

"It was just a party. There were some people doing drugs and stuff. I wasn't doing anything, but when the cops came everyone freaked out. Deals and I didn't get out in time because things were getting crazy and people were running everywhere. Finally they just arrested everyone who was left."

"But if you weren't doing anything, how could they arrest you?"

"Delia was. She had a bag of marijuana, and she put it in my pocket when the cops came."

"She didn't. Oh, Sam, I'm—"

"It's fine. Since it was my first time being arrested for real, the cop let me off with just some community service, not reporting the pot part. Just a drunk and disorderly." He looks up at me, meets my eyes, then quickly looks down. "But I'm done with Delia."

Cue the hallelujah chorus. There is a God. And yet . . . my mind races.

"The whole thing was weird. From the day she moved to San Francisco. Like, she invited me to this cabin for the weekend with her family, but then when we got there it was just us in this little romantic room with only one bed, and she was telling everybody it was my idea. And she started introducing me as her boyfriend, and I didn't know how to tell her we were just friends." I shoot him a look that says, Oh come on! "Lily, whatever. I mean, maybe not like, just friends, but certainly not boyfriend-girlfriend either. She was . . . I don't know," he says, shaking his head. "It was starting to scare me. I just wanted to hang out with an old friend, but she apparently wanted a whole lot more. And then she set me up . . ." He breaks off and looks in my eyes. "I saw what an ugly person she can be, and how low she was dragging me, and it scared me." He looks away. "I realized that's not what I want."

I feel like I should be excited, but I don't actually think I'm happy about this, deep down. When it comes down to it, it's just sad.

"I'm sorry," I say, and I really mean it. I'm sorry for him and for who he has become.

"I'm fine," he says, shaking his head. "I'm fine. That's not why I came in here." He lifts a wrapped package onto the counter. "I brought you this."

"What is it?" I ask, touching the shiny silver paper.

"I had the gift-wrap department do it for me," he says, laughing nervously.

I slide my finger under a flap and rip the tape. Carefully, I unwrap it and slide the box out of the paper. "A Chia pet?"

He grins shyly.

"Wow. Uh, thanks," I say, laughing.

"I figured even *you* can keep this alive."

I turn the box over. "It takes three to five days for the seeds to sprout? The commercials always made it looks much faster."

"Don't believe everything you see," he says. "That's the lesson of the day." He nods. "I was going to get you the Clapper too, but clapping to turn your lights on and off just seems way too lazy." He is trying to joke, but it falls flat. His voice is too full of pain.

"Agreed. And this is . . . Well, this is something. Um, thanks."

"Maybe next Christmas I'll get you a George Foreman grill or a Magic Duster." He laughs softly, turning to leave.

"Sam?"

He turns back slowly.

"Merry Christmas."

He smiles at me, then walks away.

"*H*e gave you a what?" Reagan asks, her perfectly groomed eyebrows arched. She puts down her spoon. The café is mobbed thanks to the holiday rush, and I'm in a hurry. I couldn't find Tricia to tell her I'm on break, so I need to get right back to my station. The Silver Spoon is now a madhouse, but I needed some advice.

"A Chia Pet. You know, Ch-ch-ch Chia!" She laughs when I sing the jingle from the commercial. "I know. It's weird, right?"

"Hm," she says, taking a bit of frozen yogurt. It's peppermint, which they only make for the holidays, and which they shouldn't make ever. It's disgusting, but Reagan loves it. "This could mean one of two things."

"And they are?" I ask, looking skeptically at her.

"Either he actually likes terra-cotta animal shapes that grow grass 'hair,'" she says, shuddering at the thought of the Chia Pet, "or he wanted an excuse to talk to you."

"Hardly. He said it was so simple even *I* could handle it."

"You do have a particularly hard time keeping plants alive," she says, nodding. "But really. Why else would he bother?"

"He broke up with Delia."

"What?" A blond woman in a floor-length fur turns, but no one else seems to even hear Reagan's outburst.

"Yeah. I guess things went bad."

"Hm," she says. "Well, that's a new development." She mulls it over. "But good for you. And it seems he's not as over you as he thought. That's what this gift proves."

"It was just a dumb present."

"I don't know," she says, shrugging. "But speaking of gifts, I got you a Christmas present," Reagan says, pulling a small parcel out of her purse.

"Reagan," I whine. "We said we were taking each other out to eat for Christmas."

"We're still doing that. This doesn't count. I didn't spend a single penny on it." I sigh and shoot her a look.

"Thanks," I say and start unwrapping the box. "Where in the world did you find Snorks wrapping paper?"

"EBay," she says. "My seller threw it in after I bought a whole collection of Strawberry Shortcake dolls."

"Of course," I say, shaking my head.

She shrugs.

I open the box and see a picture frame inside. I gasp, putting the lid back on the box quickly. "Reagan!"

She's cracking up. "I thought you might need a visual."

I pull up the box lid again and try to look at the picture frame, which is only half the problem. The frame itself is an awful pink plastic frame that Reagan has decorated with rhinestones and written all over in paint pens of varying fluorescent colors. It says "Rest in Peace. The Old Lily" across the top. But the picture inside is, well, frightening. It's a newspaper clipping of *the* picture of me. The one the *Chronicle* ran that started my entire makeover process. I stare at it in shock. I look awful, and what's more, I look like a little scared mouse.

I lift the picture out of the box and show it to her. "I really can't believe this is me."

"Me neither," she says, laughing.

We both dissolve into hysterical laughter. "No wonder I never had a date," I say at last.

Reagan shrugs. "I always knew you had a glamorous girl hidden somewhere in there."

"Did I ever say thanks for helping me out?" I ask.

"I don't know." She cocks her head to the side, thinking. "Hmm . . . well, thanks. For everything this year."

"Whatever. Merry Christmas," Reagan says, laughing.

"Lily?" I hear a voice from above and look up.

"Oh, hey. Mom," I say, startled. With all her jet-setting to Paris and Hong Kong, I don't actually bump into her at work all that often.

"What are you two doing?" she asks.

Reagan stands up and says, "We were just leaving."

"Reagan, yes. Please report back to work. Break's over. Lily, please follow me to my office. Tricia told me you disappeared from your shift."

I gulp. I really can't catch a break.

My mother closes her office door behind me with a firm snap.

I sit uneasily in the chair across from her Art Deco wooden desk, and she sits across from me.

"I'm afraid I have some bad news for you, Ms. Traywick," she says.

Why is my mom calling me by my last name? Our last name? I try to prepare myself for a long discussion about how much I've failed her at Traywick's. Why did I take that stupid, unauthorized little break?

"While you have been doing a fine job in Silver Spoon, I'm afraid that your position has been eliminated."

"What?" I stammer. And then it hits me. I'm getting moved to a new department. I quickly pray it's not Women's Footwear. She wouldn't be that cruel, would she? "Uh, where do you want me to work then?"

She clears her throat. "I'm sorry. I'm afraid you don't seem to understand. You're being let go."

"What!" I say, loudly.

"You're fired," she says.

Is she serious? "Is this a joke?" I ask. I thought things were so much better between the two of us.

"I'm afraid not. We'll need you to work through Christmas, and then you'll be dismissed at the New Year. There will be a severance package, of course."

I stare at her hard. She doesn't smile, she doesn't turn away from my stare, she just sits there calm as ever. This woman is unbelievable. Firing her own daughter! At Christmas! "I could, I could . . . try harder. I, I, I really think I'm getting the hang of it now." I look in my lap and remember my gift from Reagan. I hold up the picture of myself. "Look! See how far I've come?"

Mom waits until I am done as if I'm some kind of annoying child. And then she takes a deep breath and says, "Yes, we've seen and noted the changes. You look much better. But it's not really enough. Your father and I feel like this is our only option—"

I can't believe he's in on this too. What a traitor.

"—if we'd like our daughter to stop wasting her life in the store and to use her writing skills to do what she really wants to do. We decided if that's what it takes, then we'd have to do it."

What? I look up at her.

"Darling. We're very touched by your family loyalty, and you've really proven yourself to be a fine, hardworking, and even, um . . ." she casts her eyes down at the picture then back up at me, "fashionable individual. And as much as I'd love to keep you by my side the rest of your life, I know that that would be wrong. God gave you a gift, Lily. We want to see you use it. We're firing you so you will write."

I stare at Mom. What's this "God" stuff coming out of her mouth? And she's being so supportive. I never thought she understood why I wanted to be a writer. "But—"

"No buts. With the power vested in me by the Traywick's stockholders, you're fired. Plus, this way, you'll have severance to tide you over until you get steady freelance work. You can write some press releases for us to get started. Plus you'll be able to garner some sympathy in the writing world for being fired."

I laugh. "Yeah. Wow. I suppose being fired by my own mother is about all the street cred I'm going to need."

"Street what?"

"I don't want a lot for Christmas," Maggie sings sweetly into the microphone in her best church choir–trained voice. She smiles angelically down from the stage where the karaoke machine is set up, the butterfly on her shirt glowing in the bright light.

"There is just one thing I need . . ." Alex sings, dramatically clenching her fist in front of her face and closing her eyes. Mariah Carey's signature Christmas ditty will never be the same.

I can't listen to this anymore. We've already suffered through Miguel and Daniel's duet of "Rudolph the Red-Nosed Reindeer," in which Miguel sang only the "like a lightbulb" parts. But at least they were only pretending to take it seriously. Maggie and Alex are so straight and earnest they could be competing for Christian pop star of the year.

I walk around the three-foot blow-up lighted Santa and life-sized lighted plastic Nativity scene (apparently the manufacturer only makes one kind of wise man, so there are three identical statues of his distinguished figure) toward the refreshment table.

Pastor Kyle has really outdone himself this time. His idea to throw a tacky Christmas party didn't sit well with the more domestically inclined members of our group, who lobbied for white lights, damask tablecloths, and petit fours, but I am convinced it was one of his more brilliant moves. The blue aluminum Christmas tree is decorated with silver tinsel and dozens of glass balls, each with a different NASCAR driver's face and car on it, and is topped by a two-foot plastic angel with musical notes painted next to her open mouth. Shiny Mylar gingerbread men frolic around the walls, interspersed with light-up plastic Santa faces. A quaint clingy plastic, snow-covered New England village is stuck to the windows, glitter-covered paper snowflakes hang from the ceiling, and a giant cardboard cut-out of Santa's sleigh sits at the bottom of the stage, with reindeer set on the rising stairs, as if climbing into the night sky. The obligatory sprig of mistletoe hangs in the middle of the ceiling, where lots of people will have the chance to accidentally stand under it. The entire room is lit by hundreds of strings of colored outdoor Christmas lights, which blink on and off in no particular pattern. It is garishly, gloriously hideous.

I reach the refreshment table, where Bill is loading up his plate with a reindeer fruitcake cookie and some red Jell-O from a Santa-shaped mold. "I love this song," he says, smiling lovingly toward the stage. He doesn't take his eyes away. Weird. I decide it's easier to agree and hurriedly fill up my plate with crackers and a part of the cheery Christmas cheese log and dart away. I can't listen one more time to him talk about the new gaming system he expects his parents to give him for Christmas. Unfortunately, my action awakens the motion-sensitive, innocuous-looking foot-tall plastic reindeer band, and they spontaneously burst into song as I try to reach Reagan and Becky across the room. I sit down and lean in, but I can't hear what they're saying over the noise coming from the stage.

"Make my wish come true . . ." Maggie and Alex screech. Maggie is smiling broadly out at the captive audience; Alex is closing her eyes and looking upward, as if directing her comment at God himself. "All I want for Christmas . . ." they sing, simultaneously lifting their arms and pointing at the lighted plastic figure of Jesus in the manger scene, "is you . . ."

I sneak a look at Reagan, who has raised her right eyebrow but is valiantly trying to keep a straight face. Becky is chuckling under her breath until I meet her eye, when she bursts out laughing. Reagan sees us and loses it, doubling over laughing. When she tries to sit back up again, she knocks over a foot-tall plastic Santa figurine that starts blaring its mechanical music and wiggling its bottom. Reagan picks it up quickly, laughing all the harder, and finds the off switch. Alex shoots us a harsh glance from the stage, then pastes the angelic smile back on her face and keeps singing. My face reddens. We should try to be nicer to her. It's Christmas.

We struggle to talk until their song ends, and Pastor Kyle jumps up from where he is sitting in the corner, talking to Steph, to grab the microphone and announce that the karaoke portion of the night is done. Steph was released from the hospital a few weeks ago and has been recovering slowly. I had been surprised and delighted when I called her today and she said she thought she would be able to handle the Super Single Sunday Tacky Christmas Extravaganza. She has been talking to Pastor Kyle most of the night and has assiduously avoided the snacks, but I saw her eat a small slice of pizza earlier and am pleased to see her interacting normally with the church people. Although she's now been left alone in the corner, while Kyle thanks Alex and Maggie for their song. She spies us and comes to sit next to Reagan.

"Still no cute guys here, huh?" she says, looking around. I shake my head.

"None that are available, anyway," I say. "It's really a pity. I don't even know why I come anymore."

"I would have stayed in the hospital if I'd known things were this bad," she laughs. "At least some of the doctors were hot."

Pastor Kyle announces that after a brief message, we'll have our white elephant gift exchange, then asks us all to settle down for a few moments. Miguel and Daniel stop their game of Foosball (Kyle has pasted little red Santa hats onto the heads of the little players) and sit down in some folding chairs at the back of the room. Pastor Kyle talks for a few minutes about the unchanging nature of God and its manifestations at the first Christmas, and I really try to listen, but he's so hard to take seriously in his tight red leather pants, his red jean jacket, his St. Louis Cardinals baseball cap, Oakley sunglasses, and his goatee. He is, he explained to us, the postmodern Santa.

He then asks all of us to pick a present from under the aluminum tree. Daniel runs over to the pile and picks the biggest box. Alex very carefully takes the smallest, roughly jewelry-sized box, explaining to everyone in earshot that good things come in small packages. Maggie obediently takes the next smallest box. Reagan walks to the pile, her shiny, short dark green pouffy-sleeved dress, circa-1987, shimmering. Though it is not a costume party, she has taken the opportunity to parade her best tacky Christmas wear and has put on mini glass ball earrings. She's even wearing a pin that plays "Jingle Bells" when you push Santa's nose, which is remarkably similar to one Maggie is wearing. The rest of us quickly take packages and sit back down, Miguel next to Becky, Daniel next to Reagan, and Steph next to me. At least I'm not all alone at Christmas.

"This is how we got Mele," Steph says, examining her shoe-box–sized gift wrapped in the Sunday comics.

"What?" Becky asks.

"Our dog. Mele Kalikimaka. My parents got him at a Christmas gift exchange." She shrugs.

"Mellykali who?" Miguel asks, screwing up his face.

"Mele Kalikimaka," Steph says, rolling her eyes. "It means Merry Christmas in Hawaiian. That's what we named the puppy my parents got at a gift exchange. Apparently the gift giver's dog had a large litter of puppies that they weren't quite prepared for, and they were trying desperately to get rid of them." She shrugs.

"I hope I get a pit bull," Daniel says, baring his teeth and growling at his box. He shakes it, but shrugs when it doesn't growl back.

Pastor Kyle explains how the game is going to work. We'll all unwrap our presents one at a time, then we'll go one at a time and have the chance to steal someone else's gift. We can each steal twice, and no gift can be stolen more than three times.

Miguel unwraps a Mr. Potato Head doll missing all of its parts except the big red lips. Reagan opens a package of colored bendy straws. Maggie opens her little box to find a sparkplug-sized bottle of dark liquid. Alex gasps, and Maggie leans in to read the label. "Scorned Woman Hot Sauce," she reads carefully. "One hundred percent pure 'this'll teach 'im.' Then underneath it says 'Hell hath no fury like a woman scorned.'" She looks around confused. "What does that mean?" Alex shrugs.

"You should take that!" Reagan whispers. "That's perfect!" My eyes lights up for half a second, then I shake my head.

"Nah."

"Why not? It would be funny," Reagan says.

"I don't need more anger. I just want to move on," I say. Steph looks at me and smiles.

Daniel steals a bottle of Windex from a quiet girl with the unfortunate name Felice, who has been fending off Feliz Navidad jokes all night. Reagan takes the autographed picture of Linda Ronstadt from Bill. I can't believe how aggressive the stealing gets, considering we all know the Eighth Commandment. For some reason, no one wants the 1993 Yellow Pages for Los Angeles County I unwrapped, but I manage to steal a cheap, fake jewel–encrusted watch with a faux leather band. It comes in an ornate gift box, apparently a feeble attempt to make it seem valuable. Mom will think it's a scream when she finds it in her stocking on Christmas morning.

"Third steal! That's it for the watch. It's yours, Lily," Pastor Kyle announces, smiling.

"Oh," Maggie whines from the corner. "I wanted that." I look at her sweet face and am racked with guilt. She had really wanted it. To wear. "Oh well," she says, shaking her head, trying to content herself with her collection of Lego men.

I sit back and watch as the game finishes up. Reagan is ecstatic about her set of fluorescent slap bracelets that say Jesus Loves You. Steph looks dubiously at her used potato peeler. Daniel proudly holds his Scorned Woman Hot Sauce, which he announces he will drink for twenty dollars. I watch Maggie put her new Magic 8-Ball keychain into her bag a little sadly as everyone gets up and rushes toward the food and Foosball table again.

"Hey, Maggie?" I say. She looks at me. "I don't really need this," I tell her, holding out the black box. "I have lots of watches at home. Do you want it?"

Her eyes light up, and she breaks into a smile. "Really?" she asks, reaching for the box shyly. "Are you sure?"

"I'm sure," I say, nodding. "Merry Christmas."

"Thank you," she says, throwing her arms around me.

I laugh awkwardly. "Hey, it's," I try to pull away, "it's no problem." She scurries off to show Bill, who is standing in the middle of the room.

I look around slowly. Daniel and Miguel are playing tug of war with a nutcracker painted in a tie-dye shirt and wearing wooden Birkenstocks. Reagan and Steph are kicking at the giant gingerbread house, trying to knock down the Gummy Bears Kyle has stationed around the house like armies in a game of Risk. Alex is bustling around the food table, straightening the messy cracker tray. Miguel and Becky are talking quietly in the corner and laughing. And Maggie and Bill are . . . Wait a minute, they're talking together . . . under the mistletoe.

I put my fingers to my mouth and let out a high-pitched whistle, pointing at them. Everyone in the room turns to look at me, then looks where I am pointing, directing their eyes to Bill and Maggie. Bill looks around confusedly, and Maggie looks up and blushes. The group starts clapping and whistling at the two of them, until Bill leans over and plants a sweet kiss on her cheek. Maggie looks like she's about to melt. Alex looks like she is about to explode.

Bill shyly puts his arm around Maggie's waist. Maggie beams. The rest of the group looks as shocked as I feel, but the cheering only gets louder.

When the clapping finally dies down, Pastor Kyle puts on the Beach Boys Christmas album and, dancing, wishes us all a Merry Christmas.

Reagan whispers to me "I suppose any pastor who still knows how to do the Roger Rabbit has my vote."

I have to agree.

Ah, Super Single Sunday. I take a deep breath and look around. Maybe being single isn't my ideal, but being here feels so right.

Chapter 21

"*Lily, you* have to come. You promised. Please?" Becky whines into the phone. "It's my birthday!"

"Are you sure she's not going to be there?"

"I promise you. Delia was not invited. It's my party. You have to come. I want you to meet my friends from college."

"Fine," I say, taking a deep breath. "But it means I like you a whole lot because the only thing I really want to do is sit on my couch in my pajamas tonight."

"You're the best. See you at eight!" Becky says and then hangs up before I can change my mind.

"*Nuts!* I told you so! Do you see him?" I hiss at Becky over the loud dance music at the new San Francisco hotspot Dagon. Red and blue lights illuminate the bar area, and the dance floor is crowded with writhing bodies. I look up high and see a DJ perched atop a giant column with his headphones half on and half off, nodding to the beat of the thumping music.

"Who? Sam?" Becky asks, looking at the crowd. So far most of her friends have been nice, and Miguel has made a special point to introduce me to everybody and bail me out if I'm stranded alone in the corner, but still this place is just not my scene. "I don't see Sam."

"Over there," I yell, pointing near the door. "With that girl. It's him I swear."

"It is?" She exclaims. "Wow. When did he cut his hair?" I ignore her question and continue to stare at Sam. He hasn't noticed me yet. "That's my friend Amelia he's with. She's the one who knows Delia. I don't know why he's here with her. You don't see Delia, do you?" The music pulses, and she has to yell for me to hear.

"No," I say, as Amelia puts her arm around Sam's waist and guides him into the bar. "But this Amelia looks like she's hoping Delia doesn't show up either." Amelia gazes up at Sam's strong jaw, smiling. "I can't believe she's going for Sam. I can't believe she brought him to my party!" She screeches over the music, widening her eyes. "That's just wrong!"

I take a deep breath and begin to frantically pack myself up. Maybe I can still make it out the door before he sees me.

"Hey there, Becky!" Amelia yells, pushing through the crowd to greet her friend. Sam watches her run to Becky, then freezes. He has seen me.

"Happy birthday!" Amelia screeches as she leans in to give Becky a hug, then sticks out her hand for me to shake. "I'm Amelia," she says. I take her hand tentatively. "And this is Sam!" she squeals, giggling.

"Hi Sam," I say. He nods in response.

"I'm going to go get a drink," she yells, "Do you want anything, Sam?"

"Just a Coke is fine for me," he says. Amelia nods and runs off. Becky looks at me questioningly. I nod, and she walks away to the dance floor.

"What are you doing here?" I look up at him.

"This girl Amelia called and asked if I wanted to come to her friend's birthday party. She didn't mention it was Becky," he says, shaking his head. He looks around and purses his lips together. "It's really crazy in here," he says, gazing at the dance floor. He bites his lip. "What are you doing here?"

"Becky made me promise," I say. "It's her birthday and all." He looks at me and smiles. I smile back. This is so forced.

And then he makes eye contact with me and appears to be opening up. "I don't want to be here, Lily—"

"Here you go!" Amelia screams, coming up from behind Sam and putting a dark drink in his hand. "I got it special, just for you." Sam takes a sip and makes a face like he might spit it out. "Let's go dance!" Amelia says, pulling him toward the dance floor.

"What is this?" Sam asks her, raising an eyebrow.

"It's a Coke! Like you asked!" she says, laughing. "But I had them put some whisky in it too!" She giggles.

"Why?" he asks loudly. Becky turns to see what's going on.

"Oh come on. I've never seen you not drink before. I figured you must be kidding. Come on! Let's dance!"

"I didn't want alcohol. I just wanted a Coke!" he says, even louder this time.

"Why? What's wrong? I paid for it. Let's just dance!" She gives up trying to drag him to the dance floor and starts dancing close to him where they are standing. She moves her legs close to him.

"I don't want to dance," he says. Everyone around him turns to watch. "I don't want to drink either."

"Why are you being such a spoilsport?" Amelia whines, pulling back. "You love this stuff."

"I used to love this stuff," he says. "I used to, and now I'm done." He crosses his arms across his chest.

"What's gotten into you?" Amelia says, raising her eyebrows.

"I don't want to do this anymore," he says. "Who are these people? Are they your friends?" he asks, looking around. "Do they really want what's best for you?" Amelia shrugs, backing away. "I thought I wanted it too. But I don't want anything to do with it," he yells. All of Becky's friends have stopped dancing and talking in the little circle near us and are staring at him. I realize my mouth is gaping open at his outburst, and I shut it. "What is this?"

"It's just a party," Amelia yells, trying to smile.

"I don't want to party right now," he says, his voiced strained and loud. "This is everything I don't want. It's not good for me. This is all meaningless."

"Sam," Amelia says, turning red. "Everyone is staring at you."

"I don't care," he says, pulling away. "Sorry Becky. Happy Birthday anyway." He waves to Becky, then pushes his way through the crowd to the door. There is no sound until he's out the front door.

"What was that all about?" Becky asks, looking from Amelia to me. All I can do is shrug.

"He's not here."

"Did you really think he was going to be?" Reagan asks, taking a sip of champagne. The long silver strands hanging from her ears bob and glisten. "If he's all anti-party now, why would he show up here? Besides, you said that you were hoping he *wouldn't* be at Becky's party and now you're hoping he *will* be at this one?" She makes circles by her ear with her index finger to signal that I'm crazy.

I sigh. "You're right. I'm being nuts."

She nods her head to reassure me of how right I am.

"Thanks," I say. I look around. The main ballroom at the St. Francis Hotel has been transformed, to my mother's exact specifications, into a winter wonderland for the annual Traywick's Christmas party. My very last Traywick's Christmas party. The party is both a way to thank and reward the Traywick's employees for a year of hard work and an excuse to wine and dine the media and key contacts in the fashion world. Predictably, my mother has spared no expense, and the result is breathtaking. We entered the ballroom through a faux forest piled with fluffy snow the likes of which San Francisco, with its balmy winters, has never seen, and emerge from the wilderness into a glistening, glowing winter scene. The theme, of course, is Winter White, and every tablecloth, every light, every decoration, every bowtie on every member of the twelve-piece band is gleaming white. Piles of fake snow lie around, shining ice sculptures adorn every table, white tea lights and electric Christmas lights brighten the room, and everyone is dressed to the nines. It's like senior prom, only tasteful, and without the endless renditions of "Forever Young." This is the only chance most of us have to wear the clothes from the evening wear displays we see all year, and everyone is oohing and aahing over the room and everybody's clothes, all featuring the color white, due to the invitation's specifications. With so much else to take in, no one seems to have noticed Reagan and me whispering in the corner.

"But . . ." I say and then hesitate.

Reagan looks at me and says, "Fine, keep talking about him."

"Well, he certainly brought the house down at Becky's party, but I guess I thought, I don't know, that he'd make an exception and come to the corporate Christmas party. I mean, it's got chaperones for crying out loud."

"Maybe he finally just hit his low point," she says, her long silver earrings shining. "Maybe he's realized what a screwup he's become. I don't know." I look at her. She is the only person who would ever pair a sheer white Marc Jacobs slip dress with white rubber fur-trimmed snow boots, but she pulls it off. On her right wrist she wears her hot pink Jesus Loves Me slap bracelet from the church gift exchange. Somehow I feel dowdy in the simple black and white Carolina Herrera classic ball gown. I thought it was so elegant and flattering earlier. I should have worn the red scarf with it after all. "I just wouldn't count on Prince Charming's arrival at the ball, Cinderella."

I nod very slowly.

"Besides, it's better that he's not coming anyway. You've moved on, remember? Now if you'll excuse me. I need to rescue Daniel from the clutches of Lisa from Housewares," she says, nodding to where Daniel stands uncomfortably pulling at the collar of his rented tux while Lisa babbles, carefully positioning herself so he has an eyeful of cleavage. "And I see someone who wants to talk to you coming this way," she says, winking. I look around. My favorite security guard of the elevator incident is wearing a tight white tuxedo and is strutting toward us. His eyes roam over my body, and I suck my stomach in. He is smiling and, I have to admit, looks really good.

"You can't leave me now," I hiss at Reagan, but she is already walking away, chuckling under her breath.

"Hello Lily," he says, bowing his head.

"Hi." Do I sound too nervous? "Are you enjoying the party?" Men should not be allowed to be so attractive. It isn't fair.

"Of course," he says, his low voice with the slightest hint of an accent making my stomach tingle in spite of myself. "But I would enjoy it more if you'd dance with me." He reaches out for my hand.

"Oh, I'm not much of a dancer," I say, trying to think of a way to get out of embarrassing myself on the dance floor. In movies, the guy who asks a girl to dance knows what he is doing. If they don't, they ask to get you some punch or take you for a walk. Even I know this.

"I'll teach you," he says, taking my hand and guiding me to the floor in the center of the room. He places my right hand on his hip and holds the other, then shows me the basic steps to salsa.

"This isn't salsa music," I laugh. "We can't dance like that. Everyone else is just bouncing around."

"Everyone else is missing out." he says. I laugh uncomfortably.

I give in, and let him lead me all over the floor like an idiot. It's better than standing alone in the corner like an idiot. I should have brought a date after all. I had decided I was going to make a statement and show up here alone, an independent woman needing no man to escort her. I could have been independent and still have brought someone, I think as I watch Reagan and Daniel laughing at their table and see Harry the piano player and his wife arm in arm, doing the box step in the corner of the floor. I could have brought . . . Well, I bet Steph could have come or something.

He takes my hands and places them on his shoulders. He dances well, and I try to get into it, but I feel out of place on this floor. He places his hands on my waist and shows me how to move my hips, and I mimic his movements uncertainly. I look around. Reagan is watching me, giving me the thumbs-up sign and smiling. Thank goodness my mother is talking to a reporter from the *Chronicle*. He moves his hands down lower. I keep dancing, trying to pull away a little. Tricia and Charlie are whispering in the corner and laughing at Stanford from Accessories, dancing exuberantly by himself. His hands slide lower, and I pull away, but he pulls me back. I keep dancing, grimacing. He pulls me closer again, but I slip away. "Sorry. I'm done now." And then I turn away to make a mad dash off the floor, but I run right into someone.

Sam. Again. My stomach knots a little, and I tell it to snap out of it.

Sam is frowning at me. His black tuxedo hangs perfectly on his broad shoulders, and he is wearing a white vest and bow tie over his white shirt. He looks stunning. Is he growing his hair out again?

"Uh, sorry," I say.

He forces himself to smile and says, "Don't worry about it," and walks away to the refreshment table.

I snap back into action and walk over to Reagan and Daniel.

Help me, I mouth at them as I walk up.

"You guys seem to really be hitting it off out there," Daniel says, laughing.

Reagan presses her two index fingers together to make the international symbol for kissing.

"You guys are really hilarious. I wish I were as funny as you. And, hey, thanks old chums for rescuing me from that manhandler out there."

"Oh . . . you like it!" says Reagan.

I roll my eyes and plop down next to them. I spy the security guard across the room talking to another girl and breathe a sigh of relief.

"I was going to tell you when you returned from your little salsa dance lesson that Samuel March of Women's Footwear has arrived, but then I saw you almost run him over so I suppose you realize that now."

"Yup. I saw him," I say, nonchalantly. I bite my lip and look down at the floor. Reagan coughs. I don't look up.

"If you're just going to stand here and analyze what it means, I'm going to go dance." Reagan shrugs. "Daniel? You ready?"

He nods, straightens his rented bow tie, and takes her hand. "You want to come, Lily?"

"I've had enough embarrassment for a while," I say, shaking my head. "I'll hang out here and try to blend into the wall."

"Good luck with that," she says, laughing and dragging Daniel away.

I lean back in my chair and look around. How did I end up here? Still dateless. I look up and see Harry and his wife, talking quietly, completely comfortable in each other's arms, oblivious to how out of place they look on the dance floor where Stanford is now doing half-splits. He pops up and does it again on the other side. Will I ever find someone to grow old with, to dance and laugh with?

I see a shadow out of the corner of my eye and look up just in time to see Sam sit down in the chair next to me.

"Please, stay seated. I'm still recovering from our last meeting," he says.

"Hi," I say. "Sorry about that. I was fleeing the dance floor. Overzealous dance partner. I'm sure you understand."

"Overzealous? I don't know. From where I was, you seemed to be having a good time," he says, sneering.

"Not exactly. I'm a rotten dancer."

"I'm sure he'd be up for more practice. Why don't I just wave him over here," he says. He starts to raise his arm, and I grab it and wrestle it back down.

"Because I don't want to," I say, raising my eyebrows. "Is that okay with you?" Why is he acting like this?

"Fine with me," he says, nodding and looking at me. "You just looked pretty comfortable out there."

"Sam? What are you trying to say?" Is it possible? He almost sounds jealous.

"Nothing," he mumbles, looking down. "Never mind."

"Fine," I say. I pick at a hangnail. "So what's new?"

"You know what's new." He shrugs. "I flipped out and ruined Becky's birthday party. I'm done with Delia."

"I'm sorry," I say. "I don't know what to say. But I'm *actually* sorry. For you. Breaking up is hard," I say, stifling a smile. I feel so mature.

"No, Lily, that's what I'm saying," he says. "It's not a breakup. There was nothing *to* break up. She tried to make it seem like there was so much more there than there was. The truth was, we were friends, and it just went too far. Things got out of hand . . . in so many ways. I didn't like who I was becoming being around her. She was trying to get me to do things I hadn't thought about in years. It wasn't good for me," he says, shaking his head. "And I don't want anything to do with that anymore. That's what that thing at Dagon was all about. I don't want that life again."

"Sam?" I ask, resting my head in my hands. "Why are you telling me this?" He looks at me for a minute.

"I'm sorry, Lily. I messed up, and I'm trying to make it right."

I feel my eyes fill with tears, and I fight them. What is he doing? Is he just trying to get this off his chest, or is he trying to patch things up? What do I want him to be doing?

"I'm sorry too, Sam," I say.

He nods.

"But I don't know what to think," I spit. "First she was just a friend and I was being crazy, and then it turns out I was right, that she was try-ing to take you away and lead you astray." I take a deep breath. "You seemed to be okay with that, but now you're not? I just don't get you." Though I try to fight it, a tear leaks down my cheek.

"You don't get me? I've told you everything." He looks wounded.

I wipe my eyes, choking back tears. "I really liked you, Sam." I look at him. "But I don't think I really know you. I don't know what to believe."

He watches me, silently.

"Lily?" I look into his deep brown eyes. He stands up and reaches out his hand.

"What are you doing?"

"Will you dance with me?"

I look up at him, holding out his hand.

I watch him looking at me. I take a deep breath and let it out slowly.

"No," I say finally, shaking my head.

He nods, closes his eyes, and drops his arm. Silently, he turns and walks away through the illusionary forest and out the door.

• Chapter 22 •

I'm going over for dinner to my parents' house tonight, but I have an hour to kill. I still can't get over the fact that she fired me. It's so great. After I got over the shock, I felt so free. No more Traywick's. No more little Ralph Lauren suits. No more Versace patent leather shoes. No more fashion.

I check my e-mail and see something curious. Oh! That's definitely from the *Chronicle*. One of Boris's friends must have written me back with some advice about how to break in. Yes! I pump my fist in the air.

> Ms. Traywick,
>
> I'm an editor here at the Chronicle and not only have had the pleasure of working with Boris Nesterenko, but I'm also familiar with your work. I saw the article in the Weekly and cringed for you. I've known that rapscallion Arle for years.
>
> That being said, I don't hold any of that ugliness against you. Why don't you start doing some book reviews for us? We'll go from there. If both parties are happy, you can slowly work yourself up through the ranks here. It won't be like your fast climb at the Weekly, but it will at least be authentic.

Call me this week, and I'll set you up with the Book Review editor.

More than happy to help.

Best,
Marla Maroukian
Entertainment Editor

PS Not to be critical, but your e-mail to me included an error. Perhaps you should brush off your grammar books with Boris before you write your first report, hmm?

I hit my head with my hand. Oh man. I can't believe I had a grammatical error in my e-mail. Oh man! I guess when I sent it off, I was only half-earnest about doing some work for them. But now, thanks to Mom firing me, I'm very serious. I can't make a mistake like that again. Doing work for the *Chronicle* is clearly going to be a lot more difficult than for the *Weekly*, but it's a real lead for a real career and not some make-believe job at a two-bit rag. And Ms. Maroukian is right. I need to contact Boris.

Boris,

I owe you a cup of coffee, at the very least. One of your contacts, Marla Maroukian, just wrote me back and is going to be a big help.

If you think you can bear being my friend after what I did to you, I'd love to hang out. Let me know.

A very humble Lily Traywick

I send it and smile. Who would have thought I'd ever see the day I was asking a guy to be just my friend? I guess it is possible. Of course, I remind myself, with Miguel and Daniel taken, I am seriously low on male companionship these days. It's one small step for Lily, one giant leap for men of all kinds.

We sit down to dinner, and I'm shocked to see a bucket of fried chicken from KFC and all the fixings. I look around and confirm I'm at the right house.

"Ho, ho. We've surprised you, huh, sport?" Dad says.

"Yeah," I say, slowly. I'm waiting for the jig to be up.

Mom puts the appropriate serving silver in each container and has a seat. "I just thought, Let's live a little. Especially since your grandmother didn't want to cook tonight, and well, if I'm honest, I've always loved this, this, Kentucky Fried Chicken."

"Me too," Dad says, taking a big bite of a drumstick. "It's totally frigid."

I stare at her in disbelief. I look at Gran. Where is my family? Who are these imposters? "Tired tonight, Gran?" I ask. It's funny. She doesn't look tired. In fact, she looks incredible. Are those earrings she's wearing? But why else wouldn't she cook?

"Not one bit," she says. "Oh! I forgot to tell you . . ." She goes quiet, tongue-tied for the first time in her life.

Mom smiles at her mother. "She has a date tonight."

My eyes grow huge. "What?"

"I met him online, Lil. But don't worry, I Google-stalked him, and he's all right. We were both in the same chat room for nut crafters."

"Nut crafters?"

"Uh, crafts with nuts? He makes bowls from pecan shells."

We chat about Morty, my grandmother's beau, for a while. They're going to dinner in San Francisco. I'm so happy for her. She's positively glowing. And I'm happy for my mom, who has packed away two drumsticks, mashed potatoes, and a buttermilk biscuit in her bird-like body.

"How's good old Sam these days, Lil?" Gran asks, nodding.

I know she knows we've broken up so she must be making small talk. "He's fine. Whatever." I shrug. "He hurt me pretty bad, but I suppose we'll be friends someday."

"Oh, sport. I still think he is a nice guy," says Dad, smiling at me hopefully.

I sigh. Poor Dad. He's still pretty addicted to Sam. "I know he is, Dad. It just didn't work out. I was wrong, he was wrong. It just got all messed up."

"Dark and Chunky?" Steph asks. I see she's a little wary.

"Okay, so they have a gross name. It's a little too descriptive. But I know food from a box, and these are the best durned brownies on the market."

She shrugs and dumps the mix into a bowl and mixes in the eggs and vegetable oil. I'm still trying to get used to being able to hang out with Steph again. Now that she's taking a breather from med school to reconsider her priorities and work on getting better, she has all the time in the world to hang out, which is great because, as usual, my plan about taking a break from guys for a while sounded better when I made the promise to myself than it actually is. I'm sure taking a breather from guys is also helping me reconsider my priorities, but it's really dull aside from the part where you make brownies all the time and eat them in your pajamas. That part I like.

Once the brownies are out we put two hot and gooey ones on paper towels (Steph's is about a tenth the size of mine, but at least she's having a little) and head back to my bedroom. Inie had been hanging around in the kitchen in her little silk teddy, telling us all about the guy she's currently dating and how he's such a talented trumpet player, unlike some of the trumpet players she's dated before. Oh. Did she mention how practically the whole band in high school was in love with her? She didn't? Well, they were.

I shut the door to my room and sigh a relief. "Sorry about that. She's really nice, actually. If you can get past the near-nakedness and the bizarre bragging."

Steph giggled. "She's really fun in this weird way."

"I've warmed up to her. And you have to admire on some level that kind of confidence. She just seems to be born with it." I walk across the room and pick up the awful pink picture frame that Reagan gave me. "Check this out," I say.

I wait for Steph to laugh. I have decided it's hysterical and now have the picture prominently displayed in my room. When Inie saw it, she said I looked like a "big tall gooney gooney," whatever that is.

"Oh this is that picture from the paper," she says.

"Yeah. Uh, please don't ever let me walk around like that again," I say.

Steph looks at me, puzzled. "Why not?"

I suddenly feel a little uncomfortable. "Steph. You're very sweet. But *please*. I look like a monster in that picture."

"No you don't. Who made this frame?"

"Oh you know, Reagan. She was just goofing around."

Steph purses her lips. "I love Reagan. I do. But the only part of you that needed making over, Lily, was your confidence."

I force a smile. This whole niceness routine with Steph is really taxing sometimes. "Well, I like me this way."

She holds up a hand. "I don't care what you look like on the outside. You look great now. You looked great then. The only real difference I see is that you *know* you look great now."

"I never got asked out like this. When I changed my clothes, I did. I think that proves the guys like me better this way."

"Lily, I'll say it again. When you felt good about yourself, guys found that attractive. Men are so simple. If you act like you're something special, they believe you. That's what happened."

I study the picture in my lap.

"What was your big crime back then? T-shirts and shorts? So? How bad is that? A new wardrobe didn't change you into a new person, Lily. It just made you like yourself."

I swallow a lump in my throat. Why do I feel like crying all of a sudden? I look up at Steph.

"I'm sorry, Lily. I'm not trying to be mean. I think I'm just inundated with all of this body-image stuff right now, thanks to my mandatory therapy sessions with my psychiatrist. I guess this is a good sign for me." She laughs.

I nod and a tear leaks down my face. She pulls me in for a hug.

"I struggle with this as much as anybody, but you know, we all need to have confidence in how we look and who we are. God made us in his image. Who are we to judge his work?"

Even though I have heard this my whole life at every women's Bible study group I have ever attended, I think I finally grasp the enormity of such a statement.

"Just don't go off the deep end like Inie," she says, laughing. "I mean, you won't be *that* hot, ever."

Christmas Eve has been really perfect. Gran cooked a roast and bossed Mom and me around the kitchen all afternoon. Dad came home late from the store and declared Traywick's locked up extra-tight to fend off the day-after-Christmas-sales hordes from breaking down the doors. The four of us ate a big dinner and then sat in front of the fire, drinking mulled cider that Dad made. It's his specialty. I'm so blessed, and this year, I can really appreciate it. I came so close to losing it all, thanks to Earle. No, I correct myself, looking around. Thanks to my own mistakes.

I hear the doorbell ring and look at my watch. It's nine-thirty, and I'm so tired. I look at my parents for some kind of explanation.

"Are you expecting someone, Lily?" Mom asks.

"No. I thought maybe you were."

We all look at each other for a moment, and I decide to go and see who it is. When I look through the peephole, I see Reagan and Daniel. Oh man. I don't know if I have the energy for Reagan right now. I open the door.

"Hey," I say to Reagan.

She pushes past me and walks quickly into our living room. I follow behind Daniel after her.

"Mr. Traywick. Ms. Traywick. I left my wallet at work."

She's shaking excitedly. She's a nervous wreck. Daniel quickly introduces himself to all of my family and then puts a hand on Reagan's shoulder.

"Let's just get it the day after Christmas. We're both working the morning shift, and Traywick's is all locked up now. It will be fine until then," I say, trying to calm her down.

"No. No. I really need it. I'm sorry to come in here on Christmas Eve, but I've got to have that wallet. It has my driver's license, my mother's gift certificate that I got her for Christmas, my, my, my . . ."

I have never seen her in such a state. I mean, she's very excitable in general, but this is really something.

Dad stands up. "Okay, okay. It's okay, Reagan. Why don't you and Lily, and uh, right, Daniel here hop in the car and drive over to the store. I'll get the key, and write down this month's pass code for you. Lily, you know how to get in."

I want to kick him in the shin. He's too nice. I'm so tired. Why couldn't he just tell her no?

But then she turns her face to me, and I see the pleading in her eyes, and I can't say no. She's pretty hard to say no to.

"Okay, I'll do it," I say, fumbling for my house keys.

"Great! Oh thank you," Reagan says.

I kiss everyone goodbye and tell them we'll call if we have any trouble. As we walk out the door Reagan says, "Are you sure you want to wear that?"

I look down at my sneakers, jeans, and T-shirt. Only Reagan.

We are one of three or four cars in the entire parking garage. Sometimes people leave their cars here overnight. I surprise even myself by getting the three of us inside the building in fifteen minutes flat and with only one phone call to my father. We all walk through the store, which is pitch-black except for our flashlights. The shiny plastic of the little white lights that decorate the counters reflect the light back to us.

"It's really eerie in here, right?" Reagan whispers.

I flash my beam on the face of a giant Santa checking off his list in the Housewares department. He looks very sinister. "Yeah," I whisper back.

"Let's not whisper," Daniel says at normal volume. "It's giving me goose bumps."

We walk carefully through the giant store, careful not to disrupt any of the displays and trying not to freak ourselves out. When we get to the escalators we realize they're not on.

"Lily, you just stay here. No sense in all of us walking all the way up four flights of stairs just to get my stupid wallet. We'll be right back down," she says.

"That's fine by me," I say with a yawn. I'm way too tired to climb stairs, plus I sort of want to explore the first floor, the grand floor, of the building in peace and quiet. Even in the dark, the beauty of this place is breathtaking. The ceiling soars several stories above us, the shiny gold elevator doors glisten, the cool tile of the floor shines like crystal, and the live Christmas trees drenched in red and gold decorations gleam. It reminds me of the time I snuck into the church sanctuary one night when the youth group was playing Sardines in the church. It was so calm and beautiful it was overwhelming.

I hear them climb upstairs and yell after them, "No making out forever. I want to get home sometime tonight." Reagan turns and looks at me, then runs back down quickly.

I look at her. Daniel is waiting one flight up.

"One last thing," she says quietly.

"What's that?"

"Merry Christmas, Lily."

I smile. I love this holiday.

"And I don't think I ever said thanks," she says.

I rarely see Reagan serious so I'm a little baffled. I shine the flashlight in her face to see if she's kidding. She's not. "Thanks? For what?"

"For everything. For this year. I was thinking about how different my life is today than it was a year ago, and how much happier I am. A large part of that is your influence," she says.

I smile weakly. She's never said anything like this before.

She giggles. "Yours and Daniel's, that is."

"Really?" I say, teasing her. "Daniel, eh?"

She shrugs. "I *really* like him," she whispers.

"I know," I whisper back.

"Secrets don't make friends, girls!" Daniel says from the escalator above. Reagan gives me a quick hug and runs up the escalator.

I begin to pick my way around the first floor. I have a momentary impulse to hide in one of the clothes racks like I did when I was a child. Instead I go behind the glass makeup counters and peer in them. Then, some of the strings of white lights on the first floor come on. A few seconds later, another string comes to life. I blink several times, trying to get my eyes to adjust as more lights turn on.

"Lights are on now, guys!" I yell up to them.

I hear nothing and decide to walk back to the escalators to yell up to them again. I really don't want to have to go up there and tell them to turn them off. As I round the makeup counter, I hear it. The Traywick's piano.

I put my hand to my mouth and drop my flashlight. I slowly creep over to where the piano is. There are candles burning on the piano and on the floor around it. Strings of lights cast a glow around the area. I distinctly make out my favorite song, the one Harry always plays for me, "My Funny Valentine."

"Lily?"

"Ah!" I scream and turn around, only to come face-to-face with Sam. He's wearing a tuxedo and holding a bunch of red roses.

"Wait. I—" My brain is not moving as fast as I need. Why is Sam here? Why is he in a tux? Where are Reagan and Daniel? Sam moves slowly toward me as if he's scared I'm going to scream again, and I ask him the very next question that pops into my brain. "Is that Harry?"

"Yeah. I had to get him two tickets to the Giants season opener. He drives a mean bargain, that guy."

I look around the piano and smile at him, but Harry doesn't meet my eye. He closes his eyes and sways to the rhythm of the music.

"But how did you, you . . ."

He comes over to me and kisses me at the corner of my eye, lightly and gently. I can feel the warmth of his breath on my face. He nuzzles his mouth near my ear and whispers, "I'm sorry, Lily. About everything," and then he brushes my hair back behind my shoulder and kisses my neck, just once, sending chills down my spine. He straightens up and says, "What was your question?"

But my mind is a blank slate. I just hug him and bury my face into his chest. He wraps me in a big hug and holds me a little while. He smells so good, and I just stand there in his arms, working it all out. Finally I lean back a little so I can look at him. Sam then bends down and kisses me hard on the mouth, as if he's been wanting to do that for years. I kiss him gently and then say, "So the only part I don't get is, is my dad in on this?"

"Your dad, your mom, your grandmother, your best friend, her boyfriend, your favorite piano player, the Secret Service, and the ruler of a principality in Micronesia."

I giggle and fall back into his arms.

He leans down to my ear again, and his warm breath tickles my ear. "So, can we try again, Lily? From the start? I'm so sorry about everything."

I pull back. "No. Wait." I bite my lip. "I mean, yes. Yes, we can start again, but I'm sorry too." I pull back and look at him carefully. "We were both wrong," I say slowly, "but I've grown up a lot. This time, it will be different."

"I hope not too different," Sam says. "I had the time of my life, last time."

"You ain't seen nothing yet," I say, and give him a wink.

He smiles a giant lopsided grin at me. "Then will you dance with me this time?"

I remember snubbing him at the Traywick's party. "Sorry about that," I laugh and give him my hand. We walk over to Harry at the piano and start dancing, slowly. He pulls me in tight.

"Hooray!" a loud cheer breaks through the room. We look up and see Reagan and Daniel spying on us from the third floor, looking down over the escalators, cheering and waving their hands. They come bounding down the escalator, and Reagan says, "I tried to tell you not to wear that."

I look down at myself. Sam looks me over too, and then pulls me back in his arms. "It doesn't matter what you're wearing, Lily. You're beautiful."

I smile and lean in, putting my arms around Sam. I gaze over his shoulder and look around slowly. I may not know much about fashion, I think, or journalism, or even about friendship or love, but I know this: I wouldn't trade this moment for anything.